"A very tight boo[...] moving plot . . . [...] twisting, trying to [...]

"What makes *Dra[...] is that the author pulls the wool over her readers' eyes with respect to who are the good guys and the bad guys. There are quite a few surprises . . . and the ending is most satisfying."

—*BookLoons*

"*Dragon Bones* is much more than just a well-written, enjoyable story . . . I think this book could be easily classified as fantasy at its best . . . The plot has many twists and turns and delightful surprises. I wasn't able to predict any of the surprises Briggs had in store for the reader, and that's a sign of a great book. The characters are also extremely likable."   —*Fantasy Freaks Forum*

"A satisfying fantasy adventure story, a nice break from the heavyweight multivolume epics that dominate the genre."

—Don D'Ammassa, *Critical Mass*

"Heartwarming . . . Tightly written with fully developed characters and a lavish backdrop, Ms. Briggs's latest fantasy delivers a thrilling coming-of-age story."   —*RT Book Reviews*

PRAISE FOR THE NOVELS OF
Patricia Briggs

"An increasingly excellent serie[...] [...]e these books."

—Charlaine Harris,
[...] author of *After Dead*

"An e[...] [...]d turns . . . Thoroughly [...]   —Kim Harrison,
[...]or of *The Undead Pool*

"Expect [...] spellbound."   —Lynn Viehl,
New York Times bestselling author of the Darkyn series

Titles by Patricia Briggs

The Mercy Thompson Series

MOON CALLED	SILVER BORNE
BLOOD BOUND	RIVER MARKED
IRON KISSED	FROST BURNED
BONE CROSSED	NIGHT BROKEN

The Alpha and Omega Series

ON THE PROWL
(with Eileen Wilks, Karen Chance, and Sunny)
CRY WOLF
HUNTING GROUND
FAIR GAME

MASQUES
WOLFSBANE
STEAL THE DRAGON
WHEN DEMONS WALK

THE HOB'S BARGAIN

DRAGON BONES
DRAGON BLOOD

RAVEN'S SHADOW
RAVEN'S STRIKE

Graphic Novels

ALPHA AND OMEGA: CRY WOLF: VOLUME ONE
ALPHA AND OMEGA: CRY WOLF: VOLUME TWO

Anthology

SHIFTER'S WOLF
(*Masques* and *Wolfsbane* in one volume)

DRAGON BONES

Patricia Briggs

ACE BOOKS, NEW YORK

THE BERKLEY PUBLISHING GROUP
Published by the Penguin Group
Penguin Group (USA) LLC
375 Hudson Street, New York, New York 10014

USA • Canada • UK • Ireland • Australia • New Zealand • India • South Africa • China

penguin.com

A Penguin Random House Company

DRAGON BONES

An Ace Book / published by arrangement with Hurog, Inc.

Copyright © 2002 by Hurog, Inc.
Penguin supports copyright. Copyright fuels creativity, encourages diverse voices,
promotes free speech, and creates a vibrant culture. Thank you for buying an authorized
edition of this book and for complying with copyright laws by not reproducing, scanning,
or distributing any part of it in any form without permission. You are supporting writers
and allowing Penguin to continue to publish books for every reader.

Ace Books are published by The Berkley Publishing Group.
ACE and the "A" design are trademarks of Penguin Group (USA) LLC.

For information, address: The Berkley Publishing Group,
a division of Penguin Group (USA) LLC,
375 Hudson Street, New York, New York 10014.

ISBN: 978-0-441-00916-9

PUBLISHING HISTORY
Ace mass-market edition / March 2002

PRINTED IN THE UNITED STATES OF AMERICA

26 25 24 23 22 21 20 19 18 17

Cover art by Gene Mollica.
Cover design by Annette Fiore DeFex.
Interior text design by Kristin del Rosario.
Map illustration by Michael Enzweiler.

To Collin, Amanda, and Jordan.
May you always dream of dragons.

ACKNOWLEDGMENTS

To Mike Briggs, Kaye Roberson, Anne Sowards, Nanci McCloskey, and the Wordos of Eugene, who read through the rough stuff and gave me good advice. To Virginia Kidd, Jim Allen, Linn Prentis, and the rest of the folks at the Virginia Kidd Agency for their patience and wisdom. To Big Cesar (Engine #9), Sirocco, Scratch, Skipper W, Teddy, Hussan, MonAmi, Meekum, and the rest of the Terra Verde Crowd, to Gazania, and my own Nahero, who allow me to make characters of my fictional horses. As always, the mistakes are mine, but there are fewer of them because of these folks.

1

WARDWICK OF HUROG

Hurog means dragon.

BREATHING HEAVILY FROM THE CLIMB, I SAT upon the ancient bronze doors some long-distant ancestor had placed flat into the highest face of the mountain. The doors were huge, each as wide as I was tall and twice that in length. Because the ground was angled, the tops of the doors were higher by several feet than the bottoms. On each door, worn by years of harsh northern weather, a bas-relief bronze dragon kept watch over the valley below.

Below me, Hurog Keep perched on its man-made eyrie. The ancient fortress's dark stone walls rose protectively around the keep, formidable still, though there was little chance of enemy attack now. By the standards of the Five Kingdoms, Hurog was only a small keep, barely able to support itself from the meager harvest the north climate and rocky soils allowed. But from the sea harbor visible in the east to the bald-topped mountain in the west, the land belonged to Hurog. Like most keeps in Shavig, northernmost of the Five Kingdoms of the Tallvenish High King, Hurog was greater in land than wealth.

It was my legacy, passed father to son, like my blond hair and large size.

In the old tongue, *Hurog* meant *dragon*.

Impulsively, I rose to my feet and opened my crippled mind so I could feel Hurog's magic gathered around me, pulsing through my veins as I roared out the Hurog battle cry.

Hurog.

Mine, if my father didn't kill me first.

"HE'LL KILL US." MY COUSIN ERDRICK'S VOICE, though hushed, came from the river side of the trail.

The willows were so thick between the trail I followed and the river, he couldn't see me any more than I could see him. I was tempted to walk on. My cousin and I were not friendly, but the nagging certainty that I was the "he" to whom my cousin referred gave me pause.

"It's not *my* fault, Erdrick." Beckram, Erdrick's twin, spoke soothingly. "You saw her. She took off like a startled rabbit."

They'd been teasing my sister again. Erdrick might be right; I might just kill them this time.

"Next time, don't tease a girl whose brother's the size of an ox."

"Good thing he's got the brains to match," Beckram said serenely. "Come on, let's get out of here. She'll show up safe and sound."

"He'll know it was us," predicted Erdrick with his customary gloom.

"How? *She* can't tell him."

My sister was mute from birth.

"She can point, can't she? I tell you, he'll kill us!"

Time to catch them and find out what they'd done. I took a deep breath and concentrated on looking like a stupid ox instead of a vengeful brother before I crashed through the brush to the riverbank where the keep sewer emptied into the river. With my size and features, no one expected me to be intelligent. I'd taken that and played on it. Stupid Wardwick was no threat to his father's position.

They might be twenty to my nineteen, but I was a head taller than either and three stone heavier. I'd been out hunting, so my crossbow hung over my shoulder, and my hunting knife was in my belt. They were unarmed. Not that I intended to use a weapon on them. Really.

My hands worked just fine.

"Who will kill you?" I asked, untangling myself from a branch that had caught my shirt as I'd plowed through the bushes.

Struck dumb, Erdrick just stared at me in mute horror. Beckram was made of sterner stuff. His mobile face curved in a charming smile as if he were glad to see me there.

"Ward. Good morning, cousin. You've been out hunting? Any luck?"

"No," I replied.

From their light-chestnut hair, handsome features, and dark complexions to their peculiar purple blue (Hurog blue) eyes, they were virtually identical in appearance, though not in spirit. Beckram was bold and charismatic, leaving Erdrick forever Beckram's hand-wringing shadow.

I looked at the river, the trees, the keep's sewer outlet. When my eyes crossed the last, Erdrick drew in a loud breath, so I looked closer. The grate, which kept out wandering wildlife, was loose, leaving a narrow gap. A small foot had sunk ankle deep in the mud by the tunnel entrance.

I walked over to the grate and stared at it awhile. Erdrick quivered with tension. I reached up and wiggled the grate, and it slipped back easily. The gap widened into a passageway large enough for my small sister to sneak into.

After a long pause, I turned to Beckram. "Did Ciarra go in here? That was her footprint."

He turned over several answers in his head before he said, "We think so. We were just going to look for her."

"Ciarra!" I yelled down the tunnel. "Brat, come out!"

I used my pet name for her, in case the tunnel's acoustics distorted my voice. I was the only one who called her Brat. My bellow echoed in the tunnel's depths like a dragon's roar. There was no reply, but, of course, Ciarra couldn't make one.

I didn't need the muddy tracks inside to tell me that she was in there somewhere. The only thing left of my childhood gift of magic—other than a few minor tricks—was a talent for finding things. Ciarra was in there somewhere; I could feel her. I looked up at the sun. If she was late to dinner, the Hurogmeten, our father, would beat her. I took off the pack that carried my bolts and a bit of lunch.

"What'd you do to her?" I asked.

"I tried to stop her. I told her it was dangerous in there," pleaded Erdrick before Beckram could stop him.

"Ah?" I straightened and took a step nearer to Beckram.

"She's a silly chicken," sputtered Beckram, finally losing his nerve and backing away. "I wasn't going to hurt her. Just a little harmless flirting."

I hit him. If I'd wanted to, I could have killed him or broken his jaw. Instead, I pulled my punch and gave him the start of a beautiful black eye. It dazed him long enough for me to turn my attention to Erdrick.

"Really, Ward, all he did was tell her he liked her hair," he said.

I continued to stare at him.

Finally, Erdrick squirmed and muttered, "But you know how he is; it's not what he says, it's how. She took off like a startled doe and charged out the gates. We followed because it isn't safe out here for a girl alone."

Erdrick might be an irritating weakling, but he was usually truthful. There weren't any rats or insects in the sewer— some magic of the dwarves who built it, though my brother

Tosten had populated it with all kinds of monsters in his stories.

The opening the Brat had slipped through was nowhere near large enough for me. I pulled hard, but the grate only creaked.

"You won't fit," predicted Beckram, sitting up and touching his eye delicately. He must be feeling guilty, or he'd have tried to hit me back. A bully he might be, but Beckram was no coward. "Neither Erdrick nor I could. She'll come out when she's ready."

It was almost time for dinner now. I couldn't bear it when Father hit her. Wouldn't bear it again, and it was too soon for that. I wasn't good enough to defeat him yet. I stripped out of my thick leather tunic and set it down with my hunting gear.

"Take my things to the keep," I said and took a good grip on the grate and pulled. There was an easier way, of course, but an idiot wouldn't think of it. I had to continue struggling until my cousins were gone or Beckram lost patience. . . .

"Take out the linchpin, then we can pull the damn thing off," muttered Beckram. I was right; he was really feeling guilty.

"Linchpin?" I asked. I stepped back to look at the grate better, carefully not looking at the single heavy hinge.

"The bolt holding the hinge together," sighed Erdrick.

"Ah." I stared at the hinge for a good long time before Erdrick took his knife out and worked the thick old pin out of the hinges. He ruined his knife doing it.

With the linchpin gone, the iron grate popped out of the hinge, and I lifted it away from the opening.

"Damn," swore Beckram softly as I moved the grate and propped it up near the opening.

The grate *was* heavy. If I hadn't been trying to impress my cousins, I'd have asked for help. As it was, Beckram might remember this when he thought about scaring the Brat again.

This near the river, the tunnel was mushroom shaped, with walks on either side of a deep, narrow ditch that ran sluggishly with sewer water. The walkways were meant for dwarves, not hulking brutes who towered over most grown men. With a sigh, I dropped to my hands and knees and began crawling through the foul-smelling muck.

"Brat!" I shouted, but the sound just dampened in the mossy growth that covered the walls.

The tunnel took a bend that obscured the last of the daylight. In front of me, on both sides of the wall, dwarvenstones lit themselves as I approached, illuminating the tunnel with pale blue light. Most keeps didn't have sewers anymore, not even the high king's new palace at Estian. Stonework on that scale had been the dwarves' domain, and they were gone now, taking their secrets with them.

The sewer tunnel narrowed to a large tube, and I knew the outer walls of the keep were above and just in front of me. Not that I'd explored the sewers much, but there were copies of the ancient plans in the library, buried where few bothered to look. At any rate, the sewer tunnel narrowed by two-thirds so an invading army would not be able to use the sewer to undermine the walls. Not even a child could swing a pick or shovel in the narrow stone confines.

Sweat gathered on my forehead from the effort of keeping track of Ciarra through magic. I seldom used magic because it made me remember how it was to do more, but for Ciarra, alone and maybe frightened, I was grateful for what little I had left.

I crawled forward into the narrow section, trying not to think about what was in the muck I'd just set my hand in. On the bright side, my nose was showing signs of self-defense because the odors were less overwhelming.

There were dwarvenstones in the smaller tunnel, too. They weren't bright enough to allow me to see what I was crawling through, but that was just as well. Ciarra was getting farther away from me now, but she was a lot smaller and wouldn't be as hampered by the size of the tunnel.

As the eldest, I'd always looked after my brother and sister. Tosten was two years safely gone from Hurog. But since Ciarra was both adventurous and mute, her safety was a constant undertaking. Ciarra was supposed to be helping Mother today. But I knew Mother. And I knew Ciarra, too. With my uncle and cousins here, I should have stayed home, but the mountains had called to me.

We were bound to be late for dinner now, unless Father's hunting party took longer than usual. But at least with both of us equal miscreants, my father would concentrate on me instead of Ciarra. The tunnel narrowed and branched, making me rue the three fingers' height I'd gained already this summer as I scrunched into the cleaner and smaller of the two tunnels. I could see dwarvenstones shining down it where someone had activated them, while the other one, the bigger one, was dark ahead. Trust the Brat to choose the smallest way.

I scuttled ahead, fighting the feeling that the walls were collapsing. After I was well in, the tunnel tilted dramatically upward for a few body lengths before starting downward nearly as steeply. I hit my head on a low spot and stopped to think a minute. I might not be a dwarf, but I knew the sewers worked because water flowed downhill.

This tunnel had been designed to keep water out of it rather than let the water flow to the river. I closed my eyes and tried to envision what the map had indicated, but I'd found it months ago. And beyond noting a few interesting features, I hadn't given it much attention. How was I supposed to guess my sister would choose to run around the sewer tunnels?

I rubbed my head and decided that this must be an escape tunnel. All the old castles had them, a legacy from a day when Hurog, rich with dwarven trade, had been worth besieging. I was still considering it when Ciarra went from being not too distant from me to being somewhere far below. I stopped breathing.

She must have fallen, I thought as I frantically scrambled forward, perhaps through a trapdoor intended to keep besiegers from following some long-ago ancestor as he fled his attackers through this tunnel. Gods, oh gods, my little sister.

I scrambled forward like a frog, pushing with my legs and reaching out with my hands in the awkward fashion I'd had to adopt in the small tunnel, all the while thinking, *It's too far down. She's fallen too far.*

One moment I was scuttling along, and the next I couldn't so much as blink my eyes. My face went numb, and magic flooded around me. Underneath my hand, the smooth stone of the tunnel began to glow red and green, brighter by far than the faint light of dwarvenstone. It was so bright that after a moment I had to close my watering eyes against the intensity. That's why I had no warning when the floor of the tunnel disappeared out from under me and I fell.

The magic left me lying flat on my stomach in utter blackness. I pushed up, but the ceiling had closed above me, leaving me barely enough room to lift my head off the ground. My hands were trapped underneath me and, though I pulled and wiggled, I couldn't get them out. I panicked and fought ferociously against the stone walls cocooning me. I cried out like one of the silly maids, but there was no one to hear.

The thought stopped my useless struggling. If anyone had heard me, my father would have seen to it that I spent a lot more time trapped in darkness. Men don't panic, don't cry, don't grieve.

But I did. I blinked back my tears, but my nose dripped. I'd lost contact with Ciarra when the spell hit me. I *looked* for her again, hoping she'd been caught in the same spell that had held me, but she was still deeper. She wasn't moving. I had to get to her.

The tunnel was far smaller than the one I'd been crawling through. In my thrashing (well, I'd tried to thrash, anyway) panic, I'd established that the ceiling was as solid as it felt, no matter that I had just fallen through it. There was something blocking the way behind me, but cool, fresh air blew by my flushed face, so I could probably go forward if I could get my hands out from under my body where they were trapped.

Having already proven I couldn't pull them both out at the same time, I started with my left hand, which was trapped farther forward than my right. The terror at being caught with my hands pinned against my side brought on one or two bouts of panic. But when I was finished and lay sweating and shaking in the darkness, I still had nothing to do but continue wriggling my hand up. The tightest part was pulling my elbow past my chest and shoulders, and I struggled for a long time before admitting defeat.

I lay sweating and relaxed a moment. Hopelessly, I leaned my weight to the right and pushed my arm forward.

It slid out.

I stretched it above my head and wiggled it. As relief let me think clearly once more, I realized what must have happened. Relaxed, my shoulders took up less room than they did tightened with the force of my struggles. The right hand was easier than the left, but by the time I'd finished, the cold from the stone had sunk to my bones, and I was shivering with it.

With both hands in front pulling, and shifting the rest of my body as well as I could, I was able to start forward. My forearms hurt from being dragged across the rough stone each time I pulled, and my shoulders were scraped raw because they were wider than the tunnel; likely by the time I finished, they'd be a few inches narrower.

I pushed with my feet, too, or at least with my toes. Unused to such strange exercise, they cramped after a while. I stretched them as best I could, though it was maddening not to be able to bend down and rub them with my hands. It seemed as though I crawled forever before the absolute darkness in front of me let up. Somewhere ahead there was light.

Perversely, it was almost harder to go on, as if the knowledge that things were looking up made it more difficult to continue the effort. After a bit, it grew still lighter. Of course, with my luck, the light might be coming from a dwarvenstone embedded in a wall that sealed the tunnel. But pessimism lost. My tunnel curved, and I saw that the light came from a hole in the floor.

I slid my head over the edge and looked out to see, a long way below me, the floor of a large natural cave. My view was obscured by the twisted stalactites that surrounded my opening. I couldn't tell if Ciarra's body was lying below, though magic whispered that she was probably in that cave.

On the right-hand edge of my hole were two metal spikes driven into the rock. Tied to each spike was a rope. One of the ropes was about a foot long and frayed at the end; the other dangled through the thicket of stalactites until I lost sight of it. The rope looked very old, and I wasn't a lightweight. But Ciarra waited for me below, and so I reached for it and held onto it as I pulled the rest of my body out of the cave. The relief of being free of the stone embrace was almost enough to distract me from Ciarra for a moment.

The rope wasn't a ladder, though it might have been part of one once, but it was better than nothing. After I cleared the stone formations on the ceiling of the cave, I could tell that the rope only reached two-thirds of the way to the floor. I worried about what I was going to do for the last ten feet, but I needn't have. The rope broke before I got quite that far.

As I hit the ground, I rolled as my father's arms master had drilled into me until it was second nature. Even so, I hit hard. After tumbling over once or twice, I stopped against a broken outcropping. I lay there for a moment, trying too hard to catch my breath to worry about where I was. At last my air came back in a rush, and I stumbled to my feet.

I'd rolled up against the remains of a broken column that looked to have spanned from floor to ceiling in ages past. The cavern was huge, at least twice as big as the great hall in the keep. The mouth of the tunnel I'd fallen from was along the edge of the room and relatively low. In the center of the room the ceiling was much higher, perhaps as tall as Hurog's walls, though it was hard to judge. Dwarvenstones were everywhere, brighter than the ones in the sewer, making the room actually lighter than the castle was even during the day.

There was no body crumpled on the floor. Ciarra wasn't anywhere to be seen. But she was nearby.

"Hello!" I called out. "Brat?"

A small form hurtled at me and thunked her head into my ribs. I grabbed Ciarra around the waist and swung her around twice before setting her firmly on her feet and shaking her.

"You scared me to death, Brat! What idiot notion took you that you ran into the sewers?"

Ciarra's long blond hair (lighter even than mine) hung in a muddy tangle halfway down her back. She wore tunic and trousers similar to mine, and her feet were bare. She looked pitiful, but I wasn't fooled: Pitiful wasn't repentant.

"Come on, Brat," I said with resignation, "let's find our way out of here."

Though my initial relief at finding her was overwhelming, if I couldn't find a way out, she might not be any better off than if she had died. We certainly weren't going to get out the way I came in. The dwarvenstones suggested that the room had once been in use; there had to be a better way out.

Although the room was brightly lit and must once have been fairly open, the original cave formations and the rubble where great stalactites had fallen in ages past made it difficult to tell what was inside. Maybe it had once held treasure, but there was nothing here now. The center of the cave was higher than the outer edges, and there were more stalagmites and rubble. Ciarra's feet were tough as hooves since she seldom wore shoes, but I lifted her over the worst of the rubble anyway. As I surmounted a broken pile of rock, I saw what the mess had concealed.

It had long been rumored that there was treasure hidden in Hurog from when the dwarves had come here and traded their jewels and metals. Here was treasure indeed, but one I would rather never have seen. Forgetting Ciarra momentarily, I slid down rocks and stepped closer to it.

The dragon's skull, still in an iron muzzle, was as long as I was tall. Iron manacles clasped its feet, and four more sets of manacles surrounded the delicate bones of its wings. In life whatever misborn ancestor of mine who'd committed this crime had pierced the dragon's flesh to set the iron into the wings.

"Stupid!" I snarled, though the deed was long done and those who had done it could not hear me. In the cave the sound of my voice echoed and returned to me. I blinked away the tears in my eyes.

Tenderhearted, my father called me when he was most angry. It was something that he hated worse than my stupidity. A man with a tender heart could not survive here, he said, and what was worse, those around him would die, too. I believed him. Even so, I couldn't prevent the tears, though I widened my eyes so no water spilled down my cheeks.

There were no dragons anymore. Not one. It was to see the dragons living in our mountains that the dwarves had come, bearing trade gifts for the privilege and ushering a time when Hurog had been the richest keep in the Five Kingdoms.

Hurog had held the last of dragonkind. When they were gone, the dwarves had gone, too, and the lands belonging to Hurog had begun to die as the dragons had. They'd died of sorrow, the old stories said, leaving only memories and the crest of my house to remind the world that they once were and what Hurog once was.

My family had been the protectors of dragonkind; they had died to keep their preserve safe, entrusted to that task by the first high king or, some of the old tales held, by the gods themselves. *Hurogmeten* in the old Shavig tongue meant *guardian of dragons*.

All of my life I'd clung to the glory that had been Hurog's. When I was a child, I played at being Seleg, the most famous of all Hurogmetens, and defended Hurog from seaborne invaders. When there was no one but the Brat, Tosten, and me, I would take down the battered lap harp and sing the old songs of dragons and dwarven jewels as large as horse heads.

Here, buried in the heart of Hurog, was proof that one of my ancestors had betrayed everything Hurog stood for. I caressed the skull under the black iron muzzle, kneeling as was proper before the creature the Hurogs had served throughout the ages.

"She was beautiful," said a soft, tenor voice behind me.

I jerked my head up and saw a boy, a year or two younger than I. He was no one I knew, a stranger in the heart of Hurog.

He would have come up to my shoulder if I were standing, but so did many grown men. At Hurog, only my father was taller than I. The boy's hair was very dark, perhaps even black, and his eyes were light, purplish blue. The bones of his face were sharp, almost hawklike, as aristocratic as my own face was not.

He hugged himself as he stared at me. His stance reminded me of a high-bred horse ready to bolt at a loud noise or harsh word. Ciarra sat at my side, undisturbed by the strange boy, absently petting the dragon's skull as if it were the head of one of the keep's dogs. I shifted until I was between her and the stranger.

"Silver eyes," the boy said, "and a song that made many a man's heart beat faster. He should have let her alone. I told him so." His voice was breathless, shaking a bit.

I watched him, doubtlessly with the peculiar witless look on my face that drove my father thrashing mad. But I was thinking. I was in the depths of the keep, and a boy I'd never seen before was here, too. The last dragons had disappeared seven or eight generations ago, and yet this boy claimed to have spoken to the man who'd done this.

I knew who he was.

The boy who was looking at me with great, wounded eyes was the family ghost. Oh, we all knew about him, though we didn't say anything to outsiders. There wasn't a one of the family who hadn't had something inexplicable happen.

If the ghost liked you, he could be helpful. My mother's maid's knitting needles were always in her bag when she looked for them, though on several occasions I'd just seen them elsewhere. If he didn't like you . . . well, my aunt hadn't visited again since she'd slapped the Brat.

No one I knew had ever seen him, though there were family stories about people who had. I'd expected someone more formidable, not a lad with the air of a dog that had been beaten once too often—a Hurog dog, though. If his features were more refined than mine, I could still see a similarity in the shape of the cheekbones. Except for his coloring, he looked a lot like my younger brother, Tosten, and his eyes, like Tosten's and Ciarra's, were Hurog blue.

He watched me with the still alertness of an unhooded falcon, waiting for my response to his speech.

"This is desecration," I said deliberately and touched

the fragile-seeming ivory bones. Magic pounded at me through my fingertips, and I hissed involuntarily.

"This is power," replied the boy in a soft voice that raised the hair on the back of my neck. "Would you have resisted the chance to harness it? You are a mage, Ward, crippled though you are. You know what the power here means. It means food for the people, wealth and power for Hurog. What would you have done if your people were starving, and the power was here for the asking?"

Caught by the force of the pulsing magic, I stared into his eyes and couldn't speak; I didn't know what answer I could make. Ciarra's hand clamped on my forearm, but I didn't look at her. In his eyes I read desperation and terror—the kind of fear that holds rabbits immobile before the fox. I'd never seen that look in a human face before.

He waited.

At last I said, "I could not have done this."

He turned away, and my fingers dropped away from the skull. I didn't know what answer he'd been searching for, but it wasn't the one I'd given him. "Glib answers from a simple man," he said, but there was more sorrow than taunt in his voice.

I said, "You wouldn't have had to tell me this was stupid." I reached over and caught the chain that led from the thick iron muzzle to an eye hook bigger than my fist screwed into the ground. "But desperate people do stupid things all the time."

I turned back to him, half expecting him to disappear or back away, but he stayed where he was, though the fear had not left his eyes. In spite of the magic he'd used on me—if it had indeed been his magic and not the dragon bones—in spite of knowing he was centuries older than I, I felt sorry for him. I knew what it was like to be afraid.

When I was younger, I used to be afraid of my father.

"I have something for you, Lord Wardwick," he said,

holding out a closed hand. His fist was white knuckled, and there was tension about his mouth.

Still kneeling because I didn't want to intimidate him, I put my hand under his, and he dropped a ring into it. It was plain and worn smooth, with just a few bumps left of ornamentation, though the metal was platinum, much harder than gold. I knew it was platinum and not silver because it was my father's ring.

"I am Oreg," he said as the ring landed in my palm. "I am yours as you are Hurog's."

From his manner, I almost expected the lightning flashes that accompanied my father's wizard's more spectacular events, but I only felt the cool metal of the ring in my hand. "This is my father's."

"It is yours now," he said. "From his hand to yours."

I frowned. "Why didn't he give it to me himself?"

"That is not the way it is done," he said. Then he looked upward once, quickly. "Come, my lord, they are looking for you. If you will follow me?"

Holding the ring, I followed him to an opening in the wall that I must have missed when I was exploring the cave, Ciarra trotting at my heels. Through the opening was a narrow walkway that turned this way and that often enough so that I no longer had any idea whether we traveled north or south. The walls had, at some point, changed from rock to worked stone, though I hadn't noticed when the change occurred.

At last he stopped and pressed against a stone that looked, to my eyes, to be exactly the same as all the others. A person-wide section of wall swung open, and I found myself in my room. I stepped out of the tunnel with an exclamation of disbelief. The section of sewer I'd been in was underground, and I'd dropped down farther into the dragon bone cave. I'd swear on my grandfather's grave that the ghost's passageway had been absolutely level. How then was it that we'd come out in my bedroom on the third floor of the keep?

The passage door closed behind Ciarra and me, and when I turned to look, Oreg was gone, leaving me with the puzzle of our route. Magic? I hadn't felt anything more than the usual currents that were ever present inside the keep.

The door to my room swung open behind me. Ciarra, with characteristic quickness, dove under the bed.

"Ward!" exclaimed Duraugh, my uncle and the twins' father, striding in without my leave. Like my father, he was a big man, though not as large as I. In his youth, he'd covered himself in glory, and the high king's gratitude gave him a Tallvenish heiress to wed and a title higher than my father, his older brother. Even though his estate, Iftahar, was larger and richer than Hurog, he still spent a great deal of time here. My father often said, "Blood will tell. Hurogs are tied to this land."

My uncle usually avoided me; I wouldn't have thought he even knew where my room was.

"Uncle Duraugh?" I asked, trying to sound composed and suitably dull-witted. Dull-witted wasn't a stretch. Words never had tripped to my tongue, and I suppose many people would have thought me stupid, even if I hadn't tried to appear so.

His eyes traveled from the top of my head to my feet and back again, taking in the muck and blood. He held his hand to his nose; I'd gotten used to the smell, myself.

"When the twins said you were in the sewers, I thought they were joking. That's a trick for someone half your age, boy. Your presence is required in the great hall at once—though I suppose you'd better change clothes."

I noticed for the first time that he was still in his hunting gear, which was stained dark with fresh blood. He'd gone with father and a hunting party this morning.

I casually slipped the ring Oreg had given me onto the

third finger of my right hand and asked, "Good hunting?" as I stripped off the remains of my shirt. The blood from scraping my shoulders on the cave wall had dried, and the shirt didn't come off easily.

I took up the cloth that lay beside the ever-present bowl of clean water that sat on the nightstand.

"Damnable luck," he replied shortly. "Your father's horse threw him. The Hurogmeten's dying."

I dropped the towel I'd been holding to stare at him.

He looked at my face, which I knew must be blanched with shock, much more honest a reaction than I usually gave anyone. He turned on his heel and left, shutting the door behind him.

Ciarra slid back out in the open and wrapped her arms about me fiercely. There was no grief in her face, just concern. I don't know why she was worried about me. I hated him.

"I'm fine, Brat," I said, though I hugged her back. "Let me find your maid; you'll need cleaning, too."

Luckily, my sister's maid and keeper was mending clothes in Ciarra's room. She grimaced as I handed the Brat to her.

I ran back to my room, where I stripped the rest of the way, scrubbed quickly, and threw on the court clothes I used for formal occasions. The arms of the shirt were too short, and it was tight over my sore shoulders, but it would have to do.

When I opened my door, the Brat was waiting outside. She'd had time to scrub up, too, and was dressed in respectable clothing. It made her look her actual age of sixteen instead of twelve. It also made her look like Mother, fragile boned and beautiful. But it was my father's fierce spirit that burned in Ciarra, purified by her sweet heart.

"Shh," I said, taking, I was sure, as much comfort from the embrace as she did. "I understand. Come down with me, Brat."

She nodded and stepped back from me, wiping her eyes briskly with her sleeves. Then she took a deep breath, wrinkled her nose because she'd obviously washed better than I'd had time to, and held out her hand imperially. I smiled, despite the events doubtlessly unfolding in the great hall below us, and offered her my arm. She took it and walked at my side down the stairs with the regal air she adopted in front of strangers and people she didn't like.

THEY'D IMPROVISED A BED BEFORE THE FIREPLACE. My mother knelt beside it, her face pale and composed, though I could see she'd been crying. My father disliked tears.

Stala, the arms master, was still dressed in hunting clothes. She held her helmet in one hand and rested the other on my mother's shoulder. Stala was my mother's half sister. She was, as my father liked to brag, the greater part of my mother's dowry and the main reason the Blue Guard kept its reputation during my father's tenure.

She'd trained in the king's army and served two terms of service before someone noticed she wasn't a man. She returned to her family home, then followed Mother to Hurog when my father offered her the post of arms master when no other warlord in the country would have looked at her twice. Her hair was silver gray, but I remembered when it had been dark chestnut like Mother's. Stala could best my father in everything but hand-to-hand wrestling.

There was sorrow on her face when she met my gaze, but her eyes were sharp with warning. When she saw she'd caught my eye, she carefully looked at my father's wizard as he frantically scribbled on a piece of sheepskin.

I pulled the Brat with me to a place where my father could see us. His face was pale, his body more still than I'd ever seen it under the bloodstained blankets. Like Ciarra, he'd always seemed filled with boundless energy. Now the only thing alive about him was his eyes, which glared at me in futile anger, an anger that increased when he saw the silver-colored ring on my hand. I wondered if he really had given it to the family ghost to give to me or if Oreg had taken it from him.

I touched Stala's shoulder. "What happened?" Unlike everyone else in the family, Stala always spoke to me as if I weren't stupid. Partly, I suppose, because I could use a sword as well as any.

"Stygian was madder than usual," said Stala, looking up at me, her voice expressing her distaste for my father's mount. The stallion might well act wildly, but he had such power and speed I thought it was worth putting up with the rest. My aunt disagreed; she said that riding a horse like Stygian was akin to fighting with a flawed sword—it always broke when you needed it most. "He tossed the Hurogmeten onto a dead tree. None of the external wounds are serious, but it broke something inside. I'm amazed he's survived so long."

"Die at home like my father before me," grunted the Hurogmeten, staring at me.

I'd never seen him look so old. It had seemed to me that my father always appeared a score of years younger than Mother, though he was actually older. This day he looked ancient, and my mother, next to his bed, looked no older than Ciarra.

"Bad enough to leave this to an oaf," he said to me, "but still worse to die with my oaths undone. When you die, you will give to your heir what I have given you—swear it." His speech was broken but nonetheless forceful for it.

He could only be talking about the ring. "Yes," I said, rubbing it.

He gave his head a short nod, though he didn't look relieved. "Good. Are you done yet, Licleng?"

"Yes, lord," replied the wizard, spreading sand over his writings, then shaking the page and bringing it to my father.

No fool even on his deathbed, my father read the script. Then he gestured for the quill and signed his name with a bloodstained hand that shook so much his signature was mostly illegible.

"You're too young to take care of Hurog. Too soft. Too stupid," he told me. "Can't do much about the softness, though I've tried—nor the stupidity."

The stupidity is your fault, I thought, but I didn't say it. When I was twelve, he'd beaten me senseless. When I recovered, I was changed, but not entirely in the way most people thought.

After drawing a couple more pain-filled breaths, my father said, "Should have married Stala instead of Muellen, but a young man is proud." Mother made no sign that his words bothered her; she heard only what she wanted to. "The Hurogmeten can't be marrying a peasant's bastard, no matter who her father was. Can't see any child of Stala's being as soft as you. But my brother will rule Hurog until you've reached your twenty-first birthday— then Siphern's wolves deliver poor Hurog."

My father, the Hurogmeten, shoved the paper at the old wizard. The quill he crushed in a spasm of pain or spleen at the unfairness of a life that left him with his oldest son an idiot, younger son a runaway, and his daughter a mute. Too concerned with the present to worry about the future, I merely nodded my head in acknowledgment of what he'd said.

The Hurogmeten grinned malevolently at me despite the pain he must have felt. "The only thing I've left to you is Stygian. Knowing Duraugh, he'd have the beast killed. If you can't ride him, use him for breeding stock."

Stala snorted. "And breed that temper into all of his get—though I suppose none of your get ended up with yours." I'd never been sure whether Stala disliked my father or just returned his spitefulness in kind. Certainly they'd been lovers for years, though I wasn't sure if anyone but me knew that.

The Hurogmeten made a dismissing gesture with his right hand. "Duraugh?"

My uncle came forward, intent on the space where the Brat was. I stepped in front of him, blocking his way, before he could push her into the background. At something over fourteen stone, I was a good deal less movable than she.

Uncle Duraugh raised an eyebrow before he walked to the other side of the bed, edging in front of Mother. "Yes, Fen?"

"You'll take care of Hurog."

"Of course."

"Good." My father sighed. "Duraugh, Tosten will be Ward's heir. Find him, wherever he is."

"I know where he is," I replied unwisely. But I couldn't resist the impulse. It would be the only chance I'd ever have to hint to my father that he might be wrong about me.

The Hurogmeten looked at me, surprised. He'd beaten me until I bled when my younger brother had disappeared two years ago. Then he'd decided if I'd known anything about Tosten, I'd have told him; everyone knew I was too stupid to lie well.

"Where?" he asked, but I shook my head.

If my uncle knew where he was, Tosten would be yanked back here, and he wouldn't want that. I'd come across him slitting his wrists one autumn night shortly after his fifteenth birthday and persuaded him that there was a better way to leave Hurog.

"He's safe." I hoped that was true.

He sighed again, closing his eyes. Abruptly, they opened again as he fought for air and lost a battle for the first time in his life.

Mother stood up. She hummed an eerie little melody,

staring at his body for a moment, then she turned and left the room.

I felt lost and betrayed, as if I'd finally been winning a game at the expense of great effort and time, and my opponent left the playing field before he noticed I'd been winning. Which is, of course, what had happened.

Ciarra tightened her grip and leaned her cheek on my arm, her face a blank mask. My face, I knew from long practice, looked vaguely cowlike; the deep brown eyes Mother'd given me added to the general bovine appearance of my expression.

My uncle looked at me closely. "You do understand what has just happened?"

"The Hurogmeten is dead," I replied.

"And you are the new Hurogmeten, but I'll be holder in your place for two years." Duraugh's eyes hooded for a moment, and underneath the Hurog-stern face was excitement as well as grief. Duraugh wanted Hurog.

"I get father's horse," I said, having searched for the most inane comment I could make. "I'm going to go see him now."

"Change your clothes first," suggested my uncle. "When you get back, your mother and I will have decided how to honor your father. We'll have to call your brother home for the funeral."

When I'm dead and buried, I thought, but I nodded anyway. "All right."

I turned as if I'd forgotten the Brat on my arm. She stumbled, trying to keep up with me, so I shifted and hefted her under my arm, carrying her up the stairs at a rapid pace. She was really getting too old for that kind of play, but we both enjoyed it, and it reminded my fa—my uncle, just how strong I was. *Part of the game,* I thought, *part of the game.*

So did my uncle take my father's place as my opponent.

2

WARDWICK

I missed my father. I kept looking over my shoulder for him, though he was safely buried.

THE STABLEMEN WHO DRAGGED MY FATHER'S HORSE from the stall looked none too happy about it, but then neither did the horse.

"He ran back here some time before the hunting party returned, milord," said my father's stable master, Penrod. He was one of my mother's imports, a Tallvenish flatlander. He'd ridden with the Blue Guard when my father had fought in the king's battles the better part of two decades ago, before slipping into the position of stable master when the old one died. Unlike many of the higher-ranking keep folk, Penrod always treated me with the same deference he used with my father.

"We're still trying to clean the blood off the Hurog-meten's saddle," he said. "I expect it's the smell that's kept Stygian so riled."

My attention on the squealing and struggling stallion, I waited, Ciarra a small, observant shadow beside me. I could tell from his face that Penrod wanted to say something.

"He's too good to put down, milord," he said at last. "His sire was trade goods, and he died early, when your father used him to hunt bandits. We only have two of his get, and one of them was gelded before anyone realized the quality of the animals. The Hurogmeten . . ." He hesitated, perhaps remembering that I was now the Hurogmeten, at least in title. "Your father didn't want to breed him yet, thought it would make him worse to handle than he already is. So if you kill him . . ." his voice took on the impassioned plea of an artist contemplating the destruction of his finest work.

"Kill him?" I asked, as if I'd only just heard him. "Why would I do a stupid thing like that?" I laughed inwardly as Penrod fought his tongue and won.

"I'm sure I don't know, milord. But your uncle—he stopped in here just a few minutes ago. He thought it might be best."

And suggested it to Penrod, in hopes the man might persuade me. Certainly any other stable master would have hated to have such an unpredictable monster in his keeping. But my uncle had misjudged the man. Penrod was a connoisseur of horses and a good enough horseman to see that most of Stygian's madness was man-made. It would have broken his heart to kill the stallion.

I shook my head, outwardly dismissing my uncle. "No."

My father had been a rider without peer. He could stay on the worst rogue and make it do anything he wanted. He preferred to ride them until he'd battered their spirit until a lesser man could handle them. Once that was done, he'd find a different mount, or at least he had until he'd ridden Stygian. The stallion had fought him for four years, emerging, today, the victor at last.

Three softly cursing grooms struggled to hold the animal still for my inspection. It was a battle, despite the halter they had on him. Meant to control a lusting stallion, it had dull metal buttons in places that would inflict pain when the horse pulled against it. A chain wrapped around his nose could close off his breathing and drop him unconscious, if necessary.

Stygian was massive; it made him appear slow, which he actually wasn't. He was rather quicker in turning (and bucking) than in forward movement, but he'd do very well. Most animals of his build aren't much for endurance, either, but my father used to ride Stygian when his men went through two rotations of horses to keep up. He was a dark, muddy color that lightened on his belly, flanks, and nose to a rusty brown. There were other lighter patches of color near his flanks and on his barrel due to years of whip and spur.

"His bridle and saddle are here, milord. If you want to ride." Satisfied I wasn't going to kill the horse, Penrod had settled into his normal, respectful self. "Though it might be better just to turn him out." He cleared his throat. "I suggested putting him into a breeding program, but your uncle said he wouldn't have it as long as he held Hurog, said Stygian's temperament shouldn't be passed on."

"Can't breed him then," I said regretfully.

Penrod's respectful face often led smarter men than my uncle into believing that the stable master agreed with them—my father, for instance. Duraugh had probably left thinking Penrod would urge me to put Stygian down. My uncle's misjudgment might as well be turned to my good. If my uncle did well over the next two years, he would certainly win the support of the castle folk if he decided to take my place.

It wouldn't hurt to win over a few loyal men myself. Penrod already liked me, more because of how I treated his charges than anything personal. He was a smart man, or he'd never have survived in his position, given how far apart his ideas and my father's had been.

"Might shift his stall around," I said after a bit. "His is

dark. Small. I don't like small places; maybe he doesn't either." The sewer today had decided that.

The stablemen were getting tired, but so was the horse. He'd already had quite a ride. I owed the stallion for his efforts today. I wondered why I wasn't happier about it.

"That stall's the only one we could keep him in," explained Penrod as if I didn't know.

"The big run by the old stables is built to hold stallions," I said. Then, in case he didn't understand, I continued, "Have to be careful the side gate's latch is secure."

He stood perfectly still for a moment, ostensibly watching the horse. Then he looked at me. The stallion's paddock was used for loose breeding and shared a fence line with the mares' fields. If someone accidentally (or on purpose) left the side gate open, Stygian would breed whatever mares happened to be in season.

I could have left it there. He'd understood the implications well enough, but I needed him. My uncle would have two years to win my people. I would have to make sure that when the time came, Hurog's people would listen to me and not my uncle. For that, I needed Penrod to know that I might be more than they'd given me credit for, so I winked at him.

Penrod stiffened even further, shocked into turning from the horse to stare at me for a moment. It must be hard to change one's opinion of someone so quickly, but he had the added incentive of the carrot I offered him. He looked at the dark horse again.

"I'll see that he's put out in the paddock because you think that, like you, he doesn't like small, enclosed places." Underneath Penrod's bland voice vibrated a taut, fierce joy.

"Dark," I muttered. "Don't like dark."

"Right," he said with a small smile.

Once he followed my orders to disobey my uncle, he was mine. With him would come the rest of the stablemen.

It would mean that eventually everyone would know I was not so stupid, but I wasn't sure stupidity was still in my best interest. The playing field was changing.

I frowned at my father's horse. "Stygian's too hard to say." There was a flower in one of Mother's gardens that was about the same color as Stygian. I had to wait a while longer until my lips quit trying to smile at the thought of what my father would have said before I spoke.

"I'll call him Pansy," I said blandly.

Ciarra pulled away and turned to face me, her expression so incredulous it needed no words.

"Mother has a flower in her garden his color. I asked her what it was," I explained.

"Pansy," said Penrod stiffly, doubtless thinking about how it would look on a pedigree. Then, abruptly, he smiled. He nodded his head at the three tense-faced stablemen holding the stallion. "Hard to be scared of something named Pansy."

I nodded abruptly and called to the grooms, "Put him in the round corral, then take off the halter." I turned to Penrod. "I need a long whip, like the ones we use to train the youngsters. And I need five or six copper pots. You can send someone to the kitchens. And an empty grain sack."

I'd had a long time to think about what to do about Stygian . . . Pansy. No sense waiting until my father was cold to steal his horse. Some dark emotion twisted my mouth before I could banish it. I would not grieve for my father. I would not. Instead, I would spend the afternoon making his horse mine.

IN THE TRAINING RING, STYGIAN STAYED AS FAR away from me as he could, which was fine with me for now. Four years wasn't to be undone in an afternoon— or a dozen afternoons. But I might make headway if I was lucky.

I held the sack of pots in one hand, careful that they made no noise. With my other hand I held a whip twice as long as I was tall. Half the length was stick from which the whipcord dangled.

"Let's go," I said without undue emphasis once I was in the center of the ring. At the same time, I shook out the whip, and the stallion took off at a dead run after aiming a kick somewhere in my general direction.

I let him run a dozen times around the smallish pen. He thought he knew what this was about. All my father's horses started in this ring to learn simple commands like walk and whoa. But I'd brought him here to learn a different lesson, I hoped.

He started to slow to a canter, more because it was hard for a horse with his stride to gallop around such a small enclosure than because he was tiring.

"Let's go," I said again and waved the whip in his face. A green horse would have turned around and run the other way, but he'd learned too much about whips. He flattened his ears and reared at me; then, in case I didn't get the message, he charged.

I could have hit him with the whip and driven him off, but he already knew that whips hurt. It wouldn't have taught him anything. Instead, I shook the bag of cooking pots hard, yelling and stepping toward him aggressively, banging on the bag with the hard end of the whip. It sounded like the kitchen after someone vexed the cook.

The noise was too much for Stygian. He spun on his hindquarters and darted in the other direction as if a pack of wolves were on his tail, crow-hopping around the circles his size wouldn't let him negotiate smoothly. By the fourth time I turned him, his chest and flanks were covered in foam. At last he dropped his head and looked at me, not challenging, but asking for permission to stop.

I pulled the whip up and said, "Whoa."

He stopped as he'd been trained, but his hindquarters

angled toward me, so I shook the whip and sent him running again. I waited until he carried his head low once
more. This time when he stopped, he faced me. We'd both
had enough.

"Good lad," I said, setting the whip and the bag down. I
walked up to him and patted his wet shoulder gently.
"We'll turn you into a Pansy, yet, eh?"

His whole body heaved with the effort of breathing; he
was too tired and disheartened to care who I was. Dull-
eyed, he watched me, not expecting much, I thought. It
was fear, not anger, that made him dangerous. I doubted
he'd ever be a fit mount for anyone else, but he'd trust me,
eventually.

I put a normal halter on him, not his usual one. It had
taken a long time to wear him down to this point, but I
doubted anyone would have to worry about his aggressive-
ness for a few hours yet. Tomorrow would be a better
gauge of the progress we'd made. I hadn't hurt him once.
He'd remember that long after the effects of his running
were gone.

His ears twitched. I turned and found the Brat standing
right next to me. She knew better than to approach a horse
like Stygian without a good reason, so I wasn't surprised
to see my uncle standing by the fence. He scared her,
mostly, as far as I knew, because he was the twins' father
and our father's brother.

It took a heavy tug on the lead rope to get the stallion to
move—something I'd work on later. First things first. Penrod took him from me as soon as we'd cleared the gate
while another groom ran into the ring to gather pots and
whip.

"We've set the funeral for late tomorrow afternoon,"
said my uncle, approaching me. "It's too warm to wait
longer, though it means your aunt cannot make it here in
time."

I looked at him, then allowed my face to clear with

comprehension. *Ah,* he would think (I hoped), *the moron remembers his father died today.* I nodded.

He waited, clearly hoping for some further response. "I see you're not taking Penrod's advice. I talked to him after the Hurogmeten died. That beast needs to be put down."

Fat lot you know, I thought.

"He's pretty," I said. "Hot blood and small spaces. Big things like him and me need space." I thought about the tunnel leading to the dragon bone cave and the raw places on my shoulders ached in response. "Lots of space."

"He killed your father, Ward. He's dangerous."

I looked at him. "If he couldn't control him, he shouldn't have ridden him." It was father's favorite axiom with variants like, "If he couldn't beat him, he shouldn't have started the fight."

Duraugh turned as if to go but twisted abruptly and closed in until we were face-to-face.

"Ward," he said intently, "your mother may be Tallvenish, but you are born and bred Shavigman. You know that our land is ruled by magic. I've fought skellet in the high reaches—"

Ciarra darted behind me at the mention of the unquiet dead.

"—and I've seen a village the Nightwalkers destroyed." Duraugh waved a hand vaguely southward. "The Tallvenish laugh at our fear of curses, but you aren't a flatlander, are you?"

I didn't know what he was getting at, but I played along. Ducking my head awkwardly so I could meet his eyes, I whispered, "We have a curse."

And an embarrassingly poor curse it was, too. No verse, no obscure references, just something that looked as though a group of adolescent boys had scratched it into a stone wall. It wouldn't have been so bad if the wall hadn't been in the great hall. The only reason visitors didn't laugh when they saw it was that it was written in old-style runes that few people could decipher.

"Do you know what it is?"

I blinked at my uncle a moment before I decided it was something an idiot could know. "The house of Hurog will fall to the underground beast."

"The stygian beast, Ward. Stygian is the underworld beast. Fen thought it a good name for a warhorse. He picked better than he knew. That stallion is an underworld creature," he said intently. "He should have been killed long ago. Do you see?"

I'd known Stygian had been named for the beast who came from the underworld to gobble the souls of the dead who hadn't lived well enough to go dwell in the houses of the gods. Who'd have thought Uncle would take it so seriously? It occurred to me that the curse had already come to pass. Because the bones of the underground beast lay chained in a hidden cave under the keep, Hurog's riches were gone, and there were no dragons in the world.

Hurog didn't need the Stygian beast to destroy itself the rest of the way. My father was . . . *had been* a madman. My mother ate dreamroot and took little note of what went on about her. My sister was mute, though not a healer or magician could tell why. My brother had tried to take his own life.

"You *do* see?" Duraugh asked, obviously forgetting in his obsession that he was talking to the family idiot.

"I see very well," I replied to remind him. "But what does that have to do with the horse?"

My uncle was a good-looking man, better-looking than my father if not so handsome as his own sons. But anger took away from his looks; maybe that's why I enjoyed his reaction so much. The Brat buried her face against my back as he controlled himself with an effort.

"Stygian was your father's doom. If you don't see that, he'll be yours as well."

"He is a horse," I said doggedly. "And I changed his name. Stygian takes too long to say. Pansy. His name is Pansy." I liked the name better every time I said it.

OREG, THE BOY FROM THE DRAGON BONE CAVE, came to me as I got ready for bed that night. I didn't see him come in the room, but when I dried my face after washing, he was sitting on the corner of my bed. I acknowledged him with a nod, sat on a stool placed near my bed, and began trimming my toenails over the empty chamber pot with my knife.

He watched me for a while. But watching someone trim their toenails is dull work, so finally he spoke.

"Do you know what the ring is for?"

I shook my head. There was a long silence during which I switched to my fingernails.

"Do you know who I am?"

I nodded my head this time. He stood up and began to pace, muttering to himself. Finally, he stopped in front of me and put his hand over my knife to still it. His hand was warm and solid, though in the bard's stories, ghosts always have icy, ephemeral touches.

"Who am I, then?" he said, frustrated anger in his voice. I wondered if he'd watched me when I wasn't pretending. Did he know my game?

"Don't you know who you are?" I asked, widening my eyes.

He dropped to the floor in a depressed sort of flop and buried his face in his hands. The back of his neck looked vulnerable. He reminded me of my brother Tosten.

I stared at him for a long moment. There was no one I trusted with my secret. Not even Ciarra really, though she might suspect.

"Who are you?" I asked crisply. "I don't know much

more than a few ghost stories. And I don't believe you are a ghost."

His head jerked up at the difference in my voice. I put my knife away, kicked the chamber pot under the bed, and prepared to listen.

"It's true isn't it?" He whispered, more hope than certainty in his voice. "You've been pretending all these years. I thought it might be so. I couldn't tell earlier."

He watched me for a while, but I didn't know how to explain it so it didn't sound stupid and melodramatic.

"Do you know who built Hurog keep?" he asked finally.

His tone was wary. He'd already learned that asking questions was a risky business. But I'd decided he wasn't a player in the game. He was mine as Hurog was mine. I touched the platinum ring lightly with my thumb.

"No. I know he was given charge of the dragons here at the behest of the high king."

Oreg snorted bitterly. "Then you know nothing at all. The Hurog title came hundreds of years later. Hurog keep is old, built early in the age of the Empire by a true mage—not like that idiot of your father's. When the mage retired from court, he built his fortress here, where no one would bother him, because they were afraid of dragons."

He looked down and traced a pattern on the floor. "He wanted a house that would take care of itself, so he wouldn't be bothered by servants pottering about or soldiers practicing in the courtyard. He had two sons by his wife, a mundane woman who had the good sense to die when she was young. One son became a field commander and died in some war or other; the second was a wizard in his own right. I was born of a slave woman and sold to a nobleman's family, but when he gave them money, they sent me back to him here."

He stopped. I wasn't certain I wanted him to continue. I'd heard enough bards' tales to know where the story was

going, or maybe I'd just had too much experience with my
father to expect much of his.

"When I got here, he was alone; there were no servants.
He gave me a bowl of soup from a pot he had brewing in
the fireplace. I fell asleep. When I awoke, I was the keep."

I stared at him while I examined his last words. *He was
the keep,* he said. I remembered the oddity of stepping
through the hidden door into my room, though I *knew* we
had been somewhere deep in the mound the keep sat upon.
I weighed the possible responses I might make and in the
end chose to make none at all.

"Thank you for taking care of the Brat today, Oreg." If
you said something unexpected, I'd learned that you often
got more answers than if you asked questions.

His head snapped up, and he looked at me, frowning.
Whatever he thought to read in my face, I don't think he
found it. "I try to watch out for her," he said. "It isn't much.
A door that lets her escape to a quiet place where her father can't find her but her brothers can."

We sat for a bit in a companionable silence, while I
thought about what he'd meant when he told me that he
was the keep. I played idly with the unaccustomed ring on
my finger.

"You can't take the ring off," Oreg said with a start, as
if he'd just remembered what he'd come here to do. "It
gives you control of the keep. Only if you are dying will it
come off. Then you must give it to your heir."

"If I give it to someone else?" I asked, after trying to get
the ring off and failing. I wished I'd known about that
before I put it on. Rings weren't good to wear when you
fight; they change your sword grip and catch on things. At
the very least, I'd have put it on my left hand.

"Whomever you give it to becomes your heir."

"Ah," I said. "Tell me more about the spell, the ring, the
keep, and yourself."

His face went curiously blank. I recognized the look.

After all, I'd practiced it in the polished shield on my wall until it was the expression I usually wore. I wondered if he'd watched me. If he'd had cow eyes like mine, he might have looked stupid, too. As it was, he just looked secretive.

"I am a slave," he said. "Your slave, Master, bound to your ring. Soul slave to you. Whatever you ask of me, I will do if I am able—and I have much power."

I thought of what that would have meant to some of the more disreputable of my ancestors. He was a pretty boy, like my brother. Poor slave.

"If I were to ask you to sit where you are without moving, what would happen?" I asked.

"I sit here without moving," he said with bleak truthfulness, "until you die or tell me differently. I must do whatever you tell me." There was tension in his body, though if he'd been here all this time, he should know that I didn't torment people in my power. But, I supposed, that like Stygian . . . *Pansy,* it would take him time to learn.

"When you said that you were the keep, did you mean that literally? Or that you are tied to it by magic?"

"I don't think there is much of a difference," he said, examining his hands.

"Do you know what's going on in the keep?"

The boy tilted his head, his eyes looking at something other than what was before them. "In the great hall, the fire is banked for the night. There's a rat sniffing in the corner for food. Your uncle is standing before the fireplace, hands behind his back, rocking a little on his heels—"

"Enough," I said. "Can you look more than one place at a time?"

"No more than you can look at the far wall and behind you at the same time."

"Can you hear as well?"

"Yes."

I rubbed my pant legs. I could work with Pansy's fears because I understood him. I won over Penrod by the same

means. I needed to understand Oreg as well as I understood the mistreated horse. "Does it hurt you when the
keep is damaged?"

"No," he said, then continued almost reluctantly, "I can
feel it, but it doesn't hurt."

"Do you occupy the whole of the keep, or just the older
parts?"

"The whole keep, and that which belongs to it. The curtain walls, the stables, the smithy—the sewers, even."

"If you are the keep, how is it that you still have a
body?" I asked, tipping my head at his human body.

"It amused my father."

I thought about what he'd said for a while. "If the keep
is damaged, it does not hurt you. Does it hurt you when
your body is hurt?"

"Yes," he whispered, tensing.

Well, if I'd spent the last fifteen years as my father's
slave, I'd have whispered an answer, too. From all accounts, my grandfather had been worse. Deliberately, I
yawned. It was late, I needed to sleep.

"My father never mentioned you at all."

"Strategically speaking, it is better if I am secret from
your enemies—a harmless ghost that wanders the halls."
He hesitated, then ventured, "I prefer to keep my presence
quiet. I don't like people very much."

Nor would I, I thought, *after so many years of serving
Hurogs.*

"Right." I said. "Here are my orders for now. Continue
your protection of my sister. I'd like to meet you here each
night when I am alone. Other than that, do as you will."

"Do you want me to protect you, too?"

I grinned. Powerful he might be, I was willing to accept
his word on that, but he was half my weight. "I've had
years to learn to do that. If I can't, well, then I'm not fit to
be Hurogmeten, am I?"

"There are those who say you aren't fit anyway," he said, a challenge in his voice.

I couldn't decide if he was testing my temper or if he still half believed my act. Maybe he knew the truth better than I did. Abruptly, I felt tired.

"Yes. Well, now. I'd be sad if they thought me competent after all the effort I put into shoving my stupidity down my father's throat. I can hardly hold that against them, can I?"

He laughed, though I thought it was because he believed it necessary rather than because my words actually amused him. He was silent for a while then asked, "Why are you pretending to be stupid?" He hesitated and said tentatively, "I always wondered about that. It seemed so odd that you would spend all those hours in the library. But then you would read and read but never seemed to understand what it was you were reading." As he spoke, he bounced off the bed and strode oh so casually out of my reach.

"Thought I might be looking at the pictures or the pretty inks?" I asked, amused.

"What happened when your father hit you that time? If it wasn't brain damage? And even an idiot listening to you now could see that your brain is fine." He grinned shyly, a boy venturing an opinion or a slave flattering the master, but he'd put furniture between his body and me.

Like Pansy, I thought, he'd learn that I wouldn't harm him. Besides, I'd pried into his private pain; it was only fair to give him the same opportunity. "It damaged something," I said. "I couldn't speak at all." I remembered how terrifying it had been to have thoughts that wouldn't turn into words.

"You weren't just frightened?" asked Oreg.

Looking at him, I could see he knew what it was to be so frightened he couldn't speak. Pity choked my reply. "No."

"You couldn't walk, either," he said speculatively.

I nodded. "Or stand or anything else." It had taken Stala and me years to strengthen my left side until I was as fast with my left hand as I was with my right. Sometimes I dreamt that the strange, overpowering numbness had overtaken my left arm again.

"You used to do magic—make flowers bloom for your mother." Oreg was relaxing a bit. He'd settled on the bench near the door.

"I can still find things. Ciarra nearly scared me out of a winter's growth today when I discovered she was suddenly so far below me. I take it she didn't fall out of the tunnel like I did? You led her by another path?" He nodded. "But otherwise, I can't work magic anymore. I can feel it but not work it."

"But you aren't stupid. Why did you pretend?"

"So my father wouldn't kill me." I tried to put instinctive knowledge into terms someone else might understand. "My father is—was the Hurogmeten. Perhaps you know what that means better than anyone else. To him it was the most important thing a human could be, better than high king, but the title was only temporary, to be given away like this ring when he died."

"But all men must do that," commented Oreg reasonably. "His father entrusted Hurog to Fenwick. He would live on through his children."

"He killed my grandfather," I said. It was the first time I'd ever said it out loud.

Everything about Oreg went still. Then he whispered, "Your grandfather was killed by bandits. Your father brought him here to die."

"My grandfather was struck from behind by my father's arrow. My father admitted it once when he was drunk."

We'd been hunting, just the two of us, when I was nine or ten. We'd camped up in the mountains, and my father began drinking as soon as we'd set up the tent. I don't remember what led him to confess, but I still remembered the look he'd turned on me afterward. He hadn't meant to let that slip, and even then I'd known it was dangerous knowledge. I'd pretended I hadn't heard him, that his words had been too slurred. It might have been that slip that sent him over the edge, but I'd come to believe his antagonism went deeper than that.

"He saw me as a rival for Hurog. Time was his enemy, and I its standard bearer." That sounded like something my hero Seleg might have written in his journals. It also would have sounded better on paper than it did out loud, so I tried for a less dramatic tone. "My father didn't like to lose battles."

I left the bed and went to the polished square of metal hanging on the wall. I looked like my father, not so startling without the Hurog blue eyes, but a younger version of my father all the same. The size came from his mother's family, but the features were Hurog. "I was his successor, a constant reminder that he would someday lose Hurog. I'm not certain even he realized it, but from the day I first held a sword, he thought of me as a threat. You might recall, if you were paying attention, that the beating responsible for my "change" was not the first time he beat me unconscious. If it had continued, he would have killed me before I was old enough to defend myself. And I had the example of my mother to follow."

"When she lost herself in dreams, he didn't beat her as much. Or visit her bed," agreed the boy solemnly.

"My speaking problem made my father think I'd become an idiot, and I decided to take advantage of it."

"Why continue it now, after he is dead?"

I felt my way to an answer. "My uncle rules here for the next two years. Like my father, he was raised to believe that becoming Hurogmeten is the summit of what a man can accomplish. I'm not sure he'll want to give it back."

"You're so certain he's a villain? He was a nice boy . . ."

Oreg's voice dropped to a whisper. "At least I *think* it was Duraugh, but sometimes I don't remember so well."

I closed my eyes. "I don't know him, only that he has little patience with idiots. The gods know I wouldn't want an idiot in charge of Hurog, either. We live too close to the edge of survival." I shrugged and looked at Oreg, who'd somehow come to be crouched at my feet. "I don't trust him."

I'd talked more to Oreg than I ever remember talking to anyone except Ciarra. Speech was still something of an effort, and it tired me. Ironic how honesty felt much more awkward than lying."

"Trust your instincts," said Oreg after a moment. "It will harm none if you remain cautious for a while yet."

He left then, not going through the passageway or the door, just disappeared, leaving me to my memories."

My instincts, eh? My father was dead, and I didn't know if I was joy- or grief-stricken. Hurog was mine at last, but it wasn't. Should I reveal myself? Say, "Thought you'd like to know I'm not really an idiot"? I wasn't even sure that there was anything left of me but the stupid surface covering the constant vigilance underneath. I would wait.

I RESTED MY FOLDED ARMS ON THE TOP OF THE FENCE rail and breathed the early-morning air while Harron, one of the grooms, told me about the night's excitement.

Someone left the gate to the mares' paddock open, and Pansy was found snorting and charging in the paddock with my father's best mare ("Who was in season, damn the luck," Harron said cheerfully). The other mares were safely in their barns, but Moth had been restless. Penrod had thought a night in the field might calm her. He had spoken to my uncle about it.

As Harron talked, we watched most of the stable hands

and my uncle chase Pansy with halters, ropes, and grain buckets. Pansy eluded his pursuers with a flagged tail and a shake of his magnificent head. My uncle saw me and left the stablemen to their job. While he climbed through the fence, I sent Harron to get grain and a halter.

"Some idiot left the gate to the mares' paddock open," growled my uncle.

It was too good an opening to miss.

"I checked on them last night," I lied. "Pansy was in the stallion's paddock then."

My uncle stared at me.

"I checked on the mare, too," I said earnestly. I'd have to learn to be more cautious. My father saw what he wanted to see, but my uncle might not be subject to the same weakness. If I took every opening he gave me, he'd notice what I was doing.

"Here ya are, Ward!" huffed Harron, and he heaved a grain bucket in my general direction—up. On top of the bucket was the halter I'd requested.

I grabbed the bucket and rolled over the top of the fence.

"They've tried grain, Ward," said my uncle. "They'll get him eventually. Leave them to their work."

I continued walking but said over my shoulder, "Thought I'd catch the mare."

Moth, unlike the sex-ruled stallion, was greatly interested in the food. Moreover, she knew and liked me—and my father didn't ride mares. When she realized what I carried, she trotted up to me, dancing a bit with early-morning pleasure and shaking her silver gray mane.

"Liked that, did you?" I asked her, one conspirator to another. Both of us ignored the grooms chasing futilely after the stallion on the far side of the pasture. "I'd think he might be a little tough on the ladies, new as he is to this. But you have more experience. Looks like you showed him properly." She preened a bit at the admiration in my voice as she munched the treat I'd brought her with dainty greed.

She allowed me to slip the halter on her. It was too big, but with her, it didn't matter. I gave her a quick once over with my eye, but aside from a rough, dried patch of hair on her neck where he must have nipped her, she hadn't come to any hurt.

I led her out of the field and into the stallion's paddock, and she, fickle thing that she was, paid no attention to Pansy, who'd finally noticed me stealing his mare and filled the air with frantic bugling. Harron, having seen what I was about, waited at the gate between field and paddock and shut it after the charging stallion was in the smaller enclosure. By then, I'd let the mare out of the far gate and just shut it behind us when the furious stallion struck it with his hooves.

Grinning, Harron ran up and took Moth. She gave Pansy a coy look, then followed Harron quietly back to the mares' barn.

"How did you know to do that?" Duraugh asked.

"What?" I asked blinking at him.

"How to catch the stallion?"

I snorted. "Have you ever tried outrunning a horse? I have. Took me most of the day to decide that he was faster than I was." I leaned closer to him and continued conspiratorially, "Horses are stronger and faster, but I'm smarter." His face went blank at this assertion, and I laughed inwardly.

Penrod had climbed through the fence and come around as I said the last.

I nodded at the stable master and said more prosaically, "Besides, that's how Penrod caught old Warmonger whenever he got out of his pen—which he did about once a day, eh? Food never worked, but lead a mare in season by him, and he was her slave." Warmonger, the last of my grandfather's mounts, had been almost human in his intelligence and mischief.

Penrod nodded and grinned. "Damned horse could open any fastening we ever concocted. And quick, he was. Only way we ever caught him was with a mare. Finally, we nailed his door shut behind him."

I returned his grin. "Then he just jumped his way out."

So my father'd killed him. I could still see the satisfaction on his face when the last evidence of his father's reign lay dying on the ground. Penrod's humor quickly faded back into his professional mask. No doubt he was remembering the same thing I was.

My uncle hadn't followed our thoughts; his smile didn't fade. "I'd forgotten Warmonger. He was a grand old campaigner. My own stallion is from his line."

Would it be so stupid to tell Duraugh the charade I'd been playing? Maybe if he knew me, really knew me, he would like me. Perhaps my uncle could guide me in the task of ruling Hurog. Despite the midnight raids to the library and the unobtrusive, obsessive attention I'd paid to my father's method of governance, I felt ignorant. My uncle had been ruling his own lands successfully for the last two decades.

I opened my mouth, but he spoke first.

"The burial is this afternoon. I told Axiel to find you something appropriate to wear from your father's wardrobe. I noticed yesterday that you've outgrown your court clothes, and Axiel told me that you've nothing else suitable. I would appreciate it if you would go in and change. I don't suppose there's any way to get Tosten home in time for the funeral, but tell me where I can find him, and I'll send for him today."

He slipped it in oh so casually, that mention of my brother.

"Axiel's my father's man," I said.

Tosten and I were all that stood between my uncle and Hurog.

"He's agreed to look after you," explained Duraugh with obvious impatience. "Ward, where is your brother?"

Iftahar, my uncle's Tallvenish estate, was larger and richer than Hurog, but it wasn't Hurog. No dragon claws had gouged the stone of the watchtowers. I thought that even a man who owned a rich estate might hunger after Hurog.

"Ward?"

"I dunno," I said.

"But you told Fen . . ."

"Oh, he's safe," I said. "I just don't know where."

MY FATHER'S BODY SERVANT, AXIEL, AWAITED ME in my room, wearing the Hurog colors of blue and gold. He was a small man, tough as boiled leather. My mother, when I asked her, said that the Hurogmeten had brought him back from some battle or another.

When he drank enough, Axiel claimed to be the son of the dwarven king, and no one was foolhardy enough to gainsay it, because Axiel was as tough as my father.

Axiel's olive skin and dark hair had, as far as I could remember, looked the same as when I was a young child. Most of Hurog's people, including me, wore our hair after the style of the Tallvens who ruled us, shoulder length and loose. Axiel, who was not a Shavigman at all, wore his hair in the old Shavig style, roughly braided and uncut. The long braid was a disadvantage in fighting. The Shavig of old claimed it as a mark of honor that they were so skilled such a meager advantage was none at all.

He was a body servant in the Tallvenish style—a rank closer to bodyguard than valet or squire. Axiel's face showed no sign of grief over my father's death, but then he was my father's servant. Doubtless he'd learned to hide what he felt as well as I could.

"Axiel?"

"My lord." He said. "Lord Duraugh thought that it would be appropriate for you to have a body servant due your rank."

I nodded.

"I've taken it upon myself to ready the Hurog—your father's second set of court clothes for you, sir." He opened the door to my chamber for me.

There was a small room above the tallest of the shelves of the library behind the decorative curtains that covered the whole of the upper walls. I'd happened upon the little room by chance, and I thought that my father might be the only other person who knew it was there—and he didn't frequent the library. From that room I'd spent many afternoons secretly watching Axiel train with knife and sword. His style was completely different from my aunt's, and I'd found that incorporating gleaned bits of it in my fighting made me a better fighter.

If Axiel were loyal to me, I would be a lot safer than if he were loyal to my uncle. I stopped in front of the fireplace and looked at the gray remnants of last night's fire. But safe from what? Before my father died, I'd fought for my life. What was I fighting for now?

"If you would allow me?" Although he sounded as if he were asking permission, Axiel stripped my clothes off of me with great efficiency. While I scrubbed, he trotted over to my bed.

"My lord?"

I looked up from washing my face to see the servant holding two sets of clothing.

"I brought this in from your father's rooms." He held up one of the familiar gray outfits my father favored. "But someone else has been here, for I found this on top of it."

I took the tunic from the second set of clothing from

him. Deep blue velvet, so dark it was almost black, it had the Hurog dragon embroidered in red, gold, and green across the front shoulder. The velvet alone would have cost ten gold pieces, if not more, and there was no one here, other than perhaps my mother, who could embroider well enough to do the work on the dragon. The undershirt was the color of faded gold, and I didn't recognize the fabric.

"What's this made of?" I asked.

"Silk, sir. You haven't seen these before either? It's not from your father's wardrobe nor from anything I saw in your uncle's wardrobe."

"I'll wear this," I said, running my rough fingers over the undershirt, "if it fits."

"Fitting for the death of the Hurogmeten," agreed Axiel. "But where did it come from?"

"Maybe the family ghost," I said seriously after a moment's thought.

"The ghost?"

"Surely you know of the ghost?" I asked, slipping the undershirt over my head. It fit as if it had been newly tailored for me. Perhaps it had. His father hadn't wanted any other servants, he'd said.

"Yes, of course, sir. But why would it choose to do something like this?"

I shrugged, settling the velvet tunic over the silk. "Ask him." I exchanged my trousers for the loose silk ones that matched the undershirt.

I looked at the polished metal I used as a mirror and noted that the unaccustomed glory of my clothes made me look dashing and heroic. I was very careful to look stupid, too, before I left the room.

THE FUNERAL WAS A GRAND THING; MY FATHER would have hated it. But he wasn't there to object. My mother, dressed in gray velvet—her wedding gown—was

ethereal and beautiful. My uncle, beside her, appeared
strong and stalwart, the perfect man to protect Hurog.

My sister looked like a lady grown, nearly as tall as
Mother. I did some quick calculations and realized that
Mother had been married when she was Ciarra's age. Like
me, Ciarra was clad in a blue velvet gown, though her
dragon was a small embroidered pattern around her neck-
line. Oreg had been busy.

Waiting in my place at the open grave on the hillside
opposite the keep, I had a full view of the funeral proces-
sion, and they had an equally good view of me, their new
(and temporarily powerless) lord.

I'd ridden up here on a good-natured gray gelding who
looked particularly well in Hurog blue. Everyone else
trudged up the hill on foot. Stala, in dress blues, led the
pallbearers behind Erdrick and Beckram, who brought up
the rear of the family group.

Of us all, Stala might be the only one who really
mourned my father. Her face, I noticed, was still and
tearless.

I watched, standing apart from the rest of the ceremony
as the bearers lowered him carefully into the dark earth, as
my father had watched his own father put to rest. Doubtless he'd felt satisfaction as the wooden box hit bottom.

I looked across the grave at Mother, and I could tell
from my uncle's tight face that she was humming again. I
had vague memories of a time when my mother had been
gay and laughing and had played with me for hours building wooden-block towers while my father fought in the
king's wars.

The Brat watched the box with the Hurogmeten in it
settle into the soft earth. She flinched when my uncle set
his hand upon her shoulder. I thought of my brother, who'd
given up everything to leave my father.

*May the underground beast take you for what you have
made of your family,* I thought to the dead man. But per-

haps being Hurog was enough justification for the gods, too, for no dark beast rose from the shadows of the grave to devour my father's body, despite my uncle's fears.

Dismounting, I took a handful of earth and tossed it on the grave. *Stay there,* I thought at the Herogmeten. Bitter waves of fruitless anger beat at my composure. If he'd been different, I might have my brother standing beside me, to help with the overwhelming task of keeping Hurog alive. I might have a mother who could bear the burden of daily chores and free me to chase bandits and reap the fields. I would not have been standing, half mad, with tears sliding down my face as the pallbearers, men of the Blue Guard, pushed dirt over my father's grave.

In the end, I think I was the only one who cried. Maybe I was the only one who mourned. But I did not mourn the man who lay in that grave.

"DOES MY UNCLE KNOW ABOUT YOU?" I ASKED Oreg, who was stretched out on the end of my bed. From my stool, set before the fireplace, I watched him while I sharpened my boot knife. The clothes I'd worn to my father's funeral were hung up in the wardrobe. I wore instead the sweat-stained clothes I'd worn to training with the Blue Guard this evening. Not even the Hurogmeten's funeral interfered with training.

"No." Oreg closed his eyes, his face relaxed. "Your father never told anyone more than he had to."

I held the knife up so the light hit it better. I couldn't see it, but I knew the knife had developed a wire edge; otherwise it would have been a lot sharper after all the time I'd worked on it. I bent down and grabbed a leather strop out of my sharpening kit and set to work.

Oreg rolled over so he could see me better. "A man came here this evening to talk to your uncle."

"The overseer of the field with the salt creep," I agreed mildly, stropping the knife.

"Your uncle's wizard didn't fare any better than old Scraggle Beard." I'd learned that Oreg disliked Licleng, referring to him as a "self-aggrandized clerk." "There are going to be hungry folk here this winter."

I ran my stone over the edge a few more times. I licked my arm and drew the knife along the wet area. This time it sliced the hair off cleanly.

"Yes, but Hurog will survive." I decided to change the subject. There was nothing I could do about the harvest. "Thank you for the clothes. I assume you're responsible for the Brat's wardrobe, too."

He nodded. "I'm very good with clothing."

"Did you do the embroidery by hand?" I asked.

He shook his head. "Magic work. But I do sometimes, when I have the time. I . . ." He closed his eyes. "I often have too much time."

I stretched out and threw another log into the fire, which was getting low. Even in the summer, the old stone building got chilly in the evenings.

3
WARDWICK

I was caught in the web I'd spun. Instead of breaking free,
I tried to convince myself I was safer there.

"AT LEAST HE CAN FIGHT," I HEARD ONE OF THE MEN
mutter to another. I couldn't be sure who it was just from
the voice, and my eyes were occupied with my opponent.

"One on one, *when* he doesn't have to remember orders.
But in three years, he'll be giving the orders. I'm gonna be
gone by then." No mistaking the oddly nasal tenor of
Stala's second. In the three weeks since my father's death,
I'd been treated to several variants of this conversation.

A muttered curse from my opponent brought my attention back to the fight. Ilander of Avinhelle was new to the
Guard, and this was the first time he'd drawn me for all-out
pairs.

The Blue Guards drew fighters from four of the five
kingdoms: Shavig, Tallven, Avinhelle, and Seaford. If a
man lasted a few years here, he could expect to be first or
second in any guard. There weren't any Oranstonians because fifteen years ago, the Blue Guards under my father's
command had been instrumental in putting down the
Oranstonian Rebellion.

Ilander might have been new, but he understood that my aunt had trained me since I picked up the sword, so he shouldn't have assumed I'd be easy. Still, he'd watched me all week in drills after Stala had announced the participants in the weekly slaughter. But drills were drills, and all-outs were battle. During drills, I regularly "forgot" the patterns, especially if Stala changed them very often. I slowed down and refused to use all my strength against an opponent who was just interested in getting the swings right. Was it my fault Ilander thought that meant I was slow and clumsy? Ilander, who thought that playing tricks on the stupid boy was really funny.

I smiled at him sweetly as I gave an awkward twitch of my sword in a feeble-looking attempt to parry his deadly slice. It made him look really bad when my parry worked. He growled and swung overarm in the mistaken impression I couldn't hit his body with a killing stroke and still catch his blade before he lopped something important off—like my head.

Stala called it with a shrill, two-fingered whistle as soon as the tip of my sword whipped across his belly armor, but it was my blade that stopped his sword. In a serious fight, he would have been dead. If I hadn't caught his blade, I would have been dead, practice or not. He wanted to continue; I could see the rage in his eyes as I met his gaze mildly.

"Good fighting," I said earnestly, stepping back and letting his sword slide off mine. "It was good fighting, wasn't it, Stala?"

Stala snorted. "Ilander, you're not a boy. You should know better than to get angry with your opponent. When you're facing someone who has already proven stronger than you, not to mention faster, it's the height of stupidity to pull a move like that overhand. You're lucky you didn't really get hurt."

"I'm sorry I made you mad, Ilander," I said, giving him my best cow-eyed look. "I won't do it again."

Ilander, who'd been flinching under the sting of my aunt's tongue, returned to his earlier state of rage. His face flushed, and his nostrils flared whitely. "You—"

"Careful," barked Stala, and Ilander shut his teeth with an audible click. When she was satisfied he wasn't going to say anything more, she relaxed. "Go wash up. You're off for the rest of the day. Lucky will take your place on guard duty."

Lucky's position in the circle of guards was just behind Stala and to her right. Being a relatively intelligent man, he stiffened apprehensively. She didn't even look at him, keeping her eyes on the dirt in front of her. "I told you to quit fleecing money from the fledglings, Lucky. How much did you take him for?"

"A silver, sir."

"Betting that he couldn't beat Ward."

"Yes, sir."

"You know what? Sometimes I can work magic better than Licleng. Watch me. Poof!" She raised her hands in a theatrical manner. "That bet didn't happen."

He thought about arguing, opened his mouth to do it twice. "Yes, sir," was all he got out.

Lucky taken care of, Stala turned her attention to me. "Ward, you haven't even worked up a sweat."

I frowned thoughtfully, decided sniffing my armpit would be overkill, then nodded my head.

"After everyone else is through, you and I will have a go of it, eh?"

I smiled and nodded. Even if no one had thought I was stupid before, the smile would have done it. No one beat Stala. Like Lucky, I wondered just how much she knew. Did she, for instance, know that I'd baited Ilander deliberately? Did she intend our upcoming bout to punish me for it?

• • •

SWEATING ENOUGH EVEN FOR STALA, I LIMPED up the stairs of the keep. Every movement hurt, but that was to be expected. Stala was tall for a woman, and thirty-odd years of fighting had made her muscular. I was stronger, faster, and had a longer reach than she did, but Stala fought dirty. In an all-out, the only thing that mattered was winning, and she liked to win.

I rubbed my left eye cautiously, removing a few more grains of sand. I couldn't use dirty tricks without giving my act away, but I was learning them, all the same.

When I opened the door, Oreg was waiting in my room with a smirk on his face. I forgave him the smirk as soon as I saw the tub of hot water. I dropped my unpleasantly damp clothing and stepped into the water. The tub was built for my father (the only thing besides Axiel that I had appropriated), so I fit inside it. I sighed as the heat pulled the stiffness from my aching muscles.

"Do I thank you or Axiel?" I asked, reaching for a sliver of soap.

"Axiel hauled the water, but I've heated it again."

"Thanks," I said, ducking my head under the water and staying there for a bit. But the stain of what I'd done this morning still clung to me. Oh, there was no shame in losing to my aunt. Everyone lost to her—but most of them couldn't make her work for it. What bothered me was the fight with Ilander.

I came up for air.

"I watched you fight," said Oreg, sitting on my stool and balancing it on two legs without putting his feet on the floor. I wondered if his balance was that good or if he was using magic. My ability to detect magic was a vague thing, and Oreg infused any area he was directly in with so much magic, I had a hard time telling if there were small spells being worked. It felt like Hurog's magic, and I sometimes wondered if he was the magic I could always feel here or if he just tapped into it.

He used his magic a lot more than most magicians I
knew—even the good ones at court. I couldn't tell if he was
more powerful, less discreet, or just trying to impress me.

"You mean when my aunt almost eviscerated me?"

"No," he smiled at the wall beyond me. "When you
made an idiot out of the new guard. Ilandei? No, that's a
Tallvenish name and he's Avinhellish. Ilander."

My father was dead. My uncle was acting like a consci-
entious regent, handling the affairs of Hurog as well as if it
were his own estates. Better, perhaps. For the last three
days, he'd been out most of the day working to reclaim the
land the salt had taken. He'd had broken shells brought
from the sea in wagonloads and was directing their spreading on top of the salt. It wouldn't work. My several times
great-grandfather, Seleg, had tried something similar when
the creep had first been seen, but it hadn't worked. I'd read
about it in his journals.

I could have saved Duraugh three days of work. But an
idiot would hardly have read the dusty, mostly illegible
scrawls hidden on a remote shelf in the library. Guilt vied
with fear. No longer was it fear for my life—nothing so
noble.

So to distract myself from the guilt of watching Duraugh put all the effort into a losing project, I played games
with an unfortunate guardsman while my uncle struggled
to do his best for Hurog.

"You showed him," continued Oreg unhelpfully. "He
won't try that trick with oatmeal and helmets again. Not
on you. He's learned to treat the Hurogmeten with more
respect."

I watched Oreg narrowly. Was he commenting or fish-
ing? Could Oreg see the guilt that rode me? I couldn't tell.
My father's care had made certain I was very good at reading people, but Oreg was another matter altogether. He'd
been a slave for a very long time.

I grabbed another sliver of soap and used it to scrub my hands clean of the metallic odor of my sword.

"What was my uncle like as a boy?" I asked to distract him from this morning's fight.

"I think I liked him." Oreg's stool rocked back and forth. "It's been too long ago. I used to remember everything, but I stopped doing that. Now I forget as fast as I can." His face had a blank inward look that made me uneasy. It usually precluded some of his odder moments.

"You think I should let him know," I accused. "*You* were the one who told me to listen to my instincts."

He set the stool carefully down on all four feet, then slid off and away, out of my reach. Pansy was coming along much faster than Oreg, but then Pansy had only four years of mistreatment to forget. "What could he really do to you? You're not twelve anymore. I think . . . I think that the pretense is harming you more than it is protecting you."

"I'm going riding," I said, standing up in a rush of water, ignoring his flinch at my sudden movement. I took a bit of toweling and dried myself briskly. "I need to clear my head."

As I dried off, I couldn't keep my lip from curling up in a self-directed sneer. Oreg was right: Regardless of my uncle's trustworthiness, it was time to throw off the disguise, but that's where the fear came in. I didn't want to confess to my uncle that I'd hidden myself under a mask of stupidity for seven years out of fear of my father. It had been easier to tell Oreg, but then Oreg knew my father as I had. He had been here when my father had beaten me almost to death in a frenzy of jealous rage.

It was beautifully ironic. I, who had pretended for a third of my life to be an idiot, didn't want to appear to be a fool.

I laughed shortly and stalked to the wardrobe to get fresh clothing. "When I get back, I'll tell my uncle that I'm not as dumb as I look."

•   •   •

I HADN'T RIDDEN PANSY MUCH YET, AND THE RIDE
I envisioned wasn't one that would do him any good at this
stage. My usual mount for my mountain runs was a big
liver chestnut mare I called Feather for the wisp of white
on her wide forehead. She was deep chested, big boned,
and loved to run as much as I needed her to.

For her, the wild race over the side of the Hurog mountains was fun; for me, it was a necessary escape. While we
raced up narrow trails and down steep-sided gorges, I had
to keep my mind on where we were going rather than let
my thoughts twist round and round about matters I had no
control over.

While we ran, the only thing that was real was the heav-
ing of her great barrel under my calves and the thunder of
her hooves. I smelled the sweat of her effort and heard the
even rhythm of her breaths. When that rhythm broke, I
would stop.

The trail I directed her to today was challenging, full of
dead-fallen timber and abrupt twists. We both knew it well.
Usually, we stopped at the top of a craggy ridge near a
lightning-struck tree and turned back toward Hurog at a
saner pace. But when we flew past the tree, Feather was
fresh, and I was still twisting between right and embarrassment.

We tore around a sharp corner at the top of a steep
slope. I leaned my weight to the inside to help her negotiate the abrupt turn, and the soft soil under her outside hoof
gave way.

She would have fallen then, and we'd have rolled all the
way to the bottom of the mountain, except that I shifted my
not inconsiderable weight and pulled her head around to
send us galloping swiftly down terrain that was little better
than cliff face.

I gripped her with my legs and watched her ears so I
could anticipate the direction she would dodge around the
larger rocks. I had to steady her head without interfering in

her frantic attempt to keep her legs under her as our combined weight pulled us downward. If the slope hadn't been so steep, I could have thrown my weight back and asked her to slide on her haunches, but here such a move would have been fatal. There was a tangle of downed trees at the bottom, and somehow she managed to leap and jump through them at a speed no sane horse would have taken.

If she had been a fraction less bold, we'd never have made it. I honestly don't know how she kept her feet—nor for that matter how I stayed on top while she did it—but we were still upright when she stumbled to a halt. Her breathing rocked me, and the sweat of terror and effort warmed my legs.

"Shh, Feather," I said, patting her neck. "What a good girl you are, what a lady," and other such nonsense until the white left her eye and she rubbed her head on my knee with one of those incredible contortions horses are capable of.

I swung off and landed on wobbly legs. I checked Feather over thoroughly, but she only had two minor cuts and no lameness. By the time we were halfway home, she was cool and relaxed, unlike me. I'd almost killed the both of us with my stupidity. When we got home, I'd explain everything to my uncle.

THE GROOMS WERE WORKING ON A PAIR OF STRANGE horses that looked even more tired than my poor Feather when I rode into the stable yard. From the colors on their headstalls, gold and gray, they were Garranon's.

Garranon was an Oranstonian noble; moreover, he was the high king's favorite. Normally, he spent all of his time at court or hunting on the estates of various acquaintances because Oranstonian lords, even the king's favorite, were forbidden to spend much time at their own estates, a consequence of the Oranstonian Rebellion. I couldn't fathom what he would be doing here.

THERE WAS NO ONE IN THE GREAT HALL EXCEPT FOR Oreg when I came in. He stood splay-legged, hands clasped behind his back, and stared at the ancient message, the Hurog curse, carved into the wall.

There was such intentness in his expression that I stared at it, too, but it hadn't changed. The runes still looked as though they had been rough-carved with a hunting knife, but no knife I'd seen would dig into stone. In some places, the writing implement had dug in almost a finger's length, and at others, it was little more than a faded scratch. Each rune was nearly as tall as me.

"Oreg?" I said, after a quick glance to confirm that the room was empty. I was the only one who saw him whenever he was present. He used some sort of magic to keep other people from seeing him, though he usually showed himself to Ciarra, too. I'd learned to be very careful about talking to him in public places. I was supposed to be stupid, not crazy.

Magic began to gather in the room so strongly it brought a flush to my face. Much more magic than usually surrounded Oreg.

"Oreg?" I asked with a bit more urgency.

"I wrote this," he said, waving a hand at the wall. "I did it after he killed the dragon. Her eyes shimmered with silver waves, and he killed her, so I presented Hurog's future to him."

"It looks like a lot of work," I observed, trying to draw his attention. I'd begun to recognize when Oreg was about to have one of his fits. Sometimes he talked to people who weren't there or just stared blindly through me. Usually, he left abruptly, and the next time I saw him, he was fine. But once or twice, I'd been able to pull his attention to me and stop the fit.

"He couldn't read it—illiterate *bastard*." His voice hit the last word with raw hatred.

"It's in old Shavig. Not many people can read it," I commented.

"He had me beaten when I told him what it said." As he spoke, the threads of his shirt parted in a short, straight line down his back from his right shoulder to his right hip. He flinched, and another line of broken threads appeared. Incredulously, I saw blood darken the edges of the material, but Oreg didn't turn his attention from the wall.

"Oreg," I said, trying to keep my voice calm, though this time I could hear the snap of a whip as a third invisible blow hit him.

My mother could work illusions. Sometimes I'd walk into a room in the castle, and it would be filled with vines and exotic flowers from her homeland in southern Tallven. This didn't feel like an illusion: Blood dripped from his back to the dusty floor.

"Oreg, that was a long time ago. He can't hurt you anymore," I said.

"He could have killed me," continued Oreg in that unnaturally calm voice.

I stepped between him and the wall to catch his eyes, but when I saw his face, I couldn't say another word. His face was swollen past recognition, and white bone showed through his cheek.

"But he didn't. He had someone else use the whip. Do you know why?"

"No," I whispered. "Tell me."

"Because he didn't want to lose Hurog. He knew how much I wanted to die. He wore the ring so only he could kill me, and he knew that's why I baited him. So he had someone else do it."

"Oreg," I said, touching the top of his head gently, for it was the only place unmarked by ancient pain.

"Ward?" said my uncle just behind me. "Who are you talking to?" His voice was soft; it sounded very much like the voice I was using on Oreg, whom he obviously couldn't see.

So much for my plan to explain to Duraugh that I was really normal.

"I was reading the words on the wall," I said without looking around. "My brother Tosten tried to teach them to me once, but I only remember a little."

"Ah," said my uncle, sounding much relieved. "Garranon and his brother are here."

I turned abruptly from Oreg, trying not to react when he began a high-pitched keening as I pulled the shield of stupidity firmly around me. The visitors had hung back while my uncle approached, but it only took me a few strides to reach them.

"Garranon!" I grabbed his hand hard and shook it vigorously, despite his decorous attempts to escape. Then I slapped him on the back, holding him in position with the hand I still held.

He gave a muffled yelp. My uncle threw his arm around my shoulder and pulled me off unobtrusively. "Lord Garranon and his brother Landislaw have ridden all the way from court this past week," my uncle said.

Garranon was about average height with fine-boned features, curly brown hair, and thin lips that smiled too easily. He looked younger than he was, which I suppose was the attraction he still held for the king. His brother Landislaw looked very like him, but somehow Landislaw made the same features appear rugged rather than aristocratic. On Landislaw, Garranon's thin nose became strong and masculine. The narrow lips were firm, the smile charming. With the two of them together, one thought of scholar and warrior or stag and blooded bull—or so the ladies of the court said.

After I made everyone sufficiently uncomfortable by staring at them, I nodded my head. "Court is boring. I would have come here, too."

Landislaw laughed. "Truthfully said. I've enjoyed this past week more than any week at court. I'll be sorry to see it over." Landislaw was a panderer and a bully whom I disliked intensely.

Garranon was still rubbing his shoulder unobtrusively, but he had court manners. "I wish to express my condolences."

I looked at him inquiringly.

"For your father," he said.

"Oh," I said with sudden comprehension. "Yes, for my father. Died a few weeks ago."

Disconcerted at my lack of filial mourning, Garranon's practiced speech left him. I liked Garranon more than I wanted to like the high king's favorite. I liked him even better now when his presence meant I had to wait to tell Duraugh the truth.

My uncle stepped in smoothly. "Now that Ward's here, perhaps you will tell us what brings you here, my lords."

"Hunting?" I asked. Oreg had quit making any noise but soft grunts, but the sound of leather hitting flesh echoed in the hall, and the thick magic kept me from concentrating on our guests.

Garranon snorted sourly. "Yes, we're hunting—but not the kind you mean. Landislaw bought a slave from an acquaintance. Now he finds that the slave wasn't his friend's to sell." A slave? Poor abject things, they were commonplace in Estian at the high king's Tallvenish court as well as other parts of the Five Kingdoms. Shavigmen didn't own slaves.

"It belonged to his father," added Landislaw with a graceful grimace.

"*His* father," continued Garranon sourly, "is Black Ciernack."

"The moneylender?" asked my uncle, clearly shocked. Maybe he hadn't heard the rumors about Garranon's brother.

Oh, Landislaw was not in debt, quite the contrary. He brought friends from court into friendly gambling dens, just seedy enough to appeal to the jaded young courtiers. The dens belonged to Ciernack. If Landislaw's friends lost money there, it surely wasn't his fault. Just ask him.

"The moneylender," agreed Garranon. "Before Landislaw could return her, she ran away. So we've been chasing her ever since. Frankly, if Landislaw hadn't discovered that someone had been feeding her stories that Hurog is a refuge for slaves, we'd never have found her. From the tracks we've followed, she's in a tunnel down by the river. I don't know how she got in there: *We* couldn't move that grate. But her footprints continued beyond the grating."

Garranon was speaking to me rather than my uncle. It was one of the things that made me like him. Most people at court tried very hard to forget I was there, even if I was standing beside them.

I frowned at the floor. "Sewers."

Garranon snapped his fingers. "Of course. I was wondering what that tunnel was. I'd forgotten that this place—" He made a sweeping gesture around the room. "—was dwarven made."

"No," I corrected. "Just the sewers."

"Ah." Garranon nodded. "Even so. We have an escaped slave in your sewers, and we can't get beyond the grate that seems to be sealed to the tunnel mouth."

Not when I'd been there last, I thought. As far as I knew, the grate should still be off its hinges, because I'd forgotten about it. Oreg must have sealed it after the slave ran inside. He had more reason than most to care for a runaway slave. Perhaps that was what had set him off on his fit.

Behind me, the sound of the whip had become rhyth-
mical, though Oreg had quit making any sound at all.

"We left the men and dogs there and came here to see if
you had a way into the sewers," said Garranon.

"No," I said.

"You've been in the sewers, Ward," reminded my uncle
with a frown. "Certainly you know how to get into them."

I nodded. I did indeed. "No slaves at Hurog."

Garranon and his brother regarded me warily, but my
uncle began frowning. He knew what I meant; I could see
the apprehension in his eyes. I had no particular fondness
for slavery or Landislaw. If Oreg wanted to save the poor
thing, I felt no compunction about helping him.

"We followed her in," said Landislaw slowly, perhaps
thinking I'd understand it better that way. "She went in
through the grate. We could track her that far. But she
won't be able to get back out that way, since we left men
guarding the grate. We need a way in."

"Only way in is through the grates," I said mildly.

"You can open them?" snapped Landislaw, dropping his
pleasant act. He must be really worried. It didn't bother me
to see him sweat. One of the boys Landislaw had led into
Black Ciernack's nets had killed himself. He'd been a good
lad, kind to his stupid friends.

"Yes," I agreed.

"Then let's go get the slave out," snapped Landislaw, ignoring his brother's hand on his shoulder.

"There is no slave," I said, smiling at him as if I thought
he were hard of understanding.

My uncle bowed his head, shaking it slowly.

Perhaps forgetting that my stupidity was in my head
and not my body, Landislaw grabbed my upper arms.

"Wrestling," I said happily and tossed him a dozen feet
into the pack of mastiffs that usually lolled about the fireplace when no one had them out hunting. "I like
wrestling."

"Not," said my uncle firmly, "in the keep, if you will, Ward."

I looked hurt and pointed at Landislaw. "He started it."

Garranon had turned away so that I was the only one who saw his grin.

"I don't think he intended to wrestle with you, Ward," replied Duraugh in a long-suffering voice. He walked to the sputtering lordling who was fighting off the cheerful tongues of half a dozen dogs. "Here, now Courser, behave yourself. Down, Two-Spot. My lord, take my hand. You might remember that my nephew likes nothing more than a good wrestling bout. He's civilized enough if you keep your hands off him." There was cool rebuke in his voice.

Landislaw gave me a cold look, but he'd gone beyond the bounds of guest manners, and he knew it. He took my uncle's hand and climbed to his feet.

"I believe I know what Ward was trying to tell you," continued Duraugh, escorting Landislaw back where Garranon and I waited. "As someone must have told your runaway, by ancient law, there are no slaves at Hurog."

"I knew that, my lord," said Garranon, "but what does your choosing not to own slaves have to do with our slave?"

"You don't understand, my lords," apologized my uncle. He repeated himself. "There are no slaves here. If your slave has made it onto Hurog land, then she is no longer a slave."

Landislaw looked at him in disbelief. "You're jesting."

Garranon turned to my uncle, though he kept a tight grip on his brother's arm. "Lord Duraugh, surely you could make an exception this time."

"No," I said firmly, though my uncle was nodding. "There are no slaves at Hurog. As I am Hurogmeten, caretaker of these lands, there are no slaves here. All who come to Hurog are free to stay here peacefully; Hurog is sanctuary to all." It took me a good long while to get it out, not being particularly swift of tongue.

My uncle recognized the song I quoted from, one of the more famous sagas about my hero, the Hurogmeten Seleg. (Seleg hadn't started the tradition of no slavery—it was an earlier Hurogmeten who needed people to help farm the land—but Seleg had revived it.) The other two men, not being Hurogs, stared at me as if I were a cow that suddenly began talking.

"Ward, that is only a story," Duraugh said carefully. Testing, I think, to see how he could persuade me.

I smiled. "Mother told me I should be like Seleg." I could see the dismay in my uncle's eyes.

Every man who lived on Hurog lands knew the stories, and there wasn't a man here (or woman for that matter) who didn't revere old Seleg. Reminded that Seleg had taken pride in Hurog's refuge status, they would all be on my side, whether my uncle agreed or not, and he knew it. Landislaw was not going to leave with his slave. Poor Landislaw.

Duraugh frowned heavily at me. "Gentlemen, give me some time to talk with Ward . . ."

"Should be locked up . . ." said Landislaw.

My uncle raised his voice. "I'm sure that you and your men are very tired. I'll station a few of the Blue Guard at the sewer tunnel and let you and your men rest. You'll feel better after a good meal and some sleep. Ward, you need to change out of your riding gear. I'll be up in a moment to discuss some business that has come up since you left this morning."

Oreg screamed suddenly, and I couldn't help flinching.

Garronan stiffened, an odd, listening look on his face. "What was that?"

"What?" asked Duraugh.

"That sound. Like something dying . . ." his voice trailed off when he realized no one else was reacting.

"Ghost," I said casually. "I'll go clean up, now." I bowed to everyone in general and bounced up the stairs in character. As soon as everyone cleared out, I planned to go back and check on Oreg.

Axiel waited for me in my rooms. Mutely, he helped me disrobe and wash up. He didn't even comment about the new set of Oreg-sewn clothes lying on my bed ready for me to wear to dinner. I'd have to talk to Oreg about that. I didn't mind Axiel knowing about the "family ghost," but it wouldn't do to have him the topic of common gossip.

My bedroom door opened just as Axiel was tightening the lacing on my left arm—the right was already done.

"If I could speak to you for a moment alone?" asked my uncle.

I nodded. Axiel finished the lacing and bowed his head shortly. "I'll be in my quarters if you need me."

Duraugh waited until the valet left before he began pacing back and forth. "Out of the mouths of children and . . ." His voice trailed off before he added "idiots." "Where did you get your sense of right and wrong, Ward? Not from Fen, I vow. Much as I loved him, he was a chip off our father, and Da would have laughed himself to butter if someone reminded him that Hurog was supposed to be a refuge."

I stood where I was, moving my head with his pacing— something that looked particularly idiotic. I stopped when I remembered that I was going to tell my uncle the truth.

He halted midstride as if it had only been my head movements that had powered his steps. "I came up here to argue with you. If word of this gets out, we'll be a target for every runaway slave in the Five Kingdoms. We'll be laughed at in the king's court. But that wouldn't matter to you, would it?"

He didn't sound like he wanted an answer, so I didn't answer him directly. "In Hurog there are no slaves."

He sighed, but it sounded almost like a sigh of relief. He

stared past me, speaking as if to himself. "There are no slaves at Hurog. The ancient law, written into our charter by the first high king states when any slave sets foot here, they are freemen from that time forth. That my father and his father chose to forget it makes it nonetheless true. Landislaw and Garranon will just have to take their chances with Ciernack. Seleg's word still holds true in Hurog."

"Garranon's all right." I said. "Landislaw can rot."

Duraugh frowned. "You don't like him? Why not?"

This was my chance to tell him that I was smarter than he knew. But my tongue was never swift, and in the end, I just shrugged. I'd wait until Garranon was gone.

"If you had liked him, would you have declared the slave free?" asked my uncle.

I frowned at him. It was a good question. Was most of my decision based on spite? Would I have remembered the ancient laws if Landislaw hadn't been in the middle of it? I thought of Oreg mourning in the great hall and the chained dragon somewhere below the keep. Too many Hurogs had forgotten their laws over the centuries.

"There are no slaves at Hurog," I said.

My uncle gave me an odd smile and half bowed in a gesture of respect. "Indeed." He shut the door behind him.

The only slave who remained in Hurog said, "Ward? You won't turn her in?"

I turned to see Oreg standing before the panel in my wall that had opened into the passages. The cuts and marks were gone, and he seemed lucid again, though he hugged himself and shifted from one foot to the other anxiously.

I wished suddenly that I knew how to free him, too. Perhaps I'd talk to one of the king's sorcerers next time I was at court, though I wasn't sure I wanted anyone else to know our secrets. I also doubted that even one of the king's wizards could unlock an enchantment that would last so many years. Everyone knew that mages were more powerful in the Age of the Empire.

"I won't turn her in," I said.

Oreg raised his chin. "Really?"

"Really." I hoped the firmness in my voice was enough to convince him. "You've seen that she has bedding and food?"

"Yes," he whispered, "but she's still scared. I put her in the cave with the dragon bones." In a softer voice, he said, "She hasn't seen me. I just put warm things and food in the cave. I should have told you this morning."

"You've sealed her in the cave?" I asked. "She's been there all day?"

He nodded.

"I'll go talk to her," I said. "She should be all right in the keep, even if Garranon and Landislaw haven't left yet. Or she can wait there if she likes and you have no objections."

Oreg had come to me for help. Yesterday, Pansy had whickered when I came up to his paddock. Miracles do happen. Oreg stared at me uncertainly—looking as young as my brother had that last day. Sometimes I could forget what Oreg was, but not after the scene in the great room a few minutes ago. He'd come for help, but he didn't quite trust me enough to take it.

"She will be safe," I assured him.

Though he didn't move, the panel behind him slid open. He turned on his heel and walked through. I followed, and the panel slid shut behind me. This time, the passage was very short into the dragon cave, as if it were merely adjacent to my room instead of deep in the heart of Hurog. As I crossed into the cavern, I noticed two things: The first was a strange, thrumming noise inside, and the second was the magic filling the cavern like thick soup fills a pot. I could see faint glows twinkling among the rocks, and the back of my neck kept telling me that there were things watching from the shadows.

When I stopped, Oreg turned back to me and said,

"She's trying to work magic, but she isn't strong enough to break my protection of the bones here in Hurog."

We hadn't been quiet coming in, but she didn't seem aware of us as we maneuvered through the rubble to the sandy area where the dragon bones lay. She sat in front of the skull. Her hair hung in matted, filthy clumps halfway down her back. She was so dirty it was hard to tell much more about her, even in the light provided by the dwarn-venstones. The thrumming sound I'd heard was her singing, though it sounded like no music I'd ever heard.

I was watching her so closely, it took me a moment to notice that the chains were off the skeleton. I'd thought about doing it myself but had come to the conclusion that it was too much like hiding my family's guilt. A dragon's remains being found deep in Hurog would not be surprising; having it bound made our culpability clear to any who saw it. So I'd left it as it was.

"Welcome, fair traveler, to Hurog's hearth." I gave her the traditional greeting, making her status as my guest real, whether she realized it or not.

She must have been absorbed in her spells, because at my words, she jumped to her feet like a startled rabbit, and her voice choked off. Before I could say anything further, she made a throwing gesture with her right hand and a flaming, crackling *something* launched itself from her hand with blinding speed.

Then it stopped several lengths in front of us and winked out.

"Peace, little sister," crooned Oreg. "I'm sorry I had to leave you here, but I had to know what the Hurogmeten intended before I knew what I could do for you."

She lifted her chin. "I am not your sister." Her voice shook, disguising everything about her accent except that she had one.

"Why did you come to Hurog?" I asked peaceably.

"I thought Hurog was supposed to be a place of refuge,

where dragons and slaves are safe. The others laughed at me. Then I came here and found they were right." She gestured toward the dragon's chains that lay near her.

I decided she was probably from Avinhelle, though Ilander's accent was much thicker. The Avinhelle folk were given to slavery, so that would make sense. But something about her didn't ring true; she didn't sound as subservient as she should if she were a slave.

"You are safe here," I said earnestly. "You may stay at Hurog if you wish. It might be wiser to stay down here until Garranon and Landislaw are gone, but that is up to you."

"Who are you to say this?" she asked scornfully after staring at the two of us a moment. "The both of you are little more than children." The effect was ruined when her voice broke.

Lines of weariness gathered about her mouth and eyes. Garranon and Landislaw had looked tired, but they'd been on horseback. She'd been . . . I looked down and muffled an exclamation. She'd been barefoot.

"Oreg," I said, ignoring her earlier question. "See her feet?"

He looked down. "I'll get a pail of water and some of Penrod's witch hazel brew from the stables," he said and vanished.

The woman's eyes widened, and she sat down abruptly. "Who are you?" This time there was no accusation in her voice.

"Ward," I said companionably. "My father, Fenwick of Hurog, died a few weeks ago, so I am Hurogmeten—though my uncle rules Hurog until I'm one and twenty."

"And he?" She asked gesturing vaguely at where Oreg had been standing.

"Oh, Oreg?" I thought about what I could tell her. "He's a friend."

"He is a wizard," she said, almost to herself.

"Well," I confided, deep in my role as idiot, because that was how I always dealt with people, "I really don't think he's a wizard. We have a wizard here, but he doesn't look at all like Oreg."

"Wizards don't all look alike," she said in surprise.

"Uncle Duraugh's wizard and Father's wizard look alike," I protested.

"That's because they're brothers, Ward," murmured Oreg gently, returning from his errands.

I blinked at him for a moment. It was easier than usual to look stupid. I wasn't used to him popping in and out in front of me. "Oh, right. I'd forgotten that."

I motioned her to a broken slab of rock that was just a little low to be comfortable.

"I'm pretty good at this," I said, taking the bucket from Oreg and setting it on the ground at a comfortable distance in front of her. "The Brat used to cut her feet up all the time because she didn't like wearing women's slippers. Got her some good woodsmen's boots. Mother didn't like them, but she didn't have to doctor the Brat's feet, either." By the time I finished speaking, she looked calmer.

I took the pottery bottle holding Penrod's brew and uncorked it. I poured a fair portion into the bucket. Cautiously, she put her feet into the bucket, hissing when the disinfectant touched the cuts. I dipped the clean vegetable brush Oreg handed me into the bucket and pulled out a foot.

She'd done some damage. The whole bottom of her foot was raw and embedded with dirt. Knowing that there was nothing I could do to lessen the pain of scrubbing, I set about doing it well once, so I wouldn't have to do it again. When I was satisfied I'd gotten all the grit and filth out of that foot, I set it back in the water and picked up the other one.

All in all, she was a strange slave, I thought. For one thing, she'd demonstrated she was mageborn when she'd thrown magic at us. Although I suppose a mage could be made a slave, I'd never heard of one. For another, tired as she must be, she had none of the dull helplessness I'd seen in all the slaves I'd ever met.

"What will your uncle do when he knows I'm here?" she asked tightly.

"He already knows," I replied, frowning. There was some infection starting on this foot already.

"My lord?" said Oreg, his face going distant. "Your uncle is looking for you. Supper is ready."

"Can you finish here?" I asked.

He nodded, his eyes still unfocused. "If you hurry, you can meet him in your rooms."

GARRANON AND LANDISLAW WERE SEATED ON either side of my mother, across from my uncle and the Brat, while I sat at the head of the table. Garranon was his usual smooth self, but Landislaw was grim and silent.

"So," said Duraugh. "What is the news from court? I haven't been there since Winterfair."

Garranon set down the bite he had been going to eat and said, "King Jakoven is worried about Vorsag, still." Vorsag lay just to the south of the Five Kingdoms, along Oranstone's southernmost border. "The new ruler, Kariarn, is said to be unstable, and there is some question as to whether he will hold to his father's treaties."

"There was some question as to whether Kariarn's father would hold to the treaties," replied my uncle. "I've met Kariarn, and I'd say there is no question at all about him. He'll hold them as long as it suits him and not a moment more. I've heard that there have been Vorsagian border raids in Oranstone."

Garranon nodded. "I've sent most of my men back to my lands with my arms master."

"But your estate is more than six leagues from Vorsag,"

said Duraugh, his voice tautening from relaxed conversation to honest interest. "If there are bandits that far in, why isn't the king sending troops?"

"King Jakoven accepts Kariarn's claims that it's a few lone bandit clans increasing their activity, or even Oranstonians doing the raiding themselves." I'd never heard Garranon utter a word against the high king, but there was a bitter edge to his voice. "Jakoven won't declare war over a few bandit raids."

"War?" I asked, trying to sound eager, the way an idiot who was good at fighting would say it.

Garranon shrugged. "The king won't go to war over Oranstone unless the Vorsag decide to start taking land rather than riches and lives." He said it with casual ease, and I wondered if I'd imagined the earlier bitterness. He was Oranstonian, but he'd been the king's lover for fifteen years.

I turned my outward attention to my food. War would mean leaving Hurog in the hands of . . . someone . . . while Duraugh, I, and the Blue Guard traveled all the way across the Five Kingdoms to Oranstone. With the threat of bad harvest, it wouldn't do Hurog any good at all, except there would be fewer mouths to feed.

Like my uncle, I'd met the Vorsagian king, Kariarn, at court. He was one of those men who was not particularly blessed in feature or form but left you believing he was. He'd been decked with bone charms and followed about by a handful of mages. The official word was that he was a mage himself, but I thought not. His attitude about magic was wrong for a wizard; reverently obsessive, when the wizards I knew reveled in it.

"Don't you, Ward?" asked Landislaw.

I looked up. "What? I was thinking."

He smiled. "Your uncle was just telling us about your father's horse. Said it was a killer, but you have it following you around like a lady's puppy."

"Easy to get a horse to follow you," I said cheerfully. " 'Nuther matter to ride him. Had me off three times this week."

"Hmm," said Landislaw neutrally. "I was observing to your uncle that you collect misfits like the stallion. You did it at court. Remember that gawky girl last year, Garranon? Even look at your sister—though a woman who can't speak is not a bad thing. And now you're trying to add my slave."

Duraugh and Garranon smiled politely; the Brat looked nervous and tried to be invisible in her seat.

Mother looked up and said in the rambling-dreamy way she had this late in the day, "But of course he does. If he weren't the heir, he'd have been sent to apprentice with the mages, but his father wouldn't hear of it. The High King Jakoven himself commanded Fen to do it. We don't have nearly enough mages anymore. But before Fen could send him, there was that terrible accident. And then Ward wasn't at all suitable for learning magic." She turned back to her meal.

Landislaw frowned at her. "What does that have to do with Ward's strays?"

Mother chewed daintily and swallowed, then washed her food down with a small sip of wine. "He's a finder—like the ones in the stories. He finds lost things—and they find him." Her pupils were pinpoints, though the hall was only dimly lit by oilcloth-covered skylights. I wondered which of the herbs in her garden she'd been eating. Dream-root didn't affect the pupils.

I'd almost expected her to get better after Father died, but she seemed instead to lose herself in the role of grieving widow. The woman who'd made my blocks move around the room was gone for good.

"I don't think it works that way, Lady Hurog," objected my uncle. "If he were still a finder, and Fen told me that his abilities disappeared when . . ." He glanced at me, but I chewed unworriedly and rather loudly on a raw carrot. "When he was hurt. If he were still a finder, he would find things; they wouldn't find him."

"Yes, dear," said Mother, just as she had to Father. "I'm sure you're right."

I coughed, feeling sorry for my uncle. It's hard to argue with someone who slides away from your point like wet oatmeal slides around a spoon. Garranon looked particularly uncomfortable, and it occurred to me that eating at a table with Mother and me would not be a treat.

I finished the last bit of bread on my wooden trencher and got up. Duraugh looked at me and frowned, trying to remind me that it was rude for the host to leave while people were still eating. But I thought I'd let Duraugh explain that Hurog was going to hold Landislaw's slave without me.

"Pansy," I said. "He needs some carrots." I showed everyone the ones I'd stolen from the table. The Brat grabbed the remnants of her bread and jumped up after me.

"All right," I said before my uncle could say something about her manners. "You can come. Stay out of the way. If Pansy hurts you, it will make him feel bad."

4

WARDWICK

Running is an act of cowardice. Not that cowardice is necessarily bad. As my aunt used to say, "Moderation in all things."

AFTER I WAS THROUGH WITH PANSY, CIARRA followed me back to my room and manipulated me into a game of thieves and kings. The contest depended purely upon chance, and she was always confoundedly lucky—or else she knew how to cheat.

Oreg watched from his perch on his favorite stool and snickered or rolled his eyes at me as she trounced me. Oreg never hid from Ciarra unless there was someone else present.

"To bed," I said sternly when she'd beaten me yet again.

She laughed, kissed me on the cheek, and danced out of the room.

I waited until the door shut firmly behind her before I turned to Oreg. "How's our fugitive?"

He smiled lazily at me. "Sleeping. She'll stay underground until the other two leave. She doesn't like Landislaw much."

"Nor do I," I admitted freely. "I'll be happy when they're gone from here."

Someone knocked politely at my door.

"I'll just check on our sleeping guest and leave you to deal with Garranon," Oreg said and disappeared. His stool stayed on two legs for a moment before falling to the floor with a loud clatter.

I hadn't changed for bed yet, so I didn't even have to slow for my robes when I answered the knock. Garranon stood just outside the door.

"Hello," I said with an easy grin, holding the door back so he could come in.

He took the door out of my hand and closed it behind him. He stepped close to me and said, "I need your help, Ward."

I blinked at him stupidly. He needed *my* help?

"I found this in my brother's pack tonight," he said, taking a bundled cloth from his belt pouch. "I wondered if you had seen anything like it before."

As I bent down to get a closer look, he lifted the cloth and blew the gray green powder it had contained into my face. Before I fell, I saw him step back and cover his nose.

I AWOKE AND DREAMED I WAS TWELVE AGAIN AND I couldn't move. People shuffled about me, but I couldn't make sense of what they were saying. I screamed and howled in gibbering fear, but not even a whisper broke through my lips. Finally, the outside noises quieted, and for moment I thought it was because my ears had quit working, too.

Then Oreg's voice broke through the fog surrounding me.

"I had to wait until they left, Ward," he said urgently. "Don't be angry with me. Please, please don't be. I'll break you free of it. It's all right."

As the bonds of the magic Garranon used broke, I rolled to my knees with a gasp. "Ah gods," I pleaded, involuntary tears rolling down my face.

"Shh, shh," Oreg whispered, patting me anxiously on the hand. He kept his body angled away from me, afraid that I was going to hit him for not rescuing me sooner. His fear and my ability to move again brought me to myself.

"It's fine," I said. "Thank you." My voice sounded as hoarse as if I had screamed.

I wiped my face with shaking hands and realized I was on my own bed. I struggled to think. *Why had Garranon imprisoned me in a spell and then left me in my room?*

Oreg's head came up. "They're coming back. What do you want me to do?"

"Nothing," I said. "Not unless I ask you."

I could hear voices outside now. My uncle was very angry.

"Don't let them see you."

I stretched back out on the bed and closed my eyes.

"Not so stiff," warned Oreg, so I relaxed as well as I could as the door opened.

"My dear sir," said Garranon in a bored voice, "Ward is unfit to hold Hurog. To ensure for his proper care, he is to be delivered to the royal asylum in Estian as his father requested. I've shown you the king's writ. You don't even have to worry about the usual charges for this service. Knowing the state of Hurog's wealth, I have donated the fee myself."

My father had intended to imprison me in the King's Asylum?

"That was five years ago," argued my uncle. "Fenwick feared the damage to Ward was more extensive than it was."

"The Hurogmeten just didn't want to pay the fees," corrected Garranon dryly, "which I have done. The only thing you can affect now is who holds Hurog. If you help me recover the slave, I will see that you are named lord in Ward's place."

My uncle inhaled deeply in surprise or excitement.

There was a long pause. What was taking him so long to accept? Here was his opportunity to have Hurog with no blame to himself.

Garranon's voice grew slick and sweet. "The king will listen to me on such a matter, especially since Ward's younger brother has been missing for over two years. Long enough to presume him dead."

"You tie my hands," said my uncle.

"You tied your own hands when you allowed the boy to make all the decisions," replied Garranon calmly. "When we found out the girl was headed here, I thought we might need this. I know your nephew from court. He recites ballads about Seleg by the hour to anyone who will listen."

Only to the people who really annoyed me, I thought.

"I knew he would hold to the old ways. He is too . . . innocent to be negotiated out of it. Unlike you and me."

A hand came down and rested briefly on my forehead— my uncle's hand. "Do you torture puppies, too?" he murmured.

"To protect my brother I would." Garranon's voice was hard.

"I will speak to King Jakoven." Duraugh's tone held warning. "I am not without influence."

I couldn't see it without opening my eyes, but I heard Garranon's smile in his voice. "He will not reconsider. I will have that slave."

Not if Oreg had anything to say about it, I thought. Unless they took Hurog apart stone by stone, she would be safe.

"My lord Duraugh," continued Garranon, "think of it this way. How long would Hurog survive with an idiot to run it?"

From the sound of my uncle's voice as he replied, I knew he was pacing. "And what if I don't want Hurog? Look at it. It's just an old keep, smaller than my own. The only reason it's still standing is sheer Shavig stubbornness. It's too far north to do much more than to feed itself. This year it's not even going to do that. The old mines are played out and have been for generations." He was trying to convince himself, but I heard in his voice the same soul-deep hunger I had for Hurog. I wondered if Garranon noticed.

"Poor? What about the dwarves' treasure? I've heard there was gold, gems, and magical amulets," said Landislaw. I hadn't known he was there until he spoke. I couldn't tell if he was serious or if he was just making one of his idle, cutting comments—or both.

"There have been people searching for treasure since before my grandfather was born," my uncle snapped impatiently. "If there ever was such a thing, it is long gone."

"Hurog could revert to the high king," said Garranon. "His interests leave him with large debts to cover. If *someone*—" Threat added an edge to his voice. "—suggested that he hold Hurog in trust, he might sell off the horses and anything else of value and leave Hurog to rot. If you help capture my brother's slave, I'll see to it that Hurog is yours."

Silence filled the air.

"To hold in trust for my missing nephew, Tosten," said my uncle finally, giving in. "You may have the slave as soon as we get her out."

"I thought you might be reasonable, Duraugh. But you'll forgive me if I post my own guard on Ward's door. In the morning, a delegation of my men will escort Ward to the asylum. Landislaw and I will stay here until you collect his slave."

"As you wish," my uncle agreed. I heard his footfall approach my bed. He touched my forehead again and left the room without speaking another word.

"We might have trouble with him," observed Garranon.

"No," Landislaw disagreed. "The boy will do well enough in the King's Asylum with all the other noble embarrassments Jakoven collects there. Duraugh knows it. His position will hardly change at all. Hurog will be better for it, and so will I."

"You will keep your promise to me?" asked Garranon. "You will stay away from Ciernack's gambling halls?"

"Of course," answered Landislaw. "Of course."

Garranon set a guard on the inside of the door and left with his brother. Alone, except for the shufflings of Garranon's man, I examined my options.

Under no circumstances would I allow myself to be incarcerated in the King's Asylum. Father had taken me to see the poor folk who lived there once—possibly to inspect the fate he'd decided upon for me. The visit had filled me with sympathy for the empty-eyed occupants of the barred rooms.

But I knew I wasn't going to see the inside of the asylum. Garranon didn't know what he'd face getting me out of Hurog. Oreg was my secret weapon, but I expect my aunt would have no trouble stopping him, either. She wasn't one to worry about possible political consequences of her actions, and the Blue Guard outnumbered Garranon's men.

But cold fear still coursed through my heart. My father had found a way to keep Hurog from me after all. Hurog earth was in my bones, and its magic ran through my blood. When I wasn't at Hurog, there was an emptiness inside of me that nothing else could fill. Without it, I was nothing.

Stala could drive out Garranon, but the high king would not ignore treason. Eventually, Hurog would fall—destroyed by me.

I'd have to leave. And it was my own fault.

Garranon was clever; otherwise he would not have survived the war that his father had begun. An Oranstone noble of middle rank, when merely a boy he had taken down more powerful men than my uncle. He knew how the game was played.

Within his realm of corruption in the rougher areas of the royal city of Estian, Black Ciernack was as powerful as King Jakoven. So Garranon had gone after the weaker opponent: me, the idiot.

If I'd told my uncle the truth the day my father died, the whole of Shavig and most of the Five Kingdoms would have known there was nothing wrong with me, and Garranon would not have asked the king for the writ. So the loss of Hurog was my fault.

But first I would escape. Then I would kick myself for being as stupid as I pretended. After that, I'd find some way to win Hurog back.

My decisions made, I dozed lightly for a while until the guard's breathing lapsed into the slow patterns of sleep, and I cautiously opened my eyes. But I had to shut them again when someone knocked at the door.

"Who is it?" grumped the guard.

"I have food and drink for you, sir." It was Axiel.

Axiel didn't carry food. He was the Hurogmeten's body servant. Serving maids carried food.

The guard opened the door, and I heard Axiel step in the room and cross to the table near the fireplace. The guard shut the door, and I heard nothing more. No footsteps, no voices, nothing, until Axiel spoke beside my bed.

"Well, now," he said. "What did they do to you, boy?"

I felt a sudden sympathy for Oreg and Pansy. How much could I trust my father's man?

"A spell," I said, sitting up. I dropped the character of Ward the Stupid (a matter of subtle change in enunciation and facial expression) as I continued. "It's just hard to make a spell stick to a Hurogmeten in Hurog."

He stared at me a moment, and I took the opportunity to glance behind him at the crumpled form of Garranon's guard lying bound and gagged on the floor. I knew Axiel was good, but to accomplish so much without me hearing it was better than good.

I tried a smile. "I think that I'd better leave here, unless you can think of a way for me to oppose Garranon's writ incarcerating me without bringing the king's forces down upon Hurog."

The corner of his mouth turned up suddenly. "Can you define incarceration for me, Ward? Or is your intellect too deficient?"

"Guilty as charged," I said.

He laughed once, quietly. "I've watched you at practice with Stala and wondered how a stupid man could fight the way you do. I should have realized that you weren't as stupid as you pretended." His face grew serious. "We'd best go. When Stala heard that you'd been taken, she started gathering supplies at the stables and sent me here."

"There are some others who'll have to come with us," I said, having already thought through my escape that far. "Ciarra can't stay. She's turning into a pretty girl, and there are too many men who look at her as defenseless because she can't cry out, can't tell anyone what was done to her."

"And you won't be around to scare them," agreed Axiel.

"I have Ciarra and Bastilla—the ex-slave—waiting to leave," said Oreg from the other side of the room.

Axiel had his sword drawn and was halfway to Oreg before he'd finished speaking, leading me to conclude that Oreg had decided, for whatever reasons, to show himself.

"Hold, Axiel," I said, keeping my voice down in case someone was walking in the hall outside my door.

Axiel stopped but didn't sheathe his sword.

"Axiel, this is my—" I hesitated. "Cousin." Thanks to my father and grandfather, there were a lot of Hurog "cousins" around. "He's a wizard, and the reason Garranon's spell didn't stick. Oreg, this is my man, Axiel." Oreg already knew him, of course, but I didn't want to advertise it.

Oreg bowed with old-fashioned formality. Axiel nodded in return, sheathing his steel. I didn't want to give him too much time to think until I figured out a better way to explain Oreg.

"Oreg, is there a passage to the stables? There are guards in the hall."

"Of course," he said. He turned to the nearest wall, not the panel he'd used before, and pressed a stone as if there were some mechanical lever behind it. A section of the wall slid back soundlessly, answering, I hoped, any questions Axiel had about how Oreg had come to my room— even if the answer was incorrect.

The passage Oreg led us down had stairs, dwarven-stones, and dust, just like a real secret passageway would. Maybe it was. When we came to a place where the narrow corridor branched, Oreg stopped.

"It will be faster if I take Axiel to get the horses, and you get the others," he said. "They're in the cave."

"Right." I said. "Axiel, we can meet where the two boulders stick up like rabbit ears on the trail to Tyrfannig."

He nodded. With Stala's help, there would be little problem getting the horses out the gates.

I started down the left-hand way as if I knew where it led. Once I was around a corner and out of sight, I stopped and sat down, because I knew very well I wasn't going to find the cave by trailing through miles of passageway.

Unfortunately, there was nothing to do but think. What *was* I going to do? I had lost Hurog. There was no way around the king's writ except for the king. And I had neither the wealth (even if Hurog's resources had still been mine) nor influence to sway the king. I was just a stupid boy who belonged in the King's Asylum. This would never have happened to my father. He was a war hero.

Oreg didn't bother walking back but simply appeared a few paces away. He took off a money belt I hadn't noticed him wearing and handed it to me. "I told Axiel I'd forgotten some things and I'd meet up with him later. Then I stopped by the study and took money out of the strongbox. Some gold, but mostly silver and copper."

I inspected coins and did some rapid calculations in my head. Taxes would be due after harvest. There were repairs to pay for as well, and hard coin wasn't easily come by. I hadn't even realized Hurog held as much coinage as the belt contained, though it was still far less than a bribe for the king would cost. "How much did you leave?" I put the belt around my waist.

"Enough to do what is necessary. Your father had more than one strong box. This one has been hidden since his death. Hurog is not as pitiful as he liked to pretend."

"Ah," I said for lack of a better response, thinking of all the things a little more gold would have done for Hurog.

"What are your plans, my lord?" asked Oreg.

I started to speak when my thoughts, which had been lingering over my father and the substantial purse I held in my hand, gave me an idea. "My father gave me one gift that might allow me to keep Hurog: Stala's teaching. I know how to lead, to plan battles and, Siphern forbid, when to retreat. I intend to be a war hero." Like my father.

"You have training," conceded Oreg after an unflattering length of time, "but you have no experience and no army—not to mention no war."

I laughed shortly. "My whole life has been a battle. I have experience. If I can prove myself with a sword, it will go a long way to nullifying the king's writ. A nineteen-year-old idiot who is seldom at court is easily disposed of; a commander who has proved his worth in battle cannot be ignored. As for a war, there is fighting going on in Oranstone with Vorsagian raiders. If it's not war yet, it will be soon."

Oreg looked at me as if I were stupid. It was something I was used to, but I didn't like it coming from him, especially when I wasn't playing dumb.

"Commanders generally have armies," he commented. "And heroes are usually dead men. Not coincidentally, dead heroes can't conspire against kings."

I grinned at his dry tone. "Much more convenient for all concerned, I'm sure. But I have no intention of dying. With this much money—" I patted the belt. "I can hire four or five fighting men, and I have Axiel. Enough for a start."

"You'll have me, too," Oreg said. "I asked Axiel to bring an extra horse."

"What?" He had his face in the shadow, so I couldn't be certain of what I'd heard. "Oranstone is halfway to hell from here."

"I know," he said.

I narrowed my gaze at him. "I thought you were Hurog?"

"I am." He gave me a look that was half shy, half smug. "But this body can go with you as long as you wear that ring. I can even work magic—just not as well."

"Can you fight?" I asked. A wizard would certainly be helpful.

"Better than Ciarra, not as well as you."

"Yes, well, that leaves a lot of room," I said.

He smiled slyly.

"Come on then, if you're going to. Let's see to the women and go meet Axiel."

BASTILLA, THE FORMER SLAVE, AND CIARRA WERE waiting for us in the cave along with a small pile of goods. On top of the pile was my chain mail tunic. I'd grabbed my sword before leaving my room, but my hauberk had been tucked in a wardrobe. I was planning on asking Oreg to retrieve it, but he'd anticipated my need.

"Oreg," I said sincerely, "I salute your competence."

Ciarra helped me into the heavy garment, and it settled

over my shoulders like a familiar embrace. While I adjusted belts and sheaths, I explained about the writ and Garranon.

When I was through, Ciarra frowned at me. She tapped her forehead twice. *Not so stupid, Ward,* said the gesture.

"No," I said. "Do you want to come with us?"

She grinned delightedly, and I decided not to tell her I was going to try to find a safe place to leave her until I actually found one; each battle to its own day. My sister taken care of, I turned to the woman beside her.

"Bastilla, I'm sorry that I wasn't able to grant you freedom here, but I'll see to it that you don't go back into slavery."

She didn't react to what I'd said, just studied me.

THANKFULLY, THE RABBIT ROCKS WERE LESS THAN a half mile from the keep because I had to carry Bastilla most of the way. She'd have preferred to walk, but she was too slow.

Penrod and Axiel waited with eight horses behind the pale boulder that stuck up over the tops of the aspen grove surrounding them. Six of the horses were saddled, and two more bore heavy packs. Six with saddles, but there were only five of us.

"Thought you might use an extra hand," Penrod said.

Penrod had fought in the Guard, and he still trained under Stala every day with the rest of the stable hands. My father wanted everyone to be capable of defending Hurog. Three fighting men and a wizard weren't a large force, but it was a good start.

Penrod continued, "My second will tell your uncle that you came to the stables with a strange woman in tow and took the best horses. When I protested, you ordered me to go along and care for them."

"That way they won't tear down the keep looking for Bastilla," observed Oreg approvingly. He held out a hand to Penrod. "I'm Oreg, a cousin of Ward's. He's been letting me hide here while I tried to decide what to do with myself. It seems I'm going to travel with you."

Admiring Oreg's storytelling skills, I introduced Penrod to him, and then Bastilla to Axiel and Penrod. The introductions were necessarily short.

"We need to hurry," said Axiel. "Stala thinks that she can buy us time, but we want to get going."

We turned our attention to getting mounted. For the first time I realized Pansy was among the saddled horses. He snorted at me and shoved his nose in my chest. He wasn't a safe mount yet, but I was pleased to see him, nonetheless. It was Feather's presence that surprised me.

"You brought a mare with the stallion, Penrod?" I asked. Feather twitched a lazy ear in my direction as Ciarra scrambled atop her wide back. Ciarra was the only one besides me who I allowed on Feather.

Penrod chuckled as he checked the cinch on his own muscled gelding. "He knows that saddle and bridle means work. He's traveled with mares before and knows his manners. Feather would have fretted if we left her behind. There's no one left here good enough to ride her. If we end up with a foal out of it, well enough."

It took some sorting to get horses and people together. Oreg, for instance, had never ridden before—something that Penrod hadn't counted upon when he'd picked what horses to take. Finally, we changed the saddle to one of the pack animals, high-bred still, but with a calm manner, and Oreg settled on its back securely enough. Bastilla could ride, thank the gods.

There was no hiding the trail of so many, so I didn't bother to try. We needed distance more than secrecy.

"Where are we going?" asked Penrod, riding by my side.

"South," I answered. "Tyrfannig first. If we ride at a good pace, we'll make it there by morning. I think I'll buy our passage on a freighter headed to a major port in Sea-

ford, Newtonburn, maybe. Then we can continue to Oranstone and see what we meet up with."

As we rode onward, I felt the steady lessening of the
magic that impregnated Hurog. It was a dreary, depressing
feeling, and I knew it would get worse before it got better; it
always did when I left Hurog. I don't think that leaving
Hurog had affected my father the same way, perhaps because
I was mageborn and he wasn't. But it made me feel like a
drunkard deprived of his beer. After a while I'd get used to it
again, but it was always unpleasant, especially now when,
deep in my heart, I wasn't certain I'd ever come home again.

"Did I hear you say Oranstone?" asked Axiel, pushing
forward to ride shoulder to shoulder with Penrod and me.
"Why Oranstone?"

"There's a war brewing there," I said. "And I think it
might be my best chance to regain Hurog. You don't have
to join me."

To my surprise, Axiel, my father's man, who'd been in
countless battles at my father's side, didn't say any of the
things that Oreg had rightfully mentioned about the foolhar-
diness of my scheme. Instead, he grinned whitely in the darkness. "I would be honored to accompany you, my lord."

"If we're going to Oranstone," said Penrod, "shouldn't we
get passage to someplace farther south than Newtonburn?
The road from Newtonburn to Oranstone goes over several
mountain passes, and it will be late fall by the time we get
there. I've done it once, and I'll be honest, my lord, I'd not
care to do that again."

I used the conversation to distract myself from the
growing discomfort as we got farther from Hurog. "I
hadn't actually planned on traveling by sea at all. We'll
buy passage and let Garranon chase the ship while we
travel by road through Tallven to the capital at Estian and
from there, Oranstone is a straight shot south."

5

WARDWICK

I don't know that running was the right thing to do. People died who might not have if I'd stayed. People I loved. But it seemed the only option at the time.

WHAT HAD APPEARED RATIONAL AND ADVENTUR-ous in the dark of night seemed a lot stupider in the morning light. But no better plan presented itself.

As we came down out of the foothills, Tyrfannig lay ahead of us. The scattered buildings, touched by the pink light of dawn, were as familiar to me as Hurog's scarred walls.

I turned to Oreg, who was riding beside me, and murmured, "Can you tell what's going on at Hurog from here?"

"From anywhere," he said. His body relaxed, and his gaze grew faraway. "You've been discovered. Garranon is saddling horses in the stable."

"Thank you." Tyrfannig was four hours' ride at top speed. We'd taken nearer to five. I wanted us to be at least an hour out of Tyrfannig when Garranon arrived.

"Penrod," I called. When he approached, I said, "I'd like you and Axiel to buy what supplies we don't have. I'll get a room at an inn for Bastilla to rest in and leave Oreg and Ciarra there for protection while I go on a few errands of my own."

"Right," he said. "I'll tell Axiel."

When Penrod had ridden off, Oreg asked, "May I come with you?"

I wanted no company, but something in his voice made me ask, "What's wrong?" instead of refusing outright.

"I cannot be too far from you when I'm away from Hurog."

"What do you mean?"

"Unpleasantness for me," he said with a brief, apologetic smile. "Not much for you."

"How far is too far?" I asked. "My business is no more than a mile from the inn. Is that close enough?"

He stared at the tips of his horse's ears for a moment, then said with clear reluctance, "It should be all right."

SINCE NEWTONBURN WAS THE NEXT MAJOR PORT on the coast, I didn't have much trouble finding a ship going there. A ship that was leaving before the pursuit from Hurog would make it to Tyrfannig was more difficult. At last I found that the *Cormorant* was sailing with the tide, and I had to scurry to find her clerk before he left their official list of passengers at the Ship's Office.

I paid for our passage as he warned me that the captain wouldn't wait for late passengers. I assured him that there would be no trouble; if we missed it, we would catch the next one. The clerk thought me a rich fool, which bothered me not at all. Ward of Hurog's name and seven silver each for six passages went down upon the lambskin list, easy for Garranon to find.

From the docks I strode to the south side of town. The streets were a little more unkempt, the buildings smaller. I passed three taverns, several chandleries, and a smithy before turning into a cooper's shop briefly. I backtracked to a scruffy little tavern with a sign proclaiming it the Horned Lord. The name was either blasphemous (the horned god was a reviled figure from ancient times) or audacious (a horned lord could be a lord whose wife slept with other men). Either way, it was sure to appeal to sailors.

As could be expected at this hour of the day, no one was in the tavern when I entered except a ragtag minstrel too involved with the tune he was fingering on an old harp to pay attention to me. I found a clean mug on a shelf just inside the kitchen door and helped myself to ale from an open barrel.

Taking a seat, I listened to the music. The harper was better than I expected, given his youth, though he would have done well to replace the old harp with something better crafted.

"The owner will expect payment for that ale," said the minstrel at length, brushing pale gold hair out of his eyes.

"I have a few coppers," I replied.

"I heard that the Hurogmeten died." He played a few sorrow-laden notes as he watched me.

I nodded and sipped the beer. "I didn't think you'd want to come for the funeral."

He didn't say anything.

At last I set down my empty mug. "I thought to find you working wood at the cooper's, Tosten, rather than playing tunes for a rabble lot of sailors."

My brother's chin came up defensively. "I've no talent for wood. But I can play the harp. It may not be real work—"

I broke in, "Real enough with your skill. Don't confuse me with Father. Music probably pays better than being a cooper's apprentice." He looked away, so I guess it didn't. I cleared my throat. "The reason I left you with the cooper had more to do with your safety than your talents. A handsome lad like you has to be careful around sailors." He stiffened, understanding what I meant, which he wouldn't have when I left him in Tyrfannig.

"You are the new Hurogmeten." He changed the subject abruptly. I couldn't tell what he was thinking.

Tosten had always been a secretive person. I don't believe he'd ever liked me much. My loud, good-natured idiot self had made him uncomfortable, like a noisy dog and a hot-bred horse. My father's rages and beatings—though Tosten experienced them less often than I did—had been worse for him. He'd fought and fought to be what Father wanted, not seeing that Father would never be satisfied.

"No, I'm not the Hurogmeten." I stopped to consider it. Actually, I didn't know what the king's writ did with the title. "At least I don't hold Hurog right now."

I'd gotten his interest. "Why not?"

"It seems our father decided to declare me unfit, and politics have lent him posthumous aid. Unless our uncle decides to get greedy, Hurog belongs to you."

There was a long silence that stretched until the back of my neck tightened with tension. If he wanted Hurog, it was his. I didn't think he would, but he might. He was my brother; I would not fight him for it. Tosten stared through the dark wall of the tavern as his fingers, long and graceful like Oreg's, flexed on the table.

"How?" His voice cracked, as if his mouth were dry.

"After me, you are our father's heir," I said.

"I know *that*," he said impatiently, "but no one knows where I am . . . except you. I meant, how are you going to do it?"

I frowned at him. His voice laid some significance on the last two words. "Do what?"

He snorted. "You don't think I could watch you and Father spar all these years—" He sounded as if he were several decades older than he was. "—without knowing what Hurog meant to you. After you got me out, I thought about why you'd pretend to be stupid when you weren't, and I realized that you were intent on annihilating anything that got between you and Hurog. Father destroying his children; you destroying him." He set the harp aside and stood up to face me. "So you have me here alone, now. You'd better hurry, though. The tavern owner will be back soon; he's gone to get another keg of beer."

I stared at him, feeling as stupid as I'd pretended to be. I had not a clue what he was talking about. Why should I care that the owner was coming back?

"Look," I said. "I have to leave here one way or the other, or else I'll end up in the King's Asylum for Unwanted Nobles and Embarrassing Relatives. If you want to go to Estian and train at the Minstrel Hall there, I can give you money. The cooper knows people; he can find an escort for you. If you want Hurog . . . well, I *think* Duraugh's all right; but you might keep close to Stala for a while. I'll send Penrod back with you, too—" And Oreg if I could manage it. "Maybe Axiel as well." If he wanted Hurog, I wouldn't need an army. I looked around. "I don't want to leave you here, though; it's not safe. If you can think of anywhere else you'd like to go—" I stopped midsentence as I suddenly understood what he thought I was here to do. "You think I'm here to kill you."

I *was* stupid for it to take me so long. The thought that I could kill my brother was so far from the truth, it had never occurred to me he might believe it.

Tosten, watching my face, flinched.

"I'm sorry," he whispered. His hand moved as if he would reach out, but he jerked it back and wrapped it around his harp so hard it must have hurt.

I felt light-headed at the sudden insight into how he saw me: battling for Hurog, so caught up in the struggle that Father's death was the merely the final punctuation.

"If you died, the king would just claim Hurog for the throne," I said, stepping back. I needed someplace to curl up in and nurse my wounds; I needed to sleep away the nagging fatigue that reminded me I wasn't on Hurog soil. I needed to leave here.

"You left the cooper's because you thought he was my man," I said, knowing that was part of the truth, though Tosten had always loved music. "Well, enough. As long as you bring in money, the tavern owner should protect you from harm." To my surprise, my voice sounded just as it always had.

I took out the heavy bag of coins that Oreg had given me and divided its contents in half. I took one pile and slid it back into the purse. There wasn't enough left to hire a band of mercenaries, but I'd find some other way. Half would be enough to pay Tosten's way through whatever school or service he wanted.

He said my name as I walked out the door.

I MET UP WITH THE OTHERS AT THE INN. THEY WERE ready to leave, and it wasn't long before Tyrfannig was behind us. We didn't dare take the main highway to Estian; we might run into Garranon by accident. So we traveled the rougher tracks. We rode through the day and stopped before it got too dark to see.

Stala's admonitions about knowing the men fighting for you ringing in my ears, I assigned Bastilla with me to the first watch. She was still so tired she was drooping, but I was still fresh enough to stay awake until Penrod relieved us.

There was a knoll just above the camp, and I motioned Bastilla to follow me as the others were laying themselves down to sleep. She limped, but it didn't seem to slow her much.

While I sat on a fallen log, she folded her arms and leaned against a tree. Though I couldn't see her clearly in the shadows of the evening, I'd watched her as we rode today, my eye drawn to the flawless beauty of her profile. Oreg had managed a bath for her, and clean, her dark hair glinted with red highlights. She was older than I, perhaps a few years older than Mother even, but I doubted she'd seen her fortieth year.

"So," I said. "Tell me about yourself."

"What do you want to know?"

I smiled. "We may not have slaves at Hurog, but I've been to court. Slaves don't act like you. Slaves are meek and quiet. A slave wouldn't, for instance, have tried to hide how much I was hurting her when I cleaned her feet, because slaves know that making light of pain just invites more of it. Tell me who you are and why Black Ciernack would want you so badly."

She was silent.

"She's a mage, my lord," said Oreg. It was difficult to see him in the dark. I hadn't heard him approach.

"So much I did know," I said. Bastilla had looked around when he'd spoken, so I knew that he hadn't been using his trick of being unseen and unheard by anyone except me.

"I *am* a slave, whatever you believe," she said finally. "And I'm not a very good mage, but I am the only slave Ciernack has who is also mageborn. He finds me useful." She gestured, and a cold white flame appeared in her hand. She held it up and stared into my face for a long moment. Her complexion was pale, but that might have been because of the brilliance of the light she'd called. Her eyes glittered with stress. I don't know what she was looking for in my expression nor if she found it before she extinguished the light.

"I see," I said. "Where did he get you? Avinhelle?" Her accent sounded western, all soft consonants.

She hesitated, then nodded. "From the Cholyte refuge."

"You were sworn to Chole?" The patron goddess of Avinhelle demanded mages to serve in her temples: slaves in truth, but not ordinary slaves. For the first time I believed her claims. "How did he get you out?" I asked. The Cholytes were very well defended.

I could hear the bitter smile in her voice. "My life was dearly bought. I understand the Cholynn was in need of wealth to gain more power with the high king."

"She sold you to him."

Bastilla inclined her head.

"You are free to go where you will, you know. We're about as far from Avinhelle as we can get and still be in the Five Kingdoms, but I can pay for an escort home." And not much more, if the rest of us were going to make it to Oranstone.

She shook her head. "My family sold me to the Cholynn, my lord. They would be obliged to return me, and the Cholynn would simply send me back to the man she sold me to in the first place. I have no place to go. If you take me with you, I'll make myself useful." She lowered her head and shifted against the tree.

"How did you know about Hurog?" asked Oreg suddenly. "Hurog has not been a refuge for runaway slaves for a very long time. If you'd arrived few months earlier, my lord's father would have had you returned to your owner immediately."

She laughed without amusement. "Ciernack has a slave boy whose job it is to keep the fire burning in the room where the men drink. He told me that once a great lord came in and told stories about a fabled keep called Hurog. He must have listened very hard, for the boy knew three or four stories by heart."

I laughed, feeling even more stupid. "No, he probably heard them any number of times. Last time I went to court, I went to Ciernack's place several times and told those stories over and over to anyone with the misfortune to be in my company." I'd been trying to help a friend out of Ciernack's clutches. I'd failed.

So it had been my stories that caused Bastilla to come to Hurog. Even that straw in my downfall had been by my own doing.

I rubbed my face. "You are certain you want to stay with us? If you come, you're likely to find yourself in the middle of a full-scale war in Oranstone."

"Better with you, my lord, than out selling myself in the streets."

"Ah, then," I said with casual cheerfulness, "you'll just have to hire on with a mercenary band." I leaned closer to her and purred, "For you know, 'tis an ill-prepared mercenary who doesn't have his own mage to counter the magics sent against him."

There was a little silence, then she said, "How do you do that? One minute a stupid lout, the next a lord, and an instant later a . . . a . . ."

"Taveln Kirrete at your service," I bowed with more flourish than grace.

Oreg snickered suddenly. "I'd forgotten about him. He was a mercenary who came to train with the Blue Guard a few years ago," he explained to Bastilla. "Thought an awful lot of himself, and he left the day after Stala, Ward's aunt, wiped the dirt with his face. Couldn't stomach being beaten by a woman. You play him better than he did himself."

I bowed shallowly to acknowledge the compliment. Even Oreg didn't see the whole truth. Everyone I portrayed, including the lord, was an act as well. He was gleaned from stories of Seleg and from Seleg's journals hidden in the library. I hadn't been a real person since I was twelve.

"A younger son," I said out loud. "Too many people have met Taveln."

"What?" asked Bastilla.

"I can't be Ward of Hurog; he's too likely to get sent to Estian, eh? Everyone knows he's an idiot who belongs in the King's Asylum. I think I'll be a younger son in disgrace and trying to restore his good name. I took horses and money from my home when I escaped in the night with my faithful retainer. . . . Now, let's see, should that be Axiel or

Penrod? Penrod, I believe, he has that old-retainer air about him—and my squire, Ciarra, whom we shall call Ciar because it's safer for her to be a boy. Axiel will be a man we met upon the road, destitute, a fighter whose master died due to illness . . . the scourge. Oreg will be my cousin or bastard half brother or something."

"Is he?" asked Bastilla, sounding faintly intrigued.

Drawn back from my tale-telling, I frowned. "Yes, but he doesn't like to talk about it."

"I don't?" asked Oreg, raising an eyebrow.

"No," I replied firmly.

"What about me?" asked Bastilla leaning forward.

"She's the cause of your disgrace?" offered Oreg.

"No," I shook my head. "Too melodramatic. I think we hired you at Tyrfannig. An Avinhelle-born wizard stranded at a northern seaport."

"Rescued from a shipwreck?" she offered enthusiastically. "Stranded too far from home to afford passage back, so I took employment with a likely-looking group of soldiers?"

"Sure," I nodded. I liked her, and not just because she was beautiful.

"I thought you were against melodrama," muttered Oreg.

"This is strange," Bastilla said with abrupt seriousness. "I would never have thought to end up here, so far from home. Cholytes are forbidden to leave the Tower. Some of them walk around with a permanent glow from talking to the goddess. But I never felt her. The potions that we were given to help us reach her never worked on me. The Cholynn was very upset because I did neither the goddess nor the Tower any good." Underneath the stiffness, I heard shame.

Oreg snorted. "Drugged the lot of you so they could siphon your powers. You don't need drugs for the gods to touch you. Ask the ascetics at Menogue. They have Aethervon's power, enough to crisp the Acolyte Tower, and their people aren't drained husks after a year's apprenticeship."

I cleared my throat, hoping Bastilla, Avinhelle-born, didn't know much Tallvenish history.

"Menogue? The ruin outside of Estian? I was told it was destroyed in the Reformation Wars." Several hundred years ago. "And Aethervon's order with it."

There was a long silence, then Oreg said, "I'm something of a historian. Sometimes I think I live more closely to the past than the present."

Of course she accepted it. The truth was much less believable.

"How did you two meet?" asked Bastilla after a moment. "Axiel and Penrod don't know you. You're too young to be as good a wizard as you are; even the Cholynn couldn't teleport herself without a complicated ceremony, and you do it in the blink of an eye."

I assumed she was talking to Oreg, as I hadn't teleported myself anywhere.

"Oreg's one of the family," I said.

"Bastard," confirmed Oreg truthfully enough. "I'm older than I look. There was this spell . . ." His voice trailed off, then started up again briskly. "I decided I wanted to see the family estates. It was easy to get in without anyone knowing, but Ward and his sister found me out."

He lied as well as I did; use as much of the truth as you can to give the wrong impression. Perhaps it was something in the blood.

THE NIGHT WAS STILL DARK WHEN I AWOKE TO A touch on my shoulder, and Penrod kneeling beside me. I rolled to my feet with as little noise as I could and gathered my sword. I followed him into the woods and back to the rise I'd occupied earlier, where Oreg was waiting.

I saw immediately what he'd brought me to see. Not a half mile away was the unmistakable orange glow of a campfire.

"Have you checked it out?" I asked.

Penrod shook his head.

"Stay here. I'll take a look, but you keep watch. If you see a scuffle, wake the others."

Walking quietly in the woods is difficult. Doing it in the dead of night with nothing but the light of the moon proved impossible. I was fairly sure that unless the campers were deaf or asleep, they knew I was approaching before I got there.

There was only a single figure visible in the camp. He was wrapped in a thin cloak and perched on a large rock in front of the fire with his back to me. There was only one bedroll.

"I thought it would be safer if you found me than if I tried to ride all the way to your camp," said my brother conversationally, though I was fairly sure he couldn't see me where I crouched under a nearby tree.

"Staring into the fire is bad for your night vision," I commented without approaching closer. I couldn't imagine what Tosten was doing here.

"I don't want to study with the harpers in Estian," he said. "I don't want to be a cooper. I don't want to work as the entertainment for an inn. Most especially, I don't want Hurog." His voice was tight with strain. "I'm *sorry,* Ward. If not for you, I'd be buried in the hillside with the rest of our ancestors who took the easy way out of this life."

I sighed and stepped out so the light of the fire made me as visible to his eyes as he was to mine.

"Don't fret," I said. "You don't know me well, not really. Just enough to know I'm not as stupid as you thought me." I fed a small stick to his fire.

Tosten had only known what I'd shown him. Our midnight ride to Tyrfannig several years ago had been only slightly less dramatic than the confrontation last night. He'd been weak from loss of blood and I'd been in a hurry. There hadn't been time to talk.

It wasn't his fault that when I looked at him I saw the cheerful hellion he'd been as a toddler while he saw a stranger who looked like our father.

I spoke again. "Father would have done it. Would have killed you for standing in his way."

"As he tried to kill you." Tosten's voice was soft, non-judgmental. "Some Oranstonians stopped at the tavern today. They were cursing a ship that had already sailed. The older one, the dangerous one, said he'd send a man to Newtonburn, but the likelihood was that you—he used your name—were gone. He said Ciernack would have to accept money to replace his slave. It would cost more than they could afford, and the money would come out of the younger man's inheritance. Does that sound right?"

I nodded, glad to turn to less painful subjects. "What did you do, spy upon them?"

"No, I played for them. Likely that everyone heard them for a block—at least the younger man. He was vociferous about his objections to spending the rest of the year in Buril—wherever that is."

"Buril is Garranon's estate in Oranstone. Landislaw, his younger brother, is court-raised though. He'll view it as the far side of nowhere." I'd intended on avoiding Buril, but it was good to know for certain. I outlined the events that led to my escape in as few a words as I could.

"So what do you intend to do now?" Tosten asked, the firelight shifting over his face so I could not read his expression.

"I'm going to fight a war with Vorsag in Oranstone."

Tosten, like Axiel, merely nodded, leading me to question his sanity, too. "It might work. War heroes are hard to dispose of neatly." There was no doubt in his voice that I'd be a hero.

"So I thought," I agreed.

Tosten tucked his head down, hair falling over his face. "I would like to go with you."

It was guilt. He'd hurt my feelings and wanted to make up for it.

"Go learn from the minstrels in Estian," I said. "I have enough fighters."

"I'm good, Ward. You know that."

He was. Oh, not like Father and me. His technique was speed and agility not strength, but that made him no less deadly, no matter what Father had said. Tosten would strengthen our party. Five fighters and a sorceress, with only Ciarra to guard.

"If you want to help me, I could use you in Estian," I said. "I need somewhere safe for the Brat."

His face came up, and I saw the same stubborn look that Ciarra had. "I'll not go to Estian. You don't have to let me travel with you, but I'll follow. Don't forget I have plenty of money to travel."

I closed my eyes. There were many reasons to welcome him and only one to send him away. I didn't want to put my brother in danger. I'd take a look at the situation in Oranstone. If it looked too bad, I'd send him away with Ciarra. He'd go if it was to protect the Brat.

"Get your bedroll," I said. "You might as well camp with us now."

I helped him put the fire out and gather his things.

WHEN DAWN CAME, I CALLED EVERYONE TOGETHER. Ciarra sat near Tosten, occasionally patting his face as if to reassure herself he was really there. Tosten kept sliding unobtrusive glances at Oreg.

"From now on," I said, "we are a team. We work together, helping each other if we can. Every morning, we'll train. For today, Axiel will teach Oreg, Bastilla, Ciarra, and Tosten."

"Axiel," I continued, "I don't know how much Oreg and Bastilla know. Ciarra is a beginner, and Tosten, you remember, is very good at knives and hand-to-hand. Penrod and I will work out together. In the evening, I'll work out with Axiel and Penrod with Tosten. As we improve, we'll change things, but training means survival, so we're going to train as hard as we can and still travel."

THE PACE I SET, BOTH IN TRAINING AND TRAVEL, WAS brutal. We all lost weight, even the horses. A week of hard traveling saw us roughly three days outside of Estian.

"Elbow in, Bastilla." I called, watching her fight with my sister.

She'd known quite a bit about fighting, proving the reputation of the Cholytes was not undeserved, but she hadn't had my aunt as a teacher. Bastilla's footwork in particular was still rudimentary, partially because her feet were still tender. Ciarra, smaller and younger, was a much better swordswoman.

My sister hardly looked like the delicate child she'd seemed in Hurog. Hard muscle shaped her arms and shoulders as she countered one of Bastilla's swings.

Penrod tapped me on the shoulder and pointed to Tosten and Oreg's bout. Frowning, I walked across the camp and observed them.

Like Ciarra, Oreg had thrived on our journey. His horsemanship had improved until he could ride most of the horses we had with us. His fighting was indeed somewhere between mine and Ciarra's, but much closer to mine. Watching him fight with Tosten was like seeing two flitting shadows, one gold, one dark. Their hands moved so fast it was hard to follow the action, which was why Penrod had called me over.

My brother's fighting had been rusty at first, but he'd quickly improved. It was his attitude that remained a problem. Like everyone else, he'd accepted that Oreg was a bastard relative, but it only seemed to increase his resentment. In truth, Tosten seemed so unhappy, I wondered why he'd chosen to come with us. He barely spoke to anyone except Ciarra. Oreg, he despised. Had Oreg been a normal boy, I'd have been worried for him. Instead, I worried about Tosten.

Oreg was having to work at keeping Tosten's sharp blade away from his body.

"Remember, this is practice, Tosten, not an all-out," I called and watched grimly until the fervor of his strokes diminished.

Axiel looked up at me from where he was fixing our breakfast and nodded his agreement to my words.

"Axiel," I said, keeping a wary eye on Tosten and Oreg. "Tell me about the siege at Farnish Keep."

"Not Farnish Keep again," gasped Oreg, ducking my brother's sword. "Please, anything but that."

Axiel was a better fighter than even Stala, and under his tutelage, I was fast improving. Better yet, he had a firm understanding of army tactics. Penrod was quick and clever. He quite often beat me in training bouts. At every opportunity I picked their memories for campaign stories about Oranstone, about fighting battles, and about strategies for winning. They teased me about it, but they talked until they were hoarse because I asked it of them.

Axiel began with the mistakes the defenders made. I listened and learned.

After breakfast and stories, we rode through grasslands all day. The travel was easier on the horses than the rough coastal roads had been, but it was disheartening for the riders. One mile looked much like the last and the next. It was difficult to believe we'd ever see Oranstone.

After practice and dinner, I stole the last hour before

dusk to ride out alone on Pansy as always. Sometimes I used the time for hunting; sometimes I just worked with the stallion, teaching him the kinds of things a warhorse should know and a few others besides. It kept me fresh and gave me time to be myself—whoever that was. With the others, I was Seleg, my legendary hero, borrowing his calmness and leadership abilities, which only Oreg noticed with quiet sarcasm. And, as we approached Estian, I could see them responding to Seleg's calm confidence with confidence of their own—even Oreg. Only Pansy heard my doubts.

"SO, AXIEL," I PANTED, LYING ON THE GROUND BELLY first and watching Oreg run Ciarra through her paces. "What do you think of us as a mercenary band? Are we big enough, or does someone need to travel to Estian and recruit?"

"Someone trained him as an assassin," he replied with a nod in Oreg's direction. Axiel wasn't nearly as worn out as I, but I gained some satisfaction from his sweat-dampened clothes.

"Oreg, an assassin?" I watched the fight more attentively.

"I wasn't speaking of Ciarra." His tone was dry. "He's modified them, but they're assassin's moves, all the same. Where did you find him? There can't be many assassin-trained mages scattered about."

"He found me," I replied truthfully. "He's a Hurog—a bastard, but still a Hurog. I don't know a lot about his background, but I'll be damned if I'll treat him the way my father did."

"Ah," said Axiel. After a moment he said, "I don't think we need any more men. Hit and run, midnight raids—that's the best work. More skill and less chance."

"Less glory," I said. "But I suppose I don't have the

belly for close-fought battles won against the odds. Stala has seen to that."

"Never was a good general who won a close-fought battle," agreed Axiel, somehow managing to imitate my aunt's voice with his bass.

I finished the quote. "A good general never gets in a close-fought battle. Hit them where they are weak."

"Avoid them when they are strong," added Tosten, coming from the fire to sit cross-legged next to me. "Hit their supply trains and their payroll."

The fight between Oreg and Ciarra degenerated into farce when she broke into giggles at the fierce scowls he was sending her way. The sounds were atonal and odd, but they made me smile. Oreg hoisted her over his shoulder and spun around until he staggered.

6
ESTIAN: ERDRICK, BECKRAM, AND GARRANON

It was not just my story. Some of it I heard of much later. While we were still approaching Estian, events occurring in the city were to play a major role in what happened later.

NORMALLY THE TREATISE HE'D BORROWED FROM the king's library would have been enough to keep his attention, but Erdrick found himself too busy trying to ignore the sounds coming from his brother's room next door.

He shifted in his bed to get comfortable and turned the page. "At least they could be quieter about it," he muttered as a particularly shrill cry came through the walls. "It's disgusting. The queen's older than Mother." But much better looking, he had to admit.

The sex didn't bother him; he'd been ignoring his brother's mating calls since their mother's maid had first seduced Beckram. It was the thought of his brother's neck under the headsman's ax which worried him—and that was probably the very thing that had led Beckram to the affair in the first place. As usual, Beckram played, and Erdrick fussed over the risks his twin took.

Erdrick snorted in self-disgust. He'd almost jumped out of his skin yesterday when the queen mistook him for Beckram. She should have better sense than to try a little hands-on in public. After all, it wasn't only Beckram who would die if the truth came out. The queen's adultery carried the death penalty for both.

And Erdrick had squirmed under the king's regard once too often this past week. A man whose most notable accomplishment was the number of farming manuscripts he borrowed from the king's library should not have attracted so much attention—unless the king thought he was looking at Beckram. Erdrick had no doubt that the king knew. He'd tried to warn Beckram, but his brother had just shrugged. Erdrick consoled himself with the thought that he hadn't seen anger in the king's eye, merely speculation.

GARRANON TURNED FROM THE SOFTNESS OF HIS pillow to look at his father's killer and softened his voice. "The word from my estate is that the raiding is getting bad in the west."

Jakoven, High King of the Five Kingdoms of Tallvenish Rule, waved a hand indifferently and pushed the embroidered velvet spread to the floor. "The Vorsag won't stay there. The land has no value to them; they're raiders, not farmers."

"Your majesty, it is your people they are killing. Your people and mine." Though his words were imperative, Garranon was careful to keep his voice indifferent as he pulled the linen sheets straight where the bedspread had tugged them.

"My boy," purred the king with affectionate dismissal, "you worry to much. Go to sleep. You're keeping me from my rest."

Garranon buried his face in his pillow and forced his body to relax. He took his hatred and stuffed it carefully back behind the barriers he'd learned to build years ago, when he'd been dumped in Estian at twelve with his eight-year-old brother to take care of because everyone else was dead, martyrs to the cause of Oranstonian freedom. He'd learned early that lack of caution got you killed. Worse, it got your wife and children raped and killed, too. He wouldn't be like his father. He planned and nudged, changing things a little at a time. If the cost was more than he could bear, at least his brother was alive and well. Garranon's efforts wouldn't harm his family, only his soul.

And his soul hurt now for what he'd done to poor Ward of Hurog. Garranon had destroyed a harmless boy's life, and it had accomplished nothing, because the boy had fled with Ciernack's slave. If it had been possible, Garranon would have told the king he had not delivered the writ; the king had left it to his discretion. But there were spies among his men, and too many of them knew he'd taken Ward with the intention of delivering him to the asylum. So Ward was a fugitive to be caught and caged, and Garranon had used almost every penny he had to buy his brother's life—if indeed he had: Ciernack wasn't exactly trustworthy. The gods knew what damage Landislaw would do to Buril, but he wasn't safe here.

Tension tightened Garranon's stomach until it burned. King Jakoven had declared Ward unfit as much to tighten the binding on Garranon as for the gold he'd given the royal treasury. Jakoven didn't care who ruled Hurog, a keep so poor it sent its taxes in kind rather than gold. With the old Hurogmeten dead, the powerful warrior who'd held everyone in awe, Hurog was of no consequence. But the king would care that Garranon cared.

If Garranon spoke up for Ward now, there was a good possibility that Jakoven would have the boy killed. The king was jealous of Garranon's affections, be it for a person or a cause.

The sleeping king's arm fell away from him as Garranon wondered if the way he'd chosen was worth anything at all. He certainly hadn't been able to help Oranstone.

Whatever he said in public or to Garranon, the king knew that Kariarn wanted all of Oranstone. Jakoven was waiting for Oranstone to fall so the Vorsag would be forced to attack Tallven and Seaford from the mountain passes, giving the strategic ground to the armies of the Kingdoms.

It had only been fifteen years since the Oranstone Rebellion had been put down. Too many would remember fighting against her to be outraged at a "little" raiding. It wouldn't be a popular war until Oranstone was swallowed up entire by the greedy Vorsagian army. Then the Kingdoms' nobles would be angry and outraged. The strength of righteous indignation would make all the nobles of the four remaining kingdoms support Jakoven completely.

It was a good strategy, if no one worried about Oranstone. When Garranon sent Landislaw home, he'd given him instructions to begin training men to protect Buril—and to evacuate the estate if necessary.

If killing the king would have saved Oranstone, Garranon would have killed him long since. But even as a boy, Garranon had known that murdering the king would accomplish nothing but Garranon's own death. It was better to use the king than to die as a murderer, though he was aware his father would not have thought so. But if he had wanted his father's approval, he'd have killed himself like his mother had. If his father could see him playing the king's whore, he would slit his eldest surviving son's throat.

Garranon stared at the thick rug on the floor of the royal bedchamber while the king slept.

"NEWS, ERDRICK," SAID BECKRAM AS SOON AS Erdrick opened the connecting door.

The morning light streamed in and hit the parchment Beckram held in his hand. His voice had been so sober,

Erdrick expected the royal guards to be waiting at the doorway.

"What's wrong?"

Beckram tossed the letter toward Erdrick. "You read it."

As soon as he saw the script on the pages he picked up off the floor, Erdrick knew it was from his father. He read it twice.

Ward condemned to the asylum? Poor, poor, Ward. Erdrick knew what Hurog meant to his cousin, idiot or not. You couldn't be a Hurog and not know how strong the ties of the keep bound all who lived there. The Hurogmeten had reached up past the grave to hurt his son one last time. The image made him shudder; the late Hurogmeten had always scared him.

"What I want to know is how Father knew that I was sleeping with the queen," said Beckram aggressively.

You don't sleep *with her,* was on the tip of Erdrick's tongue. But his brother didn't deal well with other people's humor, so he said, "He doesn't say anything about it," instead.

"He says he wants me to use my influence on the royal household to get the king to reinstate Ward."

Time to admit it. "Hmm, yes. Well, I thought that Father ought to know you were committing the family to treason. So he'd be prepared."

Beckram made a hissing sound. "The king doesn't care about that; she has not born him, nor anyone else, an heir. He has Garranon and whoever else he can lure to his bed."

"Is that what she told you?"

Beckram gave one of his rare, real smiles. The ones that reminded Erdrick why he loved his twin. "No, it's what the king told me when he gave me permission to have her." He leaned back. "Although permission is the wrong word; it was more in the nature of an order."

Erdrick didn't know whether to be relieved or more

worried. The king played deep games. "You'd best be careful."

Beckram nodded dismissively. "What I don't understand is why Father's so worried about Ward. Everyone knows that Ward is stupid—too stupid to run an estate like Hurog. Even for the Hurogmeten, miser though he was, it was difficult to survive from year to year. Still . . ." He hesitated. "I don't like Ward—"

Because, stupid as he is, he reminds you how you should act, instead of how you want to act, thought Erdrick.

"But I wouldn't want to see him confined to a room in the royal asylum. Could you see it? I think he'd kill someone out of sheer frustration. But surely some compromise can be reached. Father would take him in. Poor Tosten has probably been feeding the fishes for some time, courtesy of our dead uncle, which would leave Hurog to Father."

"Father doesn't want Hurog." Erdrick said, knowing it would be a surprise to his brother. Duraugh had always verbally accepted the Hurogmeten's assumption that Hurog was the apex of ambition, no matter what common sense might argue.

"What?"

"It frightens him. He says it's cursed. Do you remember Grandfather? Uncle Fen was worse. He will do his duty, but he really doesn't want it. Do you?"

Beckram thought about it and grimaced. "Being a Hurog lends a certain air to a person—sort of like owning a man-eating beast. Owning Hurog, though, won't do much for my love life. Can you see any woman wanting to live in that dismal place? And as the senior estate, it would fall to me, while you get Iftahar, which is richer and warmer." He gave an exaggerated shudder. "I'll talk to her."

• • •

BECKRAM SHUT THE DOOR BEHIND HIM BEFORE HE let his smile fall away. Though he would have cut his tongue out rather than admit it, he was worried about his affair with the queen, too. The queen's last lover had been found floating facedown in the small fountain in the central courtyard—a little fact the court gossips did not speak about.

Beckram didn't know what mistake the fool had made, but he was determined not to make the same one. He'd been very careful to stay out of politics. He never asked any favors. He never talked to anyone about the queen—except for Erdrick, and that didn't count—though, of course, everyone knew.

But surely asking her to reinstate Ward wasn't a favor—just the opposite. Hurog wasn't as bad as all that. Not many people would risk their lives to give it away. Risk their lives.

Who'd have thought he would risk his life for Ward?

Well, he decided, as he walked down the corridor to the garden door where the ladies all gathered with their favored gentlemen just before luncheon, he would never tell Ward. Ward liked to hug people who helped him, and Ward's hugs were neither dignified nor gentle. There was a lilt in Beckram's step. Risk his life; he liked that.

TEHEDRA FOEHNE TALLVEN, QUEEN OF TALLVEN and the Five Kingdoms, lay back in her favorite corner of the garden and let her maid fiddle with her hair. The corner was isolated, almost out of view of the rest of the garden, and when she was in it, the rest of the ladies knew to leave her alone.

The sweet scent of the blossoming bush she'd never bothered to learn the name of was as soothing as her maid's hands. There had been one just like it outside her window at her childhood home, down to the pink tinge on edges of the white petals. With her eyes closed, she could almost hear her mother's scolding voice and her father's deeper, richer tones soothing her.

"Ah, my fair one sleeps the morning away."

Involuntarily, a smile caught her lips, but she let it widen into something more artificial as she opened her eyes. It would never do for the maid to report that her mistress looked upon her lover with tenderness.

"Beckram, my dear."

He smiled and let his eyes roll over her with admiration she suspected was partially true. He might be young, but she had the figure of a woman half her age. She wondered why the king had selected this one for her. Was he trying to test her? Onev hadn't been so young, though he'd been softer, less clever. It hadn't taken a full year before Jakoven had him killed. She hoped Beckram lasted longer. She wished she could save him, but she'd learned better a long time ago. So she would savor her enjoyment while it lasted and try not to grow too attached. It helped that he never talked of anything but nonsense. The one before Onev had liked sailing. She'd managed to forget his name after he'd disappeared, but she remembered that.

"My love, you make the summersweet blush in shame," he gestured toward her favorite bush.

"Is that what it is?" she asked, startled that she'd just been wondering, and he'd answered her unspoken question. She'd remember him now, she thought, every time she saw the bush.

He laughed. "I think so, but my brother's the one to ask. What did you do to him, anyway? He was really nervous about you this morning."

She fought to keep her public mask on. "Last night we were standing next to each other—I thought he was you. I—" Ridiculous to be embarrassed about it, she told herself. She played her role, and had for longer than this child had been alive. She managed to go on smoothly.

"—pinched his rump. I thought he was going to pass out." She rolled her eyes, though she'd been touched by his innocence.

Beckram laughed again, settling himself at her feet with the boneless grace of youth. "He takes things too seriously." He took one of her feet into his hands and rubbed it gently, with just enough pressure that it didn't tickle.

"Mmm," she said. "That feels good. Where did you learn how to do that?"

He half hesitated, losing his own mask for a moment of startled recognition. "From my cousin, Ward." He said at last. "I was twelve, and my favorite horse had twisted its leg."

No, she thought. She didn't want to know about his family. She didn't want him to be a person. But it was too late, his face was serious, somber almost.

"My brother wants to be a farmer," he said.

"Oh?" Erdrick might be a safe topic. There weren't many people more safe than Erdrick, she thought.

"And if I inherit my father's estates, we've divided up the duties. He shall farm the land, and I shall do the fighting and what politics are necessary." Beckram squinted against the bright sunlight. He looked so at home outdoors, she thought helplessly. He is a child of sunlight, and I am the black widow who has caught him. She made a neutral noise.

"The thing is, that's ruined now."

He didn't sound upset about it, so she expected some blithe comment on how her beauty would trap him here so he'd be no good at warfare. She made a more encouraging sound.

"The king's declared my cousin Ward unfit to be Hurogmeten. When they find him, he's to be incarcerated in the asylum."

"They can't find him?" She remembered Ward. He was simple but kind, a trait she found rare in men. He always danced with the ugliest girls. She couldn't imagine him in the dungeon her husband had created to house the people too important to kill—like the king's youngest brother. *Horrible, horrible,* she thought. She'd always been afraid that was where she would end up, too. But she'd had a long time to practice her public mask. Her smile never faltered, and her question had carried only polite interest.

"No. But he'll turn up." Beckram hesitated and looked up at her earnestly, all young man, not flirtatious lover. "Could you ask the king to reinstate him? He's stupid but not insane. That was my uncle."

She found herself nodding in agreement, remembering the infamous rages. She fancied her husband had been more than a little afraid of the Hurogmeten.

Beckram continued. "Neither my father nor I want Hurog. It's a nice curiosity to have in the family, but it's damned uncomfortable. I'd rather have my father's current estate, and Erdrick would rather be my manager."

She felt her maid's hands falter in her hair. A terrified stillness grew inside her. Her husband would be curious about such a request; he would want to know what Beckram stood to gain. Even after all these years at court, she could still take a boy's sincerity at face value. But Jakoven would never do that.

"Come now," she said smiling flirtatiously, trying to help him save himself. "There has to be a better reason. You must stand to gain something." She could do it for him, she thought, if he just came up with a better reason. The king had always seen to it that her lovers were well paid for their services.

Beckram shook his head. "I just can't stand to think of him confined to a room. He belongs at Hurog." He gave her a shy smile that made him look half his age. "He's big and slow—but tough." He touched his eye lightly, for no reason she could see. "He knows every rock on Hurog land, the breeding of every animal on the place. It's his home. After living with Uncle Fenwick, I think he deserves it."

Oh, poor boy, she thought, touching his hair gently. *The king will never believe that—not giving up personal gain for love of a cousin. He'll suspect you of some plan to overthrow him.* Hurog had political power if not wealth, and if she remembered that, Jakoven was sure to as well. If Shavig still had a king of its own, it would have been a man of the Hurog family, something the Shavig lords were very aware of.

But she had been Jakoven's wife for many years. She smiled. "I'll ask him, of course. But don't get your hopes up too high. He seldom changes his mind because of any request I make. Now, go find me something to drink."

He jumped up and bowed low. "Queen of my heart, it will be done."

Sheira, her maid, continued grooming her after he left, and Tehedra fought not to flinch away. It wasn't the girl's fault that she had to report everything to the king. Damn the boy for being stupid and getting himself killed.

GARRANON FOUGHT TO KEEP FROM ROLLING HIS eyes. If the Oranstone contingent at court had looked all year, they couldn't have found a worse person to plead their case than old Haverness. Morning hearings were seldom pleasant for Garranon, but this was more painful than usual.

"We are yours, my king. Sworn to you by our life's blood," said Haverness.

That oath you take much more seriously than the king, thought Garranon sadly. Haverness had to know what he was letting himself in for. Garranon had explained to the Oranstonians that the king would not help them. He'd tried to warn them that they would only make things worse by pressing. But they'd ignored him.

Havernness of Callis looked like the old warrior he was. He was the only Oranstonian at court with the courage to keep his hair in the fashion of the Oranstone nobles: shaved from temple to ear and cut short everywhere else. Garranon knew Jakoven regarded Haverness as a beaten man, a failure. If Garranon saw instead a hero, it was something he would keep to himself.

Resolutely, Garranon turned his attention elsewhere. The king held morning business in one of the larger antechambers. The Tamerlain was here this morning as she often was; she said that it relieved her boredom now that Menague was deserted. Her yellow and gold mottled body was almost shocking in comparison to all of the somberly clad nobles. She was bearlike in size and shape, but more gracile, like a giant forest cat. Her head was more catlike, too, with mobile features and sharp, white fangs. Impressive and predatory as the guardian of a god's temple should be, the only discordant note was the extra-long fluffy tail. He wondered why no one stepped on her in the crowded room, as she'd assured him years ago that he was the only one who could see her.

Her imperious yellow eyes met his over the crowd.

"Callis is besieged, your majesty. Surely you must know that these are no raiders. If they take Oranstone, Tallven and Seaford are next." There was a passionate intensity in Haverness's voice that forced Garranon to turn his attention briefly to the old general. When he looked back, the Tamerlain was gone.

"We are acquainted with the events to the south," agreed the king mildly. "But we are also acquainted with the marvelous abilities of Oranstone fighters. Why, I bet—" The ingeniousness of the king's voice made ice crawl down Garranon's neck. He kept his face blank, for there were too many people watching the king's pet Oranstonian for a reaction. "I bet that with a hundred men you could drive the raiders off yourself."

Haverness knew the king. He bowed low and started to say something, when he was interrupted.

"I'll take that bet," said a voice Garranon knew well, though he hadn't seen the king's bastard half brother in the room. Alizon Tallven sauntered to Haverness and patted his back. "Though I'd rather bet on Haverness's side. Fought against him in the last war, you know." Alizon might look the fop, but he'd been his father's general and military advisor when he was twenty-two.

The king settled back in his chair. The contrast between the two men was startling, especially since their mothers had been sisters. The king looked like all rulers should: strong-faced, gray eyes cool and measuring. He wasn't handsome, nothing so plebeian. His nose was narrow and aristocratic, with a knot where it had been broken once. His curly hair—entirely gray now, though Garranon could remember when it had been chocolate-brown—Jakoven kept cut in a short, military fashion.

Alizon, oldest of the last king's three sons, dyed his hair. Today it was a rich chestnut that spread to his shoulders. He was tall and wolf-lean, moving with comical grace. It was hard to imagine him leading an army. He had stepped down from his official post when his half brother ascended the throne. Personally, Garranon thought that was the reason Alizon had escaped the fate of Jakoven's youngest brother who was in the King's Asylum.

"You would like to bet that Haverness and a hundred can drive the raiders out?" asked Jakoven, amused.

"With the help of the Oranstone natives," agreed Alizon. "I think, too, that the choice of the hundred should be his alone."

The king chuckled, and Garranon leaned toward the belief that Jakoven was honestly amused. "What's the bet?"

"My war stallion against grandfather's sword."

Garranon saw the king tense with his first real interest. Jakoven had coveted Alizon's horse.

"Done," agreed the king. "Callis may choose any hundred men he wishes; if they can drive the Vorsagian raiders back behind their borders in the next six months, I will give you grandfather's sword. If not, you will give me the warhorse, Trueblood."

"Upon Haverness's acceptance, of course," murmured Alizon.

They had managed to turn the old warrior's plea to farce, thought Garranon, playing games with a man's honor.

"I accept your wishes as I am sworn to do." There was dignity in the old man's bearing. Garranon hoped that everyone saw it. Being of Oranstone was something to make him proud when there were Oranstonians like this. His father would have approved of Haverness.

"He's a brave man," murmured the king, looking at Garranon.

Horror knotted his belly, and a small voice inside started gibbering, *The king knows, the king knows*. But there was nothing for the king to know. He'd done nothing for Oranstone. The only thing the king could know that would harm Garranon was still secret: Only Garranon knew how much he hated the king.

"He has more courage than most." Garranon let admiration color his voice. "It is too bad that such a man is also a fool. He allows his love of Oranstone to blind him to the needs of the Five Kingdoms. Best to send him to Oranstone; he will never fight as hard for anything but his homeland."

Gratefully, he saw the king's sharp gaze grow bored, though Haverness flushed at being so described publically. Jakoven turned to his law-bringer. "Record the decision and Alizon's bet. Oh, give the man a week to make his choices and supply. We shall fund the supplies. When you are through, I will hear the next claimant."

While the king conducted the rest of the morning's

business, Garranon studied the room, wondering if the world had ever been right and fair the way he'd once thought it was.

> *Where the men of honor gone,*
> *In the fading shadow of the hours.*
> *Where the shield, the sword, the steed,*
> *To fight where coward's hero cowers.*

The sorrowful little tune drifted through his mind. Something he'd heard at an inn somewhere in that stupid chase for an elusive slave girl. *Coward's hero.* He liked that; it described him perfectly.

"STUPID OF JAKOVEN TO GIVE THE OLD BASTARD free rein like that."

The soft light of the moon only seemed to make the shadowed garden darker. Garranon turned his head, unsurprised to see the Tamerlain lounging on one of the decorative railings that served as support for a variety of climbing vines. The marble railing seemed to bow under the weight of the creature.

If she hadn't spoken, he knew his eyes would have passed her by, though she wasn't concealing herself. The brightly mottled fur, so startling in the daylight, blended perfectly in the junglelike shadows of the garden. A mythological, magical beast who'd showed herself to a frightened boy for reasons he'd never understood. Boredom, she'd told him when he'd asked.

The Tamerlain was the Guardian of Menogue, but no one believed in her anymore, especially since Menogue had been destroyed. She'd once said Menogue's fall had been fated, though her tail had snapped like an angry cat's while she said it. With travelers to Aethervon's broken temple so few, she interested herself in the doings of the Estian court and the king's Oranstonian lover.

"The king stupid? Why do you say that?" he asked, knowing that they were alone in the gardens by her relaxed manner.

She rolled over on the handspan-wide rail and twisted, rubbing her spine against the hard surface without losing her balance. "Why is it that Oranstone cannot defend herself against the Vorsag, though she's done it before?"

"Because the—" the progression of that thought caused him to hesitate briefly. "—the lords who should be at their seats are stuck here in Estian and have been since the end of the last war. But it's not that easy, Tamerlain. It's been fifteen years. There are no trained men on the estates, because we're not allowed to have armies. Most of the experienced lords were killed—then or by later mysterious means. The only reason Haverness hasn't fallen off his horse or been mistaken for a deer while he rides out in the woods is because there's not a duplicitous bone in his body. Not even a patriotic idiot would recruit him for an underground movement, because he'd tell the king as soon as the words reached his ears."

"Many men will follow him in war," she purred soothingly. "He is a hero—and perhaps not as absurdly honorable as you believe. And there are others here: you, for instance."

"He's not likely to choose me after I embarrassed him in public like that."

"Perhaps not," she allowed, flipping herself off the rail and onto her padded feet. Her claws clicked on the brick walk. "But your question was why the king is a fool. Think what will happen if Haverness succeeds with his hundred men. All of the Five Kingdoms will know that it was spite that made the bet. Everyone loves an underdog who triumphs. It might be enough to shake his grip on the throne.

If I had been the king, I would have killed Alizon long ago. Intelligent men are dangerous."

"Why do you care so much?" he asked suddenly. "What do the events here matter to you?"

She changed suddenly, as he'd seen her do only once before. A human seemingly rose out of the bulk of her animal body. Her skin was dappled as her pelt had been; otherwise, she could have been any other naked woman he'd ever seen. Even her eyes had changed to a warm amber. It surprised him again how young she looked. If she'd been human, he'd have said that she was less than twenty.

The Tamerlain stepped forward and touched his cheek. "The time is coming, Garranon of Buril. It has been dark for a very long time, not just here, but among the other creatures of magic. The dwarves have huddled down in their reaches, but disease and disharmony are rife among them. Something tainted the magic of the land long ago. Now the land may be saved."

"Defeating the Vorsag will change the taint?" he asked. She'd spoken often of tainted magic but never so specifically.

She smiled. "I don't know, but it might. The future is hard to divine, even for Aethervon."

"Aethervon?" Garranon looked at her in surprise.

"Just because Menogue lies in ruin does not mean that Aethervon forgets his promises." The Tamerlain lowered her eyes, looking more cat than bear. "In return for giving his followers Menogue, Aethervon promised the high king to look after his kingdom." Her eyes went unfocused briefly as she sniffed the air. "He is coming." She took up her more usual shape again and gave him her usual words of parting. "Fare thee well, child."

Uncertain what he should do with what she told him, Garranon sat on the rail she'd occupied and brushed at a chipped area with his thumb.

"Garranon," said Jakoven. "I remember you sitting

there just so when you first came to me. What makes you so sad?"

Garranon sat upright, though the king's hand encouraged him to lean back against Jakoven's shoulder. *Enough lies,* he thought. *They wouldn't work anyway.* "Oranstone, my liege."

His answer displeased Jakoven; the hand on his shoulder tightened. "Your father abandoned you to fight for Oranstone's freedom. Abandoned you so there was no one to defend you when the soldiers came, killed your sister in front of your eyes. And they raped you and your brother, didn't they? If your father had followed his oaths, he would have been there to save you."

From you, thought Garranon with sudden violence. For a moment he was terrified he had said the words aloud. But the king's hold softened.

"You were so hurt when you came to me," Jakoven murmured. "So small and terrified. It hurt me to see you, to see the fear in your face. So I made it better," he nuzzled Garranon's neck.

Not fooled by the loverlike tones, Garranon knew the reminder of what had happened had been deliberate. Especially the reminder of his brother's fate. But his brother was in Oranstone, safe from Jakoven. Perhaps, he thought while his body responded to the king's caresses, perhaps he would join Haverness. It would be good to see his wife and lands again.

7

WARDWICK

Aethervon has always been a curious problem for devout Tallvens. If he was really a god, why did he allow the destruction of his temple? Fortunately, most Tallvens are not given to worship anything except gold so, on the whole, they aren't much troubled.

"TELL ME AGAIN WHY WE'RE TRAVELING SO CLOSE to Estian, Ward," said Tosten, swinging his sword my way.

"Because the best path through the mountains is straight south," I replied, parrying. "From what you said, Garranon has given up finding his brother's runaway. He'll have taken the faster road to Estian, so we won't meet him."

We were doing patterns he and I had practiced since we could hold a sword. Stala encouraged talk during patterns, said that engaging the mouth demanded the body operate from reflex. I wasn't certain of that, but I did know I didn't have to worry about him missing a link in the pattern.

"Think we'll reach Estian today?" asked Tosten, increasing the speed of his strokes so I had to as well.

"Should." I increased my speed a little more than he had.

"Wouldn't traveling have been faster if we practiced less?" he said with a gasp, but he set the pace even faster.

"Yes. But we need to be ready by the time we reach Oranstone." I managed all that without a breath and

matched his speed, too. I added, "I don't want anyone
kill—" gasp "—killed because they don't know how to
handle a sword." To make up for the loss of breath, I quickened again. From the corner of my eye, I saw the others
had stopped fighting to watch.

"Why does Ward look faster?" I heard Bastilla ask.

"Because he is." Axiel's voice carried satisfaction like a
proud father's. "He has a longer distance to move to meet
Tosten's blows. That's why a big man is almost always
slower than a small man."

"It always surprises me to see Ward fight," added Oreg.
"He always talks slowly—sounds almost stupid, even
when he's not trying to appear that way. Moves that way,
too."

"No," Axiel disagreed. "He just moves well. It usually
makes him look slow, like Penrod's gelding. Fastest horse
in the bunch, but he looks as if he's traveling half the speed
of the others." He raised his voice, "Ward, Tosten, slow
down. Someone's going to get hurt."

"Want to really show them?" asked Tosten, grinning.
The expression took me aback. He'd never been given to a
quick smile.

"What do you have in mind?" It would have to be quick,
because I couldn't keep the pace up much longer.

"Close your eyes."

Stala had us do that. We all used wooden blades and full
armor so that, barring total incompetence, the worse risk
was a nasty bruise. Usually, she blindfolded only one of
the sparring partners and the patterns were taken at half
speed.

"You, too?" I asked.

He closed his in answer, so I did also, and neither of us
slowed the pattern. The worst thing about closing my eyes
was that it always threw my balance off until I got used to
it. On the other hand, it increased my focus immeasurably.
The greatest sensory input came from my sword, until I al-

most felt like Tosten's sword was hitting my arm instead of the silver blade. It was exhilarating, better than running down the cliffside on Feather—and about as smart.

We kept it up until I heard a raggedness in the rhythm of metal on metal; one or both of us was tiring. "Done on three," I whispered.

"One," he said as softly.

"Two," I replied.

"Three," he said.

I jumped back out of range and opened my eyes to see that he had done the same. Dizzy with the sudden addition of sight to my heightened senses, I had to sit on the ground before I fell.

"Idiots," said Axiel. "That kind of horseplay will get you killed."

Tosten and I exchanged unrepentant grins, and I felt the old bond of brotherhood settle over us for the first time in a long while.

Our attitude didn't help Axiel's temper. "I told Stala that blindfolding was stupid. It encourages the *steran* to do stupid stunts like that display."

Feeling less dizzy, I rolled back to my feet and held out my sword to Axiel, as a repentant student is supposed to do.

He shook his head in refusal but gave me a reluctant chuckle. "I wouldn't have missed it for all the sheep in Hurog—but don't you tell anyone."

"What's a *steran*?" asked Oreg, with such innocence in his voice that I looked at him sharply. He was pointing out something to me, but I didn't know what it was.

"Foolish young boys," answered Axiel with such well-concealed discomfort I might not have noticed without Oreg sharpening my attention. I knew several languages, as any lord who lived in the Kingdoms had to. *Steran* wasn't a word I was familiar with.

"Fretsome old dwarf," taunted Oreg softly.

Axiel's face set, but before he could say anything, Tosten jumped in, as he did at every opportunity to attack Oreg. "Poor-mannered bastard," he said. "You need to show respect to your elders."

A look of unholy glee spread across Oreg's face.

"Time to break camp," Axiel said abruptly. It was the first order he'd given outside of the morning and evening exercises. It might have been to keep Oreg and Tosten from fighting, but I wondered if it was Oreg's remark about dwarves.

I thought about pursuing the matter but reluctantly decided to leave Axiel to his own counsel. He'd earned that much by his long years of service to my family. Besides, I never liked playing someone else's games, not even Oreg's. Just how unlikely was it that Axiel's father was a dwarf? About as unlikely as Oreg being as old as Hurog. I could accept dwarven blood; it was the other part that I would choose to disbelieve. When he was really, really drunk, he claimed his father was the dwarven king.

PANSY WAS FEELING GOOD AND SHOWED IT BY dancing and snorting. The warm sun felt good to me as well, and for the first time since leaving Hurog, I started to feel normal again. My broken bond with Hurog still made me feel like I was missing some vital part of myself, but it was bearable, a healed-over scar of a missing limb.

"My lord," said Oreg diffidently, riding to my side.

"Yes?"

"Where did you intend to camp tonight? We won't reach Estian until late this afternoon."

"The trail we're on meets up with the main road in a few miles. My father liked to ride into Estian in the morning. I thought we'd just camp where we always have and ride past the city tomorrow."

"Is it possible to camp at Menogue instead?"

"In the interest of a scholarly visit?" asked Bastilla who was riding beside me.

Oreg gave her a pleased smile and nodded his head.

Bastilla had blended into my odd group much better than I had expected a beautiful woman to do. She was, I think, sleeping with both Axiel and Penrod, but managed it without friction.

"Menogue is northeast of Estian. It's at least five or six miles out of our way," I said. "That means over ten miles altogether."

"I know," he replied. "I'd still like to stay there overnight. You told Tosten that speed isn't important."

"The ruins are haunted." The track was wide enough here for Tosten to come up on my right. "Axiel knows all the stories. He's scouting, but I'm sure he'll be happy to tell us all about it tonight."

His tone was congenial. Something about this morning's sparring had made him happier.

"Haunted?" I put some tremolo in my voice and managed not to glance at Oreg. "I'd forgotten about that. Maybe we shouldn't stay there after all."

Tosten humphed, "You needn't fake it, Ward." He grinned at Bastilla. I could see she'd worked her magic on him as well. "We've a ghost at Hurog, too. I've never seen it, but you should have heard my aunt—Lady Duraugh, not Stala—when it visited her." Bastilla hadn't met Stala, but she'd heard us all telling stories.

"It's easier to dismiss ghosts in the daylight," I said. "Not so easy at night when the ruins come alive around you."

Penrod had ridden up to see what was going on. "Ruins?"

"Oreg wants to stay in the haunted ruins of Menogue," explained Bastilla.

The old horseman grinned, "Spend the night in haunted ruins? Sounds like home."

•   •   •

IT WAS AXIEL WHO FOUND THE PATH WE NEEDED TO
take. I would have ridden right past it. There were signs of
the great road it had been, but I doubted there would be any
trace in another hundred years. Rumors of hauntings and
curses had kept the curious away. And to think the Tallvenish were so quick to point fingers at us Northlanders for
being superstitious.

Truthfully, had I not known what Oreg was, I would not
have agreed to it. As my uncle had said, no one knew like
a Northlander how bothersome real magic was. Neither
Axiel nor Bastilla showed much enthusiasm. But Tosten
practically brimmed over with excitement, which was what
had finalized my decision. This was the most cheerful I'd
seen him.

Our path twisted between trees that hadn't been there
during Menogue's reign but now towered over us, shadow-
ing the path. Blackberry brambles hid the remnants of broken stone benches and statuary.

The horses were tired after a full day of riding, and
they huffed and sweated, hauling us up the steep hill.
Penrod kicked his feet loose of the stirrups and slid off.
Axiel ahead of him and Ciarra beside him followed suit.
I laughed a bit at myself as I slid out of the saddle, because I didn't want to walk up the hill very much, but if
Penrod, who looked as fresh as he had this morning
though he was at least twice my age, was walking up the
hill, then so was I.

The moment my feet hit the soil, I stopped laughing as
the hair on my arms rose and gooseflesh covered my body.
It wasn't the same here as it had been at Hurog. The magic
in the hill didn't flow through me like the sea, filling the
hollows in my soul, but it was definitely here. And it was
curious.

I don't know why I thought that. I'd always been taught
that magic was a force, like the wind or the sun. But at
Hurog the magic welcomed me, filling me with strength

and peace when I needed it—though it didn't answer my call anymore. But whatever touched me through the soft dirt under my feet was inquisitive and . . . not that welcoming. Oreg stepped beside me and gripped my elbow, pulling me forward before the others had realized I'd stopped.

"Yes," he murmured quietly so the jingle of harness and clomp of hooves would cover his voice. "You feel it, don't you? Bastilla doesn't. How curious."

"It's like Hurog," I murmured back.

He smiled grimly. "Yes, and no. They are both places of old power."

"What power?" asked Tosten, coming alongside as he frequently did when Oreg and I talked, though he seldom addressed Oreg directly.

"Menogue," I answered, nodding my head to the ruins that rose darkly above us.

Tosten rubbed his arms and said, "This place makes me nervous, as if something not very friendly is watching us."

"Come on, hurry up," called Bastilla, "you're blocking the trail. If we've got to camp on this forsaken hill, let's at least make camp while we've light to do so."

I glanced back and saw that Bastilla, unencumbered by pride, was still mounted. But I quickened my pace without a word. She was right.

Walking put a stop to my inquiries for lack of breath—something I'd have felt badly about except that no one else could talk either. When the slope began to get steeper, I let my reins loose on Pansy's back and dropped back to use his tail to help me over the rough stuff. It was an old mountaineer's trick, and I forgot until I grabbed his tail that Pansy wasn't used to such familiarity. But when he didn't kick and kept following Penrod, I quit worrying and gratefully accepted his help. Glancing back, I saw Tosten had done the same, though Oreg scrambled up without apparent effort. Bastilla had dismounted at last and fallen behind. Feather, bearing a lighter burden than she was used to, hauled Ciarra past us as if she were walking on the flat.

The crest of the hill loomed ahead like a beacon in a snowstorm. Pansy felt it, too (or maybe it was the humiliation of having Feather pass him) and increased his pace until I had to jog to keep up with him.

Though the top of the hill was still light, trees shadowed the path, and I stumbled over the rough ground. Rather than have Pansy drag me the rest of the way up, I let go of his tail and caught a broken stone pillar that was part of the ruins.

I woke up flat on my back with a stranger leaning over me. He wore none of the tattoos of our order, nor were his robes familiar. There was something about his face . . . he looked like a Hurog . . . I saw a dragon in the sky, fierce and frightening, deep blue scales edged in gold.

Hurog.

It was Tosten who leaned over me, his eyes concerned. "Are you hurt, Ward? What happened?"

It seemed like a good question, but tingling from toes to forehead, I didn't have an answer. I must not have been there long, because I heard Oreg and his horse approaching in a rush.

"What's wrong?" asked Oreg.

"I tripped," I said, though it had been the pillar, not whatever I'd stepped on that laid me out. I forced a quick grin. "It just feels so good to lie here on the grass, I thought I'd stay here a while."

Noticing that my hand was still touching the base of the stone, I pulled it away. Blessedly, the pulsing tingle faded within a few heartbeats. Nothing hurt except my head.

"Nothing's wrong," I said rolling to my feet. My head bumped into Pansy's, which did neither of us any good, and he stepped back indignantly. "Let's get to the top."

I hoped the shadow hid my face, because I didn't want anyone to see my fear. What had sounded like an adventure this morning was turning into something else, and I'd just developed a serious mistrust of whatever Oreg had in mind for this visit.

"I hope you know what you're doing, Oreg." I said softly.

He smiled faintly but gave no other reply.

When I reached the top, Axiel, Penrod, and Ciarra had already unsaddled their horses and were grooming them briskly. Pansy whickered and joined the other horses, waiting for me to get his hot, itchy blanket and tack off, too.

"Can we explore a bit and see if the monks left anything?" asked Bastilla, fastening the hobbles on her horse.

Penrod took a good look at the sky. "We won't have daylight for much longer."

Ciarra looked at me expectantly, bouncing on her toes. She'd already hobbled Feather. I knew what Ciarra wanted to do, but after my experience with the pillar on the hill, I wasn't sure the ruins were safe.

"Right," I said reluctantly. "Just for tonight, no practice. Go ahead and look around. But remember, this place was dedicated to a god. Be respectful, and don't touch anything."

Before the words had left my mouth, Bastilla and Ciarra were off. As soon as he was finished with his horse, Tosten followed with Penrod beside him. Axiel took the small shovel off the pack saddle and began digging a firepit. Oreg, looking uninterested, gathered dry sticks that were lying around on the ground.

I took my time, grooming Pansy until his coat gleamed and only a slight roughness showed where his cinch had rubbed. Finally, he stamped his foot, impatient to go out and graze with the others. I put his brush away in a saddlebag and let him go. I didn't hobble him; he'd stay with his herd.

"I'm going to look around," I said. Axiel grunted, but

Oreg left his pile of dry tinder where it was and followed me.

Penrod or Axiel had chosen a camping ground some distance from the main buildings. That put us on the northern edge of the hilltop, farthest from Estian with the remains of the temple tower between us and the city.

The top of the hill was a flat field encompassing about six acres. Though the sides of the hill had been covered in tall trees, the top was a grassy meadow. Once, I supposed, most of the acreage had been paved. Now there was soil over the old stones, but it was too shallow for anything but grass.

"Why did you bring us here?" I asked when we were alone.

Oreg ducked his head so I couldn't see his face. "Wait and see. It might be important, most likely not."

I stopped. "Is this dangerous?"

He smiled a little. "Life is dangerous, my lord. Death is the only safety. But the Tamerlain keeps evil spirits away from here. It will be fine, Ward."

I stared at him for a moment. The Tamerlain was the legendary guardian of the temple, a great predator who fed upon the night demons and lived only on the mound of Menogue. Sometimes I wasn't certain whether Oreg was mad or not, but he seemed calm and sincere about our safety. I nodded briefly, mostly because I didn't really want to trek down the hill again, and continued toward the place where the largest section of walls remained standing.

It was a tribute to the Tallvenish fear of Menogue that most of the temple was still here, not carted off as building stones for more humble dwellings. There were stories about nasty things that happened to people who took things away from Menogue, plagues and ill luck. My father had once observed, cynically, that access to a trove of building materials would have upset the natural order of things. Peasants would have had good stone houses just like the merchants. They'd have gotten above themselves. Much better to make the stone off limits to the peasantry, and superstition has always been the cheapest guard.

The end result for us was that as Oreg and I approached the standing walls, we had to scramble over a lot of loose rubble. Some of the fallen bits were taller than I was, and a fair number showed carving, mostly cracked and broken. Even so, I marveled at the quality of the stonework.

"Did the dwarves carve these?" I asked Oreg.

"Eh?" Then he grinned. "You believe the dwarves' claims that they're the only ones who know how to carve stone, too? Not that they weren't masters—they did the carving in Hurog's library—but there were skilled human masons, too, like the ones who carved this. But stone carving fell out of fashion a couple of centuries ago. Plaster and wood carving are cheaper and faster."

The piece of standing wall I approached would have towered above the highest roof at Hurog. At one time it would have been even taller, but the top had tumbled to the ground. The wall was gently curved and layered in four-foot-tall sections, each one a little farther inset than the one below it. I imagined that at one time it was part of a dome. The sections were covered in stone carvings but we were still too far away for me to see them in any detail in the growing shadows of evening.

We skirted a few piles of stone and crawled over another into a small cleared area right next to the wall.

"This was the inner temple," said Oreg a little sadly. "It was painted in brilliant colors, blue and purple, orange and green. There was nothing else like it anywhere."

After he spoke, I could see that the wall had been painted once. Where the panels were undercut, protected by the weather, the paint was obvious. The bottommost panel contained a series of comically exaggerated people who seemed to be occupied holding up the next layer with their stone hands. Upon closer examination, each of them

differed in feature and clothing. Some were standing on
their hands and supporting the top with their feet instead of
the other way around. The lip of the upper layer even bent
upward a little where a particularly stout little man pushed
on it. Near the first break in the wall, one of the little fellows had a particularly sly look on his face. Upon closer
inspection, I could see that neither of his hands were
touching the slab above.

The second tier of panels were trees, but they were trees
I wasn't familiar with. The one above that . . .

"Siphern," I exclaimed, sending Oreg, who had been
waiting patiently for me to notice, into a fit of laughter.

Like most Tallvenish gods, Aethervon was deity of two
opposites: sorrow and merriment. The folks in the third tier
looked very merry indeed.

I examined one particular scene. "I didn't know that
was possible."

"Only if the woman is very flexible," smirked Oreg.

I looked at him doubtfully. "I don't think I'd want to be
this fellow if she loses her balance."

"Some risks," he asserted with all apparent seriousness,
though his eyes still danced with fun, "might be worth
taking."

I shook my head at him and continued on in my explo-
rations, leaving Oreg to the carvings of the inner temple. I
found Ciarra standing on a wide section of broken wall
staring at Estian far below. I stepped up behind her to make
sure she didn't fall.

"Big, isn't it," I said. Ciarra had never seen Estian
before.

She shook her head and made a shrinking motion with
her hands. I looked down again and considered what she'd
said. Estian was an old city, maybe older than Hurog. Oreg
would know. From this height, successions of city walls,
each added as the population outgrew the safer space inside, gave the impression that the city had been laid out by

a spider of some sort. The older inner walls were softened by the buildings that had been built against them.

I frowned. The outermost wall was narrower and shorter than the wall that had preceded it. There were few buildings between the outer two walls. For the most part, the space was filled with the blackened remains left by the fire that had ravaged Estian near the time of my birth.

Ciarra was right. Estian was shrinking.

I SLEPT BADLY THAT NIGHT; I KEPT HEARING BELLS. But when I sat up and looked around the first two times, everyone else was asleep. The third time, Ciarra and Oreg, who were on watch, were both gone.

I woke Tosten up and moved to Axiel, while Tosten woke Penrod. Axiel opened his eyes before I could utter my whispered warning, but neither he nor I could wake Bastilla, who slept as one drugged.

"I'll stay with her," offered Penrod in our whispered conference.

I nodded at him, and the rest of us set off to look for Ciarra.

"It's too dark to track," whispered Axiel. "We need to split up and meet somewhere."

"Let's meet at the wall," I said pointing to the silhouette of the tallest section of wall where the comical men held the tower upon their shoulders. I knew where she was; I'd *found* her and Oreg some time before. My magic was telling me that if they weren't at the wall, they were somewhere very close to it. But, for some reason, I knew I wanted to go there alone first. It was such a strong feeling that later I decided it hadn't been my own. So I sent Axiel and Tosten off.

The summer night was alive with the sounds of insects and night hunters going about their business. The white, ghostly shape of a haar owl flew above me, making the dis-

tinctive sound for which it was named. The scattered
stones made it impossible to run, but I wasted no time
heading for the wall.

Ciarra stood on top of the wall where she had been earlier this evening. The cool night wind ruffled her hair as
she stared at Estian. Oreg lay curled into a small ball on the
ground at the base of the wall.

"Ciarra," I said kneeling next to Oreg's huddled form.
"Oreg, what's wrong?"

"I can't," he cried out. "I can't stop it, master. I tried, I
tried . . . Aethervon . . ."

"Ciarra, do you know what happened to him?" I asked.

She faced me then, and the hairs on the back of my neck
crawled, and a chill clenched my heart, for her eyes glowed
a brilliant orange in the night. She put out her hand and
something materialized in the darkness, a great beast that
made Ciarra look even smaller than she was. It shoved its
head under her hand, like a cat asking for a scratch. I was
close enough to smell the predatory odor of its breath.

"Ciarra?"

My sister smiled gently and spoke. "Wardwick of
Hurog, there will yet be dragons if thou art willing to pay
the price." There was no tone to her voice at all, it could
have belonged to a man or woman, child or grandfather.

"Hush," I said to Oreg, who was still muttering soft,
broken words to himself.

"Child of the dragon killer, choose thy path carefully,
for in the end it will be thy choice upon which everything
rests, but the heart of the dragon is rotten through." Her
voice this time rang with bass overtones; it might have
been my father's.

Numbly, I recalled the stories I'd heard of Menogue.
There had been a seer here who would speak at the god's
dictation. The last seer had died when Menogue was razed.

"I didn't find . . ." Axiel's voice fell silent as he came
around a large block of stone to see us.

"Son of the dwarf king, what brings thee to this circumstance?" She was all female this time, with a sensuousness that had never belonged to my sister.

"Prophecy and necessity," he answered plainly after a moment in which he took in the scene before him. "My people are dying."

"Thy father dreamed a dream," agreed Ciarra, now sounding like a child much younger than she was. "And you are necessary for the cleansing."

"Ciarra!" It was Tosten, sounding out of breath as if he'd been running.

"Singer," she said in a musical tenor.

He stopped dead at the sound of her voice.

"Dig out thy knowledge and use it well. Minstrels have always been close to the way of the spirit, and melancholy touches their heels. But be thou a warrior, also. This world has need of song and sword."

"What have you done to Bastilla and Oreg?" I asked, tiring of Aethervon's games. Oreg was shuddering and shivering against my hands, whispering to himself, and it made me angry.

"The woman woke before times," said Ciarra, this time in my mother's light, faraway tone. "She'll sleep until morningtide under Tamerlain spell." The big animal pulled away from Ciarra's touch and dropped to the ground.

Unblinking eyes caught mine and tried to pull me into them. I tugged my gaze away and turned back to Ciarra. "And Oreg?" My mouth was dry; ignoring the bear-sized predator standing almost on top of me wasn't easy.

"Quit, now, Tamerlain. Thou'lt never catch a dragon so," chided my father's voice, rich with amusement. "That one tried to overreach himself and needed a reminder of what he is." Oreg flinched at each sound Ciarra made, reminding me of the day he'd inflicted wounds upon himself in Hurog's great hall.

It made me angry, the way I'd been angry when my father hit Ciarra. I surged to my feet with a roar, startling the Tamerlain into backing away. "Enough! You have no need to torment him so. Leave my sister."

She looked at me through ember eyes, and still in my father's voice said, "Can you make me?"

Rage shook me, and magic from the foundations of the ancient temple came to my call, flooding me from my feet to my head as it forced a searing path through my body and mind.

She smiled, waved her hand, and the magic was gone as if it never had been. My body felt as if someone had filled it with ice water rather than blood, and I dropped to my knees, holding my head against the pain of it.

"Ward!" Tosten's warm hands closed on my shoulders.

"Not with my power, you can't." Ciarra's voice changed back to the first sexless whisper. "This is not the dragon's eyrie."

Ciarra closed her eyes, and her body toppled off the wall toward us, rather that down the hillside. Axiel caught her before she landed on the ground. Her body was limp, and she didn't awaken when Tosten patted her cheeks. The Tamerlain twitched its tail twice and disappeared.

I forced down panic and the throbbing headache that kept me on my knees. "Axiel and Tosten, take Ciarra back to camp and keep her warm. Oreg and I'll follow you."

"Are you all right?" asked Tosten in a low voice.

I nodded and gritted my teeth. "Yes. Fine. Go."

Tosten threw his head up at my tone like a young horse trying to evade the touch of the bit.

He looked at Axiel, said, "Let's go," and stalked off without looking at me again.

Axiel looked after him thoughtfully and glanced at Oreg. "If you're not careful, Tosten's going to hate Oreg— if he doesn't already."

"I'll deal with Tosten," I said shortly. "You take care of my sister."

Axiel nodded and followed Tosten into the darkness with my sister laid over his shoulder. I should have been tending to Ciarra, but she had Tosten and Axiel, and Oreg had only me. Aethervon said he'd reminded Oreg of what he was.

"It's all right," I told him, settling uncomfortably on the ground, for every muscle in my body hurt. "Aethervon's gone. You're safe." What was Oreg? A slave? Hurog?

He flinched away from my touch, pressing his face cruelly hard into the rock. "He wouldn't leave her." He said. "I tried, and he wouldn't leave her. It's my fault, my fault, my fault."

"Shh," I said.

"You told me to protect her, and I couldn't. It hurts, it hurts . . ." he moaned.

I was in pain myself, and it distracted me. I almost didn't catch the import of his words. "Trying's enough," I said, my throat tight. "Do you hear me, Oreg? Trying is always enough. I don't expect that you'll be able to protect her from everything."

I'd told him to protect her, I remembered. He had to follow my orders. I hadn't realized there would be consequences if he could not. At my words, his body relaxed, and he quit banging his head into the stone. After a moment, I realized he was unconscious. The pain that the Tallvenish god had inflicted on me seemed to have settled into the sort of muscle aches I got from training too hard. Resigned, I pushed myself to my feet and gathered Oreg over my shoulder for the walk back to camp.

I found Axiel, Penrod, and Tosten at the fire. Neither of them commented when I set Oreg on his blankets and covered him up. When I came up to the fire, Tosten walked pointedly back to his blankets and rolled up in them, his back to me.

Axiel watched him, then said, "I told Penrod what happened. Bastilla and Ciarra seem to be sleeping now. Hopefully, they'll wake fine after they've slept it off."

"I wish we could get them out of Menogue," I said. "I won't feel safe until we're well away from here."

Penrod nodded.

"Did Aethervon tell you anything helpful before I got there?" asked Axiel.

"No," I answered. "All he told me was something about the heart of the dragon rotting—as if I haven't known that Hurog is in trouble." He'd revealed that the stories about Axiel were true, though. Pushing aside my smoldering anger at the suffering of Oreg and Ciarra, I thought more carefully. "He said something about the return of the dragons if I choose carefully."

Penrod shook his head, but Axiel stiffened to alertness, like a hound at the sight of a leash. A small, satisfied smile touched his face.

AFTER EVERYONE WENT TO SLEEP, I CUPPED MY hands and stared at them for several minutes. At last a small silvery light hovered, cool and bright, a few inches above my fingertips—a child's exercise in magic. Untrained as I was, I could do no more with my magic. But it was my magic once more.

8

WARDWICK

The Oranstonians had a difficult time deciding who they'd rather fight, we Northlanders or the Vorsag. They didn't like either of us much.

MY FATHER ALWAYS SAID THAT YOU KNEW YOU were in Oranstone when the wind picked up and it began to rain.

Tallven, through which we'd been traveling, was mostly flat with a few rolling steppes, good grain country. Oranstone was more like my native Shavig in that it was rocky and edged in mountains. But Shavig had never been this wet.

Axiel slowed his horse until I was riding beside him. Mud-spattered, he looked nothing like the son of a king. He hadn't said anything about being a dwarf prince, so I'd left it alone.

"If the land's flat, and there's no road through it, likely it's marsh. We'll have to stay on the road until we reach the mountains," he said.

Penrod, on my other side, nodded. "Just wait until night falls and the mosquitoes come out," he said cheerfully.

As we started down the old road through Oranstone, the wind picked up, and it began to rain. About midday, wet and miserable, we passed by the first village.

I sneezed. "We're short on grain. Penrod, you and Bastilla bargain, and we'll set up camp just down the road. Get news about the raiders, if you can."

Penrod nodded, and the rest of us continued on. We found a stand of trees in a rocky outcropping (as opposed to marsh) and set up our tent for the first time. Because we didn't carry tent poles, we had to find two trees the right distance apart so we could stretch the tent between them. I left Axiel and Oreg to it and had Ciarra help me with the horses, who were as miserable and wet as we were.

I'd just taken off Pansy's saddle when he stiffened and stared down the trail. After a moment, I heard someone coming at a thunderous gallop.

Penrod beat Bastilla into the camp, but it was Bastilla who called, "Bandits. In the village—a dozen or so."

"Saddle up," I commanded, and I threw the saddle back on Pansy and tightened the cinch. I hadn't expected to run into bandits this far from Vorsag, which was stupid of me. Any land as neglected as Oranstone was sure to be rife with raiders, Vorsagian or otherwise. Pansy, sensing my excitement, danced and tossed his head as I swung my leg over his back. I'd often hunted bandits with my father, but this was my first time being in charge.

As the rest of them mounted, I said, "We'll stay together until I tell you differently. Be careful of the villagers—if you're not sure if the man you've got is a villager or a bandit, don't kill him. Anything I've forgotten Axiel?"

"No, sir," he said.

"Penrod?"

"The men must be working elsewhere, because the only men I saw were bandits," he said. "The main street is cobbled under loose dirt. The horses won't have good footing there. Don't be afraid to dismount and fight. These aren't Vorsagian troops, just poorly armed common bandits. The likelihood of any group of thieves being as well trained as even young Ciarra is almost nothing."

"Ciarra," I said, reminded of her presence. "You stay in your saddle. You don't have the weight to go up against a full-grown man, no matter how poorly trained." I wanted to tell her to stay here, but Penrod was right: As long as these were normal bandits, she would be fine. More importantly, she wouldn't have stayed if I told her to. Stala always said that a good commander never gave orders he knew his troops wouldn't obey.

I glanced around and made sure everyone was mounted, then said, "Let's go."

So we galloped back to the village. There was no one in the streets as we entered, but a woman screamed, and we followed the sound as we wove between a row of huts.

There were, perhaps, fifteen bandits, scruffy and dirty. One man held a crude bow that wouldn't have hit a keep wall at twenty paces; the rest were armed with battered swords that looked as though they'd looted them from a fifteen-year-old battlefield. They'd been distracted by the entertainment, and hadn't even heard the horses until we were upon them.

The bandits had the village women gathered in a tight group. In front of it, on the bare, cold ground, lay a young girl held by a pair of men while a third was untying his breeches.

I forgot to give the signal for attack. Pansy charged into the fray, and with the force of his speed I beheaded the would-be rapist with the first stroke of my sword. The body fell on the girl, but that couldn't be helped. Following my lead, if not my orders, Axiel got another of her attackers, but the rest of the bandits scattered.

"No mercy," I called and set Pansy after one of the men.

It was butcher's work. None of the men I killed even tried to parry, let alone attack. After I killed the third man, who was old enough to be my grandfather, I couldn't find anyone else to chase. Most of my people had scattered with the bandits. The only one nearby was Penrod, who'd dismounted and was throwing a body over his horse's back.

I rode to him but had to sit through Pansy's tantrum at being asked to halt when he was having such fun. "Why take the body back?" I asked. With Penrod there was always a reason.

"We need to search them and return anything belonging to the village," he said. "Then we should burn the dead, Oranstonian fashion, so their spirits don't linger here."

I should have known that. I'd hunted bandits with my father, but my job had been to ride back to the keep with news rather than help with cleanup. I said, "I'll tell the others. Axiel's chasing one who made it into the trees. Bastilla stayed with the women. Did you see where Tosten, Oreg, and Ciarra went?" A good commander in a real battle would have known.

"Tosten and Oreg followed the three who ran the other way through the village, back toward our camp. Ciarra was behind me, but I think she stayed in the village with Bastilla."

"Right," I said. "I'll go round them up if you'll tell Axiel we need the bodies."

"Likely he already knows," replied Penrod, "But happen I'll tell him anyway."

"I'll be back to help as soon as I find the others." Pansy willingly bounded into a gallop.

At my approach, the village women bunched in a group with the children, including the bloodstained child molested by the bandits, in the middle like a herd of mares facing down a pack of wolves. I looked around for any of my missing companions and saw Bastilla emerging from the woods.

Pansy danced in place. War-trained, the smell of blood excited him rather than scared him. To me, it smelled like butchering time in the fall, and I purposely ignored that it was men not beef we'd been slaughtering. You learn to do that or be sick at every fight.

"Bastilla, have you seen Ciarra?"

"Not since she chased one that way," she motioned through the huts with her bloodied sword.

I took Pansy back through the line of huts and onto the main street. Feather stood ground-tied in front of a sturdy-looking building across the way and snorted at our approach. There was no sound of battle inside the hut.

Raw fear made my ears pound with the sound of my pulse and converted to anger. I'd *told* her to stay on her horse. I dismounted slowly. Speed didn't matter, because whatever had happened in that hut was already over.

I opened the door and stepped into the doorway. At first, my eyes, adjusted to the sun, I couldn't see anything at all. Something attacked me, hit me hard in the ribs.

My attacker was too close for a sword, so I tossed mine and grabbed my dagger before I saw it was Ciarra I held, her head buried against me. I hauled her out of the hut and looked her over quickly. Her sword was covered in drying blood as was her clothing from chest downward. Her whole body shook, but I wasn't much better: I'd almost stabbed her.

"Are you hurt?" I said, my voice angry and raw.

She shook her head and then pointed urgently at the hut.

I grabbed my sword from where I'd tossed it and cautiously stepped into the hut. It was little bigger than one of the stalls at Hurog. A rope bed was strung up in the left corner, the fireplace in the right. In the close quarters, the smell of sliced entrails was unmistakable, but I had to wait until my eyes adjusted to the darkness before I saw him.

The bandit was curled around his belly wound, but his eyes were open and alive. Ciarra had gotten the first blow in, and it was fatal, eventually. Underfed, he was probably Tosten's age, but his beardless, tearstained face looked younger.

My anger at Ciarra's recklessness fled far too easily and left me weak with horror.

"Please," he gasped in some heavy Oranstonian dialect.

I saw in his eyes that he knew his wound was mortal. He knew what awaited him if my courage wasn't high enough. Seleg, I thought, Seleg wouldn't have left him here to suffer. I raised my dagger, then let my hand drop. Seleg would have saved him. Killing children was for brutal men like my father . . . and me.

I renewed my grip and slid the dagger's sharp blade into the base of his brain, just as Stala had taught me. For a man of my strength and speed it was the fastest, surest way to kill. He didn't even have time to flinch.

I wiped both my sword and knife clean on his shirt and sheathed them. Then I picked him up and carried him out of the hut. Ciarra looked at me, then turned her face into Feather's mane. Her shoulders heaved with silent sobs. I left her there.

Bastilla was trying to talk to the women when I came around the hut. From the frustrated look on her face, she wasn't getting very far; I realized that she couldn't speak Oranstonian, and they were refusing to understand Tallvenish. There were three bodies in a pile, and I set the boy I carried beside them.

"Leave them, Bastilla," I said in clear if simple Oranstonian. My father had been baffled by my ability to pick up languages, though he said I sounded as stupid in one as I did in any other. "They'll settle down after we leave without hurting them. If you killed anyone, you need to bring the body here. We need to burn the corpses so they won't haunt this place." I repeated what I said in Tallvenish for Bastilla's sake. My voice sounded strangely harsh in my ears.

Oreg and Tosten rode in at that point. Tosten's horse was dripping mud and trembling.

"Fell in a bog," Tosten said shortly.

"We need to gather the bodies," I said.

Tosten gave me an exasperated look. "My horse isn't up to it."

"I'll get them," offered Oreg, glancing from my face to Tosten's and shaking his head slightly at me.

I bit my tongue on what I'd been about to say. It wasn't fair to take out my horror on Tosten. He looked pale and shaken. Unless tavern life in Tyrfannig was more interesting than I thought, Tosten had killed for the first time today.

Bastilla looked cool and professional, like she'd killed bandits before. Either her time as a slave had hardened her to death, or there were things going on in the Cholyte temples I didn't want to know about. Oreg, like Bastilla, looked as if he killed on a daily basis. The thought of picking up the bandits' dead bodies hadn't bothered him at all.

Tosten threw a leg over his horse's withers and slid off. He gave me a humiliated look, stuffed his reins in my hands, then bolted for some bushes. I patted his horse's neck and led him a bit to make sure he wasn't lame. The terrified looks I was getting from the village women were making me uncomfortable.

Tosten looked paler when he came to take his horse, and he wouldn't meet my eyes.

"Stala says some of the most hardened soldiers she knows are sick after every battle," I said. It didn't seem to help, so I gave him something to do. "Ciarra needs you. She stabbed a man in the stomach. I finished him off, but it was rough. She's over there." I pointed to the other side of the huts.

Maybe they'd do each other some good.

Eventually, we got all the dead bandits gathered. Oddly enough, given our disorganization (my fault), we'd gotten them all. Axiel, Penrod, and Oreg searched them and stripped them of everything but their clothes. The leader had a silver and amber pin on his sleeve. When Oreg set it on the small pile of loot, one of the village women took an aborted step toward it before she caught herself.

I sent Bastilla to tell Tosten and Ciarra to go back to our camp before someone came upon it and made off with our pack horses and gear. She returned, leading Pansy—or being dragged by him. I'd forgotten I'd left him with Ciarra.

"That's the last of them," commented Axiel, wiping his bloody hands on a ragged shirt he'd saved out. "Now we have to find fuel to burn them."

"No," said Oreg. "I can do it." He gestured at the pile, and the corpses began to smolder as if they were made of wood instead of flesh.

Bastilla joined him, touching his arm. Almost instantly, a wave of heat touched us all. Magic, Hurog magic, hit me, and I staggered back a step. For a moment, I almost felt as if I were home again, and the terrible hollow feeling left me. I was whole. It felt glorious.

"Sss, not so much, girl," snapped Oreg. He glanced at me worriedly. "I'm sorry, my lord," he said; then the magic ceased.

I almost cried out with the pain of it. Luckily, no one but Oreg was watching me, so I had a chance to recover. Until that moment, I hadn't understood that Hurog and Oreg were really the same. He'd told me, but I'd really still thought of him as a person tied to the keep—like I was, only closer. But it was different; I felt it in his magic. He *was* Hurog. I wondered what would happen if he were killed in battle; something I should have been worried about sooner.

"Licleng couldn't have done this on his best day," commented Penrod in awe.

His voice pulled my attention back to the bandits. Where they'd lain, there was nothing but scorched earth. It had taken less time to reduce the bandits to ashes than it would to take five deep breaths.

"That's not saying much," said Axiel. "Licleng couldn't light a candle without a flaming faggot to aid him."

"It was Bastilla," said Oreg keeping his worried gaze on me.

"Let's go," I said. "The horses are tired. And the sooner we leave, the sooner the village can start recovering." I nodded my head at the cluster of women and children.

OUR CAMPING SPOT WAS NOT TOO FAR FROM A clear-running creek, and we all washed up in it. Tosten and Ciarra had finished setting up the camp, so all we had to do was groom horses and prepare dinner. Neither Tosten nor Ciarra ate much.

Ciarra avoided me, clinging to Tosten's side. It hurt, but I understood. If I could have escaped from myself, I would have. I didn't regret putting the boy out of his misery, just the necessity of it—and the reminder that pretend as I might, I was my father's son.

People often wondered why my father, who clearly disliked Tallvens more than Oranstonians (because he didn't have to pay a sovereign's tithe to the Oranstonians), had fought so hard for the Tallvens in the Rebellion. *I'd* known why since I'd killed my first bandit. Once my sword bit into flesh, I loved it: loved letting go and swinging with the full force of my body. Even killing the boy hadn't robbed me of battle euphoria entirely. Sometimes I wondered when I was going to wake up and discover that I *was* my father.

I gave Tosten and Ciarra third watch together, taking second myself with Oreg for company. I didn't plan on waking them for their shift. If they could sleep, I'd let them.

I waited, wide awake, until Penrod came to wake me for my watch. When he and Axiel appeared to be asleep, I crouched beside Oreg, who was mending his shirt by the light of the fire.

"What happens if you're killed in battle?" I asked.

"The walls of Hurog will fall, until not one stone stands

upon another." After delivering his bardic lines dramatically, he tied off a thread and said in a different tone, "Do you really think if my father had left me such an easy way out I wouldn't have taken it before? I can be hurt, but only the ring bearer can kill me."

"Ah," I looked out into the darkness. That was right. He'd said something like that before. "Only me."

"Talk to me," he said after a moment. "You're more tense than old Pansy gets when a mare walks by."

I hesitated. "Battle always surprises me. The way men die so easily. But every time I unsheathe my sword, I expect it to be different. That it should be . . ." No matter how I said it, it would sound stupid.

"Like the songs? Full of glory and honor?"

I was right. It sounded stupid. So why did I still believe it?

"This wasn't a battle," said Axiel quietly from his bedroll. From his manner, I decided he'd only heard the last part of the conversation. "This was vermin hunting."

"I didn't mean to wake you," I apologized.

He shrugged and wrapped his arms around his knees. "I get restless after a fight, anyway."

"The boy I killed," I swallowed because my throat was dry. "He should have been farming the land with his family, not out thieving for survival. Where is the overlord for this land?"

"The boy was a pit viper, Ward," said Axiel. "Doesn't matter how old they are, they'll kill you just the same. He'd have cheered and left you if you'd been in his place. Real battles are . . . both better and worse. They strip you raw, tear all the pretenses, all the surface off of you. You can't hide from yourself in battle. Take Penrod: He learned that quiet self-confidence of his on the battlefield. For others . . . you know the high king?"

I nodded my head, though it hadn't really been a question.

"His father was such a warrior that men still speak his

name in awe. Your father fought under his command. King
Jorn had a rare combination of courage and wisdom, and
his heir, Jakoven, was smart as a whip. He could look at a
battlefield and evaluate it like a man twice his age. He was
good with a sword. He should have been a fine commander, but he just didn't have it in him. The first battle he
fought, he killed most of his men because he lost his
courage. His father put him in a command post after that,
somewhere safe where his talents would be of use. But we
all knew Jakoven failed. I think it twisted him. Not just the
loss of courage, but that we all knew."

"This was not battle," said Axiel. "But it was necessary.
First, we saved this village and all the other villages they'd
have destroyed. Second, if you are planning on taking this
group into battle—there were too many of us who had
never fought to kill. It's different from training."

"No one broke," I said.

"No one broke," agreed Axiel, pushing a strand of dark
hair from his face. "Ciarra will be fine, and Tosten, too."

THE NEXT MORNING WAS GRAY AND MISERABLE.
Everything was damp. It hadn't rained overnight, but there
was a thick mist overlaying the land. The firewood was
damp, too. If we hadn't had Oreg with us, we'd never have
gotten a fire going. After breakfast, we settled into practicing. Yesterday's fight made everyone more serious than
usual—or else I was so grim no one felt comfortable light-
ening the mood. Even Oreg was uncharacteristically silent.

Axiel called an abrupt halt to our fighting. I nodded at
Penrod, my erstwhile opponent, and went to see why Axiel
had stopped us.

A tall, rawboned man waited a cautious distance from our
camp, a packhorse beside him. Clearly he'd decided to let us
come to him rather than the other way around, a smart way
to approach fighting troops. Any Hurog farmer would have

just hailed the camp and tromped right in; but then Shavig hadn't been attacked in living memory. At my gesture, the others stayed back while I went to meet the man.

"My lord," he said in respectable Tallvenish as soon as I was within comfortable speaking distance. "My wife told me we owe you and your men for their safety."

He said it all without the histrionics the words implied. He could have been talking about the weather. I noticed he had a sword. Oranstone peasants were forbidden edged weapons by a law enacted just after the Rebellion. Moreover, it was a *good* sword, not the sort belonging to the average man-at-arms. I took a closer look at him.

He was about the same age as Penrod, though the years hadn't been as kind. He wore a woolen hat pulled down around his ears. It might just be to keep him warm, but it would also disguise that distinctive haircut that used to be worn by the Oranstonian nobility. But what really gave him away was the packhorse. Small, slab-sided, and narrow-chested, the beasts prized by Oranstonian nobles could travel for weeks on little food.

The horse he led was old. Someone else would have thought it half-starved and fast approaching death. But my father had brought back one of the horses from his campaigning, so I knew what I was looking at. Straight legs, high-set tail, and swan neck told me that this animal had never been bred for a peasant.

A nobleman, I thought. *One of the ones who'd refused to capitulate at the end of the war.* How terrible to owe his wife's life to the enemy. No wonder he appeared so calm. I bet he wanted to take that sword and ram it down my throat—but he had to act like a peasant.

"Something amuses you?" he said then added quickly, "my lord."

"I was thinking that you probably would have been happier if we'd managed to kill each other off," I said candidly. "If it helps, we haven't a Tallven in the party. Most of us are Shavig born and bred—and we've come to fight the Vorsagian scum." I added "my lord" to the end of my speech, too.

He looked at me a moment, then he smiled thinly. "It helps. It also helps that it was my daughter you kept from rape. My name is Luavellet." He offered his hand, and I took it. "My wife also says that you are traveling, and probably came to trade for food and grain. We decided that provisioning you was the least we could do. I also brought a few things you might not have, being from a dryer climate."

"My thanks," I said, meaning it. "You will let us pay you, of course."

He raised both his eyebrows in a manner that reminded me of my grandfather at his most haughty. "I will hear of no such thing." We'd both stopped my lording each other.

"Money we have," I said. "Let me trade with you, then you can give me information for the rest. I've come to find out what the Vorsagian bandits have been doing."

"Why do you care?" he asked, though there was no hostility in his voice.

I found myself trying to answer him honestly. "I don't like bandits, but I wouldn't have traveled half the kingdom to fight them. I need to prove myself to my family, and this seemed the best way to do it."

"There's going to be a war, boy," he said.

I nodded. "So there is, and I'll have been here for a while before the king sends troops."

He smiled up into the sky, though his eyes were sad. "Why are they always so young? Boy, the king's not going to send troops. He'll wait until the Vorsag have slaughtered us all. Then he'll close flanks on them and make them fight from the wrong side of the mountains."

It made sudden sense. I'd known there would be war, just from listening to Garranon explain the situation in Oranstone. If *I'd* seen it, anyone with any eye to strategy

knew it, too. Axiel had said King Jakoven was a strategist.
He was also a cold-blooded bastard.

I could extrapolate even further. If Luavellet, isolated in
his village, knew what the king was up to, it stood to reason
that the Vorsagians knew it as well. Were they just after Oranstone? If so, they'd try to take the mountain passes and then
dig in. If not, they'd split their forces and attack on two
fronts, probably on the Seaford coast—unless King Kariarn
was an idiot. What that meant for me, I wasn't sure yet.

"You just paid your debt to us," I said after a moment.
"You'll have to let us pay for the supplies."

THAT EVENING, WE SHELTERED FROM A RAINSTORM
on the oiled drop cloth Luavellet had provided. There was no
question of practicing in the slick mud. If it persisted, I'd
have to come up with something, but we took the night off.

Axiel retold a few more battle stories, then Tosten
brought out his harp. With Ciarra leaning against his shoulder, my brother proved he was right to give up coopering
in favor of the harp. His music wrapped around me like a
warm blanket.

Penrod produced a small soldier's drum from somewhere
and joined in. Bastilla sang in a pleasing, if thin, alto, but it
was the blending of Axiel's bass and Tosten's golden tenor
that completed the magic. I hadn't heard its like since the last
time I was at court. I leaned against one of the trees the tent
rope had been tied to and relaxed, closing my eyes. Someone
pulled a damp blanket around my shoulders.

"Careful," Penrod said in hushed tones. "I don't think
he's slept since before the fight."

9
ESTIAN: BECKRAM, ERDRICK, GARRANON

My father always said that Jakoven was an evil, sly, dangerous coward. If it hadn't been for the cowardice and the annual sovereign's tithe the king demanded, I think the Hurogmeten might have liked the high king.

"JUST FOR ONE NIGHT," IMPLORED BECKRAM. "Ciernack's brought in an Avinhellish sword dancer."

Erdrick crossed his arms and sat on his bed. "That's what you said the last time we switched places. It took three days."

"Please, Erdrick." Beckram smiled winningly. "You do it so well."

"I don't do it well," said Erdrick in driven tones. "You know I don't." He saw the triumph in Beckram's face and knew he should have stuck to a simple "No." Now the argument had slipped from his willingness to his ability.

"Your court manners are flawless, and you know it. Everyone is expected to be on their best behavior tonight. You can even retire early with a headache or something."

"You aren't ever on your best behavior," snapped Erdrick. "If you start now, everyone will be suspicious."

"No," Beckram sounded unexpectedly grim. "They'll just think I've put on airs since the king confirmed Father's hold on Hurog."

"It's not your fault. You tried," Erdrick left the bed and touched his twin's shoulder.

Beckram rubbed his hand over his face. "Then why did the king smile at me when he made the announcement? I should have left well enough alone. Waited until Father could talk to him."

"Father wouldn't have done any better than you did."

Beckram smiled to acknowledge Erdrick's support, but the warmth didn't touch the desperation in his eyes. "I put my foot in it somehow, Erdrick. You know it, and I know it." He rubbed a spot on his linen sleeve. "All else aside, Erdrick, I just can't face them tonight. I need to go somewhere I don't have to play games. Just tonight. I need to take my mind off the king, off the queen, off of Father. He's worried sick about Ward."

"So are you," commented Erdrick.

Beckram's eyebrow rose in disbelief. "I don't even like him."

"You envy him," corrected Erdrick shrewdly. "Stupid or not, he's a good man. You like him better than you like yourself."

Beckram flushed with temper. "He's an idiot. If he hadn't been a moron, none of this would be necessary."

"Father will straighten it out," Erdrick said. "Father's good at this sort of thing."

Beckram nodded and gripped his twin's hand. "Thank you, Rick. Wear my blue and gold outfit; everyone knows it. They'll look at you in it and see me."

Erdrick watched Beckram stride energetically back to his room and wondered how he'd ended up agreeing to this. He reviewed the conversation in his mind and couldn't suppress a grin when he realized that he hadn't agreed to it. Trust Beckram. Erdrick put the book he'd been reading back on the shelves. He'd hoped to finish it tonight, but it looked like he'd be strutting with the court peacocks instead.

•   •   •

GARRANON DUCKED UNDER HAVERNESS'S SWORD
blade and drew his arm back to deliver a mortal blow, but
Haverness's knife swept out of nowhere to touch his throat.

"Your fight," Garranon said with a smile to show he
held no grudges. Actually, he was pleased he'd managed to
fight the old man off as long as he had. Stupidly forthright
Haverness might be politically, but few could compare
with his swordsmanship.

Haverness withdrew his knife and sheathed it. He
looked at Garranon grimly. "Now you will tell me what
this was about. I trust you didn't call upon me in your father's name for a bout of sword and knife?"

Garranon looked around the training grounds. Though
the ancient room was empty, he said, "Let's walk." That
way no one could listen in.

The old man stiffened. "You play games."

"I grant you that. But I'm the one at risk if the king
finds out why I've approached you. Please, walk with me."

After an insultingly long hesitation, Haverness sheathed
his sword and gestured for Garranon to lead the way.

Garranon didn't talk as he strode down the halls that
would bring them, eventually, to the gardens where the
sound of running water would cover their voices. No one
they passed looked twice; their weaponry and sweat gave
answer to why the newly named Champion of Oranstone
would walk with the king's favorite.

The smell of sweet blossoms was almost overwhelm-
ingly strong when they left the musty halls for the gardens
at the heart of the keep. It was early yet, and the gardens
were deserted.

"Are you serious about taking a hundred men to defeat
the Vorsagians?" asked Garranon abruptly.

Haverness's eyebrows rose in mild inquiry. "I am his
majesty's most obedient servant." If the old man felt bitterness, Garranon couldn't hear it in his voice.

"Who is going?" Garranon almost winced after he

asked the question. That hadn't been what he'd meant to ask, and he wasn't surprised when Haverness's face went blank.

"My clerk has a list, but I can't recall offhand."

Garranon waved his hand in dismissal and sought another course. "What I wanted to know is, do you have space for me? In my father's day, Buril had three hundred trained men. I cannot do so well, but there are sixty armsmen, and I can gather another hundred raw recruits."

"Oh, is that what you think I'm doing?" whispered Haverness almost to himself. His features hardened into a cold mask.

"It's what I hope you're doing," replied Garranon steadily. "It doesn't matter if the king knows it or not, though he seems to be more concerned with his queen's affairs right now. He cannot withdraw his approval now."

They paced once around the outside of the garden before Haverness spoke again. "You look like your father."

"Yes."

"Askenwen refused to consider coming." Askenwen was the richest of the Oranstonians, a young man who relished court life. "He likes Tallven just fine. Oranstone is too wet, he said. Do you know what his father was called during the war?"

"The Direwolf," replied Garranon with a thin smile.

"The Direwolf stood off an entire army with a score of men for three days to let our armies disperse so we could retreat to our holds and protect our families after we knew the war was lost. His son prefers to get drunk in Shadetown at Black Ciernack's tavern." Haverness shook his head, his mouth twisted in a bitter smile. "Don't get excited about winning this war. Jakoven has done too good a job of gelding our young men. I suspect we'll all be valiant martyrs for use as rallying cries when Jakoven finally decides to defend the Kingdoms."

"Being a martyr is highly overrated," observed Garranon. "Useless lot for the most part—my father included, begging your pardon, sir." He took a deep breath. "Askenwen's younger brother, Kirkovenal, started a fight yesterday."

"Indeed?" Haverness sounded lost in his own thoughts.

"He was fined for disturbing the peace, as the king did not find defending the honor of Oranstone a sufficient reason to beat the stuffing out of a pair of loyal Tallvenish subjects." Garranon let his gaze linger on a small pond where lilies floated. "He has been running Grensward for his brother since he was old enough to hold a pen."

"He's a boy."

"Eighteen. Old enough to hold a sword, eh?" Garranon reminded Haverness gently. "Old enough to rally Grensward . . . against her enemies." Not just Vorsagian enemies.

Haverness caught the leading pause. "The Rebellion is dead."

Not as long as I live, thought Garranon. He said, "Yes. But if we don't defeat the Vorsag, Oranstone will be dead, too. I can help."

Haverness started to say something, but he was interrupted by a royal page.

"My Lord Garranon, sir," panted the boy before he stopped to get his breath. "The king requires your presence at his breakfast in his rooms."

Garranon watched Haverness's face freeze and could have cursed. The old man had been about to accept him before the page reminded him who Garranon's bed partner was.

Garranon drew a deep breath and sent the boy on his way with a few courteous words. Before Haverness could speak, Garranon said, "The streams in here are a marvel, do you not agree. A tribute to Jakoven's skill."

"A tribute to the king's mages."

Garranon shook his head and met Haverness's eyes firmly. "No, a tribute to the high king. He has his secrets,

our Jakoven; do not underestimate him. Now, King Kariarn of Vorsag would like you to think he's a wizard, but
he's not. He does have, however, at least four adept mages
in his employ."

Haverness swallowed the information about Jakoven
but said, "There aren't four adept mages in the whole of
Vorsag."

Garranon shrugged. "Nonetheless, four adepts serve
Kariarn, according to Arten, Jakoven's archmage. I have
other information you might find useful . . . if you bring
me with you."

Haverness nodded thoughtfully, his eyes hooded. "I'll
consider that."

"Of course," replied Garranon with more calm than he
felt. Bleakly, he knew he'd be standing on the king's right
when Haverness rode out of Estian with his hundred.
"Thank you for the bout. Pray excuse me, the king commands my presence."

ERDRICK LOOKED IN THE MIRROR AT HIMSELF
wearing Beckram's green and gold court outfit. He closed
his eyes and imagined pulling Beckram's reckless self-
assurance around his shoulders like a cloak. *This is the last
time,* he thought, and couldn't tell if he were serious or not.
There was freedom in being Beckram, freedom and exhil-
aration. When Erdrick opened his eyes, he looked at Beckram in the mirror, tugged the neck of his tunic straight, and
strolled out of his rooms.

DESPITE HIS PROTESTS TO BECKRAM, ERDRICK WAS
comfortable in his brother's skin. In the crowded court he
flirted and charmed the ladies and exchanged half-barbed
quips with the men. But he couldn't force himself go near

the queen. Let his brother make up with her afterward if she chose to take offense.

At dinner, Alizon, the king's half brother, sat at the empty place next to him. "So, your father has been named Hurogmeten in his brother's place," he said in a bored tone.

"Damnable thing," Erdrick agreed in Beckram's lazy drawl. "Poor Father. Hurog's cold in the winter and damp in the summer. Half the peasants are freeholders—serfs are much easier to deal with. Most of the time, it's all the Hurogmeten can do to see that the people are fed; the rest of the time, they're not fed."

"The title's an old one."

"That and a half copper will buy a loaf of bread. The worst of it is—" Erdrick managed exactly the right put-upon tone. "—my younger brother gets the better end of the bargain. Iftahar is richer and warmer than Hurog."

"So you didn't ask the king to settle Hurog on your father?" asked Alizon, glancing up.

"Do I look stupid?" replied Erdrick indignantly. "Why would I do that? I don't want Hurog."

After Alizon left, Erdrick wiped the sweat off the back of his neck. The king's half brother was entirely too unnerving. This was absolutely the last time he took Beckram's place.

He drained his cup of wine and gathered another from a passing servant. When he finally stood up to retreat to his room, he could feel the effects of the alcohol. So instead of taking a shorter route, he walked through the courtyard gardens. The cool night air did a lot to restore his sense of balance.

Next to the library, the garden was his favorite part of the castle. The sound of the flowing water from the fountains and artificial streams reminded him of home. He smelled the petals of a flower that stood out ghostly white in the darkness. He was disappointed to find it had no scent at all.

When someone grabbed him by the shoulder, he was still thinking about flowers.

IN BLACK CIERNACK'S TAVERN, BECKRAM COUGHED suddenly and swallowed a hefty draft to counter the sudden pain in his throat. It worried him for a moment, but when it dispersed so quickly, he decided it must have been just a muscle cramp. Beckram turned his attention back to the dancer who was in the process of sheathing her sword in a way no man ever could.

JAKOVEN JUMPED BACK AWAY FROM THE SPRAY of blood, waiting for the writhing body to grow still. He licked a drop of the dark liquid dripping from his knife, then threw it on the ground beside the boy. The knife wasn't distinctive, though that didn't matter. Everyone would know who'd done it.

"No more lovers for my lady queen," he said out loud. He nudged the body with his toe, but the boy didn't move. The high king stared at the pale face. "Not even a stupid Shavig boy was safe enough. So, Beckram, what do you think? Should she commit suicide when she hears of your death? Or should she choose to sequester herself at one of my country estates? Not much help, are you? Never mind, I'll decide tomorrow."

In the shadows, Alizon, who'd arrived just a moment too late, clenched his fists and thought, *Too many bodies, Jakoven.*

BECKRAM WHISTLED CHEERFULLY AS HE CHANGED his clothes. The sword dancer had been as good as she was touted and more. He might have stayed longer, but some niggling worry about his brother sent him home early.

Maybe it was just guilt at making Erdrick take his place again.

He popped open the door to his twin's room and found it empty. It was later than Erdrick usually stayed out, but the festivities would last until dawn.

"Well, brother mine, did you seduce some lass? Got to be careful with that, wouldn't want the queen jealous . . ." He stopped talking when another thought crossed his mind. "No, you wouldn't, would you? Not with the queen." Maybe, he thought, that was the source of his restlessness tonight.

He glanced down at himself to make sure his clothes were something Erdrick would wear and pulled the yellow scarf off his knee. Then, slouching a little, Beckram paced down the hall.

There were a lot of people still in the court hall, so it took Beckram a long time to see that Erdrick wasn't there. When he saw the queen gossiping with one of her ladies, he relaxed. Not that he'd believed his brother could betray him, not really.

"Erdrick?"

He was better at being Erdrick than Erdrick was at being him. Beckram didn't even hesitate in responding to his brother's name. "Lord Alizon?"

The older man looked tired. "You don't usually come to the dances, Erdrick."

Beckram gave his brother's soft, half-embarrassed laugh. "Well, I'm looking for Beckram. He borrowed one of my books to press a crease out of a scarf, and now I can't find it anywhere."

"Ah," the king's brother shrugged. "I haven't seen him here lately. After dinner, he said something about catching some air."

"I'll check the courtyard, then," said Beckram.

Alizon nodded. "If I see him, I'll tell him you're looking for him."

When the Shavig boy wandered away, Alizon sipped his water to wash the foul taste of his brother's business out of his mouth.

AT FIRST, BECKRAM THOUGHT THE COURTYARD WAS empty. It was a little chilly, not yet fall but soon. The unease, which had brought him home earlier than his comrades, hadn't dissipated with the reassurance that Erdrick hadn't poached his lady.

He stood in the middle of the courtyard and tapped his toe impatiently. To bed, he decided abruptly. There must have been something odd in the ale he'd had tonight that produced this feeling that something was wrong. The damned palace was too big to search for his brother, who was probably passed out on some forgotten couch somewhere.

Beckram started for the entrance nearest his rooms but stopped when he smelled blood. As the air brought the rich scent of it to his nose, something within him died as a sudden certainly grew within him. Something had happened to his twin.

"Rick?" he called anyway, answered only by a faint breeze that made the leaves whisper together.

A dizzy feeling of unreality swept over him as he stepped through the carefully planted bed and followed the scent of death to the shape that lay half hidden in shadows. Shock was replaced first by grief, then by rage, as he stared at his twin's dead face. He remembered the pale face of the queen's last lover after he'd been drowned and cursed himself for asking Erdrick to take his place. He should have known better.

The urge to kill Jakoven was overwhelming. He knew he could do it, too, despite the king's reputation as a swordsman. Who would be so stupid as to defeat the high king? Beckram's sword work had been polished by Stala.

Yes, he could kill Jakoven. There were places the king didn't bring his guards.

But if he did, his father would lose both of his sons, one to murder and the other to the headsman's ax. Beckram held that thought and rode the pain it brought: There could be no overt revenge. He would have to hold to the oaths he swore to the king for his father's sake.

Carefully, Beckram closed his twin's eyes. He kissed the cool forehead and muttered a few words of love. Then he slid an arm beneath Erdrick's shoulders and under his knees, gathering him close.

It wasn't easy getting to his feet, for Erdrick weighed no less than Beckram, and neither of them were small men. Beckram staggered a bit, adjusting to the weight, then began to walk.

BECKRAM STOOD MOMENTARILY UNNOTICED IN the entranceway and looked around. His gaze drifted over Haverness and found a dozen more nobles who were just the kind of men he was looking for. Men whose loyalty to the throne could not be doubted nor could their word be bought.

Satisfied, Beckram strode in with measured footsteps, the beat of his pulse dictating his steps. He could tell when they saw him, the hundred or so people still dancing at this hour, because a hush fell over the crowd. Everyone in this room knew about the queen's previous lover. Everyone knew Beckram had been her lover. Everyone knew they were watching Erdrick carry Beckram's body before the king who had killed him.

The king remained where he was, expressionless. Beckram heard the small sound the queen made, but he had eyes only for Jakoven. When the king was five paces away, the traditional space for fealty swearing, Beckram knelt and set his brother on the white marble tiles. He remained kneeling.

"My king," he said, using his voice as his father had taught him so it carried to the far corner of the room. "Hurogs have served the Tallvenish rule since there have been high kings. My father, his brother, their father before them served you. It is my intention to do the same. Haverness?"

O, brave man, thought Beckram as he saw the Oranstone nobleman approach out of the corner of his eye.

Haverness waited to answer until he stood behind the king. We are all doing this by tradition, thought Beckram with that same eerie calmness that had claimed him from his entrance into the dance room.

"Hurog?" asked Haverness.

It startled Beckram to be called that; he'd always been addressed as Iftahar, after his father's holding, but it was appropriate. Surely his soul was encased in the cold black stone of Hurog.

"How many men go with you, Haverness?" Beckram asked, not taking his eyes from the king.

"Eighty-four."

"And you leave when?"

"Ten days' time."

"Would you consider taking me?"

"Hurogs are rare men. I would be honored."

For the first time since he'd entered the room, Beckram looked away from the king. He stared at his twin's gray face and black blood. *No more dusty books,* he thought.

Beckram returned his gaze to the king's face, wanting to watch his reaction. "Then you may put down the name of Beckram of Hurog on your list."

A gasp of surprise traveled around the room.

"First though, I must take my brother Erdrick to Hurog for burial. He met with an accident in the courtyard— or maybe it was suicide." Beckram looked at the gaping wound, then looked around the room. "No, I suppose it was an accident. He tripped and cut his throat on a thorn in the garden." Beckram scooped his brother off the floor— the body seemed much lighter—and strode to the nearest door. It wasn't until he was in the corridor that he realized Haverness and Garranon paced beside him.

"When are you leaving?" asked Garranon.

"Now," Beckram replied shortly.

"Do you have enough gold to hire horses along the way?"

"I'll manage."

Garranon pulled his belt purse loose and tied it to Beckram's belt. "That should be enough."

"I'll have two of my men ride honor guard," said Haverness. "They'll meet you at the stables."

"I won't wait."

"If they're late, they'll catch up."

They left him then, and he walked the rest of the way to his rooms alone. He had to set Erdrick down to open the door, and it was harder to pick him up again this time. The strength of anger was seeping away, leaving only guilt.

Beckram lay Erdrick on the bed while he packed. He took Garranon's pouch and put it in his saddlebags, then stared around the suite at a loss. What was appropriate to pack?

In the end, he just wrapped Erdrick in the top quilt of the bed and staggered out with near-empty saddlebags. He didn't bother waking the grooms but settled his burden on a pile of hay and saddled both horses. The Hurog-bred geldings snorted a bit at the dead body, but Hellebore, Erdrick's war-trained mount, stood steady while Beckram heaved the wrapped body over the saddle and secured it with rope.

Mounting his own steed, Beckram started out. He passed a couple of men wearing Haverness's colors running to the stable, but he didn't stop. He would spend no

more time than he had to in the home of the man who mur-
dered his brother. He didn't even notice it was Garranon
and Haverness who opened the palace gates and let him
through.

"HAVERNESS, I NEED TO RIDE WITH YOU," SAID
Garranon hoarsely. "If I stay here longer, I'll slit Jakoven's
throat myself—which fool act would do Oranstone no
good at all."

Haverness gave him an odd look, then shifted his gaze
to watch his two men galloping after the Shavig lordling.
"Foolish indeed. Very well, Garranon, ride with us for
Oranstone."

"Oranstone lives." Garranon made a sign with his fingers, an old sign of the Oranstone rebels.

Haverness returned the signal easily and switched to his
native tongue. "Oranstone free."

Garranon wondered if everyone hadn't been a little too
certain of Haverness's loyalty to the king.

BECKRAM'S RENTED HORSES WERE STAGGERING BY
the time Hurog appeared, dark and foreboding in the morning skyline. Two days and three nights of riding, eight
changes of mounts, and most of Garranon's gold had gotten him this far. He hadn't seen Haverness's men since the
second night.

Just in front of the gate, Beckram drew his horse to a
halt. When he'd ruined a friend's horse by jumping it reck-
lessly over a fence too high for hurdling, his father had
paid for the animal. This time there was nothing his father
could fix.

Exhausted, Beckram laughed, though there was nothing humorous about it. He'd been bringing his brother to

Hurog for his father to fix, and he hadn't even realized it. He let the horses plod ahead.

The sound of hooves on the pavement in front of Hurog alerted the sentries, but they recognized him and opened the gate. Although it was barely dawn, his father was in the bailey talking to one of the farmers when Beckram rode in.

"Erdrick?"

Beckram blinked stupidly, wondering how his father had jumped across the bailey so fast. Then it occurred to him that he'd closed his eyes for a bit.

"Erdrick? What's wrong? Who's . . . who's on the horse?"

Beckram slid off his horse and continued to fall until he knelt on the cool ground.

"I'm Beckram," he said clearly. "Erdrick's dead. My fault." He stared at his father, waiting for the news to hit, waiting to be punished as he deserved.

"SO THE KING KILLED ERDRICK BECAUSE YOU WERE sleeping with the queen? After he'd all but ordered you to do so?"

Beckram wondered that his father's voice was so calm. They sat in a small antechamber, where no one could hear.

Beckram was still tired, but he'd slept, drugged with mulled wine and exhaustion, until the dreams had driven him from his bed. For the third time he said, "The king killed Erdrick, thinking he was me. If I hadn't talked Erdrick into taking my place, he would be alive."

Duraugh closed his eyes. "I saved that young fool's life once, did you know? Saved it so he could kill my son." He sighed. "We'll bury Erdrick tomorrow. Your mother's here."

"She'll want to bury him at Iftahar."

His father heard the need in his voice. "He'll be buried here unless you wish it differently."

"Here. Hurog will protect him from murderers and fools." He hadn't meant to say that, it sounded silly aloud.

His father merely nodded.

Beckram relaxed a bit. "I'll leave the next day for Estian."

"You're still set on joining Haverness in his fool's errand?"

Beckram picked at the table covering. "I need something to do. If I don't, I'll kill him."

Duraugh's mouth tightened. "Don't think I haven't considered it. If it were fifteen years ago, I could do it. Young Alizon was popular, and the world was used to war. But Jakoven has gotten rid of most of the men who could stand against him, and Alizon's a useless fop outside the battlefield." He sighed. "Very well, go. But I won't send you alone. I'll talk to Stala. She and fifty men will accompany you, fighting under your command."

"I can't take them," said Beckram. "Haverness only has leave for a hundred men. I believe I'm the eighty-fifth."

"You'll take them," said Duraugh, standing up. "The Blue Guard's motto is 'We fight as one.' You will only be one."

"The king won't accept that."

Duraugh smiled coldly. "I'll talk to him. Leave it to me."

10

WARDWICK

Death is a wretched business, and rain only made it worse.

SEVERAL WEEKS INTO MY QUEST, MY SEARCH FOR glory seemed fruitless. We looked for Vorsagian raiders as we neared the southern reaches of Oranstone, but only came upon a few more groups of ragged bandits and the burnt-over villages where the Vorsag had been. It rained all the time—except when it hailed or sleeted. Oreg's gelding and one of the packhorses had developed hoof rot, despite the oil we used. Everyone's temper was short from being constantly cold and damp.

Tosten, as always, was the worst, seldom speaking except in answer to direct questions. The cold damp caused an old wound in Penrod's shoulder to act up, making practice visibly painful, but he didn't allow me to release him. When Axiel forced him to stop, he and Penrod almost came to blows—would have, except for Bastilla's intervention. Axiel, son of the king of dwarves, watched me like a sheepdog watching his shepherd but said little. Even Oreg was subdued.

We stopped at a village one midafternoon for provisions. It wasn't much, but I sent Penrod to find the head-man and talk to him. Oreg took the opportunity to wander off, exploring.

"They say they haven't seen any raiders, nor heard of any," said Penrod when he returned. "They also say that they've no grain for sale, nor any other foodstuff."

We'd heard that often enough. If it hadn't been for Luavellet's provisions and our own woodcraft, we'd have been starving. Oranstonians had a long memory.

"Did you tell them that the village east of here was burned to the ground when we passed it?" asked Tosten.

"I did," said Penrod. "I'm fairly sure they think we're the ones who did it. Where's Oreg?"

"He went to look at Meron's temple," I said. "I think he went to ask her to stop the rain."

"It'll just sleet, then," said Axiel sourly.

This village was larger than the last we'd been in, but that was all to be said of it. There had been people going about their business when we came. Upon seeing us, they'd sought shelter in the small stone and thatch huts that were set in circles off of the path that served as the main road.

The temple of Meron the Healer, goddess of growing things, was a little larger than the other buildings, and some time ago someone had painted it; there were still flecks of blue and white on the orange stone. It had no door, just a bit of ragged oilcloth hung from the doorframe.

"He went to look at the artifacts. Meron's temples are filled with them," explained Bastilla. "I don't feel much magic from the temple, though."

We had gone from being mercenary warriors here to save Oranstone from the evil Vorsag to being unwanted tourists. I rolled my eyes at the thought.

"There isn't very much magic in Meron's temples," I told her. "Not really. Most of the nobles worship Vekke, the god of war. Meron's priests might demand magic as tribute, but that usually means homemade charms from some hedgewitch. Peasants can't afford real magic."

"Silverfells is not far from here," said Axiel, "I recognize that rock formation." He pointed toward an outcropping on a hill. "I think we passed just west of here last time we came. If you're looking for interesting magical items, Silverfells has a stone they claim was once a dragon."

Penrod snorted. "The Hurogmeten said it was as much a dragon as he was a horse when we stopped by there."

Axiel shook his head. "I don't know. It was steeped in magic, I could tell that much." I hadn't known he could detect magic.

Oreg ducked under the cloth door of the temple and sloshed his way to his horse. "Where do we go next?"

"Silverfells," I said. *Let's go be tourists,* I thought bitterly.

"To see the dragon?" asked Oreg. "Splendid."

PANSY'S BIG HOOVES SPLASHED WATER FROM THE puddles high enough to splatter my already soaked boots. It was hard to say if there was a creek running through the path or a path running through the creek.

At least Pansy was happy. I rode in the lead where he liked to be rather than with the rest of them. The last time I tried to cheer Tosten up, he made a few nasty comments, and I thought I'd better stay by myself until I was able to control my tongue.

The rain didn't bother the stallion, as it did some of the other horses. Pansy ignored it as if he were too arrogant to be troubled by such a little thing as weather.

I wondered if I should send everyone else home. Penrod needed to be back in the dryer climate of Shavig, where his shoulder wouldn't bother him. Ciarra was too young for this, and Tosten was too soft: not in body, but in spirit. He felt the death of every body we burned, whether it was a bandit we'd killed or a villager killed by raiders. Even Bastilla would be better off elsewhere. She had claimed to be a poor wizard. I was no judge of such things, but although she was certainly not as good as Oreg, she was far better than Licleng, Father's mage. She lit a fire every night with wet tinder and wetter wood while Oreg dried our bedding. She could make a living in any noble's house, especially in a wet climate. She didn't need me.

Oreg belonged at Hurog where he and Hurog were safe. It was almost painful to be around him; he was my daily reminder that Hurog was not mine nor, I'd come to believe, would it ever be.

That left only Axiel, my father's man, the dwarven king's son. Of us all, he was most suited to doing something other than wandering aimlessly through this godsforsaken swamp: Any noble would hire him as arms master. But, according to Aethervon, Axiel was here to save his people because his father had had a dream. Axiel had been with my father for at least sixteen years, maybe longer, but he thought *I* was the reason he'd been sent to Hurog.

Pansy snorted suddenly and collected himself: a warhorse ready to do battle. The change pulled me abruptly from my absorption. Heart thrumming, I searched the woods for signs of watchers.

With a nudge of my knee and shift of my weight I spun Pansy in a tight circle, but I didn't see anything except that the rest of my party was some distance back, with Axiel in the lead and Oreg hindmost. Tosten and Bastilla were engaged in animated discussion. Penrod was rubbing his shoulder under Ciarra's concerned gaze. Axiel was watching me, his hand on his sword.

I held up my hand flat, signaling him to wait. When he nodded, I set Pansy ahead on the narrow track, which wound through high mountain marshes. Pansy minced forward, twitching his ears this way and that. I was just ready to turn back when the path wove through some willows and into the remains of a village.

Thank the fates I had kept the others from following me, was all I could think. I didn't want Ciarra or Tosten to see this. This didn't look like any of the raided villages we'd come to before.

The Vorsag had demolished the village houses and piled the wood and thatch along the road. The bodies of the villagers were laid out very carefully on top. Someone had tried to start a pyre to burn the dead, but the rain had gutted it before any of the bodies had been more than scorched. It was the smell of wet char and blood that must have alerted Pansy.

I dismounted and led the stallion behind me.

Though we'd seen the results of Vorsagian attacks before, I hadn't seen anything like this. At the other villages, there were survivors who'd run at the first sound of trouble. If the Vorsag hadn't killed every living soul in the village, they'd certainly tried. The Vorsag, like Shavigmen, buried their dead, but they hadn't been, up to this point, concerned enough with the possibility of the Oranstonians' unquiet spirits haunting their village to burn the dead. I didn't think that they had suddenly started now.

My father said he learned the most about the enemy when they broke away from their usual actions. What was different about Silverfells?

They had a temple with a stone dragon.

I backed away from the pyre and looked for the temple—or for where it had been. The Vorsag had ravaged the village for the wood in their pyre, and there weren't many buildings standing. In the end it could have been any of four sites, but I couldn't tell for certain. But there was nothing that could have been Axiel's stone dragon unless it was smaller than my fist.

Who was calling the shots for Vorsag? Kariarn was only a few years older than me. Normally, that would mean that he was either ruled by or at least was guided by his advisors. But I'd met Kariarn. If someone else was pulling the strings, then they were more devious than I was. Possible, but not likely.

When Kariarn had been in Estian, he'd had his people scour the countryside for artifacts purported to be magical. What if that was what he was doing now? What if they raided the villages with temples dedicated to Meron, took the artifacts, and then burned the villages to disguise what they had done?

Most of the temples had only junk, but that was not always true. Oranstone, like the other kingdoms, was an old land. There were ruins that yielded unexpected treasures. Some of the temples held powerful magic. I searched the ground carefully, but there was nothing to indicate that a large object had been moved: no wagon tracks, no deep hoofprints. But the Vorsag had been here, more than fifty of them, perhaps even a hundred. The falling rain obscured the tracks.

It *had* been a long time since Axiel and Penrod had been here with my father. It was possible that since that time the stone had been moved, but I was convinced it was Kariarn who took it.

Just how much power could Kariarn gather that way? I'd been taught that the days of great magic were past with the passing of the great Empire. The theory was that there was only so much magic in the world, and gradually it had been used up. My father had claimed that there never was an age of great magic, just great storytellers.

But what if the magic was stored in thousands of artifacts? What if one person collected all of them and found a way to get the magic out? I had to find Oreg.

I started back, but stopped when I neared the stacked bodies. If the Vorsag had tried to burn them, it was not out of respect for their enemies; it was to hide something the villagers' bodies might tell.

There were seventy-two men, women, and children laid out singly on the wood pile. Most of them were naked, facedown, and blindfolded with strips of rags (probably from their own clothing), and bound hand and foot. Those that weren't bound looked as though they'd died in the fighting when the Vorsag had first attacked. There were no flies—the one blessing the rain brought.

I was born and bred to prevent things like this. Being Hurogmeten was more than owning land—it was taking care of the people who lived there. Responsibility was bred in my bones, and the high king's failure to protect these people enraged me.

If this land had a lord to oversee it properly, no Vorsagian troop as large as this one would have come here and had the time to do this. But the rightful lord of this land had died in the Rebellion, and King Jakoven had not seen fit to replace him, leaving Silverfells unprotected.

I turned over the body of a young girl. Her face was smudged with the dirt of childhood broken with clean trails of tears that the rain began to wash away. Her body was cool to the touch. The only wound I could find was a slit as wide as two of my fingers in her throat. There were runes drawn on her torso. Some of them were done with paint and started to run as soon as the rain touched them, but others had been cut into her skin. *Seventy-two Oranstonians,* I thought, glancing at the rest of the bodies. *This must have taken a very long time.*

I inspected the skin under the bindings at her wrists and ankles to see what they had to tell me. Her wrists were raw, but the bindings on her ankles had cut almost to the bone. That and the lack of pooling blood where she'd been lying told me she had been hung by her feet so the blood would drain from her neck more completely, just like a hog at slaughtering time.

It was the analogy that tore the cap off my rage. Deep within me, my anger fanned a fire that had smoldered since

Aethervon had awakened it at Menogue. It poured through my chest, down my arms, and out my hands. I couldn't see the magic I felt thundering in my veins, but the wet wood and thatch lit when I touched them. Pansy snorted and backed as far from the burning, smoking mess as he could without pulling on the reins, as the fire traveled rapidly through the wet fuel, releasing the spirits of the dead for their journey beyond.

Son of my father, I'd never sworn fealty to a god nor taken much interest in religion. I knew little of Meron and less of the war god, Vekke. And, after what Aethervon had done to Ciarra, I would not give these people to him. They needed justice. A prayer my nurse had sung to me when I was a child came naturally to my tongue. A Shavig prayer was out of place in these wetlands, but I closed my eyes and sang to Siphern, god of justice and balance, as the flames roared higher.

And he came. I didn't see him, even when I opened my eyes, but I felt him: felt his anger at the village's death, felt him gather their frightened spirits to his bosom, felt his touch on my forehead as he left.

When I finished my song, I felt peaceful, even empty. And in that emptiness came clarity and honesty. The reason for my foul mood the past few days wasn't the rain; it was the growing knowledge that Hurog was lost to me. Even if I won glory defending Oranstone (which was unlikely, even under better circumstances), the king cared nothing for this kingdom. Witness how he failed to protect these villagers. My uncle would care for Hurog better than my father ever had, and his sons after him.

But for the first time, I had an attainable goal. I would help these people who had no one else to help them.

"Lord Wardwick?" Axiel's voice sounded breathless, and when I turned to look at him, he was on his knees with his head bowed.

His posture alarmed me, so I reached down and tugged him to his feet. "I thought I ordered you all to wait."

Hope and wonder lit his face when he looked at me. "We waited for a quarter mark, but we heard nothing. Since I can take care of myself a bit better than Penrod and the youngsters, I came ahead while the others still argued about what to do. I imagine they'll be along soon." He drew a breath. "When I came through the trees, my lord, I smelled evil as I haven't known for centuries—blood magic. Then I heard you sing Siphern all the way from the Northlands for these people. He cleaned this vale of evil for you, my lord. My father told me that our hope was in Hurog. I did not know until now he dreamed true."

I squirmed under his regard. Truthfully, I didn't know what I'd done to invoke it. Lighting the pyre was something Bastilla or Oreg could have done with half the effort. And . . . had he said *centuries?*

"Centuries?" I squawked.

He grinned sheepishly and rocked back on his heels. The awe was gone from his expression, but it had left his face altered in its wake. The watchful caution that was the usual aspect of his countenance had given way to a silly grin that was out of place in the presence of so much death.

"Yes, well," he said. "My father's people tend to live a bit longer than humankind. I was sent to Hurog half a century ago to find hope for my people, the salvation of dwarvenkind."

Salvation of dwarvenkind? I wanted to ask. Instead, I said, "You don't look like a dwarf."

"I take after my mother. My father is so tall—" He raised a hand to his shoulder. "—and twice my weight."

White, steamy smoke and the smell of burning flesh billowed off the wet tinder. The smell reminded me of the mystery of what had happened here at Silverfells. I grasped onto it hard, a task to fill the emptiness Hurog's loss had left me with.

I asked, "Do you remember how big the stone dragon was?"

"A bit larger than Pansy," he said after a moment. "It didn't look like the dragon in the Hurog coat of arms, but it didn't look like much of anything else, either. It was more like a piece of stone a good mason had started working into shape, but there weren't any chisel marks."

"It's not here," I said. "Or at least I couldn't find it. I also couldn't find any sign of it being moved."

Axiel coughed and moved away from the fire. "That's odd. I suppose someone could have moved it since we were here."

"I don't know a lot about magic," I said focusing on the burning bodies. "What if I told you that most of the villagers were bled dry like slaughtered sheep, and I couldn't find any great dark places in the dirt where so much blood had flowed?"

Axiel frowned. "I'd say that it *was* blood magic I smelled earlier, and it would take a powerful one to consume this much blood. The king's best mage is no more powerful than Bastilla. Of all the human wizards I've seen lately, only Oreg could work the kind of magic that would require so much blood."

Axiel thought Bastilla as powerful as the high king's mages? I knew she was better than she claimed, but I couldn't recall seeing her do anything spectacular. I opened my mouth to ask, but Pansy tossed his head and called out a greeting as the rest of our party emerged from the trees.

Oreg stopped his horse near me but didn't dismount. "Impressive," he said looking at the fire. "You build this yourself?"

"No," I said. "The Vorsag. Oreg, Bastilla," I said, as the others crowded around. "The dragon stone is gone. Axiel says it was as big as Pansy, but I could find no sign of anyone dragging it off. The villagers were hung and bled out, their bodies covered with arcane runes." I should have waited to light the pyre, but I had been feeling more than thinking.

Oreg tilted his head, staring at the pyre with dreamy eyes as an odd half smile tugged the corners of his mouth. "I smell dragons," he said.

"Axiel said he thought there was blood magic involved."

"There is a taint to blood magic," replied Bastilla. "And I don't feel it here."

I didn't feel up to explaining about Siphern. Weariness from working magic and from the knowledge that the hole in my spirit where Hurog belonged was permanent made me want to keep it as simple as I could. "Could a mage or a group of mages drain an object of magic and use it for themselves?"

"Yes," said Oreg at the same moment Bastilla said, "No."

I raised my eyebrows at them, and Bastilla finally shrugged. "I suppose it's possible. Theoretically. But the stone would still exist—just not magic."

"Not this stone," disagreed Oreg, still in that strange, dreamy state. "I smell dragon."

"Could they have transformed the stone?" asked Penrod.

"That stone felt like dragon magic," said Axiel. "Could something have transformed a dragon into the stone, and the Vorsag released it?"

A cold chill ran down the back of my neck just before the steady drizzle of rain turned to a torrential downpour.

"Kariarn has a *dragon?*" asked Tosten.

"Someone has a dragon," said Oreg peacefully.

Part of me was chanting euphorically, *I knew there were still dragons, I knew it, I knew it,* while the rest of me tried to figure out what Kariarn would do if he controlled a dragon.

"Where do we go from here?" asked Bastilla.

Good question. I put the thought of the dragon aside for the moment. That done, the question was fairly simple to ask. I only needed one more bit of information to test out my theory about the Vorsagian attacks, and I knew where to get it.

"Axiel," I asked, "Do you know how to get to Callis from here?"

"Callis? Yes, I think so. Why Callis?"

"Because I need information. And if anyone has information on what's been going on here, it's that old fox Haverness. Last I heard, he rules at Callis still." Haverness's people would know if the other villages the Vorsag hit had held better artifacts than the ones that had been passed by. They would know where other likely targets would be. My father had said that Haverness knew more about what the king's troops had been doing than the king had for all the old fox tramped about court looking as though butter wouldn't melt in his mouth.

THE POURING RAIN EASED A BIT AFTER AN HOUR OR more. For lack of a better place, we set up camp in a relatively sheltered spot under some trees. The fire smoked and sputtered, but it was good enough to cook over. It was my turn to do the cooking.

Oreg had gone hunting and produced a pair of rabbits. I had them spitted and turning over the fire when Ciarra came to sit beside me and took one of the spits, more because she wanted decent food to eat than out of any desire to help me.

"So you're not avoiding me anymore, eh?"

She grinned at me and tapped my face.

"Me? Grumpy?" When she raised her eyebrows, I said, "It rains all the time here, and we've been running around not accomplishing much for the better part of the summer."

She shook her head at me and pointed to the sky, then to my face.

"I know it's still raining," I said. "But now I know what we need to do." It was true. Kariarn had a dragon and possibly more magic than the world had seen in an age, an entire village had been slaughtered, Hurog was lost, but I felt better because I knew what I was going to do. "You're turning the rabbit too fast."

She leaned against my shoulder but didn't noticeably slow the spit. Her rabbit was perfect; mine was too pink in the middle. Not that it mattered, as hungry as we were.

We all went gathering wood after dinner except for Ciarra who, armed with a hunting horn to call us, stayed with the horses. Usually we all traveled separately, but this time Oreg came trotting by my side. He was quiet for a bit, but I could tell from the bounce in his step that he was just biding his time.

"So you decided to be a hero, again," he said finally. I couldn't decide if there was sarcasm in his voice or not.

"Oranstone needs a hero," I said, kicking a stone out of the path with a little more force than necessary.

"Are you going to free the dragon?"

"Oreg. Gods, there are seven of us! What do you think we can do?" And there, I thought, was the problem with my scheme to help the Oranstonian villagers. I wasn't a legendary warrior like my father; I wasn't Seleg; I had no army. It was like the story about the fly who declared war on the horse who took no notice.

"He *can't* be allowed to keep her," he said with sudden heat. "There were no flame marks where the dragon fought. They must have it under a spell."

A spell? My mind boggled at the thought of how much power it would take to control a dragon. "Could you break a spell strong enough to hold a dragon?" I asked.

His silence answered me. At last he said, "What are you going to do?"

"I'm going to Callis. From there, I'll send a message to the king, my uncle, and Haverness, so something is done to stop Kariarn—if anything can stop him now."

"They'll try to kill it, Ward." Oreg said in a low tone. He meant the dragon. "They can't afford to let him use a dragon."

"And just tell me what else they can do." I said, knowing he was right.

We walked a few more paces, Oreg's face turned away from me.

"*Seleg* didn't need an army to kill a dragon."

I came to a full stop. "What do you mean?"

"If one Hurogmeten killed a dragon, why shouldn't you?"

I scarcely noticed the sarcasm as a cold knot settled in my stomach. "*Seleg* chained the dragon?" My hero killed the dragon in the cave?

Protect those weaker than yourself, he'd written. *Be kind when the opportunity is given.* Ideas that no one else in my father's home would have said aloud for fear of being laughed at. Seleg set forth the ideals I'd tried to follow. But it was impossible to disbelieve Oreg's truth.

"And killed her so he'd have the power to defeat the invading fleet. He was scared. Frightened he'd lose Hurog." There was something wrong with Oreg's voice, but I didn't pay attention to it.

It hurt to breathe. If Seleg'd killed the dragon, he'd also had Oreg beaten for protesting it. I'd seen the beating myself in the great hall the day Garranon had come to Hurog. How could I feel betrayed by a man dead for centuries?

"Oreg . . ." I stopped when I saw his eyes, glowing with an uncanny lavender light. Despite the ring I wore and the disparity in our sizes, I backed away.

"Did killing the dragon make your life easier?" he whispered to me. "Do you hear her scream every night like I do?"

"Oreg, I haven't killed any dragons." Chills crept up my back, and I stepped another pace away.

He laughed like the autumn wind in a field of corn. "I warned you what would happen. Your children's children's children will pay the price for what you have done."

Oreg's episodes weren't insanity. Warrior's dreams, Stala called them, battle visions. Sudden visions of past battles so strong that they overwhelmed the present, terrifying when they hit an armed man but doubly so when that man was also a wizard. A wizard of Oreg's power made the dream real enough to bleed.

"Oreg," I said. "It wasn't me."

A soldier in his lifetime could amass a lot of horror and shame; how much more numerous were the memories Oreg had. He'd told me once that he tried not to remember things.

Oreg stared at me, breathing heavily as he fought the vision off.

"It's done with, Oreg," I said. "The dragon died a long time ago."

"Ward?"

"Yes." The terror in his eyes hurt me. Was he afraid of his memories? Or was he afraid of me? I turned away and began walking. "We need to hunt for wood."

After a moment, I heard his footsteps following me.

"Sorry," he said. "You look like him, you know. He was a big man, too. And filled with magic—like you've been since Menogue."

I shrugged.

We gathered wood for a bit. There wasn't much to be had that hadn't rotted in the damp. The woods looked as if they'd been gleaned already. We were too near Silverfells.

"After I killed that boy on the Oranstone border, I pretended to be my father," I said abruptly. "He was good at killing." I needed to talk to someone. Bastilla was a better listener, but Oreg had known my father.

"Not like your father," Oreg said, as if convincing himself. "You've never been like him."

I thought about the swift easing of my knife into the boy's neck, the way I couldn't lend words of comfort to my brother when he mourned the loss of his innocence; and I knew Oreg was wrong.

"When my father died, do you know why I really didn't want to drop my role as an idiot?" I asked.

"No." His reply was too easy. He'd increased the distance between us, oh so casually, reacting to my body language, I thought, and I tried to loosen up.

"At the time, I thought it was mostly embarrassment. But that wasn't it entirely. You see, I'd played an idiot so long, there wasn't anyone else to be. When I left Hurog, I tried being that mercenary, but it wasn't right. So I picked Seleg."

He was quiet for a long time. I didn't look back for him, just paced forward, away from camp. We'd been talking too much to find any game, but given any luck, Tosten or Axiel would bring something back.

"You do Seleg very well for a man who didn't know him." His voice was tentative. "He wasn't all bad—not until he grew old and frightened." The gap between us closed. "He wasn't as smart as you are, nor as kind. Just be yourself, Ward." We marched through the muck side by side now.

There isn't any me, Oreg, I thought. Just bits of my father, a stupid mercenary who charmed everyone he met except my aunt, and an ancestor who left too many journals for me to read.

Oreg grinned at me suddenly, shaking off the gloomy mood. "I know you. You talk slow and fight hard. You're smart and kind to small children, abused horses, and slaves. You're the Hurogmeten. That's more than most people know about themselves."

I smiled at him, a grateful smile, as I'm sure Seleg

would have had. The idiot talked slow; my father fought hard. Seleg was smart, arrogant, and kind—and Hurog wasn't mine. I was so good at playing roles, I'd even fooled Oreg. I would just have to make sure I didn't start fooling myself.

I'D INTENDED TO SHARE THE WATCH WITH OREG, BUT after our talk in the woods, I changed my mind. I'd said too much, and it had left me raw. I gave him first watch with Penrod, which left me with Penrod's usual partner, Bastilla, for second watch.

A rise in the ground not far from camp allowed a fair view of the trail from both east and west. After Oreg and Penrod retired to their bedrolls next to Ciarra and Tosten, Bastilla and I settled on a boulder large enough for the both of us.

"You came back from the village as if it gave you new direction." She shifted uncomfortably on the hard surface.

"Knowing your enemy and understanding your allies is the best way to win a war, according to my aunt." I gave her a wry look. "Not that we have any chance of winning a war against Vorsag, mind you, but I've an idea of what they may be after."

She laughed and took a bit of bread and cheese out of a small pack she'd brought and handed to me. "Eat this. Axiel gave it to me for you. He said if it didn't get eaten tonight, no one could eat it, and you've been eating less as the supplies get lower. You've started to lose weight again."

I nibbled the stale bread with all the enthusiasm it deserved. How could something be dry and moldy at the same time?

"So you think the Vorsag are after artifacts?" She laughed at my expression. "You asked me if a mage could harvest magic from artifacts."

I put down the food without much regret. "I hope Haverness's people will be able to tell me for certain."

"It will be good to do something else besides slogging through marshes," she said wryly. "I prefer fighting."

I laughed softly. "Me, too." That was my father in me.

She touched the corner of my lips with a finger. She hadn't been flirting, so I was unprepared for her touch.

"I keep expecting you to be stupid, do you know?" She traced a line from my mouth to the corner of my eye. My breathing grew ragged despite the effort I expended to steady it.

"It's the eyes. Hard to look smart with cow eyes. And I talk too slowly," I said.

The feather-light touch of her fingers on my face caused my belly to tighten. It wasn't the first time she'd indicated she would be willing to sleep with me. It was one of the reasons I'd always paired myself with Ciarra or one of the men. Penrod and Axiel might be able to couple without commitment, but I'd never gotten the knack of it.

"I would have thought listening to you would make me impatient," she breathed, "but your voice is like a velvet drum. I always feel so safe with you." She held my head with both of her hands while she came up to her knees to kiss me.

She desired me for my body. Women had liked it even when they had thought it belonged to an idiot. Maybe especially when they thought it belonged to an idiot. But she liked me, too. That would make it more than sex, a gift between friends.

Or at least she liked the man she thought I was: strong, competent, honorable, smart.

The echoes of my earlier conversation with Oreg kept me from falling into her spell. As I drank in the smooth-wine flavor of her mouth, I fought for the strength to pretend for a few hours more. One of the things the game with my father had taught me was that half of the success of the disguise was in the mind of others. My father thought I was stupid, so he ignored signs that I might be something else. Bastilla thought me a hero; the role should have been easy, but it wasn't. I pulled away reluctantly.

"Ward?"

Breathing hard, I rested my forehead on hers, trying to find a reason for my restraint that wouldn't hurt her or me. It was easier knowing I was more recreation for her than serious prey. The Avinhellish were freer about such things than we Shavigmen.

"We can't do this, Bastilla. We're on watch. If we get any further, I won't care if a hundred Vorsagian raiders come galloping down that road." It helped that the excuse was true.

She snickered and allowed me to break the mood. "A hundred, eh?"

I nibbled down her neck once, regretfully. Then I bounced to my feet and took several steps back. "Maybe a thousand. I'm going to run the perimeter." I pointed at her. "You stay here."

She was still smiling when I left, but I knew that I had just put off a problem I'd need to deal with later.

CALLIS LOOKED AS DIFFERENT FROM HUROG AS POS-sible, given that they were both fortified keeps. Hurog was square, where Callis was round. Callis was perhaps three times as large and built out of native stone. The gray green lichen covering the walls turned the orange stone to a muddy brown.

The gates were closed and barred. Persuading the young warrior in charge of the gate to let me inside proved to be significantly more difficult than finding Callis had been.

His lord wasn't there, which I knew.

We looked like mildewed bandits, which I also knew.

Far worse, we looked like Shavig bandits. We'd grow old and rot before he'd let us in, he informed us with a few pithy adjectives. Judging by the grins from his fellows (who'd gathered around as soon as they noticed something interesting was happening at the gate), they'd be pleased to help us along.

Well, he wouldn't be left on guard for more than half the day. I'd wait and see how the man who replaced him on wall was before I tried any more desperate measures.

We'd picked a few apples from an orchard not far down the road, and Axiel handed me one. It was green and sour but better than stale bread and moldy cheese.

"Where'd that apple come from?" called the guardian of the gate suspiciously.

"Bought it from a man down the road." I took another bite and smiled around the sourness.

"No Oranstonian would sell our good apples to a North-lander."

"Well," I stared at the apple a bit. "I'd not call it good, but he said it was the best Oranstone had."

The snappy retort lost a little because of the distance the wall put between us, but I saw from his grin he was ready to give as good as he got. The guard was bored, and so was I. Neither he nor I really wanted a confrontation, just a few minutes of stupid Northerner/Southerner, all done in good cheer. Unfortunately, one of his fellows, a young new-comer to the conversation, didn't understand the game.

"That apple's too good for Shavig scum like you!" The hothead had a crossbow, and he nocked it.

My aunt always said you had to watch out for the young ones as they are generally too stupid to understand what's really going on. It had always amused me when she told *me* that.

I caught a glimpse of the gate guard's horrified face and knew that he'd be almost as unhappy if the young man shot me as I would. The walls at Callis weren't as high as

Hurog, maybe only twenty-five feet. Luckily, I was faster with my apple than the guard was with his crossbow. He mustn't have had a good grip, or the apple would just have spoiled his aim rather than knock the bow out of his hand. His weapon fell only a few feet from me.

The gate guard, as senior on the wall, turned on the rash and bowless guard. I couldn't hear what he said, but the boy wilted.

"What's going on here?" The voice rang clear as a bell, though I couldn't see the man who spoke. Judging by the sudden attention of everyone on the wall, it was someone very senior.

I picked up the bow, disarmed it, and tossed it up and over the edge of the wall. I was hoping it would land at their feet just when the senior man approached them. Maximum embarrassment for them, possible entrance for me, as I had stopped the boy without hurting anyone and returned their weapon.

After a few moments, a new face appeared at the wall. His head was shaved from the top of his ears to the nape of his neck in Oranstonian traditional style, but he'd allowed his beard to grow out white and full like a Shavigman. It was a distinctive style and made him easy to recognize.

Haverness's right-hand man, I thought in surprise. I didn't know his name; I don't think I'd ever heard him say more than four words together. He was always at Haverness's side, and so should have been at Estian. Haverness was only allowed at Callis for a fortnight at planting and a fortnight at harvest, which was still a month or more away this far south.

He frowned at me. "Who are you, son, and what do you want?" He asked it in Tallvenish, so I replied in the same language.

"Ward of Hurog. I have some news about the Vorsag."

"Wait here." He scattered the guards back to their posts and then left.

Oreg handed me another apple. "So, are we in?"

I took a bite. "I think so."

If the old fox's shadow had been here alone, he'd have had the authority to open the gate at once or send us on our way. That he'd left the wall implied he was going to speak to his superior, Haverness.

Haverness had always been kind to me. Of course he might not feel the same way when he found out I wasn't an idiot. I wondered what he was doing here; had King Jakoven finally decided the raiders were a threat?

The gate rattled and began rising slowly.

"Mount up," I called, following my own advice.

We rode through the narrow passage into the bailey proper. Most of the expanse between the walls and the inner keep was cobbled; I suppose they'd have to because of the rain. Spring at Hurog left our bailey half a foot deep in muck. Here it would have been year-round.

Straw had been piled along the edges of the bailey, and tents were set up all along the walls. A quick glance led me to estimate that Callis held at least two hundred more men than she'd been built to. Had the king allowed Haverness to come home and defend his land? I couldn't believe that the old fox would break his word and return without the king's permission. We were met halfway to the keep by Haverness himself and a few servants.

"Ward," he said. "What are you doing here, boy?"

I started to give him my stupid cow look out of habit but restrained myself. It would be a deadly mistake to let Haverness think I was stupid now. His dislike of lies and broken promises was the stuff of legends.

"The same as you, I imagine," I said. "Fighting the Vorsag."

The warm smile left his face at my crisp reply. I dismounted, loosened Pansy's girth, and continued talking to give him time to think. "I think the Vorsag are raiding rather than conquering right now, though. Kariarn has always lusted after magic. I've just come from Silverfells, and the raiders had left there not a half day before us, killing everyone in the village. My men tell me that the last time they were there—fifteen years ago—Meron's temple at Silverfells claimed a large stone dragon, which is not there anymore."

"Oranstone seems to have had a beneficial effect on your intellect," he said.

I gave him a slow grin. "We'll have to recommend it." I could see from his face it wasn't enough, so I continued more soberly. "My father killed his father to get Hurog, and he half killed me. I was afraid he'd finish the job."

Shock came and went quickly on his face. Slowly, he nodded his head; he knew my father. "Survive how you can," he said. "Would you introduce me? I see several Hurog faces, but I can't place them."

"Haverness," I said formally. Oranstonians dislike titles, so I gave him none. "These are my men, Axiel and Penrod, who fought under my father's banner and now follow me." Normally, one wouldn't introduce one's troop to a man of Haverness's standing, but he'd all but ordered me to do so. "And my sister Ciarra." She gave him a gamine smile in return for his courtly bow. "You're supposed to curtsy, you mannerless ruffian." She rolled her eyes at me, then bobbed quickly up and down like a serving maid, and Haverness chuckled.

"My brother Tosten."

Haverness's gazed sharpened on my brother. "I thought he was dead."

"Who said that?" I asked. I hadn't heard that bit of gossip.

"Your father, I believe."

"Pleased to meet you, sir," said Tosten, bowing. "My father was mistaken."

"Bastilla of Avinhelle," I continued the introductions. "Mage and warrior."

Bastilla smiled and sank into a graceful curtsy that managed to look ladylike despite her moldering fighting leathers.

"And our second mage, Oreg, my cousin or some such, who tells me it is possible that Kariarn plans on draining the magic from his artifacts to perform great magic. Also that Kariarn's mages have managed to transform whatever was in the stone dragon into something real. He thinks it was a dragon."

"Ward?" The voice was familiar, but it was so out of place I couldn't attribute it until I saw one of my cousins hurrying over to us. I could usually tell them apart, but in some strange way, this man looked like neither of them. He'd lost weight, and he looked as if he hadn't slept in weeks—nor smiled in all that time. "As I live and breathe," he said, sounding as astounded as I felt. (What was my cousin, whichever one it was, doing here?) "It is you. Where did you come from?"

There were no bright scarves tied in odd places, but it was the neatness of his appearance that finally made me guess. "Beckram? What are you doing here?"

He clapped me on the shoulder and ignored my question. "Father will be glad to know . . ." His jaw dropped. *"Tosten?"*

"Good to see you again, Beckram," he answered.

"I'll leave you to your greetings." Haverness nodded at us. "Beckram, see that they are settled in."

11

WARDWICK

I wasn't entirely sure whether I'd gotten myself into a war to defend Oranstone from the Vorsag, or a war against the high king. Either way, it suited me.

THE BLUE GUARD WAS CAMPED ALONG A SOFT stretch of turf against one wall. I whistled when I counted the tents, which included Stala's distinctive one. Three Blue Guardsmen were walking a lazy patrol around the perimeter. The rest were probably out practicing somewhere, knowing my aunt.

"What are you doing all the way out here with Stala and half the Blue Guard, Beckram?" Tosten asked my question, which seemed wise, given how Beckram felt about me. "Did the king decide there was a war going on at last?"

Beckram snorted. "The king misspoke himself and fell into his half brother's trap."

"Alizon?" I said.

"None other. The upshot is that Haverness was given leave to bring a hundred men to quell the problems here in Oranstone."

"And he chose the Blue Guard?" I said doubtfully.

Beckram stopped walking toward the tents. "No, that's another story. Ward, what happened to you?"

He sounded concerned. I fought back the impulse to list my nicks and bruises; old habits die hard.

"My father died." I said. "It improved my outlook remarkably—as well as my intelligence."

He smiled slowly—not his usual brilliant smile—and I wondered for a minute if he were Erdrick. They switched places sometimes, and it was surprisingly difficult, even with their widely disparate personalities, to tell which was which.

"Erdrick was right," he said. "He told me once that he didn't think you were as stupid as everyone thought you were."

"Stupid enough to lose Hurog," I returned.

He shrugged and resumed his rapid pace toward the distinctive blue tent. "Do you have camping equipment?"

"For the woods. But there are no trees here."

At Beckram's gesture, a couple of men took the horses to be stabled while we saw about our packs. After a bit of rearranging, we stored our goods in a tent vacated for us.

When the work was done, Axiel settled a hand on Penrod's shoulder. "We'll go see what Stala is up to and tell her you're safe, Ward."

"Bastilla and Ciarra should go with you and tell her that they've moved into her tent," I said.

Ciarra nodded her head enthusiastically and patted her sword; then she dashed off, leaving the rest to follow.

As soon as they were safely away, Beckram turned to my brother and gave him a bear hug. "It's good to see you, Tosten. I see you still have that harp I gave you."

Beckram always could charm the birds out of the trees, and he managed to charm a smile out of Tosten. I hadn't known the harp was my cousin's gift.

"He was supporting himself at a tavern at Tyrfannig," I said."

Beckram raised his eyebrows. "At Tyrfannig? I'm surprised you didn't find him before this."

"He took me to Tyrfannig in the first place." Tosten turned his smile to me.

"To a sailor's inn?" Beckram looked at me. "Maybe you're not as smart as I thought. . . ."

I shook my head, but Tosten jumped in to defend me before I could say anything. "No. He left me with a cooper."

Beckram laughed. "He would. And he'd expect you to stay there, wouldn't he?"

"The cooper was a good man," my brother replied hotly. "If I'd had no other place to go, I could have been happy there."

Tosten was defending me? I couldn't be sure; maybe it was the cooper.

"Who's this?" Beckram nodded at Oreg, who was trying his best to be part of the scenery.

"Another Hurog," I said. "Oreg, this is our cousin Beckram. Beckram, meet Oreg."

"You never told Ward what the Blue Guard is doing here," said Oreg softly, without acknowledging the greeting. Of course he knew Beckram already, and Oreg wasn't happy about the way my cousin teased Ciarra.

Beckram gave Oreg a cool, assessing look, then smiled tightly at me. "You did a better job of guarding your brother than I ever did mine. Erdrick's dead." I sucked in a deep breath, but he continued before I could say anything. "I was sleeping with the queen and misstepped somehow. Jakoven killed Erdrick by mistake, because he looked like me. It was ride out with Haverness or kill the bastard." His voice was light and quick, belying the bloodlust in his eyes. I saw then that the expression he wore to greet us was a mask covering a core of soul-deep rage. I reached out and touched his shoulder, but there was no room in him for comfort, and he stepped away from me.

Erdrick was dead; it didn't seem possible.

"When I took my brother's body back to Father, he sent the Blue Guard back with me."

"So Haverness took the Blue Guard as his hundred?" I asked, changing the subject because that seemed to be what Beckram wanted.

"No, he already had most of them picked out."

"The king made a mistake," commented Alizon, stepping around a tent. The king's half brother had discarded his usual court robes and colors. Dressed in hunting leathers, he looked much more dangerous than I'd ever seen him. I couldn't tell if he'd been listening to us or if he'd just happened to come upon us, but I knew which one I'd lay odds on.

"He chose to kill Beckram," continued Alizon, "knowing that Hurog is a not very important, virtually penniless holding in the lands of the northern barbarians." Alizon's voice showed that he, clearly, was not so stupid. I was. It sounded like an accurate description of Hurog to me. "He believed Hurog's strength vanished with the death of the remarkable bastard who ruled it for so many years. So Duraugh gave him an example of the power of the Hurog name. He brought half the nobles of Shavig with Beckram to the capital and shoved the Blue Guard down my brother's throat. 'Hurog fights as one,' indeed." Alizon grinned, a boyish expression that belied the cleverness in his eyes. "Shavigmen have a long memory. They know who their king would be, though there hasn't been a king in Shavig for centuries. It was obvious to everyone that Duraugh was perfectly willing to begin a rebellion right then and there. He wanted the king's hide nailed to the wall, but he was willing to settle for adequate protection of his remaining son."

"Better the king count himself lucky my father wasn't still with us," I said. "The Hurogmeten would have killed Jakoven and let politics take care of themselves."

"And he had many other fine qualities as well," murmured Oreg.

"What are you doing here, Ward?" asked Alizon suddenly. "And I might add: My, how you've changed."

"I'm told that Oranstonian air has that effect." Tosten looked at the ground as he spoke. "Or maybe it's the apples."

"My father's death seems to account for most of it," I said. "Being too smart didn't seem healthy while he was alive. As to what I'm doing here: I heard about Oranstone's troubles, and thought to myself, what they need is a Shavigman to show the Oranstonians how to fight. I ended up with a few more volunteers than I needed. Two Shavigmen are worth a few hundred Vorsag, eh, Tosten?"

Alizon's gaze narrowed abruptly on my brother.

Tosten said, "He's been saying that we should have left a few behind, but who knew the women would be such fighters. We've considered conquering Oranstone and holding it as a fiefdom as well as Vorsag, but Ward tells me it would be rude to conquer a country twice in a century." Tosten had broadened his speech into rough Northlander.

Beckram's flashing smile lit his face at last. He slapped Tosten on the back. "Fair sounds like a proper Shavig barbarian. Now that we've got him here, we've nothing to worry about."

"Better not let the Oranstonians hear you talk like that," said Alizon repressively.

"No one likes to hear the truth," said my Aunt Stala. I'd been aware of someone approaching, but since they were wearing the Blue's colors, I hadn't paid much heed.

"Stala." I caught her up, armor and all, and swung her around.

"Put me down, boy," she said, though I could tell she was pleased. "I'd hoped that old Axiel would have better sense than to allow you to play soldier down here."

I set her down. "He didn't have much say in it."

"You've lost some weight."

I shrugged, and Tosten said, "Oranstonians don't like selling supplies to Shavigmen. Last time Northlanders were down here, we did a fair job of alienating the villagers."

I guess Stala hadn't noticed him when she'd approached, because her jaw dropped and she said, "Tosten?" in a small voice.

He hugged her self-consciously and stood a little awkwardly when her arms tightened fiercely rather than releasing him. At last she stood back and looked him over.

"I have all my fingers and toes, Aunt Stala," he complained mildly.

"So you really did squirrel him away someplace?" Stala didn't look away from Tosten as she spoke.

"He needed to get away, someplace safe." I said. Not even to her would I tell Tosten's secret, though the memory of his blood lying between him and me like some pool of awful truth was as clear in my mind as if it had been a moment ago.

"I'm hungry," Oreg said. "I wonder if there's anything we can scrounge to eat."

AT SUPPER, I SAT AT THE HIGH TABLE WITH HAVERNESS, Alizon, and Beckram. The rest of my troop ate with Stala and the Blue Guard. Haverness set a fine meal, and not the least of its attractions was his daughter. Oh, there were sweet maids aplenty here, many of them daughters and wives of Oranstonian nobles, sent here for safekeeping. One beauty with flaming hair cascading in waves down her back stole shy glances my way and then blushed when I nodded at her. But it was Haverness's daughter who caught my full attention.

Tisala was more akin to my aunt Stala than to the prettily clothed maidens. Curly dark hair trimmed short as a man's covered her well-shaped head. Her face wasn't pretty. She shared her nose, a slim, too-long blade, with her father along with his square build and tall frame. Her hands were swordsman's hands and bore the scars of someone well used to fighting, and for all that, she wore a woman's confining gown with grace.

I remembered hearing that Haverness left his lands in his daughter's hands while he was at court, but I hadn't expected that she would be more than an administrator. She hadn't gotten those scars arguing with clerks.

Once the course had been served, she looked me over and said, "What's an idiot doing in the middle of a war?"

I smirked at her, liking her instantly. "It takes an idiot to get into the middle of a war," I pointed out. "Especially when it's not even on my own lands." I glanced around and noticed Bastilla watching me, an odd look in her eye. When I nodded to her, she turned her attention back to her food.

Haverness snorted. "You see why I never took her to court."

"My father wouldn't have taken me if he'd been given a choice," I said. "Have you had a chance to look at the villages the Vorsag have hit?"

He nodded, sobering. "Every village had a temple to Meron. That's not really surprising, since almost every village has some sort of temple. But—" He pointed his knife at me. "—all the ones that were hit had some object of real power. I've spoken to my mage and my priest, and they are putting together a list of other villages that fit your conditions."

We ate for a while: real food, hot and well seasoned. As we waited for the next course, Haverness said, "I'm going to send out armed parties to each of the villages on the list, keeping the larger forces here at Callis until I can pinpoint where the bastards are. They've got a base in Oranstone; they're too deep in country for anything else."

I grunted and finished swallowing a piece of duck. "My troop has come this far, we might as well be of use. Give us one of your villages."

"I hoped you'd say that. I don't have an unlimited number of trained men, and just the one wizard. Most of the men I brought from Estian are readying their own estates to face a Vorsagian invasion."

"Uhm," I ate another small piece of duck. "You'll forgive my question, but isn't building up armies on such scale illegal?"

"Demons take Jakoven, and his laws," said Haverness heavily. It had taken a lot, I saw, for him to break his oaths of loyalty, but Jakoven's refusal to rescue Oranstone had done it. Jakoven had, in fact, broken his oath first.

"By the time the king can do anything about it," Alizon said, "we'll have driven the Kingdoms' enemy out of Oranstone, and he'll have nothing to do but congratulate these men for saving his throne. If he prosecutes, he'll have the nobles of all the lands against him—and he's just smart enough to know that."

I nodded. "Especially since you'll tell him so."

"Exactly, so," murmured Alizon sweetly.

"YOU LOOK LIKE YOU STAYED UP AND CELEBRATED last night," said a raspy woman's voice, frigid with disapproval.

I opened one eye and looked first at Haverness's daughter, who stared down her long nose at me, then around the empty tent and attempted to remember what I'd been celebrating last night.

"Your men are up and at practice already. The small man who seemed to be in command told me I could find you here. My father has a village for us to go to."

I hadn't been carousing, but Stala and I had talked late into the night about Erdrick's death and Oranstonian politics. My body was trying to insist that it needed a few more minutes to recover, but it didn't appear that Tisala was going to let me rest. I rolled stiffly to my feet, bent and touched my toes a time or two to stretch. "Oranstonians have confounded long names, and they never shorten them," I said to distract her from my condition. "I suppose I could call you to Tissa or Lally."

"Not if you want to keep your tongue," she tossed back. I thought I caught a glimpse of a dimple, but her voice was serious.

"YOU LOOK STUPID," COMMENTED TISALA, RIDING beside me. I learned Haverness's definition of small was an order of magnitude larger than mine. In addition to my troop's seven, Haverness had sent his daughter and her fifty sworn men.

"Stupid," she said again, shaking her head.

I thought about crossing my eyes and drooling at her, but she didn't need any encouragement from me to continue.

"I think it's the eyes. No one expects brilliance out of a man with eyelashes like that." Her disapproval was plain.

I wondered what she thought I should have done about my eyelashes.

"Thank you," I murmured. "But I thought it was the color, myself." She had brown eyes, too. I wondered if she'd catch the insult.

"Maybe it's your size," she went on, turning her face to scrutinize the forest around us, but not before I caught sight of a betraying dimple.

"Large means stupid?" I relaxed in enjoyment as I realized she was teasing me. It gave me something to wonder about instead of dead cousins and the aching eyes from too little sleep.

"Everyone expects big people to be slow and stolid," she said. I didn't see any tension in her, but her thin, narrow-hipped war stallion arched his neck and sidled. If the stallion weighed half what Pansy did, I'd have been surprised. On its back, Tisala did look oversized. Funny I hadn't really thought about her height, but she was as tall as her father, who was accounted a tall man, though not nearly as tall as I. For a woman, being as tall as a man was no light thing.

"Slow, eh? And stolid?" I asked.

She must have heard the comprehension in my voice because her chin tilted up and her formidable brows lowered.

I grinned. "It would help if you had a real horse, rather than a skinny, cow-hocked pony." He wasn't cow-hocked much, just enough to make her sensitive—and steer our teasing to a place less painful for her.

"Better to ride a cow-hocked pony than a dullard plow-horse." The chill in her voice would have frosted a potter's kiln.

Dullard? I thought. Looking at Pansy, I supposed her observation had merit. He was paying no attention to her stallion, walking with a relaxed air that might, indeed, have belonged to a draft animal. The image was helped by the long threads of grass hanging from his mouth. He must have snatched it when I wasn't paying attention. Not much left of the murderous beast who'd terrified my grooms—not this morning.

"His name is Pansy," I said with painful dignity. "If you're going to insult him, you ought to at least know his name."

On my other side, Ciarra snickered.

Tisala looked from my sister's face to mine, nodded her head to Ciarra, and said, "Your brother is a terrible tease."

Ciarra raised her eyebrows.

"No, I'm not," Tisala snapped. "I'm blunt and rude. Just ask anyone."

Ciarra smiled broadly and tilted her chin at me.

"I have to agree with her, Ciarra." I said sadly. "Anyone who calls my poor Pansy a dullard must be blunt and rude."

"Rat," commented Tisala. "I can't believe you carried

it off. How many years did you fool them that you were stupid?"

Ciarra held up seven fingers.

"Seven," Tisala shook her head. "Seven years of holding your tongue. It would have killed me."

"Probably," I agreed.

She laughed. "Is he always this bad?"

Ciarra shook her head firmly, then raised her eyes to the sky.

"Not possible," said Tisala. "He couldn't have been worse."

There weren't many people who could read the language Ciarra spoke. Penrod, used to the silent speaking of his charges, could talk to her almost as well as I. Tosten could a little. But Tisala was the first woman who'd conversed with her with such matter-of-fact ease. Bastilla tended to avoid Ciarra, as if my sister's inability to speak made her uncomfortable.

I'd been avoiding thinking about Bastilla.

When I was fifteen, the daughter of one of Penrod's grooms had been the love of my life. She had been twenty, gentle and cheerful. When I was sixteen, she broke my heart by marrying a merchant in Tyrfannig. I understood her reasons and knew they were good ones. I even liked her husband, though that had taken me a good long time. After her, I'd slept with a few who had taught me that the act without love was dreary indeed.

I felt nothing more for Bastilla than I did for . . . Axiel. Less perhaps. Given that, I should have refused her outright rather than leaving the possibility open for some later time. I hadn't had the chance for private conversation until now, but the ride was too good an opportunity.

"If you'll excuse me, ladies," I said, "I'll desert the field of battle, for no man wins a war with a lady's tongue."

Ciarra stuck her lady's tongue out at me.

The trail we were riding through the overgrown forest

was wide enough for a wagon, so Pansy and I had little trouble working back to the rear ranks where Bastilla rode with Oreg.

I turned to ride beside them. "Go talk to Ciarra, Oreg. See if Haverness's daughter is any happier with you than she is with me."

"She finds you objectionable?" Bastilla sounded amused.

"I believe it is my eyelashes."

Oreg batted his eyes at me. "Mine are prettier than yours are, Ward. She's bound to like them."

When he'd ridden off, I slowed until we brought up the rear. I switched to Avinhellish, which I spoke with a terrible accent but well enough for my purpose, which was to ensure that no one overheard what I had to say to Bastilla.

"I believe I owe you an explanation, Bastilla."

Her marvelous eyes sparkled in the dappled light, and she smiled. "An explanation for what, Ward?"

"For my refusal of your offer the night before we came to Callis."

Her smile fled as if it had never been. "How so?"

"If we had not been on duty that night, I would have taken you up on your offer. And it would have been wrong."

"Ah." Her gelding bowed his head against her white-fingered grip on the reins. "I am too old for you? Perhaps Tisala suits you better?"

I shook my head. "Not too old." I couldn't let her think this had anything to do with Tisala. "For you, sex is a game—one you play very well. But I cannot view it that way."

"You sound like a virgin bride." Her voice was brittle with hurt.

I shook my head. "My first lover taught me that love only works between equals." And she had been right. She had led and I followed, unable and unwilling to break out of my idiot act, even where I loved. "You and I are not equal in this; you can sleep with Axiel and Penrod without causing them to fret. Anyone who can do that is far more skilled than I am. My second lover taught me that coupling without love is worse than nothing—at least for me."

"And you don't love me."

"Do you love me?" I wouldn't have asked it if I hadn't known the answer.

Her chin went up, and she didn't say anything.

"I should have said this that night. There is no love between us, lady. Respect and lust, yes, at least on my part. But not love."

"You will regret this," she said with a careful smile to hide the hurt in her eyes.

"Lady, my body already does," I said ruefully. "But it is the right thing. I will not play games."

She did not reply. After a few moments, I decided it might be best to give her some time to herself. As I rode past Penrod and Axiel, I jerked my head, and both of them fell back to ride behind Bastilla.

THE PRIEST LOOKED AT US BLANDLY. "WE ARE HERE to protect these things. They are dedicated to Meron, and we must keep them in her temple."

The temple in question was a little timber building, half the size of the peasant huts of the town. The priest, Oreg, Bastilla, Axiel, and I were the only ones inside, as there simply wasn't room for anyone else. Tisala had tried to talk to the priest for a few minutes before throwing her arms up and stalking off to get the rest of the little village into packing up and leaving. I hoped she was getting further than I.

"Except for the armband, they're not much," reported Oreg from the altar where he and Bastilla were getting a better look at the items in question. "What magic they had upon them has faded. The armband was powerful once, but there's no shape to the magic anymore."

The priest was visibly displeased with Oreg's assessment.

"They are not worth your life; even the goddess knows that," Axiel said. I'd left the negotiations to Axiel, once Tisala left, since he looked the least like a Northman and spoke Oranstonian.

"I know that, my son." The priest set aside his irritation to smile gently at the dwarf king's son. "But my word *is* worth my life. If I die in her service, I shall be with her forever."

"You're aiding the enemy," said Oreg unexpectedly. "These don't seem to be powerful, but if the Vorsag gain enough of them, and if they have the right sort of knowledge, they can use this to destroy even the memory of Oranstone and the Great Healer, Meron. If you take them to a fortified place, they will still be hers." But the priest would lose his power outside this village, and he knew it.

"You imply Meron cannot protect her temple," chided the priest.

Oreg moved to my side. "There are rules the gods must follow, or they invite destruction. If she steps in to protect this temple, the Vorsagian gods can act on their behalf, too."

"Perhaps the Vorsag serve Meron, too. Perhaps she has decreed that they shall have the sacred objects." The priest was enjoying this.

Stala said that to persuade someone, you had to know who they were and what they wanted. What made a priest of Meron? They were a peasant group, loosely knit with little higher organization. As Oreg continued to argue, I thought about what we must look like to the priest. Shavigmen, or at least not Oranstonian. But he'd been no more ready to listen to Tisala.

The followers of Meron were men of the land, farmers and herdsmen. Peasants. If a peasant had spoken to a nobleman's messengers the way that this priest was, my fa-

ther would have him whipped until he couldn't stand up.
But a priest was different.

I looked at the priest's calloused hands; he helped in the
fields. Perhaps he had his own herds.

"Eh," I broke in, interrupting Oreg rudely. "They're
mages, what do they know about the way of the Healer?
Good with a fancy argument, they are." I'd heard enough
peasant Oranstonian to know I'd gotten the accent close to
right. "Nobles who sit in stone halls don't understand the
goddess. I worked the land myself, before I took up the
sword, and didn't I feel her hand guide my plow?" I
thought my father's head herdsman might be a man of the
priest's ilk, and his mannerisms weren't difficult to adopt.
"Doesn't mean I don't think you ought to take whatever
the goddess holds sacred and save it for her." I nodded at
the armband that held its place of honor on the altar. "Hate
to see that on the arm of one of those heathens who burned
Silverfells and stole the dragon stone."

For the first time, the priest looked shaken in his con-
victions.

"If you take them with you to Callis," I said, "as soon as
Kariarn turns his attention elsewhere, you can return them
to their place." I heard something odd outside.

He took a deep breath. "I suppose . . . temporarily . . ."

It was the faint clash of steel on steel I'd heard. I left the
priest dithering to Oreg and took a quick step to the temple
door and peered out. It required no more than a glance.

"To arms!" I bellowed, as if I wasn't the last person to
see. "Raiders!"

They had doubtless meant to sneak up on the village.
But had met with a few of Tisala's men who'd been on the
outskirts of town. I tore out of the temple and was on
Pansy's back before I'd finished speaking.

The first few men hadn't slowed the mass of Vorsag
down much, but by the time I arrived at the fighting, they'd

run into the larger block of our troops and their forward progress had slowed to a crawl.

Pansy screamed, a harsh, shrill stallion's warning, and plunged into battle. And time slowed. Everything in me was concentrated on each moment, each block, each blow, each life lost. I became gradually aware that Tosten fought on my left and Penrod my right, but it had no meaning beyond the moment.

I loved the battle, even when it was against scarecrow bandits. Here, where sword met sword and I tested myself against the mettle of my opponent, it meant something when my sword sank deeply into flesh. Pansy told me with twitches of ears and muscles where he was going to move, and he listened in turn to my shifts of weight. We brought death to our enemies, and I loved the power of it. And that final love, one I shared with my father, frightened me more than any battle ever could.

Axiel had been right; a real battle was different. The knowledge that here at last I was facing my own kind, warriors trained in martial arts, added the sweetness of competition to the fray. These men had a real chance of killing me as the bandits we'd fought before did not. For these were regular army men, for all they wore outlaw's rags over their armor.

Stala would have told me to pull the men, because our armies were too evenly matched. There would be no victor here, just dead men to litter the ground. But there were villagers behind us, unarmed women and children I'd been sent to protect.

A long-fought battle has a flow to it. Fierce speed when I was in the heart of the enemy army followed by almost peaceful moments when Pansy and I broke through the battle lines and there were none to come against us. I held Pansy there to give him a rest and saw that there were others doing the same.

In one such pause, Tisala joined me, meeting my grin

with one of her own before the years of command fell back upon her shoulders.

"We're evenly matched," she said.

I nodded, moving my right shoulder to try to restore some feeling to my arm. "I hope that occurs to the Vorsagian commander soon. We can't let them through to the village, but if the Vorsag don't pull back, there won't be many of either side left."

She scanned the battle and pointed to a group of her men who were cornered. Without another word, we both put our horses at the enemy.

Her stallion was as hot for battle as Pansy and nearly as well trained, but Pansy's heavier build made him a more effective weapon. When he shouldered a Vorsagian horse, the other horse went down with its rider. Tisala's style of fighting was different from my own, with flourishes designed as much to cow the enemy as anything else, but she killed as quickly as I did.

At another lull in the fighting, I noticed the sun hung low in the sky, though I'd have sworn it was still early afternoon. Pansy's head hung low, and I rocked back and forth with the force of his breathing.

"The commander's breaking off." Penrod rode up to me, his teeth flashing white in the dark blood and gore of his face. "They weren't expecting a troop of fighters here. They outnumber us, but not enough to make this anything but a bloodbath for us both."

"A good general never wins a close fight," I quoted my aunt. "He pulls his men out before his losses are high and hits the enemy another time."

"Your aunt never left her troops behind."

I followed his gaze and saw that the man who'd been commanding the Vorsag was escaping through the trees, while his underlings were organizing a retreat in a slightly different direction.

"Shall we go after him?" I asked. Without waiting for

his reply, I sent Pansy leaping over a slippery mass of bodies, and we galloped after the fleeing man.

Beyond the growth of trees was a short limestone cliff. Pansy and I drew up beside it just in time to see the Vorsag scarper over the top. He'd abandoned his horse, so I jumped off Pansy and dropped his reins to the ground. I could hear Penrod doing likewise behind me.

"Do you think he's gone up here?" I said. No one answered.

Something hit me in the arm. I spun around, sword upraised, and saw Penrod with a surprised look on his face. In his hand was a dagger red with my blood. Behind him, my brother pulled his sword out of Penrod, and the horseman slid to the ground.

"Penrod?" I said blankly, for the scene was too strange for understanding. "Tosten."

Tosten dropped his sword and looked at me. "He was trying to kill you," he said, sounding as shocked as I felt. "I followed you and saw him raise his dagger to stab you in the back."

Warm blood wet my hand, attesting to Penrod's attack.

Penrod lay faceup on the ground, the terrible wound hidden underneath him. He smiled palely at me. "I'm glad . . ." His voice was a hoarse echo of itself. "I couldn't stop."

I had to drop to my knees to hear him, but he didn't say anything more. His body convulsed, and he died in the messy way all men do. Tears gathered in my eyes, and I blinked them away.

Tosten bent down slowly and picked up his sword, cleaning it on the bottom of his shirt as he stared at the dead man. "I didn't even realize it was Penrod until I struck him."

Penrod had been a mainstay of his childhood, too. What there was of it.

I looked up at Tosten. "He died fighting the Vorsag."

"Yes," he said, understanding perfectly without further

explanation. Penrod's name wouldn't be blackened by betrayal. He bent and closed Penrod's eyes, then knelt beside me. "Siphern guard his path.

"Why would Penrod try to kill you?" Tosten asked.

I shook my head, feeling incredulous, although the evidence of Penrod's attempt at murder was throbbing painfully. It made no sense.

"Some wizards can control people for a brief time," said Bastilla's voice thoughtfully. From the way Tosten started, he hadn't heard her approach, either. She walked up to us in her blood-splattered leathers. "But to do that, the wizard has to be nearby." There was something wrong with her voice. She and Penrod had been lovers, but she sounded as detached as the huntmaster looking at the stag he'd just brought down.

Bastilla leaned over me to get a better look at Penrod and balanced herself with a hand on my shoulder. I remember a flash of energy gathering there between us, then blackness claimed me, and I knew no more.

12
CALLIS: BECKRAM

Commanders are used to losing people on the field of battle, but usually there's a body.

THE ONLY THING BECKRAM COULD WORK UP ENthusiasm for were the daily practices with Stala. There he could focus on the fight and the aching grief and guilt faded, leaving only the empty hole where his brother had been. Stala no longer let him fight with the other men.

She forced him to pay attention to his defense by hitting him with the flat of her blade. "Do that in battle, and you'll be missing an arm," she snapped.

He responded with a swift thrust and a series of moves that kept her too busy to talk for a few minutes. Only after she disarmed him did he realize that he'd followed no pattern, and if any of his swings had connected, he'd have killed her. Which was, of course, why she'd quit letting him fight with anyone else.

He made no move to pick up his sword, just swayed a little on his feet and concentrated on not falling down. "Sorry."

"Let's try it again." He noticed that she wasn't even breathing hard.

Slowly, he picked up the sword again and faced her.

"I am not going to take the news to your father that he's lost another son, Beckram." Her voice was not unkind. "If it takes a few bruises, then that's your choice not mine."

When she was through with him, he staggered to his tent and collapsed on his bedroll. Sometimes when he was this tired, he didn't dream. If no one disturbed him, he might sleep as long as an hour. He closed his eyes, but it wasn't sleep that came to him, but thoughts of his cousin.

All in all, he thought, Ward's sudden recovery of his wits made him even more unlikable. Instead of a fool, he was a manipulator. All those incidental remarks in public that caused Beckram to squirm had been deliberate. Not that he'd been the only one to suffer.

Despite himself, Beckram grinned, remembering Lord Ibrim's widow's face after she'd made the mistake of propositioning Ward in a public place a few years ago. Even then, Ward had been as large as a man full grown. Beckram'd felt a great deal of satisfaction at her embarrassment, as she had gone out of her way to torment Erdrick the night before. Tittering with her gaggle of friends over the hick who'd worn a shirt with a stain on it to a formal dinner, she'd reduced Erdrick, sixteen, to public tears.

Beckram's smile died as he realized that Ward had witnessed that little incident, too. Had Ward been defending Erdrick? He remembered the look on Ward's face when he'd told him about Erdrick's death. Shocked sorrow had been followed by cold rage that chilled Ward's eyes until they didn't look like a cow's at all.

If he'd met Ward just this week, he might have liked him. Yesterday over dinner, Ward told the story of how he'd escaped Hurog and reduced the whole table to tears of mirth—even Alizon. Lying now in the dimness of the tent, Beckram doubted any of it had been funny at the time. The whole lot of Ward's band looked worse for wear, their clothes not much more than well-mended rags.

"Beckram!" called a familiar voice outside his tent.

"Kirkovenal?" The Direwolf's second son was one of Beckram's few real friends, so he sat up instead of sending him away as he would have anyone else. "Come in."

Kirkovenal stepped into the tent and tied the flap closed behind him. His red hair had been recently shorn in the traditional Oranstonian manner, leaving a pale strip of skin above both ears.

"Someone told me your cousin was here," he said abruptly.

"That's right." Beckram crossed his legs and gestured for Kirkovenal to sit beside him. "And it appears my uncle's death left Ward strangely recovered from his mental affliction."

"What's he doing with Ciernack's Bastilla?"

Beckram snapped his fingers. *"That's* where I'd seen her before. I don't think I ever knew her name."

"So what's she doing with Ward?"

Beckram frowned at his friend's obvious agitation. "You knew Ward lost Hurog because he tried to stop Garranon from taking back one of Ciernack's slaves."

"Bastilla was that slave?" Kirkovenal sounded dumbfounded, as if it had never occurred to him.

"It's not as if Ciernack has more than ten or twelve," Beckram said. "What's wrong?"

The Oranstonian rubbed his hands over his face. "Did you ever pay attention to what went on in Ciernack's tavern? Did you notice how many of the patrons were Oranstonian?"

Beckram shook his head. "But now that I think on it . . ."

"I didn't notice either," confessed Kirkovenal. "Not until Garranon cornered me a couple of years ago. He told me that since I was determined to drink myself to death, I might as well make myself useful while I did it. It was he who pulled together what Ciernack's game was."

"Ciernack's working with the Oranstonian rebels?" guessed Beckram.

"No." Kirkovenal's voice was low. "He's working for Vorsag."

"What?" Beckram shook his head to see if that helped connect a wild bunch of useless Oranstonian lordlings with Vorsag.

"Who do the Oranstonian lords hate more than Vorsag?" asked Kirkovenal.

"The Tallven," answered Beckram instantly. "Siphern guard me. . . . Do you mean that we have *Oranstonians* helping the Vorsag?"

Kirkovenal shook his head. "Not as you mean it, anyway. Think about the men at Ciernack's. They're all like me—orphans of the Rebellion with no power, not even over our own estates. They don't have the ability to help the Vorsag. But some of them might not mind giving information."

"But you were talking about Bastilla."

To Beckram's surprise, Kirkovenal gave him a sick smile. "Yes, I was. Because I was working for Garranon, I paid attention to what went on at Ciernack's. And I noticed a few things. Bastilla is a mage."

Beckram nodded. "That's what Ward says, too."

"Didn't you ever wonder how a mage got to be a slave? I did. And I noticed that Ciernack never gave her an order, never crossed her in any way."

"All right," said Beckram. "I didn't notice her much one way or the other. I'll accept your word that Bastilla was an unusual slave, but I don't see what has you so upset about her being with Ward."

"Do you like your cousin?" he asked.

Beckram laughed shortly. "I was just wondering that myself, but I think the answer might be yes."

"Do you remember Paulon?"

"The lad who was killed by robbers in Shadetown last year? Of course I do."

"About a month before he died, he approached me at my apartments. He was three sheets to the wind, and it was only midmorning. I cleaned him up and found a spare bed for him, but before he passed out, he told me that Bastilla had raped and tortured him." Kirkovenal shut his mouth abruptly and looked away. "I didn't believe him—he was drunk. Who's ever heard of a man being raped by a woman?"

Beckram was so sensitized to guilt that he could read it in someone else at fifty paces. "You think he was killed deliberately? Because he told you that Bastilla had hurt him?"

Kirkovenal smiled tightly, released it, and drew a shaky breath. "I think someone, maybe Paulon himself, told her that he'd talked to me. The last time I went to Ciernack's—"

Abruptly, he surged to his feet, hands clenched at his side. "I haven't told anyone this. I don't know if . . ." He began pacing back and forth. "Did I ever tell you that your cousin did me a good turn once? I was in Shadetown and ran into a few thugs looking for easy money. One of them knocked me to my knees, and the next thing I know, the whole alley is full of motionless lumps. Your cousin patted me on my head and asked if I'm dead."

Kirkovenal stopped, his back toward Beckram. "I went to Ciernack's shortly after Paulon died. I didn't think there was any connection because I still didn't believe Paulon's story. The next thing I knew . . . I, she . . ." Kirkovenal stumbled to a halt. He grabbed the bottom of his shirt and pulled it up, turning so his back was to Beckram.

"Gods," swore Beckram. Even the dimness of the tent couldn't disguise the severity of the scars on Kirkovenal's back.

He jerked his shirt back in place. "It wasn't the worst part of what she did to me. I thought I was a dead man."

"Why didn't she kill you, too?" Beckram asked.

"She had me there for two days. I convinced her Paulon

never said anything to me. That I thought I'd paid her to . . . hurt me while I was drunk, as if I'd paid women to do that to me before. I said she had to keep it quiet, that my brother would cut me off if he found out I'd been paying to have women beat me. It seems to have worked. I'm alive." He turned back to Beckram. "I haven't had so much as a drop of wine since."

Beckram stood up. "Thank you. Ward needs to know this. Do you know who I should ask to find out where Ward is? He rode out this morning—with Bastilla—and I can't for the life of me remember where he told me he was going."

Kirkovenal nodded. "I'll find out. Then I'll take you there myself."

TISALA NURSED HER LEFT ARM AS SHE LISTENED TO her sublieutenant list the men who had died and the ones who were wounded. She knew every man in her command down to his favorite color, and losing them was hard. Fourteen of her fifty were dead today. Another dozen were seriously wounded, and the rest were all sporting cuts and bruises.

She directed the sublieutenant to see to the gathering of enough wood to build a pyre for the dead. She would see to mounting a guard herself. No sense being caught unprepared if the Vorsag decided to return unexpectedly. Then she sifted out ten of her men who were still whole to mount a patrol. She'd just finished with her orders when the priest came shuffling up to whine at her.

"The goddess's artifacts need an escort to Callis," he said.

"We'll all be going back to bring this news to my father," she said. "You and the people of the village are welcome to come with us when we leave tomorrow morning."

"There are not enough riding animals in the village—"

She interrupted him impatiently. "We'll mount who we can, but the rest will have to walk. Tell them to pack lightly because they'll have to carry what they take."

He looked disappointed. Did he want to leave half the village behind?

Exasperated, Tisala turned on her heel and strode to the pyre to see how far they'd come in laying it. Before she made it there, the slender, dark-haired wizard who traveled with Ward of Hurog caught her arm.

"Have you seen my lord?" he said urgently. "Penrod's horse was caught running loose, and I can't find him, nor is there any sign of the Hurogmeten."

She frowned. Some battlefields seem to swallow the dead, but this one wasn't that big. "Just before the retreat, I saw Ward chase off into some trees. I think some of your people were following."

"Which trees?"

Tisala looked at the strain on his face and compared it to the work she still needed to do. "I'll show you. Let me get my horse."

One of Ward's men lay in the shelter of the woods, killed by a clean sword thrust from behind, and Oreg almost fell off his mount in his scramble to examine the fallen man. "Penrod?" He checked pulse points, but she could see that the man had shed too much blood to live. While the wizard fiddled with the body, she paced out the clearing. Here that big beast Ward rode had stood for a short while—impossible to mistake the size of hoofprints. The ground was too soft with rain and dense with grass to hold many indications other than the most obvious. She couldn't distinguish the human footprints from the general muck.

"The horses went off this way. . . ." She let her voice trail off when she got a good look at the wizard.

She took half a dozen quick steps and thrust a shoulder under his arm before he fell. "Are you wounded?"

With an eerie keening sound, he became a dead weight.

The bushes behind them shook. Tisala dropped the wizard and drew her sword, but it was only another of Ward's people, Axiel. She only remembered his name because her father had said it was dwarven, and the dwarves used to trade at Callis.

Axiel took a quick look at the dead man before he knelt beside the wailing boy. "Oreg?"

"Does he do this often?" She had to raise her voice to be heard.

"Never seen him do this." Axiel took the younger man's face in his hands. "Oreg, what's wrong? What happened to Penrod?"

The mage jerked away and curled into a fetal position, but he quit wailing. "He's gone. My fault, he's gone."

"Who?"

"Ward, I think," answered Tisala when Oreg didn't reply. "We came out looking for him and found Penrod here. Ward's stallion has been here as well as a couple of other horses, but I can't tell much more."

Without a word, Axiel began to pace the little clearing as she had. After a moment, he returned and nodded. "If we'd had a foot or two less rain in the past few months, I could do better. Someone took three horses off in that general direction and set another free—probably Penrod's. All three of the horses were big, which means that they belonged to our group rather than yours. Oreg's here. Penrod's dead. Ciarra is helping with the wounded. That leaves Ward, Tosten, and Bastilla."

"They left together?"

He shrugged. "Their horses did, anyway. Maybe they took off after the man who killed Penrod."

"And they'll be back when they're finished."

Axiel grunted as men do, and Tisala decided to take it as an affirmative. "Right. Then we'll take Oreg and bed him down with the rest of our sick men. I'll send someone back for Penrod." She'd seen enough men in battle to know that battle fever and its aftermath took people strangely sometimes. As long as Oreg wasn't wailing and sobbing tomorrow, he'd be no worse off than any other soldier she knew.

"I'll come back and get Penrod after I'm through with Oreg. Penrod and I've been comrades for too long to leave him to other hands." Axiel picked up the young mage without visible effort, though Tisala doubted there was a stone of weight between them.

"I'll find Ciarra and let her know what's going on." She held Axiel's gelding while he dealt with the difficulty of getting Oreg on his tall horse. She bit her lip and didn't say anything disparaging about the Northern horses. Some people you could tease, and others you didn't. Despite her father's comments, she did actually know which were which, and sometimes she even cared.

AXIEL COVERED OREG WITH THE BLANKETS FROM both of their bedrolls, but it didn't stop the shaking.

"I've got to go get Penrod's body."

Oreg didn't appear to hear him. After a moment, Axiel stepped into his saddle. His horse let out an almost human sigh, but made no other protests.

"That's it Foxy Lad," he told his horse. "I don't know why the aftermath of battles are always more a trial of endurance than the battles themselves, but that's how it is."

Axiel was tired, too. There was some basis for human rumors of dwarven endurance, but he was half human, and his arms told him that he'd been in a fight. A dull ache in his ribs let him know that he hadn't come out unscathed, but it would have to wait until after Penrod was taken care of.

You'd think after all these years, Penrod would have learned to watch his back. Axiel stopped himself. Much easier to just accept death rather than rail at it, and he should have learned that by now.

Penrod's body lay undisturbed. The growing shadow gave the glen an unsettling feel, though it might just be that he was here alone. Axiel bent down to pick him up.

"Sleep well, old friend," murmured Axiel. He hefted the body as carefully as if Penrod had been wounded.

CIARRA CRIED SILENTLY AS THE FLAMES CONSUMED Penrod. Axiel rested his hands on her shoulders, but his eyes were dry. Penrod was neither the first nor the last comrade he'd fed to the fire. He watched the bodies of the fallen blacken, dwarven eyesight letting him see what the flames concealed from the humans around him. When Ciarra turned away and buried her face in his chest, he wrapped his arms around the child.

"Come, lass," he said. "Let's get cleaned up and set up the tent. If we don't hurry, we'll be doing it in the dark. Your brothers will be back soon and ready for sleep."

IT WAS NEARING DARKFALL WHEN BECKRAM AND Kirkovenal came upon the camp. The dying embers of the funeral pyre told them that there had been a battle long before they arrived, so Beckram was careful to hail the camp before riding in. No one he asked knew where Ward was. But a delicate hand caught his sleeve while he was talking to yet another Oranstonian.

"Ciarra?" he said. Then, when he got a closer look at her, "What's wrong? Did something happen to Ward?"

She started to shake her head, then shrugged instead. Tightening her grip on his arm, she dragged him behind her. Kirkovenal dismounted, too, and followed them.

Ciarra took them to the center of the camp, where Beckram saw Axiel at the cooking pot.

"Beckram," Axiel said. "What are you doing here?"

"Looking for my cousin. Do you know where Ward is?"

Axiel handed off his ladle with a "Mind you keep stirring, or it'll burn on the bottom."

"We're not sure where Ward's gotten himself off to," said Axiel. "As far as we could determine, he, Tosten, and Bastilla went off chasing Vorsag. We had a minor skirmish with the Vorsag earlier today. Afterward, we found Penrod dead in a small clearing on the far side of the battlefield. From the tracks, the three of them took off south. What do you want him for?"

Beckram had the whole ride from Callis to put Kirkovenal's information together with Ward's storytelling and had come up with a few theories.

"Ciernack in Estian has been selling information to King Kariarn and probably his father," he began. "At first, it was military information, but the new king of Vorsag wanted more; he wanted magic. So the people working at the tavern bought artifacts and probably stole a few, too. A couple of years ago, about the time Kariarn's father became ill, Ciernack got several new workers, including a slave girl, Bastilla. Except she wasn't really a slave at all; she was working for Kariarn."

"Bastilla was working for Kariarn?" asked Axiel.

"It's the only reason we could come up with for her to run to Hurog," explained Beckram. "Bastilla was no slave running for her freedom. Kirkovenal knows of at least one man she had killed and another she tortured. Ciernack didn't give her orders, she gave them to him. We think that Bastilla heard the stories about Hurog's treasure and went to check them out for herself—with her lover, Landislaw, in pursuit to make sure she made it back."

Axiel shook his head. "I saw her feet after she ran to Hurog. I saw the scars on her back."

Kirkovenal spoke. "I have seen her slice the skin off a man's back for the sheer pleasure she took in it. I've seen Black Ciernack, who the king himself is careful with, flinch from her anger. And I've seen her pretend to be an innocent maid or a whore, as it suits her."

Beckram broke the silence that followed. "Before Bastilla 'escaped' to Hurog, Landislaw cornered me and asked me about the treasure of gold and magic the dwarves are said to have left at the old keep. It's nonsense, and I told him so—but Bastilla could have been sent to check it out. The only thing I don't know is why she stayed with Ward." Even as he spoke, a possible answer came to him. "Unless she found something. Something that she couldn't get right away. Ward rescues her and tells her he's headed to Oranstone, and she decides it might be the easiest way to get her information back to Kariarn."

"Haverness thinks that the Vorsag have an enclave in Oranstone," said Kirkovenal abruptly. "You said Ward, his brother, and Bastilla left here headed south. Buril isn't too far from here."

"Garranon's keep?" asked Beckram.

Kirkovenal nodded. "Where Landislaw has been holding court. Bastilla's lover, Landislaw."

"Who hates the king much more than he hates Vorsag," said Beckram.

"You're speculating," said Axiel. "What proof do you have?"

"When did Ward leave?" asked Beckram.

"Right after the battle was over," Axiel replied.

"I ask you, would any commander trained by Stala desert his men after a battle to go chasing after a few enemy soldiers?" asked Beckram. When Axiel made no answer, Beckram said. "No. He wouldn't. I think Bastilla believes there's some treasure at Hurog, but she can't get to it without Ward, and she intends to use Tosten to make Ward help her get it."

13

WARDWICK

Obsession is a strange thing. It can be the fire that forges a true blade, but more often it is the flaw that causes the sword to break.

I DREAMED OF HUROG. IT WAS SO REAL I COULD SMELL the musty books in the library where I stood. *Dusty tomes in languages no one could read anymore lined the shelves. Somewhere there was a map of the secret ways, but the long, shallow drawer that held all the maps was gone. If I couldn't find the map, they would kill my brother.*

Tosten cried out, his voice muffled and distant, but it still hurt me.

"You take care of Tosten and Ciarra," my mother said. "I have to tend my garden."

"All right, Mother," I said. Tosten's hand was warm in mine. Ciarra was a heavy bundle in my free arm. The sun was warm and bathed the flowers of the garden in a rich orange hue. . . .

"Where are the dragon's bones?"

Tosten screamed. His voice echoed in my head until the garden disappeared, and I found myself in the dragon cave, deep in the heart of Hurog. I had to get out, but without Oreg, I was trapped. I'd come in through the sewers.

Through the small tunnel that clamped down on me like a vise.

"Hurog's magic's been poisoned, child," whispered Oreg's voice in my head. *"It seeks out weakness in the blood of the dragon. Dreamers lose their way. Anger becomes berserker rage. Ambition becomes obsession. Hatred eats your soul."*

Hurog, I thought. *Hurog means dragon.*

HUROG WAS GONE WHEN I WOKE UP. GONE SO FAR that all I could feel was the empty place that was left, and I could have cried at the agony of the loss. My right hand was so cold it hurt; icy waves traveled up my body from the battered platinum ring. I tried to pull my hand to tuck it in my armpit to warm it as I did in the winter months, but all I did was rattle some chains.

I was in a small, dark cell with a high ceiling. A tiny window two bodylengths up the wall let in a little light, but didn't do much to cut the fumes rising from floor rushes, which should have been changed a decade ago.

At first I thought I was alone, but when I lowered my gaze to the floor, I saw a broken form lying in the moldering rushes.

I forgot my discomfort.

"Tosten?" The hand I could see was swollen and misshapen. I thought of hearing his screams in my dream and realized it hadn't been a dream at all.

"Tosten!" I shouted it. I needed him to move, because I couldn't tell if his ribs were rising at all. I couldn't bear it if he were dead.

As if in answer to my cries, the cell door opened, and Kariarn stepped through. He looked very like the boy I remembered, a year or so older than I was. His fine brown hair was trimmed neatly at shoulder length. His clothing was expensive without being ostentatious. But it was his companion I stared at.

I almost didn't recognize Bastilla in the self-effacing woman who stood just behind the Vorsagian king, her eyes lowered and her head bowed submissively. Gone was the ragged warrior, and in her place was an immaculately groomed slave wearing a wisp of ivory silk that did little to hide her body. What had Kariarn done to her?

"Ah, the guard told me you were awake, Ward," said Kariarn.

I looked at him.

"Sorry about your brother." Kariarn nudged Tosten with his boot. If I hadn't been chained, I'd have killed him. "The magic wasn't working against you. My archmage swore there was no one who could stand against it, but Bastilla said you were a stubborn Northman, and it might not work." He reached back and patted her on the top of her head like a huntsman patting his hound after a kill. I kept waiting for her to turn on him and almost didn't follow his next words. "Which is why she brought both of you. She was right; you couldn't talk fast enough, once he started screaming. It's too bad you didn't know what we needed. Who'd have thought that the lord of Hurog wouldn't know how to reach his treasure without a wizard to guide him?" Kariarn gave me a chiding look. "No matter. Bastilla left a bit of hair in the chamber so my archmage can use that to locate it. A waste of power—but with the dragon's bones, that will hardly matter." The lust in his voice when he said "dragon's bones" reminded me of the way my father sometimes stared at a new chambermaid.

I swallowed to wet my dry throat. *Bastilla?* Behind his back, she smiled at me. It was a smile I'd never seen on her face before, sly and triumphant.

I said, "You're telling me all of this because . . ."

He smiled. "I'm tired of all the old men who think they know better than I. I need young men, men who understand youth doesn't mean stupid or weak. Bastilla tells me that your wizard will follow you, no matter which ruler you choose."

He stopped speaking, perhaps waiting for me to confirm or deny what he said. But I was distracted by the cold that numbed my arm. It didn't hurt anymore, and that worried me. Had they done something to me? Why just that arm? Had they tried to steal the ring?

"I can take Hurog, Ward." The mention of my obsession turned my attention back to Kariarn. "I have magic at my fingertips that will knock down her dark walls and leave her in ruins, to get my dragon bones. Or I can take you there and give you Hurog instead. You could swear fealty to me instead of the boy-lover Jakoven. What do you owe him? He killed your cousin and took Hurog from you. Look what he's done to Oranstone. A man like that does not deserve the throne. Look beyond what is, Ward. Five Kingdoms dwindling into slow death in the hands of Tallven blood could be six flourishing lands under me. I could make you king of Shavig, Ward—as you should have been."

I could hear my aunt patiently explaining how a war could be lost before the first blood was shed. The worst of it was that Kariarn was right: Jakoven wasn't fit to manage an estate, let alone the Five Kingdoms. *Kariarn* wouldn't stand by while another country ravaged his lands; he would protect what was his. I even understood his obsession with magic far better than I would ever understand Jakoven, for I was obsessed, too—with Hurog.

At my feet, Tosten moved his hand briefly.

Kariarn must have seen the direction of my gaze. "Bastilla can heal his wounds; that's another of her talents. I see she didn't tell you of it. I'm sorry I let her play with him a little too long, but she'd earned her reward. She likes hurting things, and I indulge her when I can. As I said, she can heal the damage done to my allies."

I bowed my head, staring at Tosten's hand that might never again touch a harp string. I thought numbly, *Bastilla did this? Bastilla enjoyed my brother's pain?*

"Show him your pet, master," said Bastilla suddenly.

He jerked on her chain, roughly pulling her to her knees, coughing and choking. "Speak when I ask, slave. Have you been gone so long I must train you over again?"

She shook her head quickly, and it seemed to satisfy him. He rocked back upon his heels. "The timing is not right. Let him think a while."

She recovered control of her breathing, but she didn't get to her feet. Instead, she knelt in the molding rushes and kissed his boot. He raised her up with a finger under her chin, and she kissed his hand as she stood. I could see her face for a moment, and the blind adoration in it made me feel ill. I didn't understand. She could have stayed free of him. She was strong—a wizard, even.

I may not have loved her, but I had liked her. I stared at her for a long moment and wondered if she might be faking this.

But Kariarn said that she'd been the one who hurt my brother, that she'd enjoyed it. I couldn't imagine the Bastilla I knew hurting anyone except in battle.

She was a better actor than I was.

I looked away and met Kariarn's amused eyes. "She is my chameleon," he said, reading my mind. "She is whoever suits me best—a gift from my archmage. A human succubus. She belongs to me, body and soul. Don't you, Bastilla?"

"Only to you," she answered.

Kariarn held my gaze. "Haven't you met a Cholyte before? When they enter the order, they give up their will to Chole's prophetess, the Cholynn, or whomever she bestows them upon. The Cholynn gave Bastilla to me as a present when I turned thirteen."

He left, leading Bastilla behind him. I heard a bar slide into place on the other side of the closed door.

After a moment, Tosten groaned again and sat up. "Did he mean that magic turned her into that?"

"I don't know," I said."

"Pox rot you," he snapped weakly. "Don't look at me like that. You didn't have a thing to do with it."

"I should have spoken sooner."

"Most of this happened after you talked." He looked away from me and into the shadows. "Gods, Ward. I thought she was my friend. She broke my finger, then kissed me as if my pain were one of Mother's aphrodisiacs. She licked the blood from my back." He shuddered. "Kari-arn had to drag her off of me." Tosten bowed his head and spoke as if the words were dragged from his throat. "Tell me that it was magic that made her that way. Tell me that she's possessed by demons."

"I don't think that even the gods can change someone completely. Some people just like others' pain," I whispered. "Father was like that." I remembered a dark night when I held my lover while she cried and told me that my father had raped her. I said, "After he beat me, he used to go straightaway to his bed with whatever maidservant happened to be closest."

Tosten buried his face in his knee and laughed. "Aren't you supposed to be reassuring me at this point? You know, taking care of the helpless?"

"I can't protect you from knowledge," I said at last. "You have to acknowledge evil, or you give it too much power over you. Look at Mother. She's spent most of her life running from what our father was, so she left her children unprotected against him." I hadn't realized how angry I was with her, with the passive way she'd watched Father cut Tosten with a tongue that bruised as well as his fists, until Tosten had tried to kill himself to get away from it. In my dreams, Oreg had excused her by telling me that

Hurog's magic twisted her—but she should have fought for her children.

"She had you to protect her children," said Tosten unexpectedly. "Me, I'm like Mother, clinging to my troubles. All the way here . . . all the way from Tyrfannig, I've been hurting you because you like Oreg better than you like me."

"A wise man told me once that horses kick and bite because they are afraid or hurt more often than because they are angry." It hurt to use Penrod's arguments.

"I am not a horse," he huffed.

"But are you afraid and hurt?" I asked. He did not reply. "You can't blame a horse that strikes out in pain or fear. You just see what you can do to relieve the cause."

Tosten laughed, a real laugh this time. "Or you slit the poor animal's throat."

"I have to admit there have been times . . ."

If someone had been listening, they'd have thought we were idiots, laughing ourselves to jelly in a filthy cell, me chained to the wall and Tosten so badly injured he yelped now and again as he laughed.

"So how are you going to rescue us?" He asked finally. "Are you going to switch allegiance from the bastard who killed poor old Erdrick?"

"To Kariarn?" I snorted. "Now, that's a good choice. Like the chicken who went to live with the foxes because she was afraid of the farmer's dog. No."

"So we'll sit here and rot?"

I looked at the silver ring on my numb hand. "I think I have a better plan."

I called Oreg to me, as I'd summoned him often in Hurog, though I'd never tried calling him outside of Hurog's walls. Since the pyre where I'd burned the village dead, I hadn't tried any more magic, because untrained magic can be deadly. Even so, I hadn't really expected the power that flooded my call. The ring vibrated with magic and sent warmth burning through the numbness of my hand and arm and made them mine again.

I could all but smell the magic that coalesced slowly into Oreg's huddled form, which looked very much like Tosten's huddled form had, except Oreg was shaking. He twisted awkwardly until he was clinging to my leg.

"Don't leave again. Please, please . . . don't leave again. It was too far." His toneless, despairing whisper set the hairs on my neck on edge, and I wanted to kill whomever had done this—but Oreg's father was long dead. Oreg was the only person I knew whose father had been worse than mine. Perhaps that, rather than the ring was the true heart of our bond.

Tosten stared at Oreg.

"No. I won't leave," I promised. "I didn't do it on purpose, Oreg. Are you all right?"

He buried his face in my leg and shook like a dog who'd been in cold water too long.

"What did you do to him?" There was abhorrence on Tosten's face.

Oreg's actions reminded me uncomfortably of Bastilla and Kariarn, too. "I did nothing to him. Give him a moment, and I'll explain."

Tosten glanced from Oreg to me and then turned painfully away, muttering something that sounded like, "It had better be good."

"Where are we?" asked Oreg after a moment. He didn't loosen his grip on me, but his voice sounded almost normal, if a bit muffled.

"Buril," answered Tosten when he saw that I didn't know. "Garranon's estate."

Garranon was dealing with the Vorsag? It didn't fit what I knew of him, but neither did Bastilla's new persona.

"How did you get here?" Oreg asked. "Where's Bastilla?"

"Bastilla brought us," I said as conversationally as pos-

sible when chained up with a man clinging to my leg.
"She's responsible for the damage to Tosten. And she's not
Ciernack's slave, she's Kariarn's. He seemed to indicate
that she'd been altered somehow by the Cholynn—to turn
her into his loyal creature. Can that be done?"

"Only if she consented first," he said.

"Did you know that she wasn't what she seemed?"

Oreg pulled away and looked at me finally. Even though
the room was dark, his pupils were pinpricks. "I knew she
was a mage as soon as she stepped onto Hurog land,
stronger than she knew or at least stronger than she would
admit to. Beyond that . . . once such altering as you spoke
of is done, it is not an easy thing to detect, not even if you
know to look for it."

I nodded. "She fooled me, too. Kariarn called her a
chameleon." I smiled at him. "She's like me. She can be
anybody she wants to be."

"No." Tosten interrupted abruptly. "Not what *she* wants
to be. I've been thinking about that. You wanted someone
to rescue, Penrod and Axiel wanted a lover with no strings.
I . . . she let me talk to her, about how . . . about things. She
stayed away from Ciarra because she couldn't understand
what Ciarra wanted. That was how her act worked. As long
as we saw what we wanted to see, we didn't look any further."

Oreg nodded, releasing his grip on me entirely so he
could look at Tosten. "Ward becomes exactly what *he*
wants to become, usually to the vast irritation of the people around him. He can't get rid of the stubbornness or the
honor."

"Or the belief that he has to take care of anyone he
meets." Tosten sounded both superior and pleased.

"Tosten," I said. "There are some things you should
know—in case you get out of this and I don't. Oreg is not
one of Father's by-blows. He was bound to Hurog the day

it was built. He's our family ghost—though he's more a mage than a ghost."

Oreg turned betrayed eyes to me—though how else he expected me to explain his recent actions, I don't know. Tosten looked at me almost the same way.

"Oreg's the ghost?" Tosten said. "And you didn't tell me?"

"I didn't know until the day Father died," I replied. "And, well, it seemed as if it were Oreg's story to tell, and he didn't choose to." That didn't seem to soothe either of them, so I changed the subject. "Oreg, could you get us out of here?" I jangled my chains meaningfully.

"Yes, master."

Tosten's eyes widened as Oreg echoed Bastilla's response to Kariarn's orders.

I rolled my eyes. "Don't sulk, Oreg. Tosten, quit looking so—"

A weird mewling moan filled the air, starting high, like a stallion's shrill whistle and then dropping so deep that the stone against my back vibrated.

Oreg came to alert like a hunting dog on the scent. "Basilisk. Where did they find a basilisk?"

"Basilisk?" asked Tosten.

"Shavigmen called them—" Oreg paused, looked suddenly enlightened, and gave me a wry smile. "—stone dragons. Perhaps that is what the Oranstonians call them, too."

"Silverfells's stone dragon?" I asked.

Oreg's eyes dropped. "Basilisks smell like dragons."

"So what's a basilisk?" I asked.

Oreg relaxed gradually. "It's a lizard about four bodylengths from nose to tail and weighs at least four times as much as your horse. It's as smart as a dog or a little better and has a bit of magic."

"What kind?" I asked.

"It turns people to stone." Tosten sounded breathless,

but I expect that was as much pain as excitement over Kariarn's creature. "There are a few songs about them. Remember 'Hunt of the Basilisk,' Ward?"

He hummed a few notes that sounded vaguely familiar, so I nodded.

"Silly song." Oreg sounded smug. "What predator would turn its food into stone? What it can do is catch your eye and hold you still so it can enjoy a leisurely meal."

"You think Silverfells's stone dragon became this basilisk? I didn't think the stone carving was supposed to be as big."

"When you turn something into stone, you take out the moisture that makes most of the bulk of flesh. A really good mage could turn you into a pebble," said the really good mage before me. He looked better, though it was difficult to tell since the cell was dimly lit. His left hand still maintained contact with my leg.

"Oreg," I said after a moment's thought, "would you take Tosten back to where you were? I think I ought to stay here. Kariarn's planning something. But I need to get Tosten out so Kariarn doesn't have a lever on me."

Oreg shook his head. "I can't. I could take him out of the castle. But I can't get any farther from you than that."

His state being what it had been when he'd answered my call, I believed what he said. "Can you take him to Hurog?"

"No—nor get myself back there any way that you could not."

I stared at him a moment. "I thought you were Hurog?"

He nodded. "I can find out what's going on there, but I can't affect it from here. This body can't leave you—as you have seen—unless it is in Hurog. And Hurog is too far for my powers to take me."

Tosten shifted uncomfortably, but moving didn't seem to help. I frowned at him but asked Oreg, "Could you take us all out of here—to where Axiel and Ciarra are?"

Oreg shook his head. "Ring magic brought me, but it couldn't send me away. I could take you out of the keep, though."

"Are you sure we're at Buril?" I asked Tosten.

He nodded his head. "Apparently, Kariarn has had people stationed here for a long while."

"Garranon is hosting the Vorsag?" I muttered to myself. It still didn't sound right. Beckram had told me that Garranon had been one of the "hundred," but Garranon had no reason to betray Oranstone.

"Someone is coming," said Oreg.

"Hide yourself," I whispered.

Tosten collapsed back onto the floor just as the door opened and three men came into the room. They unchained and escorted me out of the cell without noticing Oreg as he stood beside them. Oreg had hidden that way all the time at Hurog, but I hadn't been sure he could do it here.

Conditioned by Hurog, where the prison cells were under the guard's tower, I was surprised to be led down three sets of stairs and into what could only be the great hall. The room was much larger than Hurog's great hall and smelled woodsy and damp. Kariarn and a full ten of his men awaited me near the large fireplace on one side of the room. Bastilla was conspicuously absent. I wondered where she was.

"My lord," Kariarn greeted me with a smile, as if I'd come visiting rather than from a holding cell. "How kind of you to join us. You know Garranon, of course, but his lady doesn't attend court, so you won't have met Lady Allysaian."

His men parted until I could see that Garranon was indeed there, but he didn't look happy about it. There was a bruise covering half of his face, and his hands were chained behind his back—unlike mine. The Oranstonian's feet were chained tightly to his arms and each other so that if he walked, he'd only manage a stumbling shuffle. It was

Stala's recommended method of moving dangerous prisoners. Garranon must not approve of the use Kariarn was making of his keep. It made me feel curiously relieved that the man who'd taken Hurog from me was not a traitor to his country.

At Garranon's side stood a girl a little younger than I and only a bit taller than Ciarra. She was no beauty, clad as she was in a dirty, ripped court dress, but she held herself with such pride that it didn't matter. She stood next to her husband without touching him, leaving no one in doubt of her allegiance, though she wore no chains herself.

"Garranon," chided Kariarn lightly, interrupting my thoughts, "don't you have a greeting for our guest?"

Garranon took in my chainless state in a glance and then he turned his eyes away, doubtless thinking me a traitor.

"You'll have to forgive him, Lord Wardwick," said Kariarn. "He feels that his brother betrayed him, and it has made him somewhat bitter."

"Losing your lands can do that to you," I replied pointedly after a moment's hesitation. It seemed prudent to distance myself from someone Kariarn was treating like a dangerous enemy. Trading Jakoven for Kariarn might be like the chicken who exchanged the farmer's dogs for a den of foxes, but it wouldn't hurt for him to believe I was considering it.

Kariarn smiled. "Just so. You are probably wondering why I've brought you here." He addressed his remarks to Garranon as well as me.

I inclined my head politely. The guardsmen who'd brought me watched closely, but I would never attack Kariarn until I knew Tosten was safe. Thinking about Tosten made me suddenly nervous about Bastilla's absence.

"Doubtless you intend to feed one of us to your monster and impress the Northlander," stated Garranon's wife in cool tones. She obviously liked Northlanders no more than she liked the Vorsag.

Kariarn inclined his head to her. "Lady, I'm certain you'll enjoy the show just as much." He nodded to one of his men, who hurried out of the room. "You see, Garranon, your brother was of the mistaken opinion I was going to set him up as king of Oranstone. I *had* considered it, but he doesn't have the ability to lead men. He had months here without you, while you played catamite with Jakoven, when he could have won the hearts of your people and your wife. Instead, he alienates everyone. If I put him in your place, your people would kill him as soon as I left."

It was not wise to admit he made promises he didn't keep in front of me, to whom he also expected to make promises. But he was young, and he knew, because Bastilla knew, how badly I wanted Hurog.

The grunting sounds of a struggle turned my attention to a doorway. Two of Kariarn's men dragged Landislaw, bound much as Garranon was, into the room. Instead of bringing him to us, they took him to the center of the room and held him there.

Kariarn's eyes followed Landislaw's progress, but he continued speaking. "Because of Landislaw's inability to win over the people here, I'll have to leave one of my generals in Buril now, and a good portion of a full army. Landislaw will have to pay for his bungling."

Kariarn wasn't watching Garranon, so he didn't see the Oranstonian open his mouth to speak. Garranon's lady put a firm hand on his forearm and shook her head. Garranon closed his mouth without uttering a sound, but there was black hell in his eyes as he looked at his brother.

The hall shook with that strange, reverberating cry I'd heard earlier. I shivered, and Kariarn saw me.

He clapped a friendly hand on my shoulder. "Don't worry. My wizards have control of the beast. It takes two of them, but I have many."

On the tail end of his words, the two large doors flew open with a bang. Briefly, I could see the bailey grounds beyond, lit by the early-morning sun. A monumental form blocked the entire doorway briefly and then skittered into the great hall with a light motion that belied the creature's size. It stopped motionless a full body length from the door, allowing us all to look our fill.

It was as tall as Pansy in the shoulders, but most of its bulk was in length. Disregarding the size and a few other details, the basilisk looked a lot like the lizards that played in the king's gardens at Estian. Green scales the size of my palm covered it from tip to tail. Emerald eyes blinked unconcernedly at us from the front of its head like predators everywhere, but lizardlike, the eyes didn't appear to track in concert. Remembering Oreg's words, I averted my eyes hastily from the creature's and continued to study it.

A braided band wrapped twice around its middle with black-painted runes obscuring the natural brown of leather—wizard's work. Likely that was how they controlled the beast.

Black horn spikes studded the forked tip of its tail and continued up the ridge of its back until they disappeared in the improbable ruff of scarlet feathers encircling its neck. A tongue as large as my arm flicked out of its mouth momentarily.

I was so fascinated by the basilisk I almost didn't see the two wizards who had entered in its wake. Like my father's wizard, Kariarn's affected the uniform dress of wizardkind: long beard, close-fitted tunic of black broadcloth, and brilliantly dyed panel skirts that swept the floor. Armsmen walked to either side of the wizards, holding them by the elbows to support their weight. If they were able to control the basilisk, it wasn't without effort. A deep fear I'd held inside eased. These two would never be able to maintain such concentration during an actual battle, so Kariarn couldn't use the basilisk without risking losing as many men as his enemy.

"Direct its attention to its food," commanded Kariarn.

One of the men by the nearer wizard bent down to speak into the wizard's ear. And the guards holding Landislaw turned their heads away from the beast.

The basilisk turned toward Landislaw, who had closed his eyes and continued to struggle against the grip of the men who held him. Either their grip loosened when they turned away from him, or terror granted him extra strength, because Landislaw broke from his keepers and shuffled toward us on bound feet.

"Garranon!" He cried.

His brother made an attempt to go to him, but Kariarn's guards gripped him.

The basilisk moved suddenly, so fast that my eyes almost couldn't track it. One moment it was near the door, the next it was beside Landislaw. The noise it made drew Landislaw's attention. I knew the moment its gaze captured Garranon's brother. He stopped moving as suddenly as if he were a puppet whose strings were cut.

The basilisk kept one eye on its food and allowed the other to swivel over us. Only after the cold gaze passed over me did I realize I should have looked away, but it hadn't been interested in more food. If I stood frozen, it was not from any magic of the basilisk's gaze but from the knowledge that there was nothing I could do. Without a weapon, I stood no chance against the creature, not to mention Kariarn's guards. With my brother captive, I could not throw away my life. But standing there was the hardest thing I'd ever done in my life.

Apparently reassured it wouldn't have to fight any of us for its dinner, the basilisk butted Landislaw with its jaw, knocking him over. It opened its mouth to reveal small, triangular teeth no larger than a dog's. Swiveling its head, it engulfed Landislaw's upper body, and then the reptilian nose jerked upward, forcing the limp man to slide into its maw.

One of the guards who'd been holding Landislaw turned to the side and began vomiting helplessly. Landislaw wasn't dead. Held by the basilisk's terrible magic, he would be slowly digested while he yet lived.

I'd never liked Landislaw, but no one deserved that.

"What happens to the chains?" I asked in a casual tone. I was counting on the dimness of the hall hiding my paleness.

Kariarn's eyebrow raised in reaction to my casual tone. "It vomits up the hard tissues after a few days."

"Like an owl," I said, holding my voice level. Never let the enemy know what scares you. I kept my gaze on Kariarn's face, not wanting to witness Garranon's pain. "Where did you find out how to control it?"

Kariarn smiled as if he'd found a soul mate. If I could convince him of it . . . My plan was half formed at best, the better to accommodate the changing situation.

"The Cholynn was very helpful. She is tired of Tallvenish rule. Without Jakoven, the Cholytes could take over and run the whole country. Her order has libraries that date back to the time of the Empire, and she has sent me several mages—though none as useful as Bastilla has proved."

"Why did you bring me here to see this?" I asked.

"Bastilla thought you might be interested in my stone dragon, since Hurog was once the home to dragons." He smiled suddenly. "Do you know that the emperors had dragons in their service? I am the first since the ancient times to own a dragon."

He was the first what? *Emperor?* He did not have his empire yet.

I nodded thoughtfully. "Tell me, Your Highness, how do you intend to return Hurog to me?" There was no need to fake my feelings for my home; doubtless even the impassive-faced soldiers heard my lust.

Kariarn laughed, "Directly to business. Why the change of heart?"

"You expect me to lose face before my brother? Eventually, he'll come around to the idea that I did it to save Hurog. But it will take time for him to adjust. I know the

Tallvenish king will never return her to me, and I have little love left for him after he killed my cousin. My question
is: What is your price?"

"Nothing you cannot pay," he said quickly, afraid his
fish would slip the hook. "You will give me loyalty and
taxes as you now do to Tallven."

"I've made vows to Tallven," I said letting the thought
trouble my brow as if I'd just realized what accepting Kariarn's help would mean. "A Hurog does not break vows."

"No one holds to vows that are already broken," he said.
"Jakoven Tallven broke the bonds his ancestors forged
with Hurog so many years when he stole Hurog from you
on a whim. You owe him nothing."

I let my jaw harden as he spoke, then widened my eyes
and let them go soft and sad. "He did. Just as he allowed
your armies to ravage Oranstone after he took away their
means to defend themselves. Such a man does not deserve
to be king."

"How easily you give away your honor, boy," said Garranon. His voice was thick with tears and anger.

"How dare you speak of honor to me!" I roared in my
father's best manner. "*You* took away my Hurog, and why?
So that your traitorous little brother could escape Ciernack's slap on the wrist? A punishment your brother well
deserved. Perhaps if you let him accept the responsibility
for his actions just once, he wouldn't have ended here. I
will not hear talk of honor from Jakoven's whore." I
wanted Garranon and his lady to escape tonight with Oreg
and Tosten. With luck, Kariarn would never believe I'd
lifted a single finger to help them.

"Take Lord Garranon and the lady back to their previous quarters," ordered Kariarn sharply.

Garranon narrowed his eyes at me, his anger a smoldering flame that momentarily blotted out the terrible agony
in his eyes. His voice was a whisper that carried through
the room. "Unlike you, my brother was no traitor. He owed

no oath to Jakoven, and he wanted freedom for his people. He was guilty of stupidity and shortsightedness. You add greed to his list of faults. I hope I live long enough to see you feed the basilisk."

He caught my gaze as tightly as ever the basilisk could, holding my eyes until the guardsmen dragged him from the room.

Kariarn patted my arm. "You are no traitor. Jakoven is no king of Shavig or Oranstone. A real king protects his people."

I tilted my chin up and turned back to the king of Vorsag. "You are right." I said decisively. "No king who deserves that name would do so little to protect his people. Now, what are you going to do about Hurog, and why are you interested in it? Hurog has no wealth."

"No, but she has great power. And I'm not speaking of just the dragon bones. Ciernack tells me that when your uncle defied the king after he killed your cousin, all of Shavig marched to his tune."

"Well, of course." I said as if it hadn't surprised me to hear of it. "Hurog is a proud name in Shavig." I let the thought collect visibly. "Oh, I see. Through me you'll control Shavig. But that won't work if they know that you put me in control. Shavigmen don't like the Vorsag."

Kariarn smiled. "I knew you were smarter than Landislaw. What if we make you the rescuer of Hurog? Defending her from her foes. We'll kill your uncle, and then you'll return and take his men, driving us out of Hurog—*after* I get the dragon bones."

"And welcome to them," I said in an absent but truthful tone. The dragon was dead, and it was the living I had to protect. "But do we have to kill my uncle?"

"He took Hurog from you, Ward. He deserves no mercy."

I took in a deep breath, as if steeling myself to a difficult task. "You're right. Yes, I'll do it. But what about my brother? I won't have him killed."

"That's not necessary—if you can convince him to follow your lead."

I nodded. "I think I can bring him around."

THEY CLEANED AND BANDAGED THE ARM PENROD had wounded before the guardsmen escorted me ever so courteously back to my cell. Even the locking of the door was done with an apologetic air. They did not reattach me to the wall. The cell had been cleaned while I was gone; stale, musty straw was replaced by fresh, flower-scented rushes.

Tosten was sitting in the corner of the room, his knees up and his head buried against them. The light from the small window high over our heads didn't let me see much more. I'd been consumed with my private guilt, having watched a man die without lifting a finger to prevent it; but my brother's state pushed that to the background.

"Tosten?" I asked. But he didn't look up.

"Bastilla healed him," said Oreg from behind me. He startled me, but it was as much the anger in his voice as the sudden appearance.

"She crawled inside my mind," Tosten whispered. "I couldn't keep her out. She stole my soul, and I couldn't stop her."

Frightened, I looked at Oreg, who shook his head and said, "No one stole your soul, Tosten. You can give it away, but they cannot steal it, not even by ruse."

"Gods," Tosten moaned.

I put a hand on his shoulder.

He stopped rocking and looked up at me. "What happened to you?"

My mind flashed back to the basilisk, and I swallowed bile. "Is there anyone listening?" I asked Oreg.

He tilted his head a moment. "Not by magic."

"Kariarn took me to watch his basilisk eat Landislaw

whole. It just engulfed him, like a snake eating a mouse."
Even saying it made me feel ill.

"Why didn't he chain you up again?" asked Tosten, who
knew who Landislaw was but had never met him, leaving
him unmoved to the boy's fate.

"Because he wants Shavig, and he thinks Hurog will
sway the other Northlanders, something we may have to
thank Duraugh for," I answered, glad to change the subject.
Much better to worry about Kariarn then to continue to
think about Landislaw slowly dissolving inside the
basilisk. "Give me a few moments to think."

They were silent as I ran through possibilities in my
head.

There was a game that my aunt taught me to play once.
It involved taking a skip-stone board and imagining all the
possible combinations of play.

Kariarn was leaving for Hurog very soon, and Garranon
and his wife would be dead before Kariarn left: He could
not afford to leave the Lord of Buril alive. So Oreg would
have to get them out of the keep.

Kariarn's abrupt delay of his plans for Oranstone after
Bastilla brought us here puzzled me. Kariarn couldn't have
had a better setup to take Oranstone. But Haverness might
discover Kariarn's people here anytime. And Kariarn was
going to risk that in order to get dragon bones out of Hurog?

Obsessions, I thought, *this is all about obsessions*. Kariarn wanted magic more than he wanted Oranstone. "What
will he do with the bones?"

"Bastilla thinks drinking powdered dragon bones could
make her the most powerful wizard alive," said Tosten.
"She was gloating over it."

"What would it do for someone who could not work
magic?" I asked.

"It could turn him into a mage for a time," answered
Oreg. "But he'd have to continue consuming the bones to
keep his powers. Eventually, it would kill him."

"Oreg, if you were at Hurog, could you keep the wizards from finding the dragon?" I asked. "Bastilla left a strand of hair in the cave."

"Possibly," he said. "How many wizards does he have?"

"How many could you defeat?"

"If I were in the keep, I could keep three or four of Bastilla's caliber out for a few days. If I could find her hair and get rid of it, much longer."

"Could you destroy the dragon bones?" I asked.

He shook his head. "No."

I nodded and dropped back into thought.

"Ward? Why did Bastilla have Penrod try to kill you?" asked Tosten. "She knew Kariarn wanted the bones, and you were the best way to get them."

"What?" asked Oreg.

I hadn't had time to think about it, but Tosten was right. It was strange. I told Oreg about Penrod's attack and how my brother had saved me.

I thought about the odd look I'd seen on Bastilla's face in Haverness's great hall while I'd been laughing with Tisala and of her reaction when I'd explained why I could not be her lover. Had she been so angry with me that she would risk Kariarn's wrath to kill me?

"I suspect Kariarn doesn't know anything about it," I said. "I wonder how much she can do outside his orders?" Oreg just shook his head, so I put the problem of Bastilla aside and thought about more immediate concerns.

Garranon, his wife, and Tosten had to get to safety. I would risk my life but not my brother's. With him safe, I could go with Kariarn to Hurog. Kariarn would destroy my home in order to get the dragon bones; if I were there with Oreg, destroying Hurog would not be necessary.

"The king," I said slowly to myself, not to my audience. "The king killed our cousin and took Hurog from me, which absolves me of oaths taken as the Hurogmeten's heir. Kariarn proposes to return Hurog to me if I support him."

Tosten staggered to his feet. "Ward . . . Don't do it. You can't trust him."

"No," I agreed mildly. "But then, he can't trust me, either. He's going to attack Hurog one way or the other. I need to be there, and the fastest way to Hurog is to ride with him."

Tosten frowned at me.

"However," I said, staring at the wall again, "when I tell you my intentions, you become enraged and hit me with—" I looked around and found a new item in the cell that had been added to increase our creature comforts. "—with the chamber pot, knocking me unconscious. You escape the cell by some ingenious method. . . ." I stared at the door, but it looked solid. There was no bar on it, though, just a large iron lock.

"Tosten spent a lot of time on the waterfront," said Oreg. "Waterfront rats have all sorts of useful skills."

I gave Tosten an interested look, and he squirmed. "All right. I know how to pick most locks if you give me a day or two."

"I can do it faster," offered Oreg.

I grinned. "So, thinking he's killed me, Tosten gets the door open and searches through the rooms up here until he finds Garranon and his lady—because Garranon knows how to get out."

Tosten drew a deep breath. "I know Oreg will go with you . . . but are you sure you don't want me, too? I make a fair backup." It amazed me, coming out of Tosten. Not the offer, but the manner in which he offered it, his quiet acknowledgment that Oreg would be more help.

"I need Oreg because of Bastilla and Hurog," I said. "I need you because you can show Garranon back to Tisala and safety. I need you because Beckram likes you, and he just might listen to you tell him a crazy tale about runaway slaves who are spies and dragon bones hidden in the heart of Hurog. Get him to gather the Blue Guard and force-march to Hurog."

He gave me a wary look and checked my face for sincerity. Then he straightened his shoulders and nodded. I'd given him a task to do. I'd gotten him out of danger, especially since there was absolutely no way he could travel all the way back to Callis, get Beckram, and ride to Hurog before Kariarn got us all on ships and sailed into Tyrfannig harbor. Geography had never been his strong point. He'd be angry, but he'd be safe.

When Oreg opened the door after a bit of magic at the lock, we could hear the guards at the bottom of the stairs. We kept quiet as we began to search the other rooms on the same floor. Garranon and his wife were in the second cell we found. Oreg had no more trouble with that lock than he'd had with ours.

I pulled the door open and stepped inside, just missing being brained with a (thankfully empty) chamber pot. Originality aside, chamber pots are heavy enough to make good weapons.

I grabbed it before Garranon's wife could try it again. "Stop it," I said in a hushed voice.

"I'm the only one who gets to brain Ward tonight," said Tosten, stepping through the doorway. He bowed to her. "I am Tosten of Hurog, and you must be Garranon's wife."

"What are you doing?" asked Garranon from the shadows. He didn't sound happy, but he was quiet. I released his wife but kept the chamber pot.

"Rescuing you," I replied. "You don't think Kariarn's going to let you live, do you?"

Oreg started working on the chains that held Garranon, and I set the chamber pot on the floor.

"I know him," said Garranon's wife, nodding at me though speaking to her husband. "But who are the other two?"

Garranon, shaking free of his chains, peered first at

Oreg then Tosten. "They're all Hurogs . . . but none that I've met."

It wasn't rudeness that kept me from making formal introductions; I just couldn't remember Garranon's wife's name, and I couldn't take the shortcut of calling her Lady Buril or Lady Garranon, because Oranstonian custom didn't work that way.

After an awkward moment, I said. "You'll have to introduce me again to your wife, sir. Then I'll make known my kinsmen."

A brief smile crossed Garranon's face. "May I present my wife, the Lady Allysaian." There was more affection in his voice than I expected, given the nature of his relationship with the king.

I bowed and waved an arm at my brother. "Lady Allysaian, Lord Garranon, may I present my brother Tosten, your rescuer."

In the cell amid chamber pots and straw, Allysaian curtseyed, and Tosten bowed. Garranon said incredulously, "He's dead."

I grinned. "Hurog has a reputation for ghosts, sir. Lady Allysaian, Lord Garranon, may I present my kinsman, Oreg, who is also a wizard."

"Indeed?" Garranon murmured. "How useful."

"Now," I said. "Is there a way out of here, or does Oreg have to see if he can spirit you out?"

"And leave Buril in the hands of the Vorsag?" asked Garranon.

"Not much you can do about it at the moment," observed Oreg.

The Oranstonian stared at Oreg, a muscle twitching in his jaw. Then he turned his attention back to me. "So you are going with Kariarn. And you rescue us because . . . ?"

"Because it is the right thing to do."

He laughed, a quiet, disbelieving sound. "I might have believed that of the simpleton you played, but you lie too well, Lord Wardwick. Kariarn has offered you the same deal he offered my brother. You have seen the results. But you're willing to risk it for Hurog, aren't you?"

Tosten drew in a sharp breath, as if he'd just realized how great a temptation Kariarn had offered me.

I nodded my head, unwilling to take time to argue. "Figure it out for yourself. My brother will take you to where Haverness's daughter's troops are gathered. She'll see to it her father knows about Buril."

Garranon's eyebrows rose. "Then you go to Hurog. Kariarn breaks in, takes whatever it is that he wants from your keep—"

"Dragon bones," whispered Oreg.

Garranon continued without pause. "—and your uncle is killed in the battle. You get Hurog."

Tosten stiffened, looking at me wild-eyed. I guess he'd forgotten about Uncle Duraugh.

It hurt that he could believe I would kill our uncle to get Hurog. But there was a part of me that anticipated my uncle's death. Oh, not that I would kill my uncle, but that he would be killed in some way I could not prevent. The hero (me) returns and triumphs over evil, and Hurog is mine. Mine.

And that's why I didn't bother to defend myself.

Garranon gave me a shadowed look and turned to Tosten. "There's a passage from the next room over."

"IT'S VERY STRANGE," SAID OREG ONCE HE'D LOCKED the two of us back in my cell and picked up the chamber pot.

"What is?" I asked.

"The way you've convinced everyone, including yourself, that the two of us can stop Kariarn and his whole army."

"I don't have to stop his army," I explained. "All I have to do is get Duraugh to evacuate Hurog rather than fight for it. All Kariarn wants is the dragon bones. He'll take them and leave Hurog."

"So you're going to let Kariarn take the bones?" Oreg tapped the chamber pot unhappily on his thigh.

"It's the only way I see for Hurog to survive."

Oreg stared at me, but in the poor light of the sputtering torches, I couldn't see the expression on his face. In the quiet, I could hear the murmur of voices as several men came up the stairs.

"The chamber pot—hit me," I said, bending my knees so Oreg could get a good angle. "I can fake unconsciousness, but it's got to be hard enough to raise a bump."

Oreg stared at the chamber pot. "I could still get you out of here. We could get Beckram and bring an army to defeat Kariarn."

I straightened. "Buril is only three or four leagues from the sea. With the wizards for communication, Kariarn'll have a fleet at the nearest port waiting for him. Beckram is at Callis. He'll have to travel overland."

Oreg worked it out for himself. "It'll take him at least a week longer to get to Hurog than it'll take Kariarn."

I nodded. "Hurog isn't ready for a siege. It won't last a week."

The guards had gone to Garranon's cell. I could hear them shouting, and I bent down again. "Do it."

"So the Hurogmeten sacrifices the dragon again," said Oreg.

I caught a better look at his face as he raised the chamber pot over his head. What I saw there told me that Oreg wasn't unhappy about the opportunity to hit me. As it turned out, I didn't have to fake anything at all.

14

WARDWICK

It always takes me a few days of sailing before I quit trying to jettison last week's dinner.

MY STOMACH TOLD ME I WAS ABOARD A SHIP BEFORE I opened my eyes to see Bastilla sitting cross-legged on the floor beside my bunk, wearing boy's clothes and looking very much like the woman who had traveled halfway across the Five Kingdoms with me.

She smiled. "Good morning, Ward. How's your head?"

I returned her smile before I remembered what she was. I touched my head gingerly but could find no bump.

"I healed you," she said. "I'm sorry Tosten was so angry that you chose to follow my master. He gave you quite a concussion. My master thought you should sleep until we reached the sea, so I let you rest."

"How do you know Tosten was angry?" I'd planned upon that interpretation, but she sounded so certain.

"When I healed you," she said, patting my knee, "I picked up on your emotions. I felt how much he hurt you."

Tosten had said she invaded his mind when she healed him. Just how much did she know?

"He doesn't understand what Hurog means to me," I

said tentatively. Her normalcy so contrasted with the picture of her kissing Kariarn's boots, it was hard to believe it was both the same person.

She nodded her head sympathetically. "He'll come around; he idolizes you. After Duraugh is dead, he can put it behind him." So she hadn't read me enough to know that Duraugh's death was one of the things I hoped to stop by traveling with Kariarn.

Everyone seemed to think that I could just throw away my uncle's life in order to satisfy my own ambitions. I don't know why I cared what Bastilla thought; maybe it was just confirmation of Tosten's opinion that hurt.

"Does King Kariarn know you tried to kill me?" I asked.

She dropped her head so I couldn't see her expression. "That was very bad of me," she said. Then she met my gaze and laughed. "Did you think you would get away with flirting with Haverness's cow after refusing me? And you suffered. I saw it on your face when Penrod died." She sounded like my mother talking about her garden. "Poor Penrod. I had thought to use him to kill your wizard, but the opportunity, with us so close to my master, was difficult to resist. He fought me, though. I don't think I could have gotten him to do more than wound you before he broke the hold, but Tosten made that a moot point, don't you think?" She smiled again at the expression on my face and ran her fingertip around the outside of my ear. "I told you that you'd regret how you treated me. But—" There was a repellent eagerness in her eyes. "—if you tell my master, I'm sure he'll punish me. Speaking of whom, I'd better tell him you have awakened."

Wordlessly I nodded.

She shut the door behind her, but I couldn't tell if she locked it or not.

Oreg appeared sitting in the same place she'd just been. "He told her to make you comfortable."

I shivered, and Oreg patted my knee the same way Bastilla had. I jerked away, because I hadn't been able to jerk away from her.

"Did Tosten get away?"

"Yes." He shifted on the bed, not looking at me. "I'm sorry I hit you so hard."

I remembered what our last words had been, and why Oreg had been upset. "Oreg, I wouldn't let him take the bones if I could see a way around it."

He nodded his head, not looking at me. "What are you going to do about Duraugh?"

Tosten, Bastilla, and now Oreg, I thought. It didn't help that the rocking of the boat had begun to make me nauseated. Thoroughly miserable and wanting to hurt him back, I said, "I'll kill him if Kariarn doesn't take care of it for me. He's the last thing standing between me and Hurog. If I have to sacrifice everyone left at Hurog to regain my birthright, well then, I guess that's what I'll do." I thought he'd catch the sarcasm, but he left instead. *Even Oreg,* I thought, *even Oreg believes me capable of killing Duraugh.*

THE NEXT FEW WEEKS WERE GRIM.

If I went onto the deck, I had to talk with Kariarn with Bastilla always nearby. I had to be very careful not to do anything that would tell her I was not Kariarn's ardent supporter. Bastilla, herself, behaved as if nothing had changed, forcing me to do the same.

I'd grown used to being less guarded, and the old cautions learned from my father's treatment sat upon me like a hair shirt. I don't think I could have done it if I hadn't wanted what Kariarn offered so much. It gave me a truth to blind him with.

Kariarn proved his reputation for charm. He asked me soft-voiced questions and listened while I ranted and

stormed about the idiots around me—the way I'd always
wanted to rant about them. I told him of my ambitions and
how much Hurog meant to me. I even told him about my
father. I talked myself so raw that when I went to my cabin
and Oreg's accusing silence, I couldn't bring myself to
confront Oreg about his assumptions.

His distrust hurt almost as much as the loss of Hurog.
Again. I'd resigned myself to it at Silverfells, but that
didn't mean it didn't hurt when Kariarn dangled it in
front of me.

I stood near the prow one evening, the setting sun on my
left sending red fingers out into the darkening sea. The air
was chill on the water and blew my hair away from my
face.

"You can't make the ship go faster by willing it," said
Kariarn, approaching me from behind.

Nor could I make it any slower. Last night I'd overheard
the Seaford-born sail master say we were making good
time.

"I'm getting tired of the food," I said truthfully.

Oreg wasn't speaking to me except when I demanded it.
I wondered bitterly if Oreg would tell some long-distant
Hurogmeten about Wardwick, who betrayed dragonkind
one final time. But Oreg wasn't without companionship.
He'd made friends of the shy trillies who lived in the dark-
est bowels of the ship: I'd seen one of the gray green, rat-
like creatures scamper off his lap when I came into our
cabin one evening.

It was shortly after that the food began to suffer from
rot, rats, and weevils. My blankets were always damp. Rats
got into my trunk and put a hole into every garment I
owned. I made Oreg repair them. It might have been just
ship's luck, but I suspected Oreg or his trillies, who were
fully capable of such mischief and weren't bound by the
ring to serve me.

"I've spoken to the shipmaster about his food storage,"

said Kariarn amiably. I gave an inward shudder and silent apology to the poor unfortunate. "I've sent a boat out to the *Sea-Singer* to get some supplies so at least we'll have good food tonight."

There were six ships, including ours. Two hundred fifty men in each ship except for the *Serpent*, which carried a hundred men, the basilisk, and fifty horses (officers' horses—Pansy had been left behind at Buril). Fourteen hundred men, of which about two-thirds were actually fighting men (the rest being cooks, messengers, smiths, grooms, and the like)—so almost a thousand men and a monster to take Hurog. Duraugh had, at best, one hundred twenty, and he was missing Stala and fifty of the Blue Guard.

I kept my gaze on the sea.

"I've always hated to travel by water," Kariarn said, setting his arms over the railing and leaning out into the wind.

"You get seasick?" I asked, though I hadn't seen any sign of it in him.

"No more than you." Kariarn grinned. I smiled back. No one knew about the night I'd spent throwing up. Oreg had helped me dispose of the mess quietly, though I'd had to order him to do it. He'd spared no sympathy on a Hurogmeten who'd betray his own. "It's just—" Kariarn said, "that I hate being dependent on something I can't control."

I laughed and turned toward him. "Me, too."

"You look sad, sometimes," he said. "Bastilla thinks that you worry about your uncle."

I nodded my head. "Sometimes. But he took Hurog from me." I met Kariarn's eye. If anyone knew about obsessions, it was he. "I cowered beneath my father's hand, gave up my very identity to keep Hurog. I won't let Duraugh take it from me."

He touched my arm, then after a moment gave me an affectionate shove. "I can't believe that you don't know where the dragon bones are." He'd said similar things before, and I gave him the same excuse as always.

"I'd just found out about them myself a few weeks before Bastilla came. Oreg belonged to my father before me." And his father before him, but Kariarn didn't need to know that. "My father's mishandling of him has made him all but useless to me. It's taken me a long time to get Oreg to trust me with the secrets of Hurog."

"So you think there are more secrets?" His response was so idle, so harmless sounding, that I had to go over what I'd said in my head to find what had triggered his oh so very casual interest.

Secrets. Plague it. To a man obsessed with magic, secrets meant magic. I'd never get him out of Hurog if he thought there was something else there, especially since there was nothing else to be found.

I nodded my head and gave him the truth. "My grandfather sold all the important stuff—four suits of dwarvenmade mail, every artifact that his wizards could find touched with magic, most of the valuable tapestries—to get Hurog through two bad seasons half a century ago. But according to the keep's accounts, there were two thousand pieces of silver left over. I know my father had access to them from his notes in the account book. There should be almost twelve hundred left, and they weren't in the regular coffers. I'd bet gems to sweetmeat that Oreg knows where it's stored. That would buy enough sheep to start a fairsized herd. It's sheep that'll restore prosperity to Hurog, you know," I confided at my usual pace. The expression of interest on his face became fixed, but I continued anyway. "My father and grandfather tried it with horses, but they are labor intensive. You don't get good money out of them unless they're trained. Sheep, on the other hand . . ." I watched the interest die out of Kariarn's eyes as I waxed enthusiastic about sheep breeding.

●　　　●　　　●

OREG WAS STANDING IN MY CABIN WHEN I PULLED my shirt off over my head, though I'd been alone when I grabbed the bottom of it.

"You usually abbreviate what you say so that you don't drive people to drink by how slowly you talk, don't you?" He observed. "Did you notice the grip Kariarn had on his knife while you told him about the difference between Northern Avinhellish sheep and Southern Avinhellish sheep?"

It was the longest speech he'd made to me since I'd awakened aboard ship. It made me wary.

"So what do you have planned next?" I asked in mild tones. This evening had been tiring, and I wasn't in the mood to ignore him anymore. "You could have the trillies rot the rope holding up my hammock so it dumps me on the floor tonight." I'd abandoned the bed for a hammock because it helped hold the seasickness at bay.

His eyes widened at my words, so I tugged hard on the top of my hammock (as opposed to the bottom, which would only dump me feetfirst) and at the second jerk, the hook holding the hammock to the upper deck pulled out of the beam. It was the wood, not the rope that had rotted.

I pulled my clothing trunk over and used it to stand on while I moved the hook to the next board over without saying a word. When I was satisfied the hook would hold my weight, I moved the chest back to where it had been and sat on it. It was time to negotiate. I needed Oreg if I were to save Hurog, so I couldn't afford to sulk anymore.

"I know you don't want to give the dragon bones to Kariarn, but I don't see any way to prevent it," I said.

"She was beautiful," he replied obscurely. "Rose and gold with a voice that made the waves leap to her music. And Seleg killed her for fear of losing Hurog. He wept and sorrowed, then justified his actions. He cursed his family even down to this generation, and he justified it because he didn't want to admit he'd been too frightened that he would lose Hurog to the invaders to try to stop them without the magic he gained from the dragon's death." Oreg took a small step away from me. "He'd learned by then what killing the dragon meant. The Hurog bloodline was thick with wizards, but Seleg was the last wizard born to your family until your birth."

I stared at him, remembering little things he'd told me, things Axiel had told me. "That's what drove the dwarves away, wasn't it? Not that the dragon had been killed. If they'd have known that Seleg killed the dragon, the dwarves would have attacked Hurog, and there's no record of it. But the dragon's death did something to Hurog. Something that made the dwarves grow ill and stunted their magic." Oreg nodded. I took a deep breath. "That's what caused the mines to quit producing and brought salt creep to the best fields. I've seen the records of the crops that used to come from those fields. We bring in less than half of that on a good year."

"Yes," whispered Oreg.

I stood up and began to pace. "It's not just the dwarven kingdoms though, is it? I stood on top of the remains of the temple at Menogue and looked down on Estian. It's shrinking and has been for a long time. It's not just Hurog that's become less than it was, but it's spreading from Hurog."

"Yes," whispered Oreg again.

"And the curse on the family isn't just that there are no more Hurog mages. I remember my mother when she was happy, but the longer she stayed at Hurog, the stranger she got. Then there is my father." I remembered what the Oreg I'd dreamed of had told me about Hurog. I said, "Hurog poisons the people who live there. My grandfather had eight legitimate children of whom only two survived childhood: my father and his brother, who were sent out for fostering at a very young age. Ciarra can't speak, and Tosten was suicidal." The strain of the voyage was telling on my temper so that the results of that ancient stupidity made me want to hit something.

"And you lost the ability to work magic."

I waved my hand, and all of the oil lamps in the room flared brightly. "Not completely."

Staring at him, I realized that the reason he hadn't moved was because he was afraid of me. I'd been agitated and ranting like my father used to, and for little cause besides stress and fatigue. I inhaled and closed my eyes and carefully pruned away the anger I felt toward Seleg, who hadn't been the hero I needed him to be; toward my father; my mother; and finally, toward Hurog, whose magic filled my soul and took my sister's voice and my mother's reason; but most of all at Oreg, who hadn't believed in me.

"Anger is stupid, and stupidity will kill you more surely than your opponent's blade." My aunt's voice echoed in my head, and so I pushed anger aside with reason. It was not Seleg's fault I'd chosen him for my hero. It was not my fault my father had hated me, and my mother had run away. When I was certain it was gone, I looked again at Oreg, who'd been betrayed far more than I.

"I can't change what Seleg did," I said at last. "There is nothing I can do to make it right."

Oreg's purple eyes were still wide with fear or some other strong emotion, watching me so he could tell which way to jump.

"I could have you get the two of us into Hurog when we are close enough. We could help my uncle hold her."

"Duraugh can't hold Hurog, Ward," said Oreg. "There are too many here. Even with all of the Blue Guard, Hurog could not withstand this many men. Not in its current state. It's not ready for a siege."

I thought again. "Could you move the bones out?"

He shook his head. "Out of the cave and its protections, every wizard within a hundred miles could find the bones, but it doesn't matter. Seleg bound me past my death to keep the bones hidden in the heart of Hurog."

"Do you see any options that would keep Kariarn from the bones?" I asked.

"No." He turned his head away from me.

"Oreg." I waited. "Oreg."

Finally, he looked at me.

I cleared my throat to hide how much his answer mattered to me. "Do you think that I would kill my uncle just to become Hurogmeten again?"

His face worked suddenly, and he dropped to his knees before me. "I believe that you would never have killed a dragon to save yourself. I believe that you would never knowingly betray a trust."

It was a powerful speech, and I wanted to believe him, but I'd been around slaves. They told their masters what they thought their masters wanted to hear, then tried to believe it themselves.

When he looked up, there was a strange expression on his face, one I'd never seen there before. It took me a moment to identify it as hope. "You would not betray Hurog," he said. "You would do the right thing, no matter what the consequences." There was something about the way he said it that made me want to question him, as if his words meant more than they said.

From the shadows beyond the chest, a shadow darted, chittering loudly, distracting me. Oreg laughed suddenly and picked up the trillie, ruffling the gray green fur behind the rodent face. He said something to it and set it down to disappear once more in the shadows of the cabin.

He pulled up his knees and buried his face in them. His shoulders shook with—laughter. "There's a rotten fish in your blankets," he said.

•   •   •

"THE SAIL MASTER SAYS WE'LL REACH TYRFANNIG tomorrow—probably very early morning," I said, watching Oreg, who lay on the hammock belly first, swinging it back and forth while he stared at the floor. It was black as pitch outside, but the little oil lamp was sufficient to light a larger space than my cabin.

"What?" he said. Apparently the floor was more interesting than I was.

"Quit watching the cracks go past, and listen to me." I paced as I spoke. Two strides, heel-turn, two strides, heel-turn. Our cabin was the second largest on the ship, but that wasn't saying much. "As soon as you can, transport yourself to Tyrfannig and warn them about the Vorsag. Have the headman send a message to my uncle and—"

"Calm yourself, Ward," soothed Oreg, rolling over and bouncing out of the hammock in one easy motion, effectively stopping my pacing because there was no more room. "I know, I'm to tell the townspeople to hide themselves until the armies have passed by. Then, as soon as we're close enough, I'll transport both of us to Hurog and you can warn Duraugh."

Something about Oreg had changed in the last few days. Perhaps it was just that he trusted me; but I'd never seen him in such calm good humor. It made me nervous. All right, more nervous. Waves of panicky self-doubt had been rolling over me since I awoke on board Kariarn's ship. My plans were so tenuous as to be laughable. Nothing I could do would guarantee my uncle's safety.

Even without experience in siege warfare, I knew that Hurog couldn't stand off a siege before harvest. So the only answer was to get the people away from Hurog and hope that Kariarn would leave with the bones. Oreg seemed strangely unworried about that part for all of his earlier histrionics. He spoke confidently of our weak plans, while *I* wasn't even certain my uncle would trust me when I told him to get our people out of Hurog.

"If I'd slept with Bastilla, she might not have gone back to Kariarn," I threw myself back on the bed, since Oreg had the hammock.

"It wouldn't have mattered, Ward. She is bound to him."

"Could you have broken the binding, Oreg?"

"If she wanted it badly enough," he answered. "But she didn't."

His reasonableness made me furious, and I curled my hands into fists, just as my father always had before he lost his temper. The thought forced me to stretch my fingers out and flatten them against the narrow mattress. "I'm sorry, Oreg. Just jitters. I just wish I knew what was going to happen."

Some fleeting emotion crossed his face. "All things happen in their own time, whether you want them to or not."

He stiffened suddenly, lifting his head and staring at nothing. "We've come farther than I thought. I can warn Tyrfannig now."

"Go," I commanded, but he was already gone.

I took in a deep, shaky breath. It had begun. I didn't know whether I felt better or worse.

THERE WERE NO SHIPS AT THE MOORING WHEN WE sailed within sight of Tyrfannig. Nor were the dockworkers there. It didn't hamper Kariarn's ships. They weighed anchor offshore and sent eel boats to transport troops and mounts to land.

"Is it always so quiet here?" asked Kariarn from the prow of our ship.

I shook my head, watching the Vorsagian eel boats. They didn't look a lot like eels, being much broader and flatter than anything a Northlander would sail. In the season of storms, they'd be capsized, but it was calm today, and they slid through the waves as if they were negotiating the southern seas.

"Where are all the people?"

"My brother must have gotten a message to Duraugh," I said without concern. "Look at that! If they're not careful, that horse is going to—ah, they got the blindfold on. Could have lost the boat."

"A message!" said Kariarn. "What message? How many troops could he muster?"

I rolled my eyes at him and said, "My uncle has a wizard, and so does Haverness. I would suppose from the results in front of us that Haverness's man sent a message to my uncle's." Inside, I felt a flash of hope. I'd forgotten about the wizards.

"Bastilla?" he asked.

She shook her head. "My sources say Duraugh's wizard is inept, and Haverness's man has no talent for farspeaking. I suppose Oreg might . . ." She looked at me.

I shrugged. "He might be able to do it; he likes to be mysterious. It doesn't matter. Tyrfannig has no fighters except ten or twenty mercenaries hired to escort merchants. This late in the summer there won't be many. My uncle has only half the Blue Guard."

"He has another estate."

"Iftahar in Tallven," I answered. We'd already discussed this. I wasn't the only one nervous about the assault—if for different reasons. It was hard to remember that Kariarn was little older than I. "Even if he had time to bring them all in, he would not have half the men you bring against him."

"If a messenger could get through so fast, so also could troops."

"Not so." I raised my voice a bit impatiently. "You know how much longer an army takes to cover so much territory. There are supply wagons that have to be taken on real roads—or at least decent trails. They'd be lucky to make five leagues a day. They won't be here for another week at the very least. By that time, Hurog will be mine, and I'll welcome them in, having supposedly driven your troops off."

On the ship nearest to us, Kariarn's wizards brought the basilisk on deck. It was longer than any of the eel boats, but they appeared to be trying to get it in one anyway. The long, slender boat swayed wildly on the pulleys that would lower it into the sea as soon as it was loaded. The basilisk was so heavy that the ship it was on dipped dangerously toward us as the creature's position threw the ship off balance. A big wave at the wrong angle would capsize it.

The basilisk remained motionless, all four legs spread out to support it against the motion of the ship. At long last, it dashed across the deck and into the eel boat. But it didn't even hesitate aboard the rocking vessel but slid over the edge and disappeared into the sea. Who would have thought stone dragons could swim?

Kariarn swore and dashed to the side of the boat nearest the beast. I followed him in time to see the basilisk dive under our ship, hitting it solidly with its tail. I grabbed the rail as the ship wallowed, instinctively grabbing Kariarn before he went over.

He didn't pause to thank me but ran to the other side. The basilisk surfaced near the rock-strewn shore and climbed out of the water. It settled on the rocks and closed its jewel-toned eyes, blending so thoroughly that if I hadn't seen him move to the spot, I wouldn't have known he was there.

A heavy hand slapped my shoulder.

"Thanks for keeping me from falling in." Kariarn grinned at me.

I grinned back and wondered if he would have drowned if I let him go over. Or perhaps I could have jumped in to "rescue" him and made certain of it. But there hadn't been time for thought, and instinct had bade me save him.

"Sire, the boat is ready." One of the sailors approached cautiously.

Kariarn waved at me to precede him. I turned, and darkness pulled over my eyes.

I WOKE UP IN A ROOM THAT WASN'T SURGING WITH the sea. My wrists and ankles were tightly knotted together.

"I'm sorry for this, especially after you've demonstrated your good faith," said Kariarn.

I focused on his face. The aftereffects of Bastilla's spell weren't as bad this time. I must have been getting used to it.

"I can't afford to trust you right now," explained Kariarn sincerely. "After we've taken the keep, I'll send some people to get you. Then Bastilla and my mages will pretend to help you take back the keep with a few impressive shows of magic. You'll be quite safe here. No one but my men will know that you've been our prisoner. Even if some of the Tyrfannig people return, I'm leaving the basilisk in the main room, just outside your door. My mages tell me that it's become harder to control and is as likely to kill my army as it is your uncle's, so it will serve as a guardian for you. To keep you safe."

I nodded my head—slowly, so the pulsing pain didn't get worse. "I understand. Just be sure you take the keep. Wouldn't want to be stuck here until the basilisk gets hungry."

Kariarn laughed and left the room, Bastilla trailing behind him.

"They made a mistake taking the basilisk here," said Oreg, emerging from the shadows after the bolt slid home. "I thought they might have trouble. The land here, even so far from Hurog, is steeped in dragon magic, which is close kin to that of the basilisk. I doubt they have *any* control of her now, whatever they think. You're not the only one who's able to play stupid."

"Did you get everyone out?"

"I carried a message from your uncle to the headman, who can read, bless his merchant's heart," he said.

"A message from my uncle?"

"Bearing his seal and in his own writing," confirmed Oreg. "Forgery is one of my many talents. At Duraugh's command, the Tyrfannig citizens have taken to the hills where they cannot be easily found." He took a slender dagger out of his boot and sliced the bindings on my wrists and ankles.

We'd decided not to send a message for Hurog. A message alone wouldn't give Duraugh cause enough to leave Hurog; I wouldn't do it myself. "Can you get to Hurog to warn them, too?"

"No."

I stopped rubbing my wrists and said, "No?" My stomach clenched. Kariarn's people would slaughter my . . . my uncle's people.

"It is too far from you. I can't do it."

I cleared my mind of panic. "Then we'll just have to get close enough to do it. When Kariarn clears out of Tyrfannig, break us out of here and . . . Why are you shaking your head?"

"She's spelled the building against your escape. It's specific, so it's nearly impossible to counterspell without alerting her. I think she suspects that you know a lot more magic than you do. Maybe it was the pyre at Silverfells."

"So you can come and go, but not far enough to do us any good. And I can't leave without alerting Bastilla. Should we worry about her?"

He nodded. "With the number of wizards Kariarn has, if they know what we're about, they can probably stop us. But she was working fast, and the spells on the doors are not holding. Doors are meant to let people in and out, and their nature fights against imprisoning spells."

"The outside door is past the basilisk," I said. "You said she was smarter than Kariarn believes. Could we negotiate?"

He shook his head. "She won't negotiate with her food. But if I can touch her for a few minutes, I can control her."

"Even here? Where there is dragon magic?"

Oreg smiled, "Especially here."

"So all I need to do is distract it for a while."

With the same magic that allowed me to find lost things, I found where the basilisk was, waiting outside about ten feet from the door. I still wasn't used to having my magic back: I knew *exactly* where it was. Surely there would be some way to use that. And, as if it had been just this afternoon that Tosten and I fought blind, I knew what I could do. Before I'd seen it come off the ship, I'd have been a lot more confident of my chances.

There was a broom leaning against one corner of the room where Oreg and I were held. It wasn't much of a weapon—more of a stick than a staff. And I would have to try it blindfolded, using my magic to tell me where it was.

"Give me your shirt," I said at last.

"Why?"

"Because I don't want to end up like Landislaw. I need to cover my eyes."

"What about your shirt?" he said as he complied with my request.

"I'd rather have some protection if it hits me. I trust you'll spell the creature soon as you can." I took the broom and gave it a thwack against the wall. It bent, but it didn't break. Beyond the wooden walls, the basilisk moved restlessly. "It sounds like there is a lot of space out there. Are we in one of the warehouses at the docks?"

Oreg nodded. "Cleaned for the new harvest."

There was no time to waste. Kariarn and his army could

be at Hurog by early evening, even on horses that were weak from the sea voyage. We had to beat him there.

I took Oreg's shirt and ripped several ragged strips off of it until I could fashion a blindfold. Oreg led me to the door the Basilisk waited behind. My knowledge of magic hadn't increased with my abilities, but *finding* had always been mine.

Where was the basilisk?

As before, the response I got back was better than sight. I hoped.

"Open the door," I said.

He threw it open, hard, and the basilisk retreated enough for me to get out into the open room.

"Yeah! Over here!" I shouted, anything to get its attention.

It moved toward me slowly. Oreg had said it wasn't stupid. I backed away from it and bumped into something unexpected: an upright timber, identified by a brush with the back of my hand. I dodged behind it, and something hit the timber hard enough to crack it. The basilisk cried out either in anger or in pain and darted forward with that sudden swiftness it was capable of. I ran at it.

Running away from it was out of the question. I'd likely brain myself on one of the support posts or run into the wall. Magic told me where the basilisk was, but I couldn't see warped floorboards or walls at the same time.

I thumped it hard on the nose, and my broomstick broke. Before I could think anything but an astonished, *help,* something my finding sense insisted was taller than me and about to hurt me badly swept in from my left. I jumped, lifting my feet as high as I could, tucking them like a horse going over a fence.

It caught my heel; the force of the blow stretched me flat out in the air and tossed me away from the basilisk. I tucked, but unable to see the ground, I landed badly, slamming my head on the ground. Instinct forced me to my feet, but I was dazed and unable to recover my sense of where the basilisk was.

Something flickered over my face, and sheer terror brought me to my senses. I'd seen the basilisk tongue Landislaw's face before eating him. Seeing me standing still, the basilisk must have assumed I was caught in its gaze.

Urgently, I called my magic, *found* the basilisk, and dove beneath its head. Blindfolded I might have been, but terror showed me its gaping jaws as I rolled on the ground beneath it.

Startled by my action, it didn't move for just long enough for me to get a firm grip on a hind leg. I hadn't realized I was still holding the broken stick until I had to drop it to secure my hold on the basilisk's leg.

I'd underestimated the creature's flexibility. It reached over with its other hind leg and caught my back with a sharp claw. If I'd have held on, I think I would have been dead. But my aunt's drills were firmly fixed in my body's reflexes, and I went with the force of the blow rather than resisting it. I let go of the leg and flung myself forward onto the ground and rolled to my feet. At which point I scurried away like a rabbit, hands outstretched to hit wall or support beam before my face did. When I reached the wall, I turned, panting.

Once again, I'd lost the sense of where the creature was. The warehouse was silent except for the slight sound of clicking scales, but I couldn't be sure which direction it was coming from. Something warm and wet dripped down my leg from my back. I couldn't tell how much damage the basilisk had done.

"I've got her," Oreg said. "You can take off the blindfold."

"Now what do we do with it?" I took off my blindfold in time to see Oreg slide down her shoulder onto the floor.

"She'll die here; the climate is too cool." He frowned at her.

"Does it eat things other than people?" I asked. I was all for helping rare creatures, but I wasn't going to inflict it on a helpless village.

Oreg slanted me a humorous glance. "Sometimes. I think I'll take the same tack some long-ago wizard did."

He drew in a deep breath and put his hands on its side. I closed my eyes, trying to hide my ecstasy as Oreg's magic swept into the room like a warm wind, filling the empty places in my soul that leaving Hurog had made. I drew that warmth around me as if it were a blanket.

"To stone," said Oreg in old Shavig. There was such power in his voice I had to open my eyes.

Magic glittered like a golden fog over the room, covering Oreg, the basilisk, and me as Oreg used it to draw patterns over the basilisk scales. As I watched, the basilisk began to draw into itself, changing color from forest green to gray as delicate scale edges blurred and disappeared.

When at last the magic was gone and Oreg and I stood alone in the storage room, the basilisk was nothing more than a boulder less than half the size the creature had been. The dirt floor under the stone was muddy.

Oreg flexed his hands and stretched his neck, as if working magic had tightened his muscles.

"We've got to go," I said.

Oreg nodded. "I'll just see that Kariarn's mages don't wake her again." He made an abrupt pushing motion, and the stone sank through the wet ground until there was nothing left of it but a dark stain on the earth that would dry in a few hours.

There was no time to look for horses. After Oreg unspelled the door and wrapped what was left of his shirt around my back, he and I ran down the path Kariarn's army had taken with less than an hour's head start. Holding hope tightly to my chest, I ran as I'd never done before, ignoring burning lungs and burning legs.

After the first few miles, I quit speculating, concentrating only on moving my feet, one after the other. There was a rhythm to running, an echo of the pulse that beat behind my ears.

When Oreg grabbed my arm, I didn't even pause, so I tripped over the stool in my bedroom, where he'd brought us, and I landed hard on the stone floor.

My room smelled musty, as if the servants hadn't aired it out in a long time. Light streaming down from the narrow windows revealed that the surfaces of the furniture had been dusted. "Oreg, where's Duraugh?"

Oreg reached for my arm again. I rolled out of reach and got to my feet before I let him touch me. I was not going to be sitting on the floor when we confronted my uncle.

I don't know what I expected Duraugh to be doing, but it certainly wasn't conferring with Stala in the great hall. Stala should only be halfway here, even if Tosten had managed to sprint all the way to Callis. But Beckram, Axiel, Tosten, and Ciarra were standing on the other side of the table from Duraugh and Stala. Gathering round behind them were eight or ten very short, very broad men. Dwarves. I was still gaping when Tosten looked up and saw Oreg and me.

"How did you get here?" I asked, betraying to Tosten that I had known they wouldn't make it. But somehow they had.

Beckram tilted his head at Axiel, a wry look on his face. "I think that's *our* question. I didn't hear the door open." But he let it go. "You know how some of the Guard say that Axiel, when he is really, really drunk, claims to be the son of the dwarven king?"

"He is," I answered.

Beckram nodded in agreement. "And they have the most interesting method of getting from one place to another."

"Beckram's told me what you've been up to, Ward. Do

you know how many soldiers Kariarn's bringing?" asked Duraugh, breaking into the conversation.

"About a thousand," I said, pulled back to more urgent matters. "And they've just left Tyrfannig. They'll be here by nightfall. Even if you've managed somehow to get the whole of the Blue Guard, you cannot hold Hurog. Unless . . . Axiel, how many of your people are here?"

"Just those you see here. The days when my people could afford to waste lives in armies are long gone, Ward. We've left the rest of the Blue Guard at Callis to come home the slow way."

"Right," I continued after drawing a breath. "So we need to get every person out of Hurog and into hiding in the mountains. Kariarn doesn't want Hurog. He wants something hidden here. He knows where it is, and once he has it, he'll leave. But there is no time to waste. The bronze doors on the mountain make a good place to gather. It's high. You can see for miles if Kariarn sends men up it, and it might be possible to defend it from people attacking from below." It was only as I finished that I realized I was issuing orders.

Duraugh gave me a considering look. My uncle had only known me while I was pretending to be stupid. I didn't know how long Beckram and Tosten had been here nor what kind of story they'd told my uncle, but it must have been something, because he only nodded and said, "If Kariarn is so close, explanations can wait. We'd best get organized."

EVACUATION TOOK MUCH LONGER THAN I WAS comfortable with, but Duraugh was thorough. He mounted all the grooms and sent them and the horses on to Iftahar. We gathered all the foodstuff and anything that could be used as a blanket or a weapon. I found my father's sword and knife in the armory and fastened them on my belt. Kariarn still had mine.

As I strode out of the armory, I came face-to-face with my mother.

She smiled at me vaguely. "When did you get back, Fenwick?"

The skin on the back of my neck crawled. "Mother, I'm Ward. Father is dead."

Her smile widened but didn't cover the blankness of her eyes. "Of course you are. And how is my baby today?"

"There you are, my lady." Her maidservant trotted around the corner of the hall. She shot me a defensive look and wrapped a heavy wool cloak around my mother's shoulders. "Let's get you out to the courtyard." To me she said, "She's been like this for a while. Mostly she doesn't even know where she is."

Oreg appeared at my side, his arms full of blankets.

I took a deep breath. "Are you through gathering things? We need to get to the bailey."

When we got outside of the keep proper, my uncle was already hard at work. Fascinated, I watched Duraugh use the Blue Guard as the base of the troop of soldiers he formed out of household servants. When he was finished, a ragged army marched smartly up the trails to the great doors high in the mountains overlooking Hurog. It was a tricky climb at best, but with such an urgent need for swiftness, I found our pace unbearably slow.

"So," said Beckram marching beside me, carrying a sleepy child of three or four who belonged to one of the kitchen maids, "Did you ever try to dig under the bronze doors?"

I think it was the first time my cousin had sought me out for conversation. I knew he could care less about the doors. It was a peace offering between us.

I accepted it. "No. After you and Erdrick dug that trench around them, my father made me fill in the holes."

He laughed shortly. "Erdrick thought it was a waste of time. *I* did the digging." The child he held peered worriedly into my cousin's face. He smiled at her, and she tucked back down against him. "Why do you think they are there?"

I shrugged and began climbing with him again. I suppose I could ask Oreg. "They've been there a long time, Beckram. I used to think they hid the dwarven ways, but I take it the entrance to the dwarven tunnels is in Hurog itself. The Hurogmeten—my father—said he thought it might have been the grave of some ancient hero." We buried our dead on the side of the hill. Perhaps it was an ancient tradition.

Just ahead of us, my mother fell and wouldn't get up when her maidservant tried to tug her to her feet. Hesitating, I knelt beside her. "Mother?" I said.

Blank eyes stared into mine.

"Aunt, you can't stay here," said Beckram, hampered by his burden.

I didn't know what to do. In my extremity, I reached for the familiar comfort of Hurog's magic. I hadn't meant to do anything at all, but I had been looking for my mother in those blank eyes—and I was a *finder*.

Cold chills crept up the back of my neck as I realized what the magic told me. There was nothing behind the blank gaze, truly nothing. My mother was gone forever.

"I'll carry her," I said, answering the maid's anxiety.

I picked up my mother's body, which still breathed and moved, and carried it the rest of the way up the mountain. I would remember my young mother who played with me while my father was away at war and not the woman who hid in her herbal potions until there was nothing of her left.

WE MADE IT TO THE BRONZE DOORS BEFORE KARI-ARN reached Hurog. I found a place to sit where I could look down at the keep. I should have been exhausted, and I was, but the flow of Hurog's magic through my flesh kept me from feeling it much. So I felt almost peaceful as, from my mountain vantage point, I saw Kariarn's massive army approach Hurog. They stopped when they saw Hurog's open gates. After a long hesitation, during which I imagined them sending a few riders to make certain the keep was indeed empty, a section of people pushed through to the bailey.

Tosten came up behind me and hit me hard in the shoulder. It was the first time he'd approached me since I'd found them all in the great hall.

"What's that for?" I whispered furiously. Sound travels oddly in the mountains, and Duraugh had warned us all to keep quiet once we'd sighted the Vorsag.

"That's for sending me to safety while you went out to get all the glory. Haverness told us there was no possible way for an army to get to Hurog before Kariarn. And you knew it, too," he returned as hotly.

I rubbed my shoulder and decided he'd a right to be angry. "So how did you get here? You could have pushed me over with a feather when I saw you in the great hall. You were supposed to be safe at Callis."

Tosten grinned at me, the expression so young it hurt my heart. "You're going to wish you'd come with us," he said. "You remember there were only a few keeps the dwarves traded with?"

I nodded.

"That's because they travel on an underground waterway, and there are only a few places where it surfaces. Hurog is one, and Callis is another." He chuckled, "You should have seen old Haverness's face when Axiel led us to an opening in the cellar."

"You should have seen my father's face when he found out I'd showed our secret ways to humans," said Axiel as he seated himself by my side. The eight dwarves who'd been following him as if they were some sort of honor guard found places to sit in front of him. He handed me a blanket, and I wrapped it around me. "I explained the situation to him, and he allowed us to bring everyone here." He looked at me earnestly, as if anxious to cement my good opinion of his father. "That wasn't without cost, Ward. The waterways take a lot of magic to traverse, and my father hasn't much power to waste."

Tosten shook his head in awe. "It was incredible, Ward. Some of the caverns looked like they were made of crystals. The boats were flat, like the riverboats the Tallvens use on their tame rivers; but the waterway isn't tame at all. I don't think we'd have made better time if we'd flown."

Beckram, wandering by with Ciarra beside him, paused to say, "It was incredible. Mostly because we all survived to disembark at Hurog."

Ciarra sat down and dragged half my blanket around her. I wrapped an arm about her shoulders, content at last. The magic of home soothed my soul; Ciarra's presence just solidified my well-being. Against all odds, Hurog would survive this intrusion as would my uncle. Kariarn wouldn't seek us out here.

I couldn't think of a time I'd been happier than when I was watching sparks that were Kariarn's torch-bearing men walking along the top of Hurog's walls. Oreg sat down at my feet. His face contained the same bone-deep peace I felt. His peace disturbed mine. He'd been so worried about the dragon bones, and now he was content to let Kariarn have them. I would never understand him.

In a dreamy voice that carried clearly to anyone who wanted to listen, he said, "They are very close to the dragon's bones. Kariarn has wasted no time."

"What?" said Axiel in a voice I'd never heard from him. "What dragon bones?"

Oreg smiled at Axiel and said innocently, "Didn't we

tell you what it was Kariarn wanted? What Ward would sacrifice to him to save the people of Hurog?"

The smug satisfaction that underlay his words caused me to shift Ciarra away from me. I wrapped the blanket tightly around her while I kept my eyes on Oreg.

Axiel turned to me accusingly. "There are dragon bones at Hurog?"

I nodded.

One of the dwarves said, in a voice like the winter wind, "Dragons eat their dead so that there will be no dragon bones for stupid humans to play with."

Axiel ignored him. "You *can't* let Kariarn have them." It was fear in his voice. I'd never heard Axiel afraid before. "Do you forget what he's done in Oranstone? The villages? He killed scores of people for a bit of power, and you would give him *dragon bones?*"

Oreg smiled at me. "Ward doesn't know about dragon bones. He was never trained in magic. Tell Ward what the dragon bones will do. I don't think he'd want to believe just me."

"For a human mage to have dragon bone is like giving a toddler a blazing torch in a grass hut." Axiel struggled for words.

"It is forbidden," said the dwarf who'd spoken before. Urgently, he came to his feet. "It gives too much power . . . corrupting power. My king thinks that's what caused this blight on dwarvenkind in the first place—that a human mage consumed dragon bone."

Seleg, I thought. *Had Seleg gotten power that way?*

"Kariarn will destroy what is left of this world, Ward." Axiel's face was pale in the fading light. "Oh gods . . . we are undone."

"They're in the cave," said Oreg, still looking at me. His gaze was intent, like a cat with a mouse. What had he led me to? And it had been deliberate on his part; he'd never attempted to tell me that the dragon bones were this dangerous. "Ward knows a way to stop them."

And I did. Oh, Siphern, I did. Oreg had told me.

"You said you could hold them off for days, Oreg," my voice was tight.

"I could have," he agreed. "But that would have just prolonged the outcome. So I helped them a little instead. You asked me, once, if there was a way to change what Seleg did."

Stala always said it is important to know what motivates your allies as well as your enemies. Oreg had once told me what he wanted a long time ago, while an invisible whip lay open his skin, but I hadn't paid attention. Oreg wanted death.

He'd planned this. Every step we'd taken off the ship. That's why he'd quit being mad at me on the boat, because he knew he could force me to this. Tears gathered in my eyes, and I fought for air. I *protected* those I loved.

"The cave is under the keep," I said. "It'll still be there if Hurog falls until not one stone stands on another."

"It won't matter," he replied. "I can see to it that the cavern falls. Ward, you can't change the past, but you can put right what is wrong." He looked at nothing for a moment, and when he resumed speaking, his voice was hurried. "You must be quick. They've found the bones. You have to do it right now." He leaned toward me earnestly. "Seleg couldn't let Hurog be destroyed, so he began the evil here. Your father would never have been able to give up so much just to do the right thing, to correct what has been put wrong. This is something that only you, Wardwick, Hurogmeten, can do, because of the ring you wear."

I drew my father's dagger and stared at the terrible triumph in Oreg's face.

"Please, Ward."

Tears blurred my eyes as I set my hand on his face. Some part of me was aware that Ciarra was struggling with her blanket, trying to stop me. I kissed Oreg's forehead, then stepped behind him. I held him as I slid my father's sharp hunting knife into the base of Oreg's skull with the hand which bore the worn, platinum ring. It was quick. It was very probably painless—for him. I felt his last breath touch my arm, warmth in the chill of the night, but I knew I'd never be warm again.

For a moment, it seemed to me that the forest around us became still, waiting. Then the earth shook with the force of the magic Oreg's passing had unleashed. The surprised cries of the men and women gathered on the mountain was drowned out by the sound below.

For Hurog keep, my home, was collapsing. The ancient stones, marred by the claws of dragons, tumbled to the ground, one by one at first. Then with a great cracking sound, the keep trembled apart, and the walls collapsed inward upon it. Dust rose, and between it and the ever-darkening skies, Hurog was mercifully hidden from view.

To me, all this was secondary, as was the feeling of Ciarra's nails tearing wildly at my bloody hand, the incredulous look on Tosten's face as he tried to drag her away from me. Even the rapid disintegration of Oreg's body, as if the years that had been artificially held at bay were absorbing his essence, was distant.

All I could feel was the wild rush of magic that surged through me, burning my lungs and heart as the land was burned clean of an ancient wrong, older far than the dragon Seleg had killed. Oreg had been incorrect. That betrayal had removed the stopper from the vial of ill, but I understood at last it was the older wrong that had poisoned the land. A crime of a father against his son.

The upheaval was over before Tosten succeeded in pulling Ciarra away from me. Below us, the once stalwart walls of Hurog were nothing but a formless heap that was soon mercifully covered by the blanket of night.

Sitting on the side of the mountain with a trace of dust

on my lap, it occurred to me that Axiel had been right. I had stopped the curse that was killing his people. And, as Aethervon had told him, I wouldn't have been able to do it without him. I would never have killed Oreg just on his own word that the dragon bones were dangerous. It had taken the naked terror on Axiel's face, he who was never afraid, to convince me.

I had just saved the Five Kingdoms from powers that hadn't been seen since the Age of the Empire. And I'd done it by becoming worse than my father. I'd killed a man I'd loved as my brother.

And Oreg was right. My father wouldn't have done it, wouldn't have seen the necessity. Seleg wouldn't have done it; he'd have been certain he could control the damage. He wouldn't have read the fear on Axiel's face and understood the danger. It was Wardwick of Hurog who killed Oreg and destroyed Hurog.

I huddled on the cold earth. Stripped at last until there was only me and no one else to be, I buried my face in my blood-covered hands and cried.

15

Stories and songs all have a final word, but in real life not even death is a true end; just look at the lasting impression my father made.

THEY TELL ME I DIDN'T SPEAK FOR SEVERAL DAYS, but I don't remember it. The healer my uncle brought in said it was exhaustion—Oreg and I had run almost fifteen miles before Oreg had been able to jump us to Hurog—and blood loss from the basilisk wound in my back.

The Blue Guard, my uncle told me later, chased the few remaining Vorsag who hadn't left on their own. My uncle's firm hands on the reins saw to it that the harvest was taken in, though the crops were indeed poor.

That winter was hard on the people of Hurog. It wasn't the food: My uncle had grain shipped in from Iftahar. But the Vorsag had fired as many of the people's cottages as they could find, and the shelters we'd managed to erect before winter weren't enough to keep the fury of the north wind at bay.

My uncle had tried to move me to Iftahar with my mother, Ciarra, and Tosten, but I would not go. I could not leave Hurog. Only the keep was gone: the people were still at risk.

My uncle understood. One night, after working all day harvesting wheat, I told the whole story of what Oreg was and why I'd done what I had to all of them: Duraugh, Tosten, Ciarra, Beckram, Axiel, and Stala. Axiel and his dwarven comrades left soon after that, having cleared a way to their underground river. Axiel promised to be back in the spring. Ciarra avoided me when she could, which bothered Tosten so much that I began avoiding both of them until my uncle left for Iftahar and took them with him before the first storm of winter.

I often took Pansy or Feather (returned to us from Oranstone several weeks after Hurog fell, along with the other horses we'd left behind) and ran the mountain trails at a pace that would have left Penrod shaking his head. When the snows made running impossible, I fought with Stala and whatever brave soul in the ranks of the Blue Guard would come against me. That wasn't enough, so I began excavating Hurog where the dwarves had left off, sorting the good stone from the broken. At first I did it alone, but one morning I came out to find Stala had organized a work party to help. We had the inner curtain walls rebuilt by the time the snow melted.

By spring, the people of Hurog treated me as if I were the Hurogmeten, though they all knew the title belonged to my uncle. Soon after the first robins returned from the south, my brother came back to Hurog.

I knew he was coming, not because of any messenger, but because the grasses of Hurog whispered that someone of Hurog blood had come back. Since I'd killed Oreg, I'd become even more attuned to the magic flows around Hurog. Once I'd needed them to complete me, but now I completed them.

I rode Feather out to greet him.

"You've lost weight," he said.

"You look better," I replied because it was true. The air of aloneness he'd carried like a cloak was gone.

"Mother's dead," he said. "Her maid found her wandering outside one night in a storm. She took fever and wasted away."

I nodded, but she'd died a long time ago.

"I came also to tell you that Beckram and Ciarra are engaged," he said warily.

Feather, impatient standing for no reason she could see, pawed the ground but quieted when I shifted my weight. Beckram and Ciarra? She was seventeen; mother had been younger than that when my father married her. But *Beckram* and Ciarra?

"Tell him I expect him to keep her out of sewers," I said after a moment.

Tosten looked away. "I tried to get Ciarra to come and tell you herself. She told me to send you her love."

I nodded my head.

"She can talk now, did you know?"

I did. "Duraugh wrote to me."

"She's afraid if she comes back to Hurog, she'll lose her voice again. But she wants you to come to their wedding this summer."

"All right," I said.

"Our uncle intends you to have Hurog. Beckram doesn't want it. Duraugh has sent a formal petition to the king."

"The king has other things to worry about," I said. Once it was clear that Kariarn was dead, Haverness's hundred had little trouble sending the Vorsag on their way. But the hundred hadn't returned to Estian when they were called upon to do so. They had retreated to their estates and were presumed to be building up armies. Jakoven might have declared it treason, except that the rest of the Five Kingdoms thought that Haverness's hundred were heroes. And heroes were difficult to prosecute.

"Don't you care?" Tosten sounded worried.

I shrugged and looked at the worn platinum ring on my finger. "Have you come to stay?"

"If you'll have me."

Feather sidestepped as I leaned toward him. "You are my brother. You are always welcome here."

TO REBUILD HUROG'S INNER BUILDINGS, I HAD FIRST to clear away the rubble so I could build some sort of support over the roof of the dragon bone cave, which had collapsed in the center, killing Kariarn and his wizards and burying them under a mound of stones. My work party had been reduced by the people needed to plant the fields, leaving only Stala's Blue Guard and Tosten when we uncovered the bodies of Bastilla, Kariarn, and the rest of his wizards. Oreg had been right; they were very near to the dragon bones.

I had them buried in the mass grave we'd dug for the other bodies we'd found in the rubble. If the Vorsag wanted proof of Kariarn's death, they would have to take my word, because the bodies were identifiable only by their clothing. I carried Bastilla's body myself.

Either by Oreg's magic or some odd chance, the dragon bones were still intact. Axiel arrived soon enough to help Tosten and me excavate them all and cart them to the field with the salt creep. The three of us ground the bones into meal and then tilled it into the ground as Duraugh had done with seashells the year before. Axiel looked relieved when the last of the white powder was covered with dirt. When the field was planted, seedlings sprang up from the once-poisoned soil.

I WOKE EARLY ONE MORNING IN HIGH SUMMER knowing something had changed. I dressed hurriedly in hunting clothes and saddled Pansy myself to get on the mountain trail sooner. Sensing my urgency, Pansy ran as if the demons of Menogue were nipping his heels, slowing only when the trail became so steep that I dismounted and walked beside him. When he stopped abruptly, eyes rolling and nostrils tasting the air with sudden urgency, I stopped beside him.

"What's up?" I asked. It took a lot to frighten an animal that had been in battle as often as Pansy.

The stallion snorted at the sound of my voice and turned to rub his sweaty head against me, knocking me sideways a step. Whatever had bothered him was gone now.

I could smell something, too. It reminded me of the blacksmith's forge: heat and metal. That's why I wasn't as surprised as I might have been when we topped the final rise and got a clear view of the bronze doors.

Axiel, when I asked, had examined them and told me he didn't think they actually opened at all. He was as confounded about their purpose as I was. Oreg hadn't been around to ask.

The doors were open now, though it hadn't happened easily. The metal was blackened on the underside, as if by a terrible fire. The left-hand door lay yards away, while the right-hand door was misshapen and bent. When I touched the door nearest me, it was still warm. When I tugged on it, I couldn't budge it an inch.

I dropped Pansy's reins and cautiously approached the hole in the mountain that the doors had covered. I don't know what I expected, but an empty hole was anticlimactic. It was just a rectangular hole, barely deeper than I was tall. If I'd put a hay wagon in it, there wouldn't be room for the team to pull it. The only odd thing about it was the exactness of the flat walls and clean corners, given that it was all just packed earth. Behind me, Pansy whickered a greeting. I turned, thinking Tosten had followed me, because Pansy didn't welcome strangers.

But Oreg was hardly a stranger.

"Hello, Ward," he said with a self-conscious dip of his shoulders.

I swallowed. "I hope this doesn't mean I'll have to kill you again," I said.

He focused on the battered wreck of Hurog and patted Pansy absently on the forehead. "I knew you were going to be difficult about this."

He glanced at my face and then quickly back to Hurog. "You've done a lot of work. What did you do with the dragon bones?"

"Sowed them into the field that used to have a bad case of salt creep," I said.

He smiled. "So I don't have to eat them?"

"I thought that was a bad thing," I said. There was something else someone had said about eating dragon bones, but I couldn't remember what it was.

Oreg bent down and grabbed a rock. He took two steps and threw it. We both watched it bounce down the mountain until it rolled out of sight in a patch of bramble. "Not if you're a dragon," he said. When he saw my face, he said, almost frantically, "I didn't know I wouldn't die. You have to believe me. I wouldn't have hurt you like that for nothing. I would have told you. Dragons don't age, but you can kill them, and I was only a quarter-blood. I thought his spell had required my death to bind my soul to stone."

My tongue was slow. I couldn't ask any of the things I wanted to. What I managed was, "The emperors of old, it is said, were served by a dragon." Kariarn had told me that.

"My father," agreed Oreg. "Dragons can take on human shape. My grandmother was young and foolish and fell in love with a human. My father belonged to neither world and chose to serve the emperors as a mage." He spoke too rapidly, anxious to please.

"What was in the hole?" I asked.

"Me," he said. "I was. I didn't know that he'd saved my body there."

I sat down and buried my chin in my hands, hoping, I suppose, to come up with a single thing to say, to feel.

"You've lost weight," he said after a while, and I remembered that Tosten had said the same.

"Yes. Well, I thought I'd killed you." I discovered that I didn't mind him feeling guilty. It assuaged the deep pit of rage I felt. A pit that trembled beneath another, larger emotion.

"Tell me what I can do," he said, sounding close to tears himself. He closed the distance between us and fell to his knees.

"What took you so long?" I asked, not looking at him.

"I was dead," he said. "Or near enough to make no difference. I don't know how long it's been, a year? Two? Not much longer, or you would have changed more. It took that long for me to awaken. My body had been lying there for . . . well since before the last emperor died, tens of centuries. Magic is powerful but not always instantaneous."

"If your father forced you to wear that body, which I killed, how is it that you look as you do now?" I asked.

He gave a half laugh. "Because the body he made took its semblance from me. Dragons can shift their shape. How do you think my father was conceived?"

I'd been angry at him for a lot longer than the past few minutes. For the first time in a nearly a year, I felt the rage slide away, out of reach.

"It's been a little less than a year," I said, answering his earlier question.

He must have read something in my voice, because he took up a more casual pose, relaxing on the mountainside. "I am surprised, really. I'd have thought it would take much longer."

"You're not a slave to this anymore, are you?" I asked, flashing the worn silver-colored ring.

He shook his head. "No."

There were things I wanted to say, but I was too much my father's son to be comfortable with most of them. So I asked for more information, just to hear his voice and know I hadn't made this all up.

"Are you the last of them, now?" I asked.

"There are other dragons, Ward, though they've always been rare. Now that the poison is gone from the magic, I expect some of them will return."

"You can do something for me," I said abruptly. "I've always wondered what a dragon looks like."

He grinned at me, suddenly, looking even more like Tosten than usual. Bouncing to his feet, he took several steps back and *changed,* the lines of his human form seeming to flow naturally into something much larger.

We'd both forgotten about Pansy, who stiffened and pulled until his reins just barely stayed where I'd dropped them. By the time I'd calmed him down, there was a dragon in Hurog once more.

He was easily twice as large as the stone dragon, and much more fantastical. His narrow muzzle was deep midnight blue as were his feet and sharp talons. Above the muzzle and its businesslike teeth, the scales lightened to violet, a lighter shade than his Hurog blue eyes, altered only in shape, which glittered against the darkness of his face. His wings, half folded, were edged in gold and black; the scaled skin connecting the fragile wing bones was lavender.

Like Pansy, I was frozen, but by his beauty, not by fear.

"I've never seen so many shades of purple," I said, and, gods deliver me, he preened, flexing the spikes that ran along his spine and spreading his wings to full extension.

The sudden movement was almost too much for Pansy, and he whistled a shrill challenge as he rose on his hind legs. Instantly, the dragon closed his wings and folded gently back into the Oreg I'd known.

"Sorry," he said. "I forgot I'd scare the horse."

Worriedly, Pansy huffed and snorted, making certain

that the horse eater had gone and wouldn't bother his people.

"Siphern's oath, Oreg," I breathed, "that was the most glorious sight I've ever seen."

He hugged himself nervously. "Does that mean I can stay here?"

Bone deep, a feeling of great contentment fell over me, washing away the conflicting rage and joy I'd been torn between.

"You're my brother," I said, as I had to Tosten. "You'll always have a home here."

As we walked down the mountain trails, I asked, "Oreg, how is it that your human form looks so much like Tosten and most of the rest of the Hurogs I know?"

He grinned and peered up at me from under his eyelashes. "Ward, I thought you knew. Hurog means dragon."